Deanne Anders was reading romance while her friends were still reading Nancy Drew, and she knew she'd hit the jackpot when she found a shelf of romances in her local library. Years later she discovered the fun of writing her own. Deanne lives in Florida, with her husband and their spoiled Pomeranian. During the day she works as a nursing supervisor. With her love of everything medical and romance, writing for Mills & Boon Medical Romance is a dream come true.

Janice Lynn has a Masters in Nursing from Vanderbilt University, and works as a nurse practitioner in a family practice. She lives in the southern United States with her husband, their four children, their Jack Russell—appropriately named Trouble—and a lot of unnamed dust bunnies that have moved in since she started her writing career. To find out more about Janice and her writing visit janicelynn.com.

Also by Deanne Anders

From Midwife to Mummy
The Surgeon's Baby Bombshell

Also by Janice Lynn

The Nurse's Baby Secret
The Doctor's Secret Son
A Firefighter in Her Stocking
A Surgeon to Heal Her Heart
Heart Surgeon to Single Dad
Friend, Fling, Forever?
A Nurse to Tame the ER Doc

Discover more at millsandboon.co.uk.

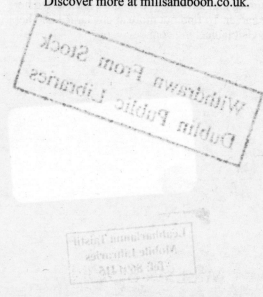

STOLEN KISS WITH THE SINGLE MUM

DEANNE ANDERS

THE NURSE'S ONE NIGHT TO FOREVER

JANICE LYNN

MILLS & BOON

First Published in Great Britain 2020
by Mills & Boon, an imprint of HarperCollins*Publishers*
1 London Bridge Street, London, SE1 9GF

Stolen Kiss with the Single Mum © 2020 by Denise Chavers

The Nurse's One Night to Forever © 2020 by Janice Lynn

ISBN: 978-0-263-27964-1

MIX
Paper from
responsible sources
FSC® C007454

This book is produced from independently certified FSC™ paper
to ensure responsible forest management.
For more information visit www.harpercollins.co.uk/green.

Printed and bound in Spain
by CPI, Barcelona

STOLEN KISS WITH
THE SINGLE MUM

DEANNE ANDERS

MILLS & BOON

This book is dedicated to all the hard-working
emergency room nurses, physicians and techs
I have the privilege to work with. You amaze me
with the care and dedication you show every day.
You have one of the hardest jobs in the hospital,
but you make it look easy.

Also, a special thanks to CAPT David Olson USNR (ret),
for founding the Combat Wounded Warrior Challenge,
and to his wife Teresa for her work with the veterans.
Your work lives on with the veterans you touched.

CHAPTER ONE

FOUR O'CLOCK IN the morning could be considered the witching hour in any ER, Lacey was sure, but for a hospital smack-dab in the middle of New Orleans, where voodoo and ghost stories were the norm, it seemed especially true.

Not that she really minded the unusual assortment of patients who seemed to find their way into the emergency room at that time of morning. If nothing else it definitely helped pass the last few hours before the sun started peeking through the windows—the first sign that the next shift would be there soon.

Unfortunately, the early-morning hours hadn't seen their usual influx of eclectic patients today, and now the hours till shift-change had begun to drag.

"What's he looking up now?" the young unit coordinator asked.

Lacey looked over to where Scott Boudreaux, one of the on-duty ER doctors, sat studying his computer screen.

"Planning his next adventure, I'm sure," she said.

Lacey had never understood the man's desire to put himself at risk for the thrill of survival, but she had learned she might as well keep her concerns to herself.

Hadn't she had almost the same conversations with her husband when he had been alive? And what good had it done her?

The two men had always been more than she could handle, with neither of them ever listening to her concerns. Then they'd both volunteered for that last deployment to Afghanistan and now Ben was gone.

There had been a time when she had blamed Scott for her husband's death, though she had known even then that it was stupid to think that way. Ben had wanted to return and help the injured soldiers on the field as much as Scott. The two of them had been like two peas in a pod through medical school, and she had finally learned to accept their adventures together, thinking the two of them would be safe as long as they were together.

She'd been wrong.

Scott had been lucky to come out with only an injury to his leg after an IED had exploded, but he'd been left with this need to always prove himself. She just couldn't understand why he felt he had to spend his life searching out thrill after thrill. Just the experience of working in the emergency room alone gave her all the taste of adventure that she needed. Add to that the trials of being a single mom and she had all the thrills she could handle.

"The next Extreme Warrior trip is only a couple weeks from now, and I think the winter trip to Alaska is pretty much planned, so he's probably working on the spring trip."

"There's a rumor that they're going to hunt Sasquatch next," the unit coordinator said.

Lacey laughed at the idea of a bunch of war veterans trying to hunt down the mythological hairy creature.

"Now, that *would* be extreme," she said, then looked over to Scott to see his reaction.

"Y'all know I can hear you, right?" Scott said as he glanced over to the two of them and then winked.

The UC let out an audible sigh and Lacey couldn't help but understand why. With his longish blond hair curling around his collar and those unusual gray-green eyes that she had always found to be seductive, he'd broken more than a few of her co-workers' hearts.

"And I'm adding the Sasquatch hunt to my list of possibilities."

Lacey laughed again when the UC's mouth dropped open. Though she knew Scott had meant to tease the girl, she wasn't sure that he wasn't totally serious. He lived to come up with new ways to challenge the group of veterans he worked with. The whole bunch of them were crazy as far as she was concerned.

When Scott had come back from Afghanistan without Ben he'd been just as lost as her. The two of them had struggled through that time together, and when he had first brought up the idea of starting the Extreme Warrior program that he and Ben had been planning before Ben's death she had been supportive.

He'd had no idea how fast the program would grow, with more and more veterans attending the meetings and applying to go on the extreme trips that Scott planned. Now, with the fast growth of the program, Scott was looking for some hands-on help, and had begun pressuring her to join the group.

Though she knew Ben would want her to help his friend in any way she could, in her heart she knew it was Ben who should have been there to help Scott, not her. The memories of sitting around the table with the two of them as they made plans to serve the military veterans in the New Orleans area just reminded her of how much of life Ben had missed out on.

The thought of her husband's death took all the humor she'd felt minutes ago out of her. She'd planned her life so carefully. She'd seen her mother struggle as a single mom, after Lacey's father had walked out on them, and she had sworn then that she'd make a different kind of life when she grew up.

So she'd gone to college and gotten the nursing degree that had allowed her to live independently and she had been happy. Then she'd met Ben, and had known right away that he was a man she could trust her heart with.

When she had married him the thought that she might lose him had never entered her head. He'd been a doctor, not a soldier. He hadn't been supposed to die so young. He hadn't been supposed to leave her with a four-year-old son who couldn't remember his daddy.

The radio on her desk went off and the voice of one of the city's emergency medical technicians began spitting out information concerning the patient they were transporting.

"Patient is a fifty-four-year-old male suffering from multiple injuries, including a laceration to the head. No loss of consciousness after a car versus light post MVA. Vital signs are: heart-rate in the one-tens, BP one-sixty-five over ninety and respirations twenty-four, with an oxygen saturation of ninety-two on five liters oxygen. ETA ten minutes, and arriving with New Orleans Police Department officer on board."

She looked at the room's tracking board, then hit the button on her radio. The EMTs hadn't called the patient in as a trauma, and the patients vital signs were stable, so she didn't want to tie up a trauma bed unnecessarily.

"Room Thirty-Two on arrival," she said, and then got up to get the room ready for the new patient.

"Am I getting a patient?" asked Karen, one of the RNs who regularly worked the night shift, as she walked by.

"No, I'm going to take this one," Lacey said.

The night had been dragging, and the fact that a police officer was aboard the ambulance with the patient might prove to be interesting. She wouldn't mind a little excitement to help the last hours of her shift pass by. She'd spent too much time tonight thinking about things she couldn't change.

At the sound of Lacey's laughter Scott pushed back from his desk and looked down the hall to where she stood with one of the other nurses. Unlike the high-pitched giggle of some of the women he had dated, Lacey's laugh had always been genuine.

It had been her laughter that had caught his attention the first time he'd seen her. With her head of dark red hair thrown back and her bright green eyes shining with humor, she'd been a vision. Never had he seen someone actually glow with happiness till that night. He'd known then that she was one of a kind, and only the fact that his best friend had laid claim to her first had kept him from pursuing her.

But she wasn't the same woman she'd been then. She was older now, more mature, yet still just as beautiful as the first day he had set eyes on her. Life had knocked her down with Ben's death, but she'd managed to get back up. It had been hard, and there had been a time when he had thought he would never hear her laughter again, which only made the sound of her laugh sweeter to his ears now.

If only his best friend was there to hear it.

As it always did when he thought of Ben, guilt slammed through him. He'd never understand why it had been him who had made it home and not Ben, who'd had a wife and son waiting for him. He knew it should have been Ben who had survived.

Watching as Lacey continued walking down to the back of the unit, he wondered if she ever thought the same thing. Did those thoughts haunt her as they did him?

Turning back to his computer, he pushed thoughts of his friend's death to the back of his mind so that he could return his focus to work. After checking the lab work on the elderly patient who was next to be seen, he picked up the man's chart and headed down the hall.

Lacey had just gotten the room stocked with the suture supplies she thought Scott would need when the ambulance crew rolled in with their patient, and a tired-looking police officer on their tail. The smell of alcohol hit her before she could even get a glance at the patient, which was enough to explain the presence of the officer.

"Thanks, Larry," she said to one of the techs as he came in, and they both assisted the EMTs in transferring the man over to the stretcher. The patient remained unresponsive as they moved him. Whether that was from the accident or the alcohol intoxication she couldn't tell.

She hooked the patient up to all the monitors and noted that the man's heart-rate and other vital signs appeared to have deteriorated from when she had gotten the initial report. She began checking the man's body for injuries. There was a cut above his right eye that oozed blood. It would need a few stitches. But her real concern was the possibility of a traumatic head injury due to whatever the man had hit his head on during the MVA.

She mentally moved the man to the top of the list of patients who needed to go to Radiology to get a CAT scan. They'd need his chest and abdomen scanned as well as his head.

"You said he didn't lose consciousness at first?" she asked the EMT who'd remained in the room, and was now filling out the needed paperwork.

"Not that we're aware of. He was awake when we got there. He passed out on the way here," he said. "His alcohol level has to be at least in the three hundreds."

She walked back over to the stretcher and rubbed the man's sternum hard enough to get a response. The man moaned and one bloodshot eye opened. He looked around the room, moaned again, and closed the eye. So he did respond to pain. But still those vital signs bothered her.

"Name?" she asked.

"James Lyons," the EMT read off his paperwork, then tore the form from his pad, handed her a copy, and walked out the door.

She looked over at the police officer who had taken a spot by the door.

"What are you charging him with?" she asked him.

"DUI," the man said. "Along with property damage and driving with a suspended license. He swiped the side of a car before he hit the light pole. It's not his first DUI. He served time for his last one. If someone had been sitting in the car he sideswiped they'd be dead now."

"Mr. Lyons, can you hear me? I need you to wake up for me."

This time the man opened both his eyes. Hopefully his unresponsiveness earlier had more to do with his alcohol consumption than injury. Or the man could be playing possum instead of dealing with the police officer in the room. She didn't have enough information to know yet.

"Do you hurt anywhere?" she asked as she shone a light into his eyes. His pupils were reactive, but she still felt there was more to his injuries than what she was seeing.

The man moaned, then grabbed his left side and looked over to the corner, where the cop was now sitting. Looking at the monitor, Lacey noticed that his oxygen saturations had dropped again, and his respirations had increased too. Pulling her stethoscope from around her neck, she placed the chest-piece against his chest and listened He was definitely moving less air on the left side.

"If you can get a line in for me, Larry, and draw the standard labs, I'd appreciate it. I'll go get some orders from Dr. Boudreaux and then we'll get over to CT," she said, as she turned the patient's oxygen up, then started out of the room. "And can you keep an eye on those vitals too? If there's any change just call me on my radio."

Not seeing Scott at his desk, she went in search of him in one of his patients' rooms and found him sitting on a stool having a conversation with an elderly man. The man's hair was pure white, his body thin and bent with age, but his smile lit his wrinkled face and his eyes sparkled with pleasure.

"Lacey, come in here," Scott said when he saw her. "I want you to meet Lieutenant Hines. He was in Europe in World War Two."

"It's nice to meet you, Lieutenant Hines," she said to the elderly man, who seemed to be embarrassed from all the attention he was getting.

"It's Frank, Miss Lacey," he said. "My days of being a lieutenant are long gone."

"It's nice meeting you, Frank," she said.

She hated to interrupt Scott, but she knew he would be tied up here for a while, talking to and examining this patient. She needed to get her new patient to CT as soon as possible, and with the increase of his oxygen needs she didn't have time to wait till he was finished.

"Can I speak to you for a minute, Dr. Boudreaux?" she asked.

"Sure. I'll be right back with you," Scott told the elderly patient before he left the room with her.

"The man's almost one hundred years old, but his mind is sharp. The things he saw were amazing," Scott said.

"What's he here for?" she asked as they moved away from the door.

"Blood sugar was reported low at his assisted living home. It's coming up, but his electrolytes are off so I'm going to admit him and get those corrected. He lost his wife over ten years ago, and they never had any children, so he's alone except for a niece who lives in California," Scott said.

He couldn't have been in the room more than fifteen minutes, but he already knew the man's life history. It never failed to amaze her how he could get people to talk to him. When depression had all but consumed her after Ben's death, and she'd been at her lowest, not only had Scott gotten her to a counselor, he'd sat beside her for hours and just let her talk. It was a gift that made him not only a good doctor, but also a great friend.

"I didn't mean to interrupt, but I've got a patient who just rolled in and I'm thinking he possibly should have been trauma-alerted. I'm putting in orders for the usual labs, but he's got a laceration on his forehead that's going to need some stitches and I've ordered a scan of his head. Can you take a look at him for me?" she asked.

"Why do you think he should have been trauma-alerted? His head injury?" he asked.

"Maybe. He's requiring more oxygen than he needed when the EMTs arrived," she said. "He's heavily intoxicated, but there's something else going on too."

"Order a portable X-ray for me. I'll be finished here in just a minute and then I'll head straight there."

She watched as he returned to the elderly man's room. She noticed that his limp was more pronounced than it normally was, but she wasn't surprised as this was the last of seven straight days on duty. The injury to his leg that he'd received in Afghanistan hadn't slowed him down a bit, and he had never let it stop him, but sometimes she wished he would. She'd have a lot fewer gray hairs if he'd slow down and quit running around the world chasing the next thrill.

She turned back toward her patient's room as she called on her radio to have the X-ray tech come down.

Scott reviewed the vital signs on the monitor, then walked over to the man lying on the stretcher as Lacey laid out the chest tube kit. While the CT scans had ruled out any brain injury, they had shown a significant pneumothorax, proving Lacey had been right to be concerned about the patient's vital signs changes and his decreased breath sounds.

Not that it surprised him. He'd been working with her long enough now to know he could trust her instincts.

"Mr. Lyons, I'm Dr. Boudreaux. You have several rib fractures from the accident and one of them has punctured your left lung, which is affecting your breathing. I'm going to need to insert a chest tube."

The man didn't seem to be paying much attention to what he was saying. Instead he seemed to be more interested in Lacey and the tray of instruments that she was setting up.

"Don't let those instruments scare you. I'm going to inject some lidocaine to numb the site on your chest where I'll insert the tube. You shouldn't feel anything," he said, and he turned toward the sink in the room and began to wash his hands.

Something crashed behind him and he turned back, expecting to see that Lacey had bumped into the stand that held the instruments. Instead he saw the patient he'd just been explaining the procedure to standing beside the bed, holding Lacey against him. The glint of steel caught his eye and he realized that the man had a scalpel in his hand.

As if he had just stepped through a time warp, he was suddenly thrown back into the war zone of Afghanistan, standing in the quickly thrown-up field hospital…

There was chaos everywhere he looked as nurses and doctors worked on the wounded who had just arrived.

He looked up and saw Ben standing in front of him. Another man held a knife to his throat while he shouted to them in a language Scott didn't understand.

Ben told him that the man had an IED, and then he watched as suddenly Ben went down and everything exploded.

He heard screams coming from all around him, and knew one of the screams was his own. A piece of metal had torn into his leg as he was thrown under one of the operating tables.

Then he heard only silence, and it took a moment for him to realize that the blast of the explosion had damaged his ears.

He crawled through the rubble, dragging his injured leg behind him as he looked for Ben. He could see the wounded as they cried out for help, but still could not hear a sound.

He made it over to where his friend lay, pulling him into his lap and propping the two of them against the side of a turned-over table. As tears rolled down his own face he tried to wipe away the blood from his friend's face.

Ben turned, his eyes no longer bright with life, And Scott watched as his friend worked laboriously to speak, concentrating on the movement of his friend's lips as he slowly formed words.

"Lacey and Alston," his friend said. "Take care of them for me."

"Always," Scott answered before his friend's eyes closed for the last time. "Always."

The tray stand crashed to the floor and just as quickly as he'd disappeared into the nightmare that still haunted his sleep he was back, watching as the man, now totally out of control, wrecked his emergency room and threatened his best friend's wife.

He took a deep breath and tried to slow his speeding heart. He didn't have time to deal with his own demons now. He had to get this situation under control before Lacey was hurt. He wouldn't let Lacey or Ben down again.

"Whoa, man, you don't want to do this," Scott said as he slowly approached the wild-eyed man.

The man's trembling hand tightened around the scalpel he held against Lacey's throat.

Scott stopped moving and held up his hands with his palms facing forward, showing the man they were empty, letting the man know he wasn't a threat. He had to find some way to get through to this guy before he hurt her.

He looked from the man's hands to Lacey's pale face. She'd gone so still he wasn't sure she was even breathing. Her green eyes were wide with a look of fear that he was only too familiar with. He'd seen it on a countless number of injured soldiers. He'd seen it on Ben's face just before that insurgent had detonated the bomb he'd been wearing. It killed him to see it on Lacey's face now.

Then her eyes caught his and her lips moved.

Alston, she mouthed, and the word was as plain to him as if she had spoken it. *Take care of Alston.*

No. He couldn't live through this again. Nothing was going to happen to Lacey. He wouldn't let it.

Did she think he was just going to stand there and let this guy hurt her? Kill her? He'd lost too many people in his life already. He would not lose Lacey. There had to be a way to get this man to let her go.

"Look, I don't know your story," he said to the man as he moved an inch closer, "but I do know that woman you're holding, and I know that whatever is going on that has driven you to do something like this is not her fault."

Scott slowly moved closer to the man. The police officer who had been with them earlier took a step into the room from the other side, causing the man to jerk Lacey up closer to him as he tightened his hand around the scalpel at her throat. One slice to her jugular and she'd bleed out before Scott could save her.

"Don't come any closer. I don't want to hurt her, but I'm not going back to jail," the man said. "I want a car outside in fifteen minutes or…"

Scott watched as the man struggled for breath. Was his color a bit cyanotic? If he could keep the man talking long enough he'd pass out with hypoxia. Only that would still leave the sharp scalpel dangerously close to Lacey's neck when the man went down…

"Do you see how short of breath you are? You need to stay here in the hospital so that we can treat you."

"She's a nurse." The man gestured with the hand that held the scalpel. "She can take care of me."

Scott had to get through to this man *now*. It would help if he knew something about him, but he only remembered the basic information. He couldn't even remember the man's name now. All he knew was that Lacey was in danger and he was going to have to get her out of it without her being hurt.

He watched as the man's hand began to shake again.

He had to do something—and now. He would *not* lose someone he cared about again.

"Her name's Lacey and she's one of the best nurses I've ever worked with," Scott said as he moved closer.

He made himself look the man in the eyes, all the while thinking about the sharp scalpel lying against Lacey's neck. His instincts told him to grab her and run, but his training told him that would put her at risk. He had to talk this man down if he was going to have any chance of keeping her safe.

"She's caring and professional and she treats everyone with respect, no matter what their background. But you'd already know that, wouldn't you?" Scott said.

The man's eyes left his and he looked down at Lacey.

Scott took another step—a larger one this time. "She's also one of the best moms I've ever known. She does that thing where she leaves notes in her son's lunchbox. Not mushy notes. The kid's eight and she knows better than that. Instead she writes down corny jokes that he reads to his friends every day at lunch," Scott said, and made a sound as close to a laugh as he could manage.

Yep, there's no threat here. I'm just a simple doctor having a conversation with his patient...

The man had gone quiet now, though whether it was from listening to him or from the lack of oxygen going to his brain Scott didn't know. But as the scalpel had moved a fraction of an inch away from Lacey's neck he really didn't care which.

Scott saw the police officer behind the man moving closer. The officer had his Taser out, but he wouldn't be able to use it until Lacey was free. They had the man boxed in now—he wouldn't be leaving with Lacey—but they didn't want him to realize that yet.

"The boy lost his dad in Afghanistan, so Lacey's the only parent he has. He's got his momma's red-haired temper, but he's a good kid and he needs his mom," Scott said, and took one more step closer to Lacey.

She was within arm's reach now. The officer behind the man nodded his head. It was time for this to end.

"Like I said, I don't know your story, but I do know that whatever or whoever you have a problem with, it's not Lacey's fault. Let her go and we can talk. Please," Scott said, as he held out his hands toward the man, "just let her go."

"I don't wanna hurt nobody," the man said, his voice slurred and tears filling his eyes. "I just wanna go home."

The officer behind the man nodded one more time. It was now or never.

Scott reached out his hand for Lacey's, felt it tremble as she laid it in his, and with one motion yanked her into his arms.

Police and Security surrounded the man as his body collapsed and convulsed from being Tasered.

CHAPTER TWO

LACEY CLUNG TO SCOTT. Nothing had ever felt as good as being held safe in his arms right then. She'd heard many a trauma survivor talk about having their lives flash before them, but she'd never experienced anything like that until now. With the sharp edge of the scalpel lying against her neck, fear had taken over her body, and with it had come the knowledge that she might have seen her little boy for the last time.

The adrenaline rush she had experienced earlier was gone now and her body had started to tremble. She looked around the hallway Scott had pulled her into. Had it all been real? Her body wanted to crumple there on the floor and curl into itself, protect her from the fear that was flooding through her.

She remembered another time when that had happened—when the chaplain from the base had told her about Ben's death. She'd sunk to the floor that day and had never wanted to get up. She'd had to fight her way up every day after that, taking it one hour at a time, then one day, one week. At first she had failed more than she'd succeeded, but with counseling, and support from her family and friends, she'd finally gotten to where she was today.

The possibility of becoming that broken woman again scared her more than that scalpel against her neck.

She gave her head a hard shake and pushed away from Scott. "I need some air," she said, then headed for the exit door.

Outside, the sky was still dark, but from where she stood she could see the city starting to come to life. Lights began to come on all around her as the early shift workers began to prepare for the day.

She leaned against the wall that enclosed the roof and for the first time in her life wished for a cigarette to hold in her shaking hands. The façade she had held on to until she'd been able to make her escape fell, and with it the tears she could no longer hold inside.

Alone in the dark, she let the tears fall as she stared out into the city. She couldn't let anyone see her like this. She had her reputation as a hard-nosed ER nurse to uphold. Laughter broke through her sobs. Some kick-ass nurse she had turned out to be.

"Lacey?"

She heard a voice call into the shadows where she hid. She mopped at the tears with the sleeve of her jacket, but she didn't answer—couldn't speak at all while she worked to hold the sobs inside her. What would Scott the mighty thrill-seeker think of her hiding in the dark, crying like some scared little rookie nurse?

She wiped at her tears again as Scott walked into her hiding place and then pulled her into his arms. The dam broke and she let the tears and the sobs take over.

"I was so scared," she said, speaking between sobs against his shoulder. "If something happened to me… Alston would be all alone…"

"It's okay," Scott said. "You're okay."

She knew that, but still she cried.

"I know. It's just…" she said.

Scott's hand ran up and down her back, his touch soothing her. Her body began to relax, her breaths becoming less ragged and her heart-rate slowing. Scott whispered in ear, sweet sounds that calmed her fears. She was safe here with him.

She knew she needed to move away from him, in case someone saw them and took what was simply the act of comforting a friend as something less innocent, but she couldn't move, couldn't leave the warmth of his body. A body that was strong and safe…one that fit so perfectly with hers. A hard body that was starting to send all kinds of tingles through hers.

Wait. Something was wrong. This was Scott. Her friend. Her late husband's best friend. There could be no tingles between the two of them.

Lacey started to push away, but Scott only pulled her closer. One of his hands cupped her face, turning it up toward him, his green-gray eyes captured hers filled with desperation.

"I would never let anything happen to you, Lacey," he promised as he looked down at her.

She knew he was going to kiss her a second before he lowered his head. She could have turned her face, could have pushed away from him, but his eyes—so earnest—seemed to hold her in place until his lips were on hers and then it was too late. There was no fighting the warm touch of his lips as they met hers.

She had felt so cold and alone before Scott had found her. Now the heat from his body drove the cold away and his arms around her reminded her that she was no longer alone. Her mouth opened and his tongue swept in, scattering all reason from her mind as desire crowded out the fear that had held her prisoner earlier.

In the back of her mind an alarm warned her. But of what she could no longer remember. Right now there was just her and this blessed kiss, which reminded her that she was alive and safe as long as she remained in the strong arms that held her.

She tasted of sunshine and hope and everything that he had been afraid of losing as he'd watched her stand there so still with that scalpel held against her throat. If that man had hurt her…if he had lost her…there would have been no hope left in his life.

He poured everything he had into the kiss, trying to reassure himself that she was real, that she was alive and safe. Her body relaxed into his, melting into him, and then he felt himself harden against her and realized he had taken things a little too far. What had started out as a need to confirm that Lacey was alive and safe had turned into a desire that he had never let himself acknowledge before.

He felt her stiffen against him and knew she had felt the change too. He eased out of the kiss, withdrawing slowly until there was a small sliver of space between them.

She blinked up at him with eyes that went from startled to horrified in a second then stared at him as if she had never seen him before.

But then she had never seen this side of him, had she? Even though the two of them were close, they'd always been careful to keep their relationship free of anything that could be interpreted as something other than friendship.

"This never happened," Lacey whispered, then backed away from him.

"Wait," he said as she continued to put space between the two of them. "We need to talk."

"No, I have to go. I've got patients. I need to call the lab."

He started toward her as she stumbled, but she held her hands up to stop him.

"Don't. I just need to go," she said, and she turned away from him and hurried toward the stairs.

He watched as she all but ran from him. What had he been thinking? He'd crossed that invisible line that lay between friends and lovers—a line that no one ever crossed without there being consequences to their relationship. A line he had never dreamed he would cross.

For the second time that day time stood still for him—except that this time, instead of a nightmare, it had felt more like a dream come true.

But nothing could happen between him and Lacey. He'd promised her husband that he would take care of her and Alston and that promise had never included anything but friendship. A friend didn't make moves on his dead friend's wife. That was just not done.

He turned east and watched the sun as it rose across the sky, creating a work of art with its blend of pinks, purples and blues that no human artist could ever truly copy. The night was over and a new day was beginning. Each day was as unique as its sunrise, and he'd learned the hard way that no one knew when a day began how it would end.

He lived his life with the motto that you had to live each day as if it was your last. There were no promises of tomorrow. You had to make the life you wanted now, because today was all you could count on till the sun began to rise again.

Only sometimes life came with unexpected complications that you weren't prepared for—and the kiss he had just shared with Lacey was one big complication.

He headed back to the ER. Maybe he should have fought off the need he'd had to kiss Lacey, but he'd needed to reassure himself that she was alive and with him at that moment.

He'd explain it to her. They'd been friends for a long time and he would never have purposely done anything to threaten that friendship. Surely she wouldn't let one kiss in the heat of the moment ruin what they had between the two of them? They were both adults and it had only been one kiss. Just one kiss.

But what a kiss it had been.

Lacey tried to pay attention to the convoluted story her eight-year-old was telling her, but her mind kept wandering back to the last shift she'd worked. She'd been able to throw off the fear that had seized her the night before after she'd gotten some sleep, thank goodness. And she'd mostly managed to file the experience with the intoxicated patient in the back of her mind, with all the other memories she hoped to forget someday.

Now she found that it wasn't the fact that she had been held hostage with a cold scalpel against her neck that occupied her mind. Instead it was what had happened later, between her and Scott. What had he...she... *they* been thinking?

They'd both been recovering from a flood of adrenaline. They'd both been scared and had needed reassurance that the two of them were safe. She could even have pushed the line a little, with the two of them sharing a hug, a kiss on the cheek, but that kiss…

That hadn't been the kiss of two friends, sharing their fear of what might have been. No, that kiss had definitely *not* been a kiss between two friends.

The feel of her fingers against her lips broke through her daydreaming and she jerked them away. Scott would be here at any minute, to take Alston to soccer practice, and she didn't need him to think she was obsessing over a kiss that had meant nothing to either one of them.

"And then Ms. Little told me to leave the class and never come back," Alston said.

"What?" she said.

She caught the glass of milk her hand had hit before it toppled over, then sent her son her most intimidating Mommy stare.

"Alston Benjamin Miller—what did you say?" She watched as Alston's face broke out into a grin.

"Gotcha!" he said, then jumped down from his seat and began dancing around in a circle, making sounds that reminded her of an injured cow.

Marching around the corner of the counter, she grabbed her son up in her arms and squeezed. He was her life, her everything. If anything ever happened to him…

She squeezed him tighter as he made fake choking sounds. He looked up at her and she thought her heart would stop. He'd been born with her red hair and green eyes, but that mischievous smile with its pair of dimples had come straight from Ben. He was growing up so fast and there was nothing she could do to slow the time down.

She gave him another squeeze, then put him back

down. "I'm sorry," she said, "I should have been pay-ing more attention."

"It's okay," Alston said.

"Tonight we'll order pizza and you can tell me the whole story again."

The doorbell rang, which sent him running for the door.

"Slow down!" she called after him.

She caught herself questioning her choice of shorts and an old hospital T-shirt. What was wrong with her? One kiss with a man and all of a sudden she was mak-ing a fool of herself. This had to stop now. She'd been kissed many times before she'd met Ben.

But you've haven't been kissed since Ben.

Her mind froze on that thought. Was the problem she was having with the memory of kissing Scott as simple as that? If so, then this strange quiver she had in her stomach at the thought of seeing him would surely go away soon.

She had just loaded the last glass into the dishwasher when Alston and Scott came into the room.

"Hurry and grab your shoes," she said to her son. "You don't want to keep Scott waiting."

She tried to make her eyes look up at Scott, but in-stead she busied herself wiping down the counters. She turned her back to him to clean the stove top, and then stopped. She was acting like an immature teenager in-stead of the mature single mom that she was.

Turning around to face Scott, she pasted her most friendly smile on her face—the one she used when a patient was really annoying, but she knew she had to play nice.

"You okay? I'm sorry that happened yesterday," Scott

said as he moved over to where Alston had dropped his soccer bag. He grabbed the bag, then moved to the counter. "I started to call last night, to check on you, but I didn't want to wake you. I figured you'd have had a hard time sleeping. I know I did."

Did he really want to talk about this now? Where did they start?

You shouldn't have kissed me?

I shouldn't have kissed you back?

What did he mean, he'd had a hard time sleeping? Had thinking of that kiss kept him awake like it had her? Did he have the same strange quiver in his stomach that she had? And he wanted to talk about it *now*? No, that couldn't be what he meant. They had to put that kiss behind them. They had a great relationship and they couldn't afford to lose it.

"We can't do that again," she said, then squeezed her eyes shut. Why couldn't her mouth get on track with her mind? She took a deep breath, then opened her eyes. "What I meant to say is that I think it would be best if you didn't kiss me again."

"Um… Lacey, I was talking about that patient grabbing you and trying to take you hostage," Scott said, his eyes now looking away from her.

Of *course* he was talking about the patient with the scalpel. He probably hadn't given the kiss they'd shared another thought. The man probably went around kissing women all the time. What would one kiss shared with a friend mean to him?

They both looked up as Alston came back into the room.

"Why'd someone grab you?" Alston asked, hands on his hips as if he was preparing to interrogate her.

Scott gave her a guilty smile, then ran his hand over her son's ginger hair. "Nothing for you to worry about," he told the boy, who was now making a show of studying the two of them.

"If someone hurt my mom I'll punch them in the nose," Alston said, and he brought his small fist up and shook it.

She watched as Scott's lips twitched and they both held back laughter.

"Mikey said his big brother punched his sister's boyfriend in the nose. He said there was blood everywhere. Mikey's mom got mad about the blood and made his brother apologize to the jerk."

"Jerk?" she asked.

"Yeah, that's what Mikey called him. Was it a jerk that grabbed you?" he asked her.

"It was definitely a jerk," Scott said. "But the cops took care of him so you don't need to punch him."

She could see that her son was ready to argue the point and she wasn't prepared for that now.

Alston took his position as the "man" of the house very seriously. He'd begun by taking out the garbage, though at first that had been more of a mess than if she had done it herself, but she'd known it made him feel like he was helping out so she'd watched him drag the trash bag out through the back door and then hurried to clean up the mess he'd left on the floor before he could return and see it.

"Y'all better get going or you're going to be late for practice," she reminded the two of them.

"Let's go," Scott said, and he wrapped his arm around her son's shoulder as they headed for the door.

"Oh, and about that other thing… If you want to

talk about it later we can," Scott said, though from the tight expression on his face she knew he would prefer not to talk about it.

"There's nothing to talk about. Everything's good. We're good, right?" she asked, and held her breath waiting for his answer.

"Yeah, sure. We're good," Scott said, and he hurried out the door with her son without looking back at her.

She took in a deep breath as the front door shut. The man was certainly not going to make this easy for her. And it was entirely that kiss's fault.

CHAPTER THREE

WITHOUT THE BUFFER of Alston between the two of them Lacey and Scott had fallen into an awkward pattern of nods and one-word comments, which were not making their work situation a good one.

She looked over at him now, as he carefully numbed her patient's arm. While most teenagers would have been looking away or turning pale on seeing the long needle, this kid was totally enthralled by the scene.

Scott reached for the suture she had prepared for him just as she reached for a four-by-four, and their hands touched for a second before they both pulled back as if burnt, the motion sending the tray stand rocking precariously.

Grabbing the stand support, she steadied the tray, then looked over at Scott. "Sorry, I'm a bit clumsy today," she said, as she tried to cover the new self-consciousness she felt when they were this close.

Scott acknowledged her comment with another of his nods before he reached again for the suture and carefully sewed the cut closed.

"Wow! Mom, are you watching this?" asked Kevin, their patient. "This is sick."

"No, Kevin. I do not want to watch," the boy's mother

answered back "And you're right. Anyone who'd want to watch *is* sick."

Lacey looked over to where the woman sat on an old plastic chair that had been pushed into the corner when she had brought the tray stand into the room. The woman, who had been handling her son's skateboard wreck well enough when they had first arrived, was now pale and diaphoretic.

Lacey felt like kicking herself. If she hadn't been so absorbed in her own feelings she would have seen this coming sooner.

Leaving the boy's side, she went over to where the woman was now hunched over with her head down between her legs. Kneeling beside her, Lacey ripped open an alcohol swab package and handed it to her.

"This will help some. I'll get you a washcloth. Dr. Boudreaux is almost finished," Lacey said.

The woman looked up and gave her a weak smile. "I'm sorry about this. I've never had a problem before," she said.

"I'll tell you a secret, but don't tell any of the other staff members," Lacey said as she moved closer to the woman. "I can handle the most gory trauma patients that come in here, but if my son gets a cut I have to call Dr. Boudreaux to handle it every time. It's just different when it's your kid that's hurt."

"Yeah, it is," the woman said.

Lacey noticed that some of her color was back and she had started to sit up now.

"Okay, I'm finished," Scott said. "Kevin, you are one tough kid. Maybe you should think about being a surgeon when you grow up."

"Maybe," Kevin said. "It would be real cool to be

able to sew people up. But I'm more interested in electronics. Especially robots."

"They are pretty cool. Did you know they're using them in surgery now?" Scott said. "Someday it might be a robot stitching you up."

The boy's eyes grew big and his mother rolled her eyes.

"Let's not plan on getting any more stitches," she mother said as she moved from the chair to the exam table.

She thanked Scott, then turned to Lacey when he'd left the room.

"He's a very nice man," she said to Lacey, "and good with kids."

"Yes, he is," Lacey said.

"And he's hot, too," the woman said.

Lacey laughed as Kevin moaned at his mother's comment, and then excused herself so that she could get the necessary discharge paperwork. As she walked back to the nurses' station she saw one of the security guards heading her way.

"Hey, Lacey!" Karen called to her. "We need some help."

"What's up?" Lacey asked, as she signed on to her computer.

"There's an elderly man in the lobby who insists his wife works here, but I've called all the units and all the offices are closed," the guard stated.

"He doesn't know where his wife works?" Lacey asked as she worked to finish up Kevin's paperwork.

"That's it—he seems very confused and I don't know what to do with him," Karen said. "He can't give me an address or a phone number so that I can call his family. I'd feel better if you could check him out for me."

Lacey looked up at the large screen hanging over the station. They were busy, but there were still a few open rooms.

"Take him to Fifteen and I'll come by as soon as I get this discharge done," she said.

Lacey finished the discharge, then headed to Room Fifteen. She'd worked with Karen long enough to know she wouldn't have asked for help unless she had legitimate concerns.

An elderly man with mocha skin and snow-white hair sat in the chair next to where Karen stood. He was dressed in gray striped dress pants and a white button-up shirt with the sleeves rolled above his elbows. The fact that he was clean and well-dressed told her that the man was not homeless—or at least hadn't been homeless for very long.

"Lacey, this is Mr. Myers," Karen said. "Mr. Myers, this is Lacey. She's the charge nurse on duty right now."

The man stood and offered Lacey his hand.

"Can you help me find my Janie?" the man asked after they shook hands.

"I'm not sure, but I'll try," Lacey said. "Karen says that your wife works here at the hospital. Do you know what she does here?"

Lacey found it hard to believe that this man's wife would still be working, if she was near his age, but they did have some older volunteers who worked at the hospital. She watched as the man tried to work through her question. She could see his frustration and understood why Karen had brought him to her.

"I tell you what, let's work through this another way.

If you can give me your first name and your date of birth I can go check our records. Maybe then I can get a phone number, and we can call her and let her know you're here to see her."

To her relief the man rattled off his birthdate without any trouble.

"And your first name?"

"Pop," the man said.

"Pop?" she asked.

"Yes, they call me Pop," he said.

"I'm going to go see what I can find out. Can you wait here for me? I'll try not to be long."

The man agreed, then sat down in the chair. She noticed for the first time the small bouquet of daisies held in the man's hand. Hoping she'd be able to pull up his information in the hospital data bank, she went back to the nurses' station.

She caught herself looking over at Scott, where he sat across from her, working on his own computer. She thought about what the woman had said before she'd left and she had to agree. Scott was hot.

He'd let his hair grow out since he'd come home from Afghanistan, and he'd pulled it back today into a stubby ponytail. She'd joked with him last week about him growing out a man bun, pulling it back from his face to show him that he was close to having enough hair to put it up. But that had been before the kiss that had made things awkward between the two of them. Somehow that now seemed too intimate.

She was letting that stupid kiss, that hot and toe-curling kiss, ruin everything. All she wanted was for things to go back to the way they had been before they'd muddled things up.

Using the frustration that filled her, she hammered the keys of her keyboard. Right now she needed to be more concerned with finding information on Mr. Myers than how she was going to work things out between her and Scott.

"What's wrong?" Scott said from behind her.

Jumping, Lacey swore, and then turned her chair around to face him.

"Excuse me?" she said.

She heard the anger in her voice and stopped. This was not the way to fix things between the two of them.

"I'm sorry. I'm just frustrated," she said. "I'm trying to find some information so I can call this man's family, but he can't tell me his phone number or where he lives. He says his name is Pop, which has to be a nickname. It's probably what his grandkids call him. Not surprisingly, I can't find anything under the name Pop Myers."

"Pop Myers? *The* Pop Myers?" Scott said, and smiled for the first time that day.

"You know him?" she asked.

"I know *of* him," Scott said. "He's an amazing blues and jazz piano player."

"That's great, but what I need right now is a number or an address for where he lives. His wife is probably out looking for him," Lacey said as she turned back to her computer screen.

"Hold on," Scott said. "I think I know someone who can help."

Lacey watched as Scott pulled out his phone and started going through his contacts. This was the Scott she knew. The Scott she was comfortable with. The take-charge-and-make-it-work Scott.

Leaving the mystery of Pop's family in Scott's hands,

Lacey went to the waiting room to call her next patient to be examined. Peeking into Pop's room as she ushered an elderly woman who was suffering from shortness of breath down the hall, she saw that he was sound asleep in his chair, his respirations even. And although he looked a bit uncomfortable, she thought it was safe to leave him alone for a little bit longer.

After getting her new patient a stat breathing treatment and ordering the needed lab work, she decided she'd better check on Pop to make sure he didn't need anything. She wasn't surprised to find Scott in his room. Pop was awake now, and showed none of the signs of fatigue and confusion she had seen earlier. Moving into the room, she noticed a younger man standing by.

"I don't understand, Pop—why did you leave the house without calling me? I could have brought you to the hospital if you weren't feeling good," the young man said, and then turned toward her and Scott. "Is he okay? He has some problems with his heart, but the doctor said all his tests were good at his last visit."

"Hi, I'm Lacey," she said. "Are you related to Mr. Myers?"

"This is his son, Jack," Scott said. "He lives with his father."

Lacey was impressed with how fast Scott had been able to locate Pop's family—but then he was Scott. The man had a ridiculous amount of contacts in the city. If Scott didn't know someone who could help someone, he knew someone who knew someone who could. It was why his local veterans' program was doing so well. He had the will and the contacts needed to make a success of it.

"Jack, your father came here to see your mother. He

says she works here, but we haven't been able to find anyone by her name."

Jack winced as if she had struck him. She watched as he took in a deep breath, then bent down in front of his father.

"Daddy, Momma passed last year. We went by the cemetery last Sunday after church—remember?"

The pain in the room was almost palpable. She knew first-hand that while grief would fade it never disappeared, and she could see the moment Pop comprehended what his son had said. The heartbreak in this elderly man's eyes touched her so much that she found herself wiping away the tears that had gathered unexpectedly in her own eyes.

As the son hugged his father he looked up at her and Scott with searching eyes. And when Pop had calmed down, Jack asked to speak with Scott. The two of them walked out, leaving her and Pop alone in the room.

What could she say that would help him? While she knew now that the man had lost his wife several months ago, to someone with the memory problems he was having it had to feel just like it had when he had first been told of his wife's death. She couldn't imagine having to live through hearing about Ben's death over and over. She had to say more than the sometimes scripted-sounding *I'm sorry for your loss.*

Kneeling down by the man, as his son had done earlier, she took his hands into hers. "Mr. Myers, I didn't know your wife, but I'd like to hear about her if you feel like talking," she said.

Talking about Ben with Scott and with her counselor had helped her deal with her loss. Maybe it would help this man too.

After a moment, with a faint smile on his lips, he began to tell her all about his Janie and the life they had built together.

Scott watched as Jack Myers escorted his father out of the ER. He'd had a long talk with the younger Mr. Myers and had recommended a local doctor who worked with dementia patients. While his father had not officially been diagnosed with the disease, Jack had known for a while that his father was having short-term memory problems. But, as most children were apt to do, he had been blaming his father's behavior on his age.

"Were you able to help Mr. Myers's son?" Lacey asked as she came up beside him.

"I gave him the name of a doctor to follow up with. And there are some medications that can help his father at this stage. He apparently started deteriorating after his wife's death. He cut himself off from his friends soon after that. He hasn't even been playing the piano since her death, which is something that has really surprised his son. Pop's been playing since he was a young kid."

"He's suffering from depression as well as the dementia," Lacey said.

Scott wasn't surprised that Lacey had picked up on that fact. She'd suffered from depression herself after Ben's death, and had cut herself off from her friends and family before he had made it back to the States and forced his way back into her life.

And now the two of them were back at square one in their relationship. Even so, as hard as it was for him to admit, while part of him wanted to forget the kiss between the two of them had ever happened, there was another part of him that couldn't forget the pleasure of holding Lacey in his arms. It wasn't something he was proud of, but it was something he needed to face if he was going to be able to set things straight between the two of them.

"It's almost as if it's better for his mind when he forgets that his wife is gone," Lacey said.

"Yeah, that's what his son said," Scott said. "I also put him in contact with a friend of mine, to set up a time for Pop to go play at his club. Jack's going to bring him around and see if maybe that will lift his dad's spirits. I think getting him back out in the clubs is just what he needs. They were setting a date when I left them on the phone. You want to come if you're off? You connected with Pop and I'm sure he'd love to see you again."

"He might not even recognize me." She started to walk away from him, then turned back. "Do you really think it'd help if I was there?"

"I do," he said.

"And he's really that good?" she asked.

"One of the best," Scott said, then smiled.

"I'll let you know," she said as she walked away.

He knew she had a weakness for elderly gentlemen. She wouldn't be able to stop herself from wanting to be there to support Pop.

Scott looked around the unit after Lacey had left to deal with the next patient. They'd held a normal conversation for almost five minutes. Maybe they could put the kiss they'd shared behind them. Maybe a night out was what they needed. A night away from everyone, where they could relax back into the relationship that they were both comfortable with.

But as he watched the redhead bend over a computer

screen as she helped one of the newer nurses on the unit, he wondered if that was really what he wanted.

Lacey smoothed down her dress as she waited for the doorbell to ring. Nerves skittered down her back as she told herself once more that this was just Scott. She had no reason to be worried about tonight. It wasn't the first time they'd been out to listen to a live jazz or blues band.

Only this time it felt different—and it wasn't just the fact that she had taken the time to dress up in her favorite strapless dress and a pair of killer shoes that she knew made her legs look great.

It was entirely that kiss's fault. But it was totally ridiculous, and she had to stop letting that one small moment in time mess up her life. She'd liked how things were before they'd crossed that line from friends to... to something more. The two of them needed to discuss things between them like adults, instead of letting things continue the way they were now, and tonight, while they were away from the hospital and out of earshot of Alston, would be the perfect time.

The doorbell rang and, as usual, Alston beat a path to get the door.

Standing up to greet Scott, Lacey suddenly felt as if she was waiting for her prom date. Blowing out a breath, she made herself head toward the door after giving the babysitter some last-minute instructions. She knew Alston would try to wait up for her, but he needed to get to bed for school the next day.

She stopped as she rounded the corner and caught site of Scott. Standing there in a simple chambray button-down and dark navy dress pants, the man was a romance novel hero come to life.

There had always been competition between him and Ben, with the two of them arguing about who was the tallest, but height was the only thing the two of them had had in common as far as looks were concerned. Ben had been the dark and dangerous type—something that had pulled her to him—while Scott, with his blond curls and light green-gray eyes, had looked more like a beach bum than a doctor.

"Ready?" Scott asked as he smiled at her. "Alston says he's got the hottest babysitter on the block tonight."

She watched as a blush stained her son's face—one of the many things he had inherited from her when he'd gotten her red hair.

"You're not supposed to tell my mom things like that. It's in the man code," her son said, then ran back to the living room where said babysitter was waiting.

"Sorry, I forgot," Scott called after him, then looked at her and winked.

"Man code?" she asked. "Why hasn't someone shared this with me? I might need to see this code before you start teaching it to my son."

Lacey let herself relax into the laughter they shared on the way to Scott's car, and to her relief the conversation between them remained on Alston's soccer schedule and Scott's work with the next Extreme Warrior challenge.

Arriving at the bar, which was named Jazzy Blues, after both types of music that could be found there, Lacey was surprised to see how many people were out on a week night.

It was easy to see that the bar had seen very little renovation in the last few years, with its scuffed-up wooden floors and whitewashed old wooden planked walls. The bar itself ran the length of the room, and a small corner stage was set into the back of the room. In the middle of the stage sat an old piano, and she saw that Jack and his father had been seated next to it.

Making a path through the crowd, she headed toward the two of them.

"Wow," she said to Scott as the two of them wound their way through, "I didn't expect to see so many people here."

"I suspect the owner, Ronnie, has told a few people that Pop is going to be here tonight," Scott said.

He had moved closer to her so that she could hear him, which put his mouth dangerously close to her ear and neck. She felt a shiver run through her. Then the movement of the crowd, as someone next to her pushed their way to the bar, pushed her back against him.

His arms came up around her, to steady her, and suddenly her knees felt weak. She paused for a second as another man passed in front of her. The feel of Scott's body against hers was tantalizing. Then, taking in a breath, she forced down her body's irritating reaction and made herself continue toward the back of the room.

She had been hoping that tonight they'd be able to slide back into their comfortable friendship, but if she couldn't get control of herself the evening would be a failure.

Finally reaching the table, they took the two seats beside the Myerses. Pop Myers sat with his hands resting on the table, looking around the room. Would the man even recognize them or should she introduce herself to him again?

"Pop, do you remember Scott and Lacey? We met them at the hospital last week," Jack said.

His father smiled at her and Scott, then went back to studying the room. She watched as the younger Mr. Myers drummed his fingers against the table, then reached for the empty glass that sat on the table. Putting the glass back down, Jack laughed.

"I don't know why I'm so nervous," Jack said.

"Don't feel bad. I'm nervous too," Scott said.

He looked from the son to the father. Had he done the right thing, recommending that Jack got his father back into the world of music? He knew he sometimes had a tendency to get carried away with his wanting to help others, but it had seemed such a simple thing to get Pop back out in the music community he had enjoyed for over fifty years.

The last thing he wanted, though, was for Pop or his son to feel pressured by something he had put in place. And it didn't help that he had brought Lacey there too.

He had thought it would be good to have her there, to give Pop and Jack the support they might need, but he hadn't known she was going to wear that sexy-as-hell dress tonight. And why did it bother him? He'd seen her in that same dress just a couple months ago, at a local art benefit, and it hadn't affected him the way it did tonight. He'd planned for the two of them to share a nice night out as friends, listening to some live music as they had dozens of times before. He needed to be thinking "friend" thoughts, not "boyfriend" thoughts.

"We never had this kind of crowd back when I played here," Pop said, startling all of them.

"You've played at Jazzy Blues before?" Scott asked.

They all waited while Pop seemed to be considering this.

"No, not Jazzy Blues… It was Norma's then, but it looks the same," Pop said. "But Norma never had this crowd. There must be someone special here tonight."

Scott wondered if they should tell him that *he* was the special person everyone had come to hear. Probably not, since that might be something that could upset the man. They didn't know for sure if he would want to play for them. Scott was only hoping he was right in assuming that since music had been such a big part of the man's life he would still be able to.

Scott recognized the owner, Ronnie, as he walked up onto the stage and a small trio, made up of a guitar player, a drummer and a sax player, followed him. Scott felt as nervous as he had once when he'd been staring down from the edge of one of Alaska's tallest mountains. He'd asked Ronnie not to make a big deal of Pop being there tonight, but apparently what he thought was a big deal wasn't to Ronnie.

Taking the mike, Ronnie welcomed his audience, and introduced the band members one at a time. "We also have a very special guest here tonight," Ronnie said, "Please join me and recognize the great Pop Myers!"

Scott watched Pop's face as Ronnie called his name. The elderly man had turned toward the rest of the audience when they'd started clapping.

"These people came to see me?" Pop asked, but his face was still calm, no sign of the panic Scott had seen when he'd been lost at the hospital. "Well, isn't that nice of them."

To Scott's surprise, Pop stood and headed toward the stage.

"Pop? You okay?" Jack said, and the panic that Scott

had expected to see in the father's face was now on the son's.

His father waved at him, then went to the piano. The tension at their table increased as Pop studied it for what seemed like a long time before he struck the first chord and began to play.

The sweet sound of blues filled the room, and soon the band began to follow the piano player's lead as the crowd of people called out encouragement.

"I didn't think he'd ever play again," Jack said, then turned toward Scott. "Thank you. It means a lot to see him up there, happy again."

Scott gave the young man's shoulder a squeeze, and then let the music relax him.

"I have to say I had my doubts," Lacey said. She leaned over toward him and her auburn curls fell between them.

He felt an undeniable urge to reach up and brush them back over her shoulder, but knew he couldn't. Their relationship was fragile right now, and he didn't want to send her running from him. He wanted to deny the attraction he felt for his former best friend's wife, but it was getting harder to do that every day.

Was it just the kiss that had changed things between the two of them? Or was it that he was only now acknowledging that he felt more?

Realizing she was still talking, he leaned further over so that he could hear her above the band.

"It's amazing that this is the same man we saw in our ER. He hasn't missed a beat and the crowd loves him," she said, as she swung her head around to look at them.

He caught a whiff of the perfume she wore. He recognized it as the scent she wore when she was dressed up, like tonight, and remembered that she had mentioned it was Ben's favorite. And she wore Ben's favorite perfume because she had been Ben's wife.

Pushing himself back from the table, he motioned to Lacey that he was going to get drinks. He didn't even have to ask her what she wanted; like many things concerning Lacey, he'd memorized her favorite drink years ago.

Scott stopped in front of Lacey's house and got out. While he had bought a loft apartment in the warehouse district, Lacey and Ben had purchased in a new gated subdivision north of the garden district, which had been built after Katrina.

Lacey gave him a speculative look as he came around the corner of the car to the sidewalk that led to her front door. "You don't have to get out," she said. "Aren't you working the first shift in the morning?"

He wasn't surprised that she was nervous about having him walk her to the door. Hell, he was nervous himself after *The Incident*, as he had come to call it. Calling it *The Kiss* had brought thoughts of Sleeping Beauty, and he knew he was no Prince Charming.

Princes didn't kiss their dead friends' wives.

"Your babysitter forgot to turn the light on for you," he said as he pointed toward the front porch. "I'm just going to make sure you get into the house okay."

"I'm not helpless, you know," she said, then turned on her heels and headed to the door almost at a run.

He started to tell her to slow down before she broke her ankle, but the view she was providing for him from the rear took his speech away.

Nope, he was definitely no prince.

She punched a code into her front door and then, breathless, turned back toward him. He could understand why Lacey had been a bit skittish these last few days, but he was starting to wonder if maybe it was more than just the fact that he had kissed her. Was there something else that was bothering her?

"I'm so glad I got to go tonight. Pop was amazing on the piano and I think it helped him to be out there. Did you see the smile on his face when he finished the set and everyone was clapping?" she said.

"I think he enjoyed the attention as well as the playing, but we both know that tomorrow he might not remember that he even played there tonight," Scott said.

"I know... But Jack said the doctor you recommended has started his dad on new medication, and he seemed very hopeful. The owner of the club was talking to Jack about having Pop perform again."

Scott felt the awkwardness between them as they stood at the door. He felt like a teenager, working up the courage to go in for his first kiss.

That thought sent him scurrying back off the porch. Now who was the skittish one?

"It was a good night," he said as he started backing away from the house. "Goodnight," he called.

He headed back to his car. Then sat in his seat for a moment after Lacey had shut her door. It was as if that one kiss they'd shared had turned on some sex-starved gene in his body and now he found himself acting like a fool every time he was alone with her. And that was not going to be tolerated. Either they worked this thing out between the two of them or...

Or what? That was the problem. He wasn't certain how they could work things out without them going either one way, in which he returned to the comfortable relationship of being her late husband's best friend, or another way, in which they moved on to something else. Something more than friends?

Shaking his head at that prospect, he turned his ignition on and headed for home, where he knew he would spend another sleepless night.

CHAPTER FOUR

SCOTT HUNG UP the phone and checked off the last number he had on the roster of volunteers who helped with events on his Extreme Warrior program.

When John, one of the nurses who had signed up to help with the swamp hike, had been called out of town with a family emergency, Scott had never thought he wouldn't be able to find a replacement for him, but it looked as if every volunteer he had was either out of town or already working.

The only person left for him to call for help was Lacey.

Up to this point the only work Lacey had done with the program had been to help with the registration and the running of the marathon they held every year in the city, with the proceeds going to help with the funding of the program. She'd always shied away from being involved in the more extreme challenges the group of veterans took part in.

She had never been able to understand why he and the others felt the need to climb the tallest mountain or shoot the most dangerous rapids. He'd tried to explain to her that he and the other veterans felt a need to prove to themselves—and, yes to others too—that they could still do all the things they'd been able to do before they had been injured, as well as things they had never dreamed of being able to do even before their injuries.

And then there was the issue they were having with being comfortable around each other now.

Things between the two of them were complicated, but he still felt sure Lacey wouldn't let him down. And, while Lacey had never claimed to be a fitness junkie, hiking some of the swamps in Louisiana was a very tame trip compared to most of the events the program sponsored.

He decided it would be better if he texted her instead of having to grovel on the phone. If he couldn't get another volunteer, another nurse to go with him, he would have to cancel the hike, and he didn't want to disappoint all the vets who had been planning for and looking forward to the hike for weeks.

Pulling out his phone, he began to type.

Hey, I've got a problem and I need some help.

He waited a moment to see if she would respond. There was the possibility that she was working and wouldn't be able to get back to him right away.

Then she texted back.

Okay. What do you need?

There's a little problem with the hike this weekend.

What kind of problem?

I need a volunteer to go with me. John had a family emergency and had to cancel.

He waited a minute. There was no sign that she was typing. If she couldn't do it he would just have to cancel. He couldn't take a bunch of beginners out without the help he would need if something happened.

Finally she texted back.

The hike in the swamp? Where there are mosquitos as big as herons and nasty water filled with snakes and gators? Do you realize how many germs there are out there in that water?

He couldn't help but laugh.

Yes, that's the one. I promise I'll protect you from any gator that decides to get frisky with you.

The gators get frisky? Nope, sorry. I am not having any part of frisky gators.

Come on, Lacey. I've called all the other volunteers and I really need a nurse beside me, just in case something goes wrong.

Yeah, it's the something going wrong with the gators that I'm worried about.

He waited for a minute. Lacey knew most of the vets on the program and he didn't believe she would let them down.

She typed back.

Did you ask Sarah?

Grandkid's birthday.

Ryan?

I've asked everyone. You're the only one who isn't either out of town or working. You're not working, are you?

No...

Alston can stay with my mom for the weekend. I'll get my sister to pick him up from school Friday. He'll love it.

He waited. No response.

Please?

She sent him a series of expressive emojis that he knew implied that she wasn't happy.

Okay, but there'd better not be any frisky gators within twenty yards of me at any time.

Ten yards...?

He laughed when she sent him an extremely rude emoji, then put his phone down and went back to his maps.

If Lacey was going to agree to come with them he'd have to do something about the second part of the trail he had planned to take. Nothing extreme…just something special that she would be sure to enjoy.

Lacey parked her car. She'd wanted to call in sick today, but how did you call in sick if you were a volunteer? Not that she'd really volunteered for this… But Scott asked so little of her that she couldn't turn him down.

Since Ben's death he'd been there whenever she had needed him. Though Scott had been in the hospital long after the explosion had killed Ben, he'd still called her every night just to see how she and Alston were holding up. And after Scott had finished rehab he'd been over to their house at least once a week, helping her with the chores that normally Ben would have done.

She had started to remind him that she had handled everything by herself before, when Ben was deployed, but she'd been able to see that it had helped him to feel that he was needed so she'd accepted his help.

He'd even driven her to her grief counselor the first time, and when counselor had recommended doing yoga he'd taken a couple of classes with her. She still had a couple photos of him trying to do the Downward Dog that she had kept for blackmail purposes.

Scott had also been there the day she'd decided it was time to pack up Ben's closet. He'd held her as she had broken down over and over again that day. He'd even broken down with her at one point. He'd been there and he'd understood what she was going through because he had loved Ben too.

It was all those things that they had shared for those first few months that had bonded them together as friends. And now she could feel that things were changing between the two of them and she was afraid of where that change would lead them.

A knock on her car window brought her back to the present. A woman she had seen at the last marathon stood by the door. Katie? Kathy?

Lacey got out of the car. It would be okay. If this woman who'd lost part of her arm could stand there with such excitement on her face at the prospect of hiking in the humid September heat, she could and would do this. She owed it to Scott and to the rest of the party to make the best of this situation and she would.

"Hello, nice shoes," the woman said as she looked down at the waterproof hiking boots Lacey was wearing—pink, covered in rubber duckies. "Scott asked me to keep a lookout for you. He seems to think you might bolt once you get here."

"Thanks—and, nope, I'm here to stay," Lacey said. "I'm Lacey."

"I'm Katie," the woman said as they started toward the group that was surrounding Scott's car.

Scott had talked about this hike while he had been planning it, so she knew it had been organized for a small group, with a combination of beginners and some of the older hikers in mind. She moved into the group and listened as Scott explained that they were taking two cars up to the Chicot State Park, where they would start the first leg of their trip, and then they would move out into the more isolated part of the hike.

When he told them he had a bit of surprise for them on the second leg of the hike Lacey moaned. Knowing Scott, a surprise on a hike through a swamp could be anything.

Scott looked over at her and smiled. Seeing how

happy he was that she was there almost made this whole crazy trip worth it.

What had gotten into her? It was as if ever since that kiss they'd shared everything between them had changed. Scott had smiled that same smile thousands of times before, but never had it made her feel so warm and gooey inside. This was not acceptable. They needed to sit down and talk things out together, though there was very little chance of that while they were surrounded by eight other people.

Scott divided the group, and Lacey hopped into the car being driven by one of the vets she had known for several years—Dennis, who was the oldest in the group, and had been injured years ago during the Gulf Wars.

Scott had met him when he'd started planning his very first trip and had been looking for someone to help coordinate transportation. Since Dennis had opened a tour company after leaving the military, he had been the perfect person to help out. Ever since then Dennis had been part of the program, lending help wherever he could.

They arrived at the park and everyone began loading their backpacks. Scott had told her he would provide everything she needed for the trip except for her personal items, so her pack was lighter than the rest of the group.

She saw Scott loading his pack and went to offer to help.

"Hey, you ready for this?" Scott asked her.

She watched him heft the heavy pack up onto his shoulders and was amazed that he could still stand upright under the weight.

"I am. Do you want me to carry some of that?" she

asked. It didn't seem right that he had to carry her provisions as well as his own.

"I've got it for now. Dennis and Max are helping too," he said, then reached into the backseat of his car. "Here, I thought you might be able to use this."

He held out a long wooden stick. It was a walking stick, with a carving of a series of alligators, going from a small one and progressing down the stick to larger alligators, till it ended with the carving of a swamp, with one large gator rising out of the water.

"Wow. Nice stick," she said.

"I thought you'd like it," Scott said. "Now if one of those frisky gators decides to go after you, you can just pop it on the head."

"Thanks," she said.

The thought of live gators being anywhere near her made her head spin, but at least now she had something to protect herself with—though she wasn't sure just how much this stick was going to help.

They headed to the start of the hiking path and Lacey fell into step beside Scott. "So how far are we hiking today?"

"Only twenty miles today," he said, and then smiled at her.

"Only twenty?" she said.

Lacey had always considered herself in good shape—she'd even run a couple of marathons back when she was younger—but walking twenty miles in the Louisiana heat was not something she was looking forward too.

One of the vets pointed out a large heron that was feeding next to the path. Its long legs allowed it to stand in the water and look down into the murky depths as it searched for prey.

As they walked the group became quieter, as if in consensus that they would try not to disturb the peacefulness of the park.

Lacey found herself looking for gators as they traveled farther into the hike, and she stopped when she spotted a head sticking out of the water. She'd swear those beady eyes were looking right at her. She gripped the stick in her hand tighter. Just let one of those monsters come toward her. She'd show them who was at the top of the food chain.

"Do you need a break?" Scott asked, and laughed when she jumped.

Looking around, she noticed that she had fallen behind the other hikers.

"Sorry. I'm good. I just wasn't paying attention like I should have been."

She'd kept her eyes on that floating head, and noticed that it had sunk back under the water when Scott had arrived. She'd rather it had stayed up above the water, where she could watch it. Now it could be anywhere.

She picked up her pace so that she could catch up with the rest of the group. There was safety in numbers, she'd always heard.

"Whoa, you don't have to run. We're doing well with our time so far. We'll make it to the campground in plenty of time to set up camp," Scott said.

"Good," she said, as the path took a turn away from the swamp and into an area heavily populated with cypress trees.

Oh, great. Now instead of gators she had to worry about snakes.

When they'd caught up with the rest of the group Scott headed back to the front of the hikers and Lacey found herself beside Katie. They walked along the path with only the sounds of their steps and the sounds of nature surrounding them.

If it hadn't been for her fear of being eaten by an alligator or bitten by a snake, she would have seen how the beautiful surroundings could be peaceful and calming. She even found herself relaxing as the sounds of birds seemed to echo through the trees. A mockingbird started its complicated song, and she searched the trees trying to locate its position.

Katie stopped and pointed over to a log, where several turtles had hauled themselves out of the water and now sat sunning themselves. Lacey watched as one more turtle tried to crawl up the log and sent another one sliding off. The splash of the water almost covered the laugh Lacey hadn't been able to hold back.

She smiled as Katie turned around and they shared the moment. Lacey had always liked turtles. They were cute and mostly harmless. The world could use more of that, she figured.

After what seemed like hours had passed, Scott stopped and they all began pulling out water bottles and sandwiches. Scott had told her the camp they were staying at the first night would have provisions ready for them for the rest of the trip.

It was the rest of the trip that had her worried.

When their break was over they started down the path again, which seemed to wind itself back to the bayou. She continued to watch out for anything that could possibly eat her, but found herself relaxing when Scott fell back to walk with her. The miles started to stretch out as the afternoon heat began to cut through the coverage of trees.

Stopping to catch her breath, she motioned for Scott to continue without her. "Don't stop...save yourself. I'll just stay here and be gator bait," she said.

She pushed the wet tendrils of hair that had fallen out of her ponytail off her face. It wasn't that she was particularly a Barbie doll kind of girl, she just didn't see the need to go outside and do things that made you sweaty and stinky—both of which she was now.

"Come on, we only have another mile and a half to go," Scott said as he looked down at his phone. "You can make it."

Lacey took in a couple more deep breaths, then straightened up. She could do this.

As Scott headed back to the front of the group, so that he could show them the course to take toward the campsite, Katie dropped back with her.

"I'm sorry I'm slowing you down," Lacey said. "You don't have to wait for me."

"You're fine," Katie said. "I'm starting to get tired too."

"You don't look it. I'm sweating like a wild pig," Lacey said. "You don't even seem winded."

Katie smiled at her. "You haven't had the training I've had. Besides, summers in Afghanistan were hot and dry. I prefer humidity."

"Wow. I've never heard anyone say they *like* the Louisiana humidity," Lacey said. "It must have been really bad over there, huh?"

"The temperature was bad, but that was definitely not the worst the place had to offer," Katie said.

Katie's face fell, and Lacey knew she was thinking

of the fighting and loss of life she had seen. Katie's life had changed when she'd come back without her arm. Lacey's life had changed when Ben had been killed. They had both lost, but the two of them were still here, still fighting to make a life out of what they had left.

For the first time that day Lacey was glad she had come on the trip. While she had always helped Scott occasionally with the program, she had been careful not to get too involved with its members. She knew that there was a possibility that some of them might have known her husband, and she didn't know if she wanted to share the memories they had with Ben.

She had still been feeling vulnerable when Scott had launched the program, and she had still been carrying a lot of anger—not only for the man who had killed her husband, but also for the fact that her husband had been over there in the first place.

Ben hadn't been a soldier—he'd been a doctor.

When they'd first met at the local college Ben had talked of coming back to Louisiana after he'd finished his residency. It hadn't been until after they had started making plans for their future together that he had brought up going into officer training with the military.

Even after he had gotten her to agree with his plans she had never considered that he might die while serving his country. She had thought that, being a doctor, he would be far away from actual danger.

She had been so naïve. But Ben hadn't been. He would have had to know that he was at risk of being injured or worse while he was overseas, but he had never told her…never discussed the possibility of his not coming back.

Lacey saw a clearing up ahead and knew it was their

camp ground when one of the other members let out a holler. Lacey dropped her pack where she stood and stared at the small buildings in front of her. They might not look like much to some people, and they definitely weren't five-star hotels, but they were a lot more shelter than she had hoped for on this trip.

Scott assigned the buildings—one for the men and one for the women—and they split up to stow their gear. They were all surprised to find a small bathroom inside the small bunkhouse, and they each took a turn at a cold shower before they headed back out.

By the time Lacey had showered and changed a fire had been built in the center of camp. An in-ground grill had been lit and a large amount of meat was grilling. She stopped by where Scott stood, beside a set of ice chests.

"Where did these come from?" she asked.

"I got one of the park rangers to bring them down from my car. We'll carry some of the bread for tomorrow night, but the rest we need to eat tonight." Scott said.

Lacey moved over to where Katie was wrapping potatoes and corn in foil. They worked together quickly, then agreed that they deserved a break after opening another cooler and finding it full of cold drinks.

As the hot sun set they gathered around the table to eat. And after everything was cleaned up around the campsite Lacey wandered over to the fire, where someone had found sticks for toasting marshmallows.

Lacey watched as Scott moved around the camp. His limp was more pronounced tonight—undoubtedly from the amount of time he had spent walking today. She knew that he still suffered pain due to his injury, though he tried to hide that fact from everyone. Watching his face, she saw the small grimace he made as he walked back over toward the fire.

"Come sit down beside me," she said.

"I didn't want to disturb you," he said as he sat on a tree stump next to her. "You've been quiet tonight. I figured you'd head to bed the first chance you got."

"I'll head that way soon," she said. "How are you doing?"

She had to be careful when asking Scott about his injury. He made every attempt to ignore it and she knew he wouldn't want her to be worried about him.

"Tired...but in a good way, you know?" he said.

"Yeah, I'm surprised to say that I can understand that," Lacey said.

She picked up one of the logs that had been left at the side of the fire and carefully placed it on top of the other burning wood. As they sat there in silence, with both of them staring into the fire, she wondered where Scott's thoughts were right then. Was he back remembering another time, before the world had changed, perhaps when he'd sat around a fire like this with his friends? With Ben? Or did the bright flames and the smell of burning wood take him back to Afghanistan? To the explosion that had injured his leg? That had killed Ben?

He'd never shared anything about what had happened that day and she had never asked. Some things she didn't need to know.

Looking around the campground, she was surprised to see they were the only two who hadn't headed into the cabins. How long had they been sitting there, just the two of them?

She looked up to the sky and saw that there was only

a small sliver of the moon shining through the clouds. She heard the hoot of an owl in the distance and heard the crackle of the fire as one of the logs broke apart into bright embers.

"I like this," Scott said.

"It's a nice area, and the cabins are definitely a bonus," Lacey said.

She reached for another log when she saw that the last one had already burned. Then she picked up one of the sticks they had used for the marshmallows and stirred the embers.

"No, I like sitting here with you," Scott said.

Lacey's hand froze. The stick in her hand began to burn and she tossed it into the fire. What was Scott saying? She felt that he wanted something more from her. More than the friendship they had shared. *Had* shared? No, they were still friends. It was just that they had complicated things between the two of them with feelings that they knew weren't right.

She wanted to beat her head against the ground till she figured out exactly what it was that was going on between the two of them, but she knew all she'd have was a headache and still no answers. She didn't want to have this conversation, but she knew that it was needed, so that they could return to the way things had been before they'd messed up.

"I enjoy being with you too, Scott," she said. "It's something that has always made our friendship special. I've never had to watch what I say or do with you. Being with you has always made me feel comfortable."

Scott knew without her saying anything more where she was headed with this conversation. She found their relationship *comfortable*. Like an old pair of shoes. Was that what she had always thought of their relationship?

He made himself stop before he said something that would make things worse. And, really, could he blame her for the way she felt? Hadn't he felt the same? If he had never kissed her at the hospital would they be sitting here now, discussing relationships and feelings?

But had it only been the kiss that had changed things between them? If he was honest with himself—really honest—he had to admit that his feelings for Lacey over the past year had been changing. He'd even stopped dating after he had started to compare the last two girls he'd gone out with to Lacey. He'd told himself that he just needed a break from all the drama that came with dating, and that his life was full with his job and the vets he worked with on the program.

And with Lacey and Alston.

They'd been a big part of his life ever since Ben had died, and at some point his time with Lacey had become less about helping Ben's widow and more about spending time with her. And that was something that was never supposed to happen and it wasn't something he was proud of.

He'd managed to put his attraction to Lacey away years ago, after Ben had come home one night and declared that Lacey was *the one* for him. And since the day he had stood as Ben's best man at their wedding he had looked at Lacey as his best friend's wife.

But how did he explain all this to Lacey without it coming out as if he was some jerk trying to hit on his best friend's wife?

"I'm not sure what to say to you," Scott said.

He always tried to be honest with people, and this

was especially true with Lacey. He didn't want to lay out all his feelings for her, but he had to at least be honest.

"I'd like to say that I'm sorry I kissed you, that I crossed the line of friendship, but I can't. We both know that I…we were both upset that night, and maybe if I hadn't experienced that fear of losing you I wouldn't have kissed you. But I did. And you kissed me back."

"I didn't mean to," Lacey said.

He watched as she picked up another stick from the ground and began raking it across what was left of the fire.

She looked over at him and he couldn't help but smile. She'd pulled her hair back from her face, and even though he was sure she'd covered herself in sun protectant a scattering of freckles was now sprinkled across her face. Her eyes were bright green tonight, as the light from the embers in the fire reflected off them. He saw that she was working through what he had said.

"But you did. I can't lie to you and tell you that I regret that, or that I'm sorry for kissing you in the first place. Whether it was fueled by the adrenaline of the night or it was something that would have happened eventually, I don't know. What I *do* know is that it was a wonderful kiss and every time I see you I think about it. And don't tell me you haven't thought about it too," he said.

"So where do we go from here?" she asked. She dropped the stick she'd been doodling with and looked up at him.

"I think that's up to the two of us," he said. "It could be that it was just a onetime fluke, and if we kiss again neither of us will feel a thing. Or it could be that there is an attraction between us that we are only just now discovering."

"And how do you suggest we find out which it is?" she asked. She was looking down at the ground now.

"There's really only one way to find out," he said.

Putting his hand under her chin, he guided her eyes up to his. She stared back at him, then her expression changed. Her chin tilted up and her eyes filled with determination.

His lips touched hers for the briefest of moments and then she pulled away quickly.

"See—nothing. No fireworks, no angels singing. We're fine," she said.

Did she really think she was going to get away with that?

"That doesn't count. I've had longer kisses from my Aunt Jo," he said. "Now, are we going to do this right or are you too scared to find out the truth?"

"I'm not scared," she grumbled.

He watched as she stuck that same determined mask on her face again. "Okay, I'm ready."

He felt like a bull having a red flag waved before him.

The hell with it all.

He moved onto the log where she sat and took her face in both of his hands. Impatience drove his lips down to hers, and before she had time to react he had pushed his hands into her hair. Tearing off her hairband, he caught the thick red mass in his hands. His lips pressed into hers and when she opened her mouth his tongue slid in.

He had no time to wait for her response. He'd spent days thinking of kissing her, and if this was his only chance he would enjoy every moment of it. He felt her hands come up between them and feared she would push him away. When she gripped his shirt and pulled him closer he would have sworn he heard those angels she'd mentioned singing.

His tongue tangled with hers and he felt the need to delve deeper, faster. His hand had found the hem of her shirt before he realized what he was doing. Cool skin filled his hand as it worked its way up her chest.

Lacey released his shirt and covered his hand. Pulling back from her, he was surprised to find that she was almost lying in his lap. He removed his hand from under her shirt and she moved away from him. Though neither of them could talk yet, Lacey's movement told him all he needed to know.

They sat there in silence as they both fought to fill their lungs with air, and then Lacey stood and walked away from him.

There was no way she could deny the attraction between the two of them, but that didn't mean she liked it. And could he blame her? They'd had a safe relationship, and they both knew that Lacey liked to play it safe.

The clouds cleared from the sky and the moon shone down through the trees, bathing the ground in a soft light. Bending over the log, he could now see what Lacey had been scratching into the ground.

Ben's name stared up at him accusingly.

He had to accept that his best friend, the love of Lacey's life, would always be there between them. She had been married to the best man he had ever known, and Scott would always just be Ben's best friend to her.

And did he really deserve to have it any other way?

CHAPTER FIVE

THE UNDER-STUFFED MATTRESS had very little to do with the fact that Lacey hadn't been able to sleep. If her mind had been muddled before the kiss they had shared last night, now it was totally scrambled.

She'd all but run after Scott had kissed her. Even now the thought of what they'd done and what she had thought about doing with Scott set her heart racing. She'd agreed to kiss him so that she could prove to him—and, yes, also to herself—that the kiss they'd shared before had just been brought on by the moment. She'd been confident that under other circumstances she'd feel nothing when they kissed. It was Scott, for heaven's sake, her husband's best friend; she couldn't have feelings or desires for him other than as a friend.

But, boy, had she been proved wrong. There was no way they could go back to being friends after what they had shared last night. Could they...?

Someone knocked on the cabin door, and let her know they were moving out in ten. She hurried to re-pack her backpack. The last thing she wanted was for Scott to come looking for her. She had a lot of things to think about today, and being near Scott would not help her understand what was going on between the two of them. She would try to keep her distance for as long as she could.

They headed back to the trail they had followed the day before, then cut away from the path after the first couple miles. They sloshed through swampy water and she was glad for her pink boots. Unlike the day before, Lacey's mind wasn't on the dangerous wildlife in the area. Now the only thing on her mind was what she was going to say to Scott the next time they were alone together.

"So how long have you and Scott been an item?" Katie asked her.

"Excuse me?" Lacey asked, not sure that she had heard the question correctly.

"You and Scott," Katie said. "How long have you been seeing each other?"

"It's not like that," Lacey said. "We're just friends."

"I'm pretty sure there's more than friendship there," Katie said, "but if you don't want to talk about it that's fine."

Lacey thought about that for a few minutes as the two of them walked together. The rest of the group was up ahead of them and she was pretty sure Katie could have kept up with them if she'd wanted to. Instead she had chosen to keep Lacey company. She felt sure that Katie wasn't fishing for information for the gossip mill. And maybe what she needed was someone out of this situation to talk to. Maybe Katie could see things differently.

"What makes you think there's more than friendship between me and Scott?" Lacey asked.

"Well, there was all the heavy breathing you were doing when you came in last night," Katie said.

The veteran gave her a bright smile.

"I'm sorry. I tried not to wake you," Lacey said. "Did I wake the others too?"

"Maybe, but they didn't say anything," Katie said.

Lacey thought about telling Katie that she had been running, then decided not to. The more she tried to explain, the guiltier it would make her look.

"What else?" Lacey asked, curious about what the woman thought she saw in them.

"Well, every few minutes Scott is turning around and looking at you," Katie said.

"He's just checking to make sure I'm keeping up. He'd be doing that no matter who was in the back," Lacey said.

"This is not that kind of look," Katie said. "Just watch him for a few minutes. You'll see."

Even more curious now, Lacey kept her eyes straight ahead, watching Scott as he talked to Dennis about something on the map, talked to the hikers behind him. He changed direction, with the rest of them following.

She was about to look away, to tell Katie that there was nothing there to see, when she saw Scott turn around. His eyes met hers and for a few seconds they were connected. She could feel the tension between the two of them. His eyes bored into hers, searching for something—but what? What was it that Scott really wanted from her? For her to admit that she was attracted to him physically? He'd proved that to both of them last night. But they both knew that their relationship had to stay platonic. Didn't they?

Unable to stand the intensity of his stare, Lacey broke the connection between the two of them. There was nothing more for her to give to their relationship.

They had to agree to go back to being friends. Only friends, nothing more.

Lacey looked over at Katie. One look at her face and Lacey knew she had witnessed the exchange.

"Told you," Katie said.

They followed the rest of the group into thick forest. Tall old cypress trees with large trunks jutted out of murky water, and the farther they walked the deeper the water surrounding the trees became. A splash in the water ahead of them reminded Lacey that this was a good place for a gator to be hunting for food. And as the water became even deeper she began to worry about whether the waterproof hiking boots she wore were going to be high enough to keep her from getting wet.

They reached an opening in the trees and saw a large lake spread out in front of them.

"I wonder why we're stopping here," Katie said.

Lacey watched as Scott worked his way through the group until he'd made it back to the two of them.

"What's up?" she asked, glancing at him for a second, then making it a point to look away.

"Yeah, why are we stopping here?" Katie asked him.

Lacey turned at the sound of the hum of a boat engine in the distance. Scott turned with her and pointed to a small dot across the lake that seemed to be coming their way. As it got closer Lacey realized it was an air boat, headed towards them. Maybe it was her lucky day, and instead of hiking they were going to be riding the second part of the way.

Lacey and Katie moved closer to the shore as the boat came to a stop. Lacey had seen airboats before, but she'd never gotten up the nerve to ride on one as they were usually used for taking people out to see the gator population—something that she had no interest in seeing.

The driver killed the engine and removed his ear protection. He offered a hand out to Scott, then pulled him into a man hug. She watched as they shared several animated moments that seemed to include an unnecessary amount of slaps on the back. Finally turning back to the rest of them, Scott introduced the man as a cousin who lived farther up the lake, and explained that they were going to take the boat over to the far side, where there was a path that would take them farther into the swamp area.

No one seemed to notice her silence when the rest of the group all cheered at this change of course the trip was taking. She wasn't surprised. She'd decided a long time ago that the people who went on these types of hikes had to be at least partly crazy.

"And this is Lacey," Scott said to his cousin. "Lacey, this is Rene. He's my father's brother's oldest son. You've probably heard me talk about him."

"You're the one who hunts gators for a living," Lacey said. Scott wasn't the only one in his family who liked to take risks.

"Ah, *chérie*. That is me. As I'm sure my cousin has told you, I'm just a poor swamper, trying to make a living off the bayou."

By the look of the large boat he was driving, she had her doubts about the "poor" comment.

Rene offered her his hand and she carefully stepped into the boat, where she found herself seated next to Scott. Reaching over her, he buckled her seat belt—something that had never bothered her before, though now it felt intimate.

Since that first kiss everything had felt more sensual and now, after the kiss they had shared last night, the attraction between them had increased to the point that every time they touched desire ignited between the two of them.

As his hands fell back into his lap she was reminded of how she'd felt last night, when she'd found herself half lying over him. There was no explanation, no excuse for what she'd done. The memory of his lips consuming hers and his warm hand against her skin sent a hot flush through her body—something she didn't need in the hot Louisiana sun.

The boat started up and began skimming over the lake, its speed making her head spin.

"You okay?" Scott asked from beside her.

No, she wasn't okay. She was about to have to end a relationship that meant a lot to her. Over the past four years Scott had become one of her best friends. The fact that they had bonded as a result of the grief they both felt due to losing Ben had never made a difference until now. Changing the rules of their relationship was not an option.

She nodded her head, and then turned her attention to the scenery around them.

Scott helped the others disembark the boat and gather their equipment. He couldn't help but notice that Lacey had headed toward the front of the boat, where Dennis was helping. From the way Lacey had left him the night before, he'd known that she would pull away from him this morning, but that didn't stop it from hurting. But he told himself to be satisfied with the friendship that the two of them had enjoyed the last few years. It had been enough before. Surely they could find their way back to that comfortable relationship?

But the truth was he wasn't sure he *could* go back. He'd gotten a taste of Lacey now and he wanted more.

It was his own fault that he found himself in this situation. He'd known he was being stupid, taking the chance of losing Lacey altogether, but he'd always been willing to take a chance when the prize was worth it—and Lacey was worth it.

He'd lived life to the fullest since he'd been injured. Witnessing all the death and destruction of war had made him see that nothing in life was guaranteed. You couldn't just sit and wait for things to happen. You had to *make* them happen. There were amazing things out in the world to experience and he didn't have the time to waste.

Lacey herself called him a daredevil, because he was never afraid to take a leap of faith, not knowing what there was on the other side waiting for him. He'd taken a chance the night before, by kissing Lacey again, and it had been just like jumping off a bridge with a bungee cord attached to his legs. He always had faith that the rope was going to hold him, and while he was flying through the air he never doubted that he'd be okay.

But he and Ben had taken a chance, returning to a war zone, and he'd lost his best friend. Now there was a chance he'd lose Lacey too. He just had to keep the faith that things between him and Lacey would work out.

Leading the group from the lake and back into the soft marshy banks that connected the lake with the deeper swamp waters, Scott made it a point to keep an eye on the terrain. He'd given Lacey a hard time about the alligators in this area, but even he didn't want to be surprised by any of the large gators his cousin had warned him about earlier.

He heard a scream from the back of the hikers and turned around to find both Katie and Lacey standing with their backs together while Lacey beat at the ground with her walking stick.

"What happened?" he asked.

"Something bit me," Katie said.

"It was a snake—I saw it," Lacey said. "I think I hurt it."

"Did it bite you too?" Scott asked as he grabbed Lacey and held her still.

Her wide eyes darted back and forth across the ground.

"Lacey, answer me. Did anything bite you?"

"No. I don't think so," Lacey said. "We were walking, and then Katie screamed, and I saw the snake so I screamed too."

"What did it look like?" Scott asked.

"It was brown and real long," Katie said, then looked at Lacey.

"And it had a yellow tail," Lacey said.

"Stay here," he said to the two of them.

Picking up Lacey's walking stick from where she'd dropped it, he began to push through the plants and logs that covered the area. If they could identify the snake, they could make the decision on the type of anti-venom Katie would need more easily.

"Which way did it go?" Dennis asked as he caught up with Scott.

Lacey pointed to the rear of the group, and Dennis and some of the others began to comb the area.

Finding no sign of the snake, Scott turned around to

examine Katie's leg—only to find Lacey already rolling up Katie's pants.

"I feel fine," Katie said, but Scott could see that she was paler than she had been a few minutes before. "I've got thick boots. It couldn't have bitten through the shoe."

Lacey pointed to the red area right above where Katie's pants met her boots.

Giving up on being able to find and identify the snake, Scott pulled out his phone and punched in the emergency number. Katie would need multiple vials of the anti-venom that the hospital kept frozen in their pharmacy for an emergency like this. Speaking to the dispatcher, he explained their situation and they discussed the closest spot to meet the chopper. Closing the phone, he was glad to see that Lacey and Dennis had spread out one of the sleeping bags on the ground and laid Katie down.

"How you doing?" Scott asked Katie.

Lacey had cut Katie's pants up the side and he could see that her leg had begun to swell.

"It hurts bad, but I've felt worse," Katie said.

"You're going to be okay, Katie. I promise," Lacey said, then looked over at him with eyes that searched his for reassurance.

"We both promise," he said as he looked down at this young woman that had already lost so much. He wouldn't let her down. He'd get Katie to the hospital, where they were waiting with the anti-venom she needed.

"Okay, I need a couple of your walking sticks. The longer the better," he said, beginning to come up with a plan.

Dennis carried over two sticks that measured at least five feet. They would work. Discussing what other items they had among them, it was decided that leaving Katie on the sleeping bag and inserting the sticks into the sides would work—if the stitching on the sleeping bag held up. One of the younger veterans handed over some rope and explained that if they tied the ropes onto the sticks it would help to support Katie's weight.

As the rest of the group worked on the makeshift stretcher, Dennis and Scott studied the map and spoke with the helicopter pilot. A clear piece of land lay two miles to the west of them. They'd hike to that point, carrying Katie, and she'd be flown to the hospital all within the hour.

"I cleaned the site, but it's still swelling," Lacey said as they began the long walk to their point of contact. "She will be okay, won't she?"

"The hospital has anti-venom waiting for her. We just need to keep her calm and get her there." Scott said, knowing that he hadn't really answered her question.

They'd both made promises to Katie and they were both worrying that it might be a promise they wouldn't be able to keep.

The people carrying the stretcher would switch out every fifteen minutes, so that they didn't tire out and slow down progress. And as soon as the stretcher was declared safe by Dennis, they set out.

No one spoke in the group. Everyone understood that getting Katie to the anti-venom as quickly as possible could mean the difference between life and death.

As the group walked Scott was surprised to see that Lacey was keeping up with the stretcher that carried Katie. She'd gone into nurse mode now, and she probably wasn't even aware that she had increased her earlier speed and was now as fast as with the most experienced of the group.

They heard the helicopter before they got to the clearing. As Lacey took a moment to check Katie's pulse, Scott gave report to the crew as they unloaded the stretcher.

"You need to go with her. If the poison affects her respiratory system you might have to intubate her," Lacey said as Katie was strapped into the stretcher.

"I know. Are you going to be okay?" he asked.

"I'll be fine—just take care of Katie. Her pulse is up into the one-twenties and the swelling is up to her knee now. If she loses that leg…"

"She'll be fine," Scott said, then called the group together.

Lacey watched as the helicopter flew toward the city. Turning around, she was surprised to see that everyone was staring at her. Scott had been joking when he'd told them she and Dennis were in charge now, right? What did *she* know about leading a group like this?

"So, Dennis, which way do we go from here?" she asked.

Walking over to her, Dennis showed her the map and explained Scott's plan to take a detour along a path that would lead them back to the lake. He would call his cousin when he reached the hospital and make arrangements for them to be picked up there. Dennis estimated that they would make it back to the original trail in a couple of hours, and with the shortcut Scott had mapped out they'd soon be back at the river.

The walk back was somber, with none of the joking

that had carried them through the trail earlier in the day. The group had lost its leader now. With all of them worried about their fellow veteran they had become disheartened and there wasn't any way for her to fix that.

Or was there?

Moving to the back of the group, she pulled out her phone and checked for service. Except for a couple texts to check on Alston, she'd not used her phone in the last two days. She typed a text to Scott and waited to see if it would get through to him. He soon texted back that Katie was responding well to the anti-venom. After getting that bit of good news, she texted him her plan and told him what she would need to make it work. Having put everything into place, she moved back up next to Dennis and let him know of the changes.

The whole lot of them were dragging by the time they made it to the bank, but in only minutes she spotted Scott's cousin's boat, headed toward them.

As they loaded onto the boat she received a text from Scott letting her know that everything was ready. It wouldn't be the same without Scott and Katie, of course, but that didn't mean that the rest of the group couldn't enjoy their last night together.

As they pulled onto the shore from where they'd started their trip across the lake, only hours earlier, Dennis explained the change of plan and they all started back to the camp ground. She wasn't surprised when a cheer went up.

While everyone else headed for the coolers that had been dropped off for them, Lacey called the hospital to check on Katie. The charge nurse on duty assured her that Katie was doing better and that the anti-venom was starting to do its job. If everything continued as it was going now there would be no danger of Katie having any permanent damage to her leg.

Lacey ended the call and shared the good news with the rest of the group.

Someone had unpacked the food and they all made sandwiches. A few complained that this was not *true* camping, but most were thrilled that they wouldn't be relaying on the dried food they'd brought with them.

Unlike the first night when the group had camped together, tonight they gathered as a group. Soon a fire was built, and as they watched the moon rise in the sky they became more subdued. This bunch of people had been through so much to get where they were today.

She watched as Zach, one of the new members of Scott's program, who'd hardly spoken for the first day of the hike, pulled up the leg of his pants and showed the guy next to him his below-the-knee prosthesis. Somehow, in just a short amount of time, this man who had been a stranger to them had been taken in by the others and now felt safe enough to share the most vulnerable part of his life.

Scott had made that possible. Their leader and her friend Scott could do miraculous things for other people. He'd been there for her when she'd been at her lowest and had never asked for anything from her until now. But now she was afraid that Scott wanted more than friendship between them, and she didn't know what to do about it.

As Lacey watched the last couple of hikers head into the cabin she realized she was sitting in the same spot where she and Scott had sat the night before. Had it only been one day since she'd shared that second life-changing kiss with him? Looking down, she saw some of the scribbling in the dirt she had done the night before, surprised to see that she could still make out her late husband's name.

She'd been so angry after Ben had been killed. She'd been angry at the people who had caused his death and angry at Ben for not sharing with her just how much of a dangerous situation he'd be in at the hospital where he'd served.

Then Scott had come home and he'd been there to listen to her, letting her work through her feelings and never judging her. The anger was gone now, and she was learning to live as a single mom. Her life was calm and safe. Until now.

It was as if with one kiss Scott had awakened something deep inside her that she'd thought had died with Ben, and then with the second kiss Scott had changed all the plans she had for her life. And she had no idea what she was going to do about it.

CHAPTER SIX

LACEY WATCHED AS her son ran off to join the crowd
of kids gathered around a table stacked with birthday
presents. She had done her best to avoid Scott for the
last week, but standing in his mother's backyard at his
nephew's birthday party she knew she wouldn't be able
to avoid him today.

She'd tried her best to come up with a good excuse
for not being able to take Alston to Jason's party, but
then decided it wasn't fair to Alston to keep him from
enjoying a day with his friends. While Lacey sometimes
found Scott's large family overwhelming, Alston loved
to attend their big family gatherings.

Scott's parents' yard was filled with activity this afternoon, with a group of teenagers playing football in
one corner while the younger kids played in the large
blow-up bouncy house that had been rented for the occasion.

Turning toward the group of adults, she had no trouble picking out Scott among the guests, and as if he
had sensed her presence he turned at that moment and
waved.

"Oh, Lacey," said a voice from behind her, "we are
all so glad you could make it today."

Lacey turned to find Scott's mother coming across the yard, carrying a tray in each hand filled with glasses of various sizes.

"Let me help you, Mrs. Boudreaux," Lacey said as she took one of the trays.

"Lacey, I appreciate your momma teaching you such good manners, but you know we don't stand on formality here. And with you and Scott… Well, he didn't want me to say anything, but it would make me so happy if you could call me Mary," Scott's mother said. "Now, if you could just take those drinks over there, by Scott, I'll carry these over to the kids' table. Make sure everybody knows that I've added a little something to the adult drinks. We don't want to get the two mixed up."

Lacey watched as the woman stopped at the first group of kids she came to and started handing out glasses. She seemed extremely flustered today, which was not like her normal composed demeanor. Was Scott's mom okay? Maybe she should mention it to him.

Of course it could be that she'd just had a few too many sips of the "adult" drinks she had specially prepared!

Scott met her as she crossed the lawn and took the tray from her. "I didn't know if you were going to make it or not," he said.

"You know Alston would never miss Jason's party," Lacey said.

"I left a message asking if you wanted to ride here with me, but you never returned my call. You barely talked to me Tuesday at work. And you've ignored my calls. Any other man would think that you were trying to avoid him," Scott said.

"Any other man?" she asked.

"My self-esteem is higher than most," he said, then winked at her.

And there it was. That little bit of mischief that pulled her in every time. No one could stay mad at this man for very long—not when he turned on that Southern charm of his.

By the time they arrived at the group of adults Lacey had relaxed. Things would be fine between the two of them. Scott was back to his normal self. They could be friends—just friends—and forget about the complicated attraction between the two of them They were adults. They both knew that a little bit of sexual desire was not enough to risk the end of a great friendship.

"Oh, Lacey, we are so glad you could make it today. It seems like every time we have a family get-together you're working. We've missed you," said Rayanne as she gave Lacey a tight hug.

Lacey pulled back and looked at Scott's oldest sister. She'd always gotten along well with Scott's whole family, but except for holiday parties and Jason's birthday parties, she'd not attended any more intimate family get-togethers.

Rayanne gave her another gentle hug. "We are all *so* glad about you and Scott," the woman whispered in Lacey's ear.

What did she mean about her and Scott? Surely Scott hadn't told them about the kiss they'd shared? Maybe Scott's sister had been drinking out of the same cup his mother had been drinking from.

Lacey pulled back and looked into the woman's eyes. They were bright and clear, with no sign that she had been into her momma's "adult" beverages.

"Mom," Alston called as he ran up to her. "Can I change and get in the pool? Scott's dad is out there."

Alston knew his mother's rules. Even though he was a good swimmer, she'd never let him swim in a pool without an adult present.

"Sure—just make sure you listen to Mr. Boudreaux," Lacey said.

"Scott? You want to swim with us?" Alston asked.

"I'll be there in a few minutes," Scott said.

"Alston is such a good kid. You know we all love that boy like he's one of our own," Rayanne said.

Lacey gave the group a smile. Unlike herself, Alston had always had the gift of making friends easily—just like his father.

"Scott was telling us about the hike y'all took last weekend," said Scott's youngest sister Leslie. "It sounds so romantic. The two of you out in the swamp, working together to save that vet…"

"There was nothing romantic about it," Lacey said, "Katie could have died out there. There's absolutely no room for romance when you're fighting to save someone's life."

"Well, surely you and Scott were able to find *some* time for romance?" Scott's sister said, with a smile and a wink that matched her brother's.

At that moment the pieces of the puzzle started to come together. The over-the-top welcome from his mother, the strange comments Rayanne had made… It all made sense now.

Scott's family had decided that she and Scott were an item. But why? After all these years of being friends, why would they suddenly think that the two of them were involved? Because they had gone together on a hike? They'd gone plenty of places together over the years, and the hike had been a planned event for the veterans, not a romantic tryst for the two of them. There was no reason for them to think things had changed between the two of them.

But things *had* changed. After they'd shared that last mind-blowing kiss everything had changed. But there was no way they could know about that. Unless...

Lacey felt the rush of blood to her face. What had Scott done? Did he think just because she had responded to his kiss that he was suddenly free to share this with his family? She'd have to straighten this out right now.

"Do you have a moment, Scott?" Lacey asked. She tried to sound casual, but that was hard to pull off when her face was glowing like Rudolph's nose. "I need to discuss something with you," she said.

Scott looked over at her, and then he looked down at his feet. The man was busted and he knew it. She'd kill him for this. There was no reason for him to have shared what had taken place between the two of them with his family—with anybody, period. *She'd* certainly not told anyone. She'd never share something that personal.

Taking Scott by the hand, she pulled him away from the rest of the group. From the look on Scott's face, her smile must be horrific. Good—let him fear for his life. If he'd shared the details of their kiss with anyone she'd kill him for sure.

Scott stared at Lacey's face. He had known he should warn her about his family, and he'd planned to do just that when they shared a ride over to his parents' house. But she had been avoiding him and he'd never gotten a chance to explain things to her.

He'd have some groveling to do now, but surely Lacey would understand why he'd done it?

"Is there something you want to tell me?" Lacey asked, once she'd pulled them inside the French doors to his parents' house.

He knew she was using her "mom voice" on him. He recognized it immediately as the one his own mom had used on him and his sisters. It was that tone of voice that could make him feel guilty without even knowing what he was supposed to be guilty of. Only this time he knew exactly what he was guilty of.

It had seemed so innocent at the time. When his sister had come to him with concerns, saying that it wasn't healthy for him to be spending all his time with his dead friend's wife and child when, according to her and his mother, he should be focusing his time on finding his own wife and family, he hadn't known what to say. If he'd tried to explain the guilt he felt that Ben hadn't made it home, or his promise to his friend that he would look out for his friend's family, it would have just upset them more.

The two of them moved aside as one of his nieces headed out the door to the pool. They couldn't discuss this here.

Now he was the one who took her by her hand and led her to the back of the house, to his old room. Shutting his door, he turned back to Lacey. Her eyes, usually full of humor, sparked with anger now. He'd have to explain everything fast, before she went off.

"Look, I'm sorry, but it started off very innocently. I didn't mean for you to find out, or to have to deal with my family. You know how they are—they're constantly trying to get in my business, especially my sisters. Living with four meddling females has never been easy."

One look at Lacey's face told him he wasn't helping matters. How was he going to get her to understand that it didn't matter? What did it matter what his family thought? But of course if it really didn't matter he wouldn't be in the spot he was now...

"I didn't mean for things to go this far," he said.

"You didn't mean for things to go this far? What did you think was going to happen? You just said that they're meddlers. Did you think that suddenly they'd leave you alone? That once they knew you'd kissed me and I had responded they would stay out of things?"

Scott stopped his pacing around the room. What was she talking about?

"Do you tell your family about every kiss you have with someone or is it just the mind-blowing ones you share?" she asked. "And I've been thinking about that. How do we even know that it was your kiss that made me respond? Isn't it more likely that the fact I haven't had sex in the past three years is the reason it affected me that way?" Lacey said, and then she stepped in front of him. "I could have responded to any man the same way."

Scott was getting tired of listening to Lacey's excuses for their attraction. He knew in his heart that Lacey would never have responded to someone else like she had to him, and it was time he proved it to her.

Crossing to the door, he locked it. He didn't want anyone to interrupt them. This see-saw of emotions would end here. He'd leave her in no doubt about whom she would and wouldn't respond to.

Turning back to her, he walked over till only inches

were between the two of them. "Is that what you really think or are you just too scared to admit that you liked me kissing you?" he asked.

She knew just as well as he did that this thing between the two of them wasn't a fluke. He just had to make her admit it, so that this argument could be set aside once and for all.

"I'm not scared," she said. "I just don't understand why you want to ruin a perfectly good relationship because of a couple kisses."

Taking her face in his hands, he slowly lowered his lips. "Do you want me to kiss you, Lacey?" he asked.

He felt the shiver that ran down her body. He watched her eyes go soft, then close.

"Yes," she whispered.

He placed his lips lightly on hers and pulled her body into his arms. He fought back the urgent need to possess her that filled his body every time he held her close to him. Instead he swiped his lips softly across hers, coaxing her to open for him. Her lips opened and he slowly let his tongue dance with hers. He felt her relax in his arms.

Moving his arms up her back, he let himself caress her. His body tightened as her arms moved around him and they moved closer together. There was no space left between them now. They moved as one as they fit their bodies together, her breasts pressed against his chest, his erection cradled against her abdomen.

He'd been afraid to let her see just how much she affected him the other times they had kissed, afraid that he would scare her away, but today she would know exactly what she did to him and what he could do for her.

His hands cupped her bottom and brought her up

against him. Their kisses were driving him crazy and they were not enough. Her body slid against him and they both moaned. Did she know what she was doing to him? Did she understand that this was more than just sexual attraction?

In one movement he picked her up and laid her on the bed, pinning her down with his body. He drew back from her. Her eyes, clouded with desire, opened slowly and stared back at him. He wanted to watch her face the first time he touched her. He moved beside her and turned her toward him. He pushed her shirt up, then moved his hand over her breast. He could feel the hard peak of her nipple through her bra.

"Could just any man do this to you, Lacey?" he asked as his other hand undid the button of her jeans. He slid his hand inside and felt her through her panties. She pushed against his hand and he knew he had her. "Could any man make you this turned on?"

He pressed his hand against her sex and watched as her eyes closed in pleasure. She was so responsive to him. *For* him. He knew what she needed—what they both needed—but with his family just outside he knew they couldn't make love. Frustration filled him and his body protested. He'd started something he couldn't finish and that hadn't been fair to Lacey.

He lowered his head to hers and kissed her deeply. Suddenly she took over the kiss, her tongue stroking his urgently with a desperation that drained him of all his good intentions. There was only one way this could end.

He moved his hand against her again and moaned. She was so wet and warm. This was going to kill him, but he couldn't stop himself.

He parted her and felt the hard bud of her core

against his fingers. He increased the friction as he kneaded it. She shook in his arms as the climax hit her and he smothered her moans with his mouth. His body was strung tight with a need he fought to suppress. If he died here, with his hand inside Lacey's jeans, his mother would kill him.

The thought of his mother helped to cool his body's demands.

Lacey lay in his arms, limp and satiated. Seeing her that way made dealing with the frustration of his own body worth it all. He needed a cold shower, but a dip in his parents' pool would have to do.

When Lacey opened her eyes he couldn't help but smile. Her lips were red with their kisses and she looked up to him with soft, welcoming eyes. He smiled again. Her smile faltered and then her lips began to tremble. Was she going to cry?

"I'm sorry," she said as she looked away.

Was that embarrassment? The two of them had always had a very open relationship. They'd shared their feelings and thoughts without any worry of judgment between the two of them. That wasn't going to change now.

"Lacey, you have nothing to be sorry about. I love the way you respond to me. I don't want you to ever be embarrassed by anything the two of us do together."

Lacey looked up at him. She still seemed unsure—something the Lacey he knew never felt— but there was some humor in her eyes now.

"I'm not embarrassed by that," she said. "It's just that you… I didn't… I mean you still haven't…"

She straightened her shoulders and looked into his eyes. Now, *this* was the Lacey he knew.

"You didn't get anything out of that. I should have done something to…ah…help," she said.

Scott broke out in laughter, and then choked when he heard his mother's voice calling down the hall.

"Scott? Lacey?"

Lacey covered his mouth with her hand and he nipped at it with his teeth.

"I told you—I saw them headed over across the street," his oldest sister said. "I think they were going to check out that old creek bed."

He had no doubt that Rayanne had seen the two of them walk into the house. He owed her a big favor for covering for him, and he had no doubt she was already figuring out what she was going to blackmail him out of.

"Shh… If your mother catches us in here I'm going to kill you. And don't think I've forgotten about the little oversharing that has caused this mess you've gotten us into," she said.

They heard the back door open and shut and both relaxed back onto the bed.

"Why in the world did you think you had to share what happened between the two of us with your family?" Lacey asked as she chewed on her bottom lip.

It was something he'd seen her do a thousand times and it had never bothered him before. Now all he could think about was those lips and all the things he wanted to do with them.

Knowing that thoughts like that were only going to make things worse, he moved away from Lacey and sat on the end of the bed.

"I didn't tell my family about kissing you," he said.

"If you didn't tell them then why are they acting so

strange?" Lacey asked as she straightened her clothes and sat next to him.

He noticed that she'd moved a little farther away from him. Was she regretting what they'd done? Or was she finding the proximity of the two of them together and the bed as much of a temptation as he was?

"You know how my sisters are always trying to set me up with their friends, right?"

She nodded her head and moved into a cross-legged position, scooting a little farther away again.

"I got tired of all the harassment from the three of them, and then one day Rayanne—who seems to think the world of you, so don't take this personally—started on at me about dating one of her husband's cousins. She said the family was worried about me spending so much time with you and Alston instead of trying to find my own wife and family. I told her that we had plans for the weekend that she was trying to set me up. She made a comment, said that the two of us would make a nice couple and it was too bad we weren't taking our relationship a little more seriously. I saw the way out of having to deal with her matchmaking and worrying my mother so I took it."

"You took it?" Lacey said. "What does *that* mean?"

She was giving him that stern momma stare again, and he felt the need to squirm. How did women *do* that?

"I just told her that she didn't know everything about my life and that maybe we *were* in a serious relationship."

Lacey shook her head at him, a look of pure disappointment on her face.

"Don't look at me that way. It worked like a charm. Not one of my sisters has tried to set me up in the last nine months. And my mom's not always calling to check up on me." He said. "It's been kind of like getting one of those 'get out of jail free' cards when you're playing that board game."

"Well, I hope you've enjoyed it—because the getting out free part has run out and now we have a mess to fix," Lacey said as she rose off the bed.

Panic hit him. If his sisters found out he'd been lying about his and Lacey's relationship they'd make his life hell. And the truth was Rayanne hadn't been totally wrong. He'd already realized that he enjoyed the time he spent with Lacey way more than time with any of the girls he had dated. He couldn't admit it to Lacey, but his feelings for her had changed months ago.

Scott had always found his friend's wife attractive, but the friendship between him and Lacey had been casual. He'd respected her nursing abilities as they'd worked together in the ER, but his real friendship had been with Ben. His friendship with Lacey had really only grown after Ben had passed. They'd both needed someone to talk to, and the sharing of their grief had been brutal for both of them.

It hadn't been until the past few months that he'd noticed their friendship was changing again. How Lacey hadn't seen the change he could not understand…

"Are you coming?" she asked, and then froze. "Although maybe it would be better if we went out separately."

Scott looked up at Lacey and grinned. He'd learned a few tricks as a result of living with his sisters. Women were always concerned about what other women thought of them. It was something he never had understood.

Men just weren't built that way. They were who they were and they didn't care what their friends thought.

"You know Rayanne knows we were in this room alone, don't you? She's probably already told Amy and Leslie by now." He watched as she nibbled on that sexy bottom lip of hers again. "If we go out there and tell them that it's all been a mistake they'll never believe us. How could they? I mean, how is it going to look if we say we were just passing the time, making out, and then tell them that we're just friends?"

Lacey looked up at him, her eyes narrow and shooting darts. Maybe that last part had been a little overkill.

"So what you're saying is that I'll look like a slut if I walk out there and tell your sisters that I was just making out with their brother, but they've totally mistaken the nature of our relationship?" she said.

He decided it was a good time for him to get up. Rising, he moved over toward the door. A little distance between the two of them might be good right now.

"That's not what I meant," he said.

No one would ever think such a thing about Lacey and she knew it.

"I know what you meant. You've gotten yourself in a pickle with your family and now you're looking for a way out. If you want my help, just ask. I'm not one of your sisters."

"Okay, I need your help. But I don't expect you to lie to them. We could just act normal and let them draw their own conclusions," he said. "Please?" he asked.

"It's not like I've got much of a choice, is it?" she said as she moved beside him. "I guess we'll just have to hope they have the good manners not to say anything about where we've been, because if they do…"

She didn't have to finish the sentence. He already knew he owed her for keeping his sisters off his back.

CHAPTER SEVEN

LACEY SPENT THE rest of the day and early evening with Scott plastered to her side. She'd wanted to needle him in front of his sisters, but she'd decided against it. If Scott needed her to protect him against his sisters' constant matchmaking, she would do it. Not that he'd really given her much of a choice.

As they moved from group to group she wasn't surprised by the looks they received from his various family members. While everyone had always been nice to Lacey, now that they thought there was something between the two of them his family seemed to have opened their arms to receive her.

By the time she had rounded up Alston and got him into the car she was looking forward to the peaceful quiet of her own home. She could feel the eyes of everyone on her back as Scott walked her to her car.

"Make sure your mother knows what a good time I had," Lacey told Scott, then leaned in closer to him and whispered, "You know everyone is watching us, right?"

"They're waiting to see if I kiss you goodnight," Scott said as he moved in closer to her.

She looked into the back seat, where Alston was buckled in and had started a video.

"I hate to disappoint them," she said—and realized too late that Scott had taken her words wrong when he dipped his head towards hers.

His lips touched hers for a moment and then were gone, leaving her wishing for more.

"That should make them happy," Scott said as he smiled down at her.

She didn't understand what was happening between the two of them. No matter how she wished it wasn't true, Scott was proving her wrong about their attraction to each other. It wasn't something that was going to go away if they ignored it, but she was afraid if they let it run its course there would only be pieces of their friendship left to pick up.

Still, looking up at him now, she couldn't help but think of what she'd experienced with him earlier. Just the thought of his hands on her sent a hot blush rushing up her face.

She turned her face away from him, hoping that he wouldn't notice. He'd proved to her that it was her attraction to him that set her on fire. She would never have been able to let another man touch her like he had, and that scared her. She'd only experienced that depth of desire before with Ben, and that had been so long ago.

If only she could accept what Scott offered her, but it was too hard for her to make that next move in her life. Was she ready for a romantic relationship? She couldn't deny the desire she felt for Scott, but where would that lead them? Their friendship was so important to both of them, and adding more to the mix, even if it was just sex, could be dangerous.

"Lacey, are you okay?" Scott asked.

She realized he'd been talking to her but she couldn't remember a word.

"I'm sorry. I must be more tired than I thought," she said.

"Do you want me to drive you home? You didn't drink any of that stuff my mom made, did you?" he asked.

He'd moved back from her now and she bent to open the car door. She needed to get Alston home. She needed to get away from Scott. A warm bath and a glass of wine would help to relax her and clear her mind. She had to figure out where she and Scott went from tonight.

"I'm fine," she said as she climbed into the car and started it up.

"I wanted to ask you if you're busy Thursday night," he said. "Jack called me yesterday and invited us to Baby Blues. Pop's playing there and he wants us to come."

Baby Blues was one of the top blues and jazz places in the city. The fact that they had invited Pop to play was amazing, and she couldn't help but want to see him perform there.

"Are you taking my momma out on a date?" Alston asked from the backseat.

When was she going to learn to watch what she said in front of her son? It didn't matter how involved he was with something else, he seemed always to be listening to her conversations—something that had gotten her into trouble more than once.

"Would it bother you if I took your mother out on a date?" Scott asked as he leaned into the car to talk to her son.

She started to interrupt him. Her son loved Scott like

a favorite uncle—which was really what Scott was to him. She didn't want to confuse him, which gave her another reason to slow down and be careful before her relationship with Scott went any further.

"If you marry my momma would that make me and Jason cousins?" her son asked.

The shock of her son's question took her breath away. No one had been talking about marriage. Where had he gotten that idea from?

"Why would you ask that?" Lacey's voice was a high-pitched squeak.

"How about we save that conversation till later? Your mother is looking a little sick right now," Scott said.

The smile he gave her took her breath away, except this time it had nothing to do with embarrassment.

"Go home, Lacey. You can tell me if you're free to go out on a *date*—" he turned his head toward Alston and winked at her son "—tomorrow at work."

Lacey put the car in Drive and pulled away, heading home to her hot bath and wine, all the while trying to make an inventory of her wine collection in her head. Because at some point in the afternoon she'd realized that Scott's family were *right* to worry about her and Scott's relationship.

Over the last few years Scott had taken Ben's place in her life everywhere except in her bedroom—and now she was considering letting him in there too. She was definitely going to need more than one glass of wine tonight.

Lacey sat next to Scott as they drove toward the club where Pop would be playing and wondered for the hundredth time why she hadn't canceled this "date" with Scott.

The ER had been busy all week, and she'd been too tired to take the time to discuss it with Scott—though she had taken the time to tell her son that she and Scott had gone out together many times, and calling their time out together by another word didn't mean that things were going to change between the three of them.

When her son had asked her again about marriage she had tried to explain to him that she didn't know if she would marry again. She'd never hidden from him the heartbreak she had gone through after his father had died.

She knew that in some ways her explanation to her son made her a coward, but unlike Scott she had never felt that was something she needed to overcome. Fear was a healthy emotion that kept you from doing stupid things that could get you hurt or killed, and there was no reason she should have to be embarrassed by it.

Scott was quiet while they drove into the warehouse district of the city, where some of the newer clubs and restaurants were located. They'd both dressed up tonight, and Scott wore a dark charcoal dress suit that showed off his wide shoulders and trim waist.

Unable to find anything in her closet that she'd felt appropriate, she'd made a quick trip the day before to one of the trendy shops in the French Quarter and bought a short cocktail dress in a dark emerald green. Putting it on tonight, she had felt like a princess, and she'd forced her embarrassed son to dance a waltz with her in the foyer before being picked up by one of their neighbors.

She'd had second thoughts about the dress while

she'd waited for Scott. The short hem and the low cut of the dress were made for seduction, and she didn't want Scott to get the wrong impression.

Or did she?

She didn't even know her own mind. The memories of Scott's hands on her as he'd brought her to orgasm had played through her memory a thousand times now, and still she didn't know how she felt about this newest change in their relationship.

She didn't like change. She liked a nice, orderly life. But now it seemed everything but orderly, with emotions she hadn't felt in years flooding through her. And while she went through this repeat of puberty she had to make sure she didn't give Scott any false hope of their relationship leading to something more serious.

Lacey would never want to hurt him, but she had no plans of marrying again. And even if she did, it certainly wouldn't be to a man who was just like her husband—a man that would put his life on the line while he had a wife and son at home, worrying about him. No, she didn't need another thrill-seeker. It had only been a year since she had been able to stop seeing her grief counselor. She couldn't take the loss of someone else she loved.

They pulled into the valet parking and she caught herself playing with the ruffled hem of the dress. She did feel like a princess tonight, and she couldn't decide if that was a good thing or a bad thing. Ben had called her the queen of his life, but she'd never understood why. She'd been an everyday wife and mother who'd spent her time washing socks and cleaning bathrooms when she hadn't been off working at her very unqueenly job of mopping up blood and dealing with drunks.

The doorman opened her car door and she stepped out into a gated courtyard glittering with fairy lights. With its big pots of blooming pink and purple flowers, the place resembled a magical garden.

Scott took her arm and they were ushered inside by the staff. Here, too, there were pots and hanging baskets overflowing with beautiful flowers.

The sound of piano music greeted them as they entered, but it didn't sound the same as the music they had heard that first night they had gone to hear Pop. This music didn't pull at her emotions like the blues she had experienced then. This music was intended to be only part of the background of the magical room they entered. The real music would start when Pop took the stage.

They were taken to a table in a corner, where they would have a good view of the stage but still have some privacy from the rest of the room.

"I thought we would be sitting with Jack," she said, breaking the silence.

"Pop's sister and his nephew's family have come into town for the show. I'm sure we'll see them before the night is done," he said, as he took the wine list from the server and then passed it to her. Scott had always been more of a beer kind of man.

She'd always been happy to let Ben choose the wine when they were out. But after Ben had died she'd gone through the wine he had stored in the small butler pantry in their house rather quickly. Though it hadn't necessarily been a healthy way to research wine, she had learned what she liked and what she didn't.

She ordered something she thought Scott would like, then handed the list back to the server. This was ridiculous. If Scott hadn't called this a date, they'd both be enjoying the night. Now everything felt magical and beautiful, but not quite the same. Where was that comfortable way the two of them used to talk together about anything and everything?

"Relax," Scott said, and then looked down pointedly to where she was wringing the linen napkin between her hands.

She made her fingers let go of the napkin and smoothed it back in place on the table, then replaced the silverware she had moved. Why was she so nervous? Maybe because all she had thought about since that day at his parents' house was how much she wanted him?

Her hand knocked against a crystal glass, splashing water onto the table.

Scott reached over and took her hand, then rested it in his palm. She took a deep breath and made her body relax. She was going to make a fool of herself if she didn't get her nerves under control.

The piano music stopped and she turned as Pop took the stage. Applause filled the room, then quieted as Pop began to play. The music he played was all blues, and it tugged at her heartstrings. A young woman took to the stage with him, and applause broke out again. When the woman started to sing Lacey began to understand the true magic of the blues.

Couples were taking to the dance floor, and when Scott rose and held his hand out to her she placed hers in his.

Lacey let the music carry her off into another world, where the blues had been born. She could see a room filled with smoke, where the smell of bourbon and whisky drowned out the smell of spicy dishes and sweat.

A younger version of Pop sat at the piano, playing, and a woman told a story of love and loss that brought tears to Lacey's eyes.

"There's something magical about his music, isn't there?" she said as they swayed together in time with the song.

"I believe so. He has a special talent. There's no way to know how long he'll be able to continue to play, but Jack's going to help his father enjoy the rest of the time he has doing what he loves, and fortunately we get to enjoy it too."

She relaxed her body against Scott's and let the music guide her.

As soon as Pop had finished playing his first set Jack brought him around to see them. Jack once more thanked Scott for all his help before returning to their table, where Pop's sister was wiping her eyes with one of the linen napkins.

The soft piano music once more in the background soothed Lacey's nerves and she relaxed as they ate, finding it easy to fall back into the kind of friendly conversation they had come to enjoy with each other. The music and the wine were doing their job and, combined with good food and conversation, she had to say that for a first date, if they were counting it as one, it had been perfect.

They left the restaurant with Scott holding her hand, and she felt none of the tension that had filled her earlier in the night as they drove to her house.

She had prepared herself for Scott to kiss her goodnight at the door, but as they stepped onto the porch she admitted to herself that she didn't want the night to end. But it had been years since she had gone out on a first date, and she wasn't really sure what acceptable behavior was now. She didn't want Scott to think she was inviting him in for more than conversation…

"Would you like to come in?" she asked as she opened the door. She tried to make her words sound casual. "I can make some coffee if you'd like."

Turning around, she found that Scott had moved closer. Without waiting for his answer she turned back and walked into the house. She felt his eyes on her body and she couldn't help but smile. Yeah, she knew she looked good in this dress. It had been worth every penny she'd paid for it.

He closed the door quietly behind them. Turning again, she admired him. He moved with a stride that reminded her of a large tiger, stalking its prey. The look in his eyes quickly told her *she* was the prey.

"Coffee?" she asked, and managed to slip through his arms right before he could have her pinned against the counter.

Moving around the kitchen, she started a pot of coffee. She'd thought he'd follow her, and was surprised to see him punching buttons on her entertainment center. He took his phone out and hit some more buttons, and a few moments later she heard the unmistakable voice of Louis Armstrong.

"Nice," she said as she moved over to the couch. Sitting down, she straightened her dress.

"Yes, *very* nice," he said as he leaned against the mantel of the fireplace and stared at her. "Did you enjoy yourself tonight?" he asked.

"You know I did," she said. "Everything from the food to the service was perfect—and, of course, the music."

The song changed and she recognized the next song—
"A Kiss to Build a Dream On"—as it filled the room.

She smiled as Scott took a seat beside her. "One of
my favorites," she said.

"I know," Scott said, then moved in closer. "Face it,
Lacey, you're a romantic."

"Me?" she said. "You're the one who picked the
music."

She'd known this moment would come when she'd
asked him in. She wanted Scott to kiss her, to hold her.
She'd had only a small taste of what sex with Scott
could be and she wanted more, even though she knew
she might regret it tomorrow.

She moved into his arms, no longer willing to wait.
His lips touched hers as Louis sang about his sweetheart's lips and a kiss that only she could give him.
Lacey let herself melt into the music and into Scott's
arms.

One kiss stretched into another as the songs changed
again and again. Desire for more filled her. Scott had
removed his coat when he'd come into the room and her
hands unknotted his tie, then moved down his chest,
unbuttoning his shirt. She felt his hand slide up her leg
and under her dress. She'd dressed in stockings and
garters tonight—something she had never done before.

Scott's mouth moved down her face, then he nipped
at her earlobe. "You are driving me crazy," he whispered into her ear.

He let go of her, then turned her so that her legs were
draped over his lap. He worked his hands up her thighs,
unhooking each stocking and rolling them down inch
by inch. Then he pulled her into his lap. The cold air

cooled her warm flesh as he pushed the straps of her dress down, exposing her breasts.

She moaned as he cupped her breasts in his hands. She wiggled in his lap and his hands left her breasts and clamped on her hips. She fought back her need to move against him, but lost.

He moaned as she moved against the hard length of him. "Lacey, I can't take anymore. Either I leave now or I stay the night," he said as he looked into her eyes. "I don't want to pressure you. If you're not ready for this, tell me now."

Lacey tried to clear her sex-fogged mind. She knew what her body wanted. It had made it clear to both of them. But what did she want in her heart?

She wanted to feel alive again. She'd spent the last few years mourning not only her husband but the life she had planned to share with him. She wanted to feel desired as a woman. She wanted to make love and have a man make love to her. Was that too much to ask for?

No, it wasn't. She was tired of fighting this thing between her and Scott.

She searched for the guilt that she had known she would feel if ever she decided to take a man into her bed who wasn't Ben, but it wasn't there. She knew she would have to take this one step at a time, but she would take that first step tonight.

She climbed out of Scott's lap and saw the disappointment on his face.

"I want you Scott, but I don't want to hurt you. Something died inside me the day I lost Ben. You know that. You saw me at my worst. I can never go back to that place again. Before we go any further, I want to make sure you understand that this—" she held her arms out to her sides "—sex, is all I have to give you. And I'm not even sure I know how to do that anymore."

She waited, feeling foolish standing in front of Scott with half her clothes off, and then he stood and walked toward her, his face unreadable.

"Come…let me show you," he said as he held out his hand to her.

She gave him her hand and let him lead her into her bedroom—the one room in her house that she felt sure he had never entered.

She hadn't been kidding. She really couldn't remember how this was supposed to go. Scott stepped behind her and unzipped her dress, letting it fall to the floor. She'd lost her stockings in the living room, and the molded top of her dress hadn't allowed for a bra. Now she stood in only the lace of her panties and her garters. She felt awkward and self-conscious.

She wrapped her arms around herself as Scott turned her toward him. He ran his hands up her sides, then took her arms and wrapped them around his neck. Her breasts brushed against the fine blond hair of his chest, the friction causing her nipples to peak. Her body arched against his as he took her buttocks and ground himself against her as his lips found hers.

Her hands found his belt buckle and undid it. Then she tackled his pants button and zipper, pushing his pants down. She might not remember everything, but she was pretty sure more than just one of them needed to be undressed if this was going to work.

She moaned as Scott's lips traveled down her neck to her breast, then made him answer her moan with his own when she reached for him and found him already thick and hard. He walked her backwards to the bed, then gave her a playful push onto the mattress that had her laughing. Yes, she remembered this now.

She caught two handfuls of his curls when he bent to her, and she took his lips with hers as she pulled him down. She felt him between her legs, then froze as she tried to prepare herself for the pain she felt sure would follow. She needed him inside her so badly, but it had been so long…

"It's okay," Scott said softly into her ear. "Relax."

She forced herself to relax and open her thighs as Scott ran his hand up her leg. He parted her with his fingers, then inserted one finger slowly as another caressed her. She felt no pain as she relaxed her body and let the motion of Scott's fingers give her pleasure. His fingers continued to pump into her, before withdrawing to circle the nub of her core, and her body bowed up off the bed as the orgasm built and then crashed over her.

Her body felt boneless as Scott moved his hand up to caress her breast, but she still wanted more. She reached down between them and guided the length of him, relaxing as his hips moved against hers. She looked up as he slowly entered her, with small shallow thrusts that went deeper every time until he was seated inside her. His face was beautifully strong and he held himself with such control.

"Are you okay?" he asked between clenched lips.

He was fighting for control, and while she knew he was only trying to be careful for her sake, she wanted him to move.

"Yes," she said. "Now move."

She wrapped her legs around him, opening herself up so he could go deeper, then began to move against him.

His lips slammed into hers and he took control of

their lovemaking as he pumped harder and deeper. Her body tightened for a second time, and this time she couldn't hold back the scream that escaped into his mouth as his own coarse moan joined hers in their climax.

Scott opened his eyes and found bright green eyes staring back at him. The night before had been more than he had ever dreamed he would have with Lacey. And, though he knew that she'd turn away from him this morning, he was thankful for the time he'd had with her.

"What do you want for breakfast? I'm starved," she said as she rolled away from him and moved off the bed.

She'd slept in the nude and he enjoyed the view as she moved away from him and went into the adjoining bathroom.

Scott stared after her. He felt as if he had entered some twilight zone. Where was the Lacey he knew? Not that he didn't like this one; she just wasn't the one he had been expecting this morning.

He got up and looked around for his clothes. Pulling on his wrinkled pants and shirt, he moved to where Lacey had left the bathroom door open. He could see her nervousness now, though she tried to hide it.

He leaned against the doorjamb and watched her brush her hair. She'd changed into a pair of pants and a tee shirt that declared her a magical unicorn nurse—which made absolutely no sense to him. What did nursing and unicorns have to do with each other?

She'd always been a beautiful woman, with that deep red hair and those green eyes that had a magic all their own. He remembered the heat in those eyes at his first thrust inside her, and then, after they'd made love, the way they had blinked slowly up at him as he'd tucked her against him and told her to go to sleep.

He watched now as her eyes seemed to dance from the mirror where she stood and then back at him. Yes, she was nervous, but she hadn't run away from him. Not yet. And nerves were something he could deal with.

It was a place to start on how he hoped their relationship would go from here—because, no matter what Lacey said, he knew she had more to give to their relationship than just sex.

Last night hadn't been just about sex, even if she wanted to believe that. He understood her reservations about opening her heart to someone else after the loss of Ben. He was scared to share his own feelings with her too, feelings that he wasn't even comfortable with himself.

"We could go by my place and let me change and then we could go out for breakfast," he offered. "What time does Alston get back from his sleepover?"

Maybe she'd feel better if they were out in public. He didn't want to scare her off, but he wasn't going to settle for just one night with her. They both deserved more than that. He just had to figure out how to get Lacey to admit that was what she wanted too.

"If you keep that up you're not going to have any hair left to brush," he said as he watched her jerk the brush through her hair over and over.

"That sounds perfect," she said, then put the brush down and turned toward him, giving him a lopsided smile. She really was trying to act like nothing had happened the night before, but she just couldn't pull it off.

They stopped by his place and he left her while he changed clothes. He thought about taking a shower, but he still feared that Lacey would run the moment her brain connected the dots and she realized that everything between them had changed once more. Lacey was a woman who liked lists and detailed planning, and he knew his spending the night with her had not been anywhere in her plans.

As they got back into his car he caught himself humming one of the Louis Armstrong songs that he had played the night before. They had gone a lot farther than one kiss now. That first kiss had changed everything between them, and last night would change them even more, but there was no going back now.

Lacey walked into the ER, dragging her feet. Alston had been home with a stomach bug, and for the last twenty-four hours she had been cleaning up after him. Single motherhood was such a glamorous job. She'd always sworn she'd never be a single mom, but she'd realized soon after Alston had been born that was exactly what she'd become. With Ben deployed, she'd been a single mom a lot of the time.

But now she needed to put a smile on her face and take care of other people's children, because that was her job. She rolled back her aching shoulders and soldiered on. She'd make it through this twelve-hour shift and then she'd go home and crash.

She heard a commotion in the first trauma room she passed and rushed in to see if she could help. A man lay on the table as staff moved around the room, each with their own job to do. Stepping in, she grabbed a pair of gloves and helped the med techs remove his clothes.

"What do we have?" she asked as she tossed the torn and bloody clothes over into a corner as she peeled them off his body, while being careful not to move him any more than was necessary. She noted an open femur fracture as she worked her way up.

"Motorcycle and car collision," answered the nurse across the room.

"Do we know who he is?" she asked Tess, the charge nurse she was supposed to relieve.

"Not yet. Paramedics called it in just minutes before they arrived," Tess said.

She looked at the table where the man lay still. An endotracheal tube protruded out of his mouth and his blond hair was matted with blood, curled around a face that was covered in road rash and cuts.

Her hand went to her chest as her heart dropped a beat. She headed for the pile of dirty clothes she'd left in the corner and found the pair of jeans she had cut from the man, went through each pocket, finding nothing that would identify the man.

She looked back over to the trauma table and forced herself to think logically. Yes, there was some resemblance between the man and Scott, but this man's build was stocky, where Scott was lean, with more defined muscles.

She took a calming breath. This man wasn't Scott.

But it could have been.

Scott had told her earlier, when he'd called to check on Alston, that it was such a beautiful day outside he was planning on riding his motorcycle to work tonight.

An ice-cold shiver ran up her back. She'd lived with all the chances Scott had taken since he'd come home from Afghanistan. She'd worried every time he'd left the country, looking for the next big thrill, the next big mountain to climb, the next extreme hike across Alaska, the next extreme cave dive. She'd made him call her as soon as he'd finished his ice climbing challenge and she'd chewed her nails down to the quick while she'd waited for that phone call.

But that feeling as if her stomach had been turned inside out and her heart ripped from her body, that feeling of total devastation that she'd had for just a moment, when she had realized that it could be Scott lying on that trauma table, was more than she could survive.

She understood why he and the other vets felt the need to prove themselves, but she had never wanted any part of that life.

She moved back as the staff pushed the patient over to get a CAT scan, then headed to the locker room to stow her bag.

A case of nerves struck her as her mind lingered on the thought that she could lose Scott just the way she had lost Ben. She'd had problems after she had lost Ben—not only with depression but with anxiety too. She'd been shattered and broken and barely able to take care of her son. She wouldn't do that to Alston again.

"Are you okay?" Scott asked as he came into the staff lounge. "Tess said you were looking a little pale. Did you catch Alston's stomach bug?"

Lacey looked up at the very man who was causing her such anxiety. How could she tell him that she'd suddenly realized she couldn't handle the chances he took? That she didn't want to lie awake at night and wait for the phone to ring and someone to tell her that he'd been killed climbing some rock somewhere, or drowned in some cave in the middle of nowhere?

She'd buried her head as deeply as possible, but she could still see that Scott had hopes of a future with her.

How could she take a step toward a future with Scott when it was too much to ask that he take a step back from that cliff-edge he seemed always to be running toward? Would it be fair of her to ask him to give up something that meant so much to him? Would it fair to her to live with the hidden fear that she'd someday have to bury Scott just as she'd buried Ben?

It wouldn't be fair to either of them.

"Lacey?" he said. "If you're sick, go home. We're not really busy right now, and I'm sure someone will come in and cover for you."

Her gut churned, and she wondered if possibly all this worry *was* just a result of her feeling ill or of her lack of sleep. Maybe after some rest she'd be able to figure out what it was she really wanted and what she could actually live with.

"Yeah, I think I'll go. I'll let Tess know and she can turn things over to the relief charge."

She walked right by him without another word.

Until she figured out what she was going to do it was better that she stayed away from Scott as much as possible.

CHAPTER EIGHT

SCOTT TRIED HARD to keep his mind on the conversation around him. He had picked Lieutenant Hines up at his assisted living facility, knowing that the group of veterans who usually attended his monthly meetings would enjoy hearing about the World War Two veteran's experiences. Unfortunately his mind kept wandering away from the discussion in the room to the one he'd had with Lacey three days ago.

He'd called and checked on her the day after she'd left work early, and she'd assured him that she was feeling better, but then she'd turned down his invitation to go out the next day. She was pulling away from him again and he didn't have a clue why. The only thing left for him to do was to confront her.

He looked at his watch. If the meeting didn't go late tonight he'd stop by her house on his way home.

He turned as the door to the building they rented opened and the woman he'd just been worrying over walked in, followed by Katie. Everyone rushed to greet Katie, and then the conversation turned back to their visitor.

Scott moved over to where Lacey had taken a seat and sat beside her.

"Do you want to talk about it?" he asked.

He'd always been attuned to the changes in Lacey's moods and he had no doubt that she knew exactly what he was asking about.

"No," she said.

He waited for her to say more. Okay, so she didn't want to talk to him about what was bothering her. Still, she was talking to him, so it couldn't be too bad.

"I'm surprised to see you here. What did Katie do to get you to come?" he asked.

"She didn't do anything. I offered to bring her," she said.

He let that roll around in his mind for a minute. Lacey had always limited her involvement in the Extreme Warrior program to just helping with the fundraisers they held, until she'd gone with them on their hike through the swamp. He'd tried to get her more involved over the years but she'd always resisted. It more than surprised him that she was willing to attend a meeting now. Maybe being out with the vets in the woods had helped her see how much it meant to them to have a challenge.

Scott had turned a lot of the administration duties he'd previously handled over to Dennis these last few months, and as Dennis now went through the minutes from the meeting the month before he knew he had chosen well.

He opened up a discussion on the next challenge they had planned, in Peru, and one of the younger vets brought up the possibility of volcano hiking in Hawaii the following year. Scott saw the incredulous look Lacey gave the young man when he began to name the different hiking trails on the islands.

"Don't worry. The volcanos aren't active," he said, and watched her relax back into her seat.

By the time Lieutenant Hines had finished answering more questions it was late and the group started to break up.

"There's just one more thing we need to discuss." Dennis raised his hand as some of the veterans groaned. "I know. This will just take a minute. I got a letter in the mail today that I want to share with everyone."

It was common that when members moved away they wrote back to their friends as a group, and everyone always enjoyed listening to Dennis reading the letters. Everyone took their seats again.

"This letter is from the City of New Orleans. I read it earlier, and it's about as dry as week-old bread." Everyone laughed at Dennis's corny attempt at humor. "Basically what it says is that our fearless leader, Scott, has gotten himself nominated for a Special Citizen award. He's been invited to attend an awards dinner two weeks from now, where they will announce the winner."

Shocked at this announcement, Scott sat up straight as the other veterans gave him a round of applause mixed in with some good-natured heckling. With all the good programs in the city, how had his gotten this type of recognition?

Most of the members came by to give him a pat on the back before they left, or in Katie's case a kiss on the cheek.

He headed to the back of the hall to lock up the back door, then turned around to find Lacey standing behind him.

"I thought you'd left already," he said.

He couldn't help but reach out and push a tendril

of hair off her face and behind her ear. He let his hand linger over the soft skin of her earlobe. He watched as she turned her face into his palm before pulling away from him.

"You love all this," she said, and she indicated the room, where posters of planned trips and pictures from past challenges hung.

"I enjoy being able to help other vets, and you know I enjoy the thrill of the challenges. What's wrong, Lacey? You've been distant all week and I think I deserve to know why," he said.

She walked away from him and headed to the far wall, where pictures of the very first challenge the veterans had gone on were shown. Next to those pictures hung a five by seven picture of Ben, dressed in his officer's uniform.

"Ben used to talk about the two of you starting up a program like this when you got out of the military," Lacey said as she ran her fingers across the edge of Ben's picture. "He would be so proud of what you've done here."

"I hope so," he said as he came to stand next to her.

"I'm proud of you too, and I would never want to come between you and this group of vets," she said, then paused.

"I can hear the 'but' coming," he said. He turned towards her and took her hands in his. "Tell me what's wrong. It can't be that bad. Tell me what's happened that has you upset."

He took her chin in his hands and turned her face up towards his. He dropped a kiss on the tip of her nose and then her forehead, then waited.

"The other day at work they brought in a trauma patient, victim of a motorcycle accident, and for a moment I thought it was you," she said.

She pulled away from him and turned her back.

"I don't understand. This has something to do with work? I don't even remember a motorcycle wreck," he said.

She was going to walk away from him and he still didn't know why.

"It was right at shift-change. Just before you came on duty. And, no, this has nothing to do with work. It has to do with the fact that I looked down at that man and remembered you had told me you were going to ride your motorcycle to work that day. It could have been you. *You* could have been lying there on that stretcher, tubed and unresponsive. It was just more than I could take," she said. "I know it sounds stupid, but it doesn't change the fact that someday someone could come to my door and tell me that something bad has happened to you. Or you could go off on this volcano hiking— which sounds crazy—and fall in and burn to death."

"Or you could have someone slit your throat with a scalpel while you are innocently doing your job at the hospital," Scott said.

His gut twisted at the memory of that night in the ER. He could have lost her.

Lacey turned toward him, surprise written across her features. Yes, he could understand the fear she was feeling. He'd experienced that same fear. Except it hadn't been about some abstract possible situation. He'd witnessed the real thing as he'd watched her life or death about to be decided by a deranged drunk.

"We can work through this, Lacey," he said. "I know that losing Ben the way you did was brutal, but have you considered all the wives who have watched their husbands die slowly in front of their eyes as disease took them? How many times have we had to tell someone that their son or mother or wife has passed away unexpectedly?"

"I know in my head what you're saying is true, but that didn't stop me from panicking when I thought it was you lying on that stretcher. You *know* what I went through after I lost Ben. You *know* what a coward I am," she said as she turned back to him.

"You are not a coward," Scott said as he walked over to her.

Would she turn away from him now? Could he have lost her before she'd even given them a chance?

"Yes, I am—but I'm trying to do better. It's going to take some work, and I'm going to need you to be patient with me," Lacey said, and then she turned toward him and walked into his arms.

He closed his arms around her. She was giving the two of them a chance, and for now that was all he could ask.

"Katie is waiting for me. I promised to take her to the hospital tonight, so that she can thank everyone who took care of her," she said against his shoulder.

He made his arms relax around her. She wasn't running away from him. Not this time.

As she raised her face up to his he lowered his lips gently to hers. Just that small taste of her was enough to set his body on fire. He knew he had to let her go, and that he had to trust they would get through this together. He was asking her to face her fears and now he had to face his own as he watched Lacey walk out the door—because right now he didn't think he could face his life without her.

Lacey tucked the little girl under the blanket and nodded to the red-eyed woman who sat at her bedside. The poor woman had been fighting her daughter's fever for hours before she had brought her into the ER and she looked like she was going to drop.

She handed the woman the extra blanket she had brought into the room. "Her fever is down. Why don't you close your eyes for a few minutes? I'll be back as soon the lab work comes in," Lacey said.

The young mother gave her a tired smile, then wrapped the warm blanket around her and closed her eyes. Lacey shut the door as quietly as possible, then headed next door to help Scott with another patient.

She could hear arguing before she walked in the room. At first she wondered if she needed to get in the middle of the patient and her husband, but it quickly became apparent that neither of them meant anything with their constant nipping at each other.

"I can't believe this has happened," the elderly woman said as Lacey watched Scott close up the laceration on her forehead.

Fortunately for her, the CAT scan had been negative, so all she would need was a few stitches.

"It was that greedy cat. She's always winding around between your feet when you're in the kitchen," the patient's husband said. "I told you this was going to happen."

The man had been grouchy since his wife had been brought in by the emergency medical techs, and Lacey had been listening to the two of them bicker back and forth for the last half-hour.

"It wasn't the cat that made me fall down. It was you, scaring me to death when you came up behind me. What were you thinking? I don't understand where your mind goes sometimes. We've been married almost fifty years now and you still think it's funny to sneak up behind me and pinch my butt? When are you going to grow up?" the woman grumbled.

Lacey watched as Scott paused with his needle in the air. Hadn't he done the same thing just last night, while she had been turning steaks on the grill?

She fought the laughter that wanted to explode out of her. Would this be the two of them fifty years from now?

The laughter died inside her. What were the chances that they would still be together in forty years? She'd spent the last three years of her life accepting that she would grow old alone, but now here she was thinking of a future fifty years down the road with Scott...

He finished the last few stitches and then, before leaving the room, he gave her a look and a smile that told her he was thinking about the night before too. Was he thinking of a future for them?

They had avoided the subject of a long commitment, which she knew was for the best while she worked through her emotions concerning Scott's way of life and his need to chase the next thrill.

She'd let him pull her into the planning of the program's upcoming challenges, and he had taken the time to show her how they worked through all the possibilities of emergencies and the strategies they used to decrease the risk of their being errors and injuries.

But was it enough to calm her fears the next time he left her to go on one of his extreme challenges? Probably not. Besides, why did *she* have to be the only one dealing with her issues so they could make this happen? Shouldn't Scott make some changes too? Would he? Or, more importantly, could he?

He lived for the adventures he went on, and if she insisted he stopped going eventually he'd resent her for it, and that wasn't what she wanted.

She gave the woman some discharge instructions, then went back to check for the lab work on the little girl.

After pulling up the lab results she walked over to where Scott was staring at his computer screen. "The lab work all came back clear on the little girl in Room Twenty. She's sleeping now and her fever is down. Can I discharge her after her fluids are in?" she said.

She waited for Scott to respond. He seemed mesmerized by what he was reading on the computer screen.

"Scott?" she said.

She bent down lower, to see what it was that had made him zone out on her, but as she moved to look over his shoulder the screen suddenly changed. An email filled the screen, all about the city's Special Citizen awards ceremony.

"Sorry," he said as he turned his chair around toward her, making her back up before she lost her balance and ended up in his lap. Again. "You were saying something about some lab work?"

'Yeah, the little girl in Twenty who came in with the hundred and three temperature. Her lab work looks good. I wanted to know if I could discharge her. Are you okay?" Lacey asked, when she saw that she had lost his attention again.

"Sure, I'm fine," he said, and he rubbed his hand over his forehead as if to clear away whatever his mind had been occupied with. "Yeah, you can let her go. I've already spoken with her mother. I suspect her daughter brought home something viral from school. She should be okay by tomorrow."

"I'll have her mom call her pediatrician if she's not better in the morning," Lacey said, and started to walk away.

"Did you get someone to cover for you for the awards ceremony?" Scott asked.

"It's taken care of. You know I wouldn't miss it," she said, as she went over to her own computer to generate the necessary paperwork for the discharge.

She looked over toward Scott as he turned back to his computer, hit some buttons, and then leaned toward the screen. He wiped at his forehead again. What was it that was bothering him? Had he just gotten that email concerning the ceremony or was it something else? They talked about pretty much everything now. If something was troubling him he knew he could talk to her.

Picking up the papers from the printer, she headed down the hallway to give a tired mother some good news and send her home to bed.

CHAPTER NINE

SCOTT LOOKED ACROSS the crowded ballroom, which tonight had been dressed up in white linen and crystal. Some of the most influential people in New Orleans had gathered there tonight, and the fact that he had been included was incredible. It was a privilege to be nominated for the city's Special Citizen award, but more importantly the attention would really help with the funding for future challenges that he was planning. The program was growing so fast that soon their annual fundraisers wouldn't be able to cover their expenses, and the last thing he wanted to do was to turn any veteran away.

He looked to where Lacey sat. She was so beautiful, sitting beside him with her hair piled up on her head. He wanted to bend toward her and kiss his way up the bare skin of her neck till he reached that one magic spot behind her ear that always made her gasp. He wanted to strip her of all her composure and expose the woman who had made love with him last night.

She chose that moment to look over at him and smile, as she laughed at something the speaker at the podium was saying. She'd worn another green dress that matched her eyes, which sparkled like emeralds with her laughter. He was so glad she was enjoying the evening—because in a few hours he'd have no choice but to ruin it.

How did he tell her that he was leaving? They'd had so little time together. Maybe they would have had a chance if this had happened later in their relationship. But now, just when she was just coming to terms with her fear of caring for someone she might suddenly lose, there was little hope that she would be waiting for him when he returned.

"Scott," Lacey said as she nudged him with her foot, "they're about to announce the nominees. Pay attention."

He forced himself to listen to the speaker as he spoke about each of the individuals nominated and their accomplishments. He recognized several of the other names, and couldn't help but be impressed that he had been nominated along with them.

When his name was announced all the people at the table where he sat clapped loudly.

"I'm so proud," said Lacey as the speaker moved on to the next nominee. "Alston was very upset when I told him only adults were invited tonight, but I reminded him of the trip to the zoo your sister is taking him on tomorrow, and he decided that the zoo would be a lot more fun than dressing up in a suit."

"Right now a trip to anywhere would be better," he said.

He really didn't like to be the center of attention. He'd rather be in the background working than have a lot of people staring at him. Lacey had made him prepare an acceptance speech, even though he knew that he wouldn't need one. She'd made him recite it to her over and over the night before, though he had told her it was a waste of time.

"And this year's winner of our New Orleans Special Citizen award is…" The man drew out the suspense while Lacey squeezed his hand. "Scott Boudreaux, founder of Extreme Warrior."

What?

He listened as the speaker read out a letter that had been sent in from one of the vets who had joined the group when she'd been at his lowest and considering suicide. Then he went on to talk about how the program had given her the confidence to make a new life in the culinary community.

Scott was shocked. It was Katie? Had she really been considering harming herself? He'd never known she was at that kind of crisis point in her life. The fact that his group of vets had helped her through that time made him proud.

The next hour went by in a blur. He stood in front of the crowd and explained the mission and vision of Extreme Warrior, and described some of their future challenges, while he tried to keep his knees from knocking behind the podium. Then he added something to his speech that he had been thinking about a lot lately but hadn't shared with Lacey.

"And while I thank you from the bottom of my heart for this honor, and your support of our local veterans, this honor really goes to my best friend and fellow officer Ben Miller, who sacrificed his life for others. This program was as much his vision as mine, and though he's been gone from us for a while now his dream of finding a way to challenge the veterans of New Orleans to be the best they can lives on in all the veterans who have taken part in this program."

He looked over at the table, where Lacey was wiping tears from her eyes.

"Thank you," he said again, then stepped down off the podium.

He shook hands with people whose names he would never remember, and was given promises of monetary support that was more than he could ever have imagined.

Lacey was working the crowd too, as if she had been born into this kind of society. He smiled as he watched her blend in with the crowd as she promoted the challenges that were planned for the program next year.

By the time they left the ballroom they were both exhausted.

For a few hours he'd forgotten that he had to tell Lacey that he was leaving. They'd both enjoyed the night and he couldn't imagine having to ruin it now. He struggled between the right thing to do and what he *wanted* to do.

The countdown of days before his departure had begun. He was running out of time. And yet something inside him rebelled against telling Lacey tonight. He wanted one more night with her. One more night to love her like she needed to be loved—one more night to show her how deep his love for her went.

As they approached her door he made his decision.

"You know, I tried that trick you were talking about? The one where you imagine everyone in the audience is in their underwear? It didn't work."

He moved in closer and turned her toward him. He bent down and kissed her neck, just above her collarbone, then ran kisses up her throat just as he had imagined earlier in the night. He'd pay the price tomorrow when he came clean with her. He'd make sure tonight was worth the pain they'd have to deal with later.

"Do you want to know why it didn't work?" he whispered into her ear, then nipped at the back of her earlobe.

"Uh-huh…" she said as she inhaled deeply and then pressed her body against his.

He didn't have her gasping yet, but the night was young.

"Because as I looked across the room the only person I had eyes for was you," he said.

He ran his hands up her neck, then entangled them in her hair, bringing his mouth to hers for a deep kiss. He poured all his longing into that kiss and then pulled back and looked into green eyes heavy with desire.

"Do you want to know what I saw?" he asked.

His body, tight with desire, begged him to take her. But if they only had this one night he was going to make it last.

"Yes…" she moaned as his lips went back to that so-sensitive spot of hers.

"I saw you there…looking so proper, with your hair piled high, your smile so sweet and innocent. Then I imagined peeling that dress off you, inch by inch, and finding that lacy pink bra…"

He ran his hands up her body and curved them around her breasts, taking the weight of them in hands.

"You know…the one that's cut down to here…"

He ran a hand down between her breasts and then moved both hands around to her back. He grasped her bottom and pulled her against the length of him.

"It has those matching panties…the ones with just that small piece of lace that hugs your bottom so tight."

Lacey moaned against him, then pulled his head down to hers. "Scott," she said between kisses, "less talking, more kissing."

He reached behind her and punched in the code for her door. Swinging the door open, he turned to Lacey and swung her up into his arms. Lacey bent her head back and laughed up at him.

Time stood still as he froze that moment into his mind. Small tendrils of hair fell around her face, framing brilliant green eyes that shone with happiness, while her bruised and swollen lips curved into a naughty smile that stole his breath. He'd thought her beautiful earlier that night, but this was the real beauty—the real Lacey. The Lacey he remembered from the first time he'd met her.

He managed to get them to the bedroom, though he stopped along the way to enjoy small tastes of her to keep him going.

How was he going to live without this woman in his life?

He made himself ignore the pain of the future. They had tonight and he wouldn't waste one moment of it.

He set her down beside the bed, then unzipped the dress and let it fall in a puddle to the floor. Standing before him in only the tiny pink bra and panties, she was sexier than his imagination could have comprehended.

Her smile turned naughty again as she peeled each piece off her body while he watched. He unbuttoned his shirt and then his pants as he tried to catch up with her.

He laid her back against the bed and took the time to freeze one more moment as he took in the vision she made stretched out before him. He'd make tonight a memory that neither of them would ever forget, no matter what tomorrow brought.

He followed her onto the bed and began to kiss her. First her lips, and then her neck, stopping at the curve of her shoulder to nip at her collarbone, then soothing the spot with a lick of his tongue before continuing his path to her breast.

"Scott…" Lacey's voice came out in a moan as she squirmed beneath him.

"Shh…" he murmured, before taking one nipple into his mouth and sucking, then moving to the next one to give it the same attention.

Then he returned to his path down her body. He would taste every inch of her tonight…

He paused at the top of her thighs, then spread them open.

"You're killing me," Lacey said. "I can't…"

"*La petit mort, ma chérie,*" he murmured as he kissed the inside of her thigh. "You will survive."

"God, I love it when you speak French," she said, then moaned again as his mouth moved higher.

Her body bucked against his mouth, and when he knew she couldn't take any more he pushed her over into her climax. Then he crawled over her and thrust inside her before her orgasm died, sending them both into that small death together.

Lacey turned the bacon and then took a long sip of coffee. She'd need a lot of caffeine to carry her through today after the night she had spent with Scott. Just thinking of their lovemaking made her heart race.

Before, she refused to call the intimacy they'd shared

"lovemaking"; instead she'd preferred to think of it as simply sex. There had been no reason to bring love into it. But last night had been different. He'd made love to every part of her body. Taking his time as he tasted her, loved her, until she'd been begging him to take her. He'd stripped her of all her inhibitions, leaving her emotions bare and open to him.

She felt the flush of heat as it curled over her body along with the memories from the night before. There'd been almost a desperation in Scott that had driven him to take her over and over during the night...

"You're going to burn that if you don't turn it," Scott said as he came into the room.

She couldn't help but stare at this sexy man, dressed in wrinkled formal wear, whose eyes, still heavy with sleep, seemed to devour her with one look.

She forced her eyes away from him and removed the bacon from the frying pan.

"Good morning," she said.

Was that her voice? Just because the man looked like sex on a stick it didn't mean she needed to lose it in front of him.

She cleared her throat, then turned back toward him—only to find that he'd moved over to the coffee pot. "I've got some grits made, and there are eggs in the warming tray."

She waited for him to respond, but he seemed to be lost in thought. Had last night touched him as much as it had her? Would he tell her that he loved her now? Could she tell him that she loved him? Was that what she wanted?

He turned toward her, and the pain she saw in his eyes stopped her dead. She set the tray of bacon down on the small round table that sat to the side of the kitchen, then walked over to where he stood.

"What's wrong?" she asked. Was he ill? He did look a little pale. "Sit down. I'll get your coffee."

"I'm not sick," he said, though she noticed that he did take a chair and sit.

He might not be sick, but something was wrong. Was it her? Them? Had last night just been a lead-up to him breaking up with her?

She took the chair across from him and waited for him to tell her what was wrong. Her stomach churned with nerves as she studied him. With shoulders slumped, he stared into his coffee cup. He looked as if he'd lost his best friend—but then he'd already done that, when Ben had died. The only other person she would have considered his best friend was her, and he hadn't lost her. She was right there beside him.

Was this about the Extreme Warrior project? Was he worried about her not being able to accept his need to lead their extreme challenges? After hearing Katie's letter at last night's awards ceremony she knew she'd never be able to stop Scott from working with the veterans. She might not understand why he felt the need to take the chances he did, but he'd showed her how he worked to keep accidents and injuries from happening. He had been right when he'd said that Katie's injury could have happened anywhere. People came in all the time with snake bites from their back yard.

"I need to tell you something," he said, never looking up from his coffee. "I should have told you earlier. I just… I didn't want to ruin the time we have left together."

"I don't understand," she said.

What did he mean? Was he saying they were over? But why? She didn't understand any of this. Last night had been magical, and she knew Scott had felt that magic too. He had managed to break down every wall she'd used to protect herself from falling for him and now he wanted to end it?

Scott looked up from the table, then stood. Was he so anxious to get away from her?

"If you want to call it quits just say so," she said as her temper began to rise.

She stood and took their unused dishes to the sink. He could at least have eaten the breakfast she'd cooked for him before he broke up with her.

"I don't want to call it quits. That's the last thing I want," he said as he walked over to where she stood. "I want us to work through this. I want you to believe that I'll come back to you. I want to be enough that you're willing to take a chance on us."

She turned around to face him. She looked up into his eyes, so full of pain. And...hope?

"Just tell me what it is, Scott," she said.

He opened his arms to her and she walked into them. It felt so right, so safe to be held by him now—something that she would never have believed a few weeks ago. Whatever this problem was, they'd work through it.

She felt his chest expand as he took in a deep breath. She held on tighter to him.

"I'm being deployed back to Afghanistan. I leave in six days," he said as he rested his head on hers.

She stood there, frozen in that spot, as she tried to make sense of his words.

Scott had finished his time in the military.

How could they make him go back to Afghanistan?

It didn't make any sense at all.

She let her hands slide down his back, then took a step away from him. She needed to understand what he was saying.

"You've been out of the military for three years now. They can't make you go back into service," she said. "Besides, you were injured. The damage to your leg was extensive."

"And it has healed now. I climb mountains and my leg holds up fine," he said.

"It still gives you trouble. You still limp when you've pushed yourself too hard. You should tell them about the limp. You should make them see that you can't be expected to be deployed again. Just tell them you're not going."

She heard the terror in her voice. She couldn't be expected to sit at home again, waiting for the doorbell to ring. Waiting for the army chaplain to tell her that Scott had been killed. Waiting for her life to be destroyed once again.

She'd wanted to scream at the men who had come to her house the day Ben had been killed. She'd wanted to tell them to shut up, to leave and never come back, but she'd known she couldn't. She'd had to be strong. She'd had to be brave. She'd had to be there for Alston and for Ben's parents.

"It's only for six months, Lacey. One of the doctors has become ill and has had to be flown home for surgery. They're working short-handed right now, and they need me to cover until he's recovered."

"Why can't you just tell them no?" she said.

She didn't know what to say to him to make him understand. She couldn't do this again.

"I only served four years. I had four years left of inactive reserves. By the end of this deployment my eight years will be completed and I won't have to worry about getting called up again. We just need to make it through those six months. They really need me, Lacey. It's hard enough in the hospitals over there without them being short. I have to go."

But she needed him too. How could he expect her to go through this again?

She thought of the days she'd lain in bed, too depressed to get up and get dressed. She had functioned the best she could, to make sure Alston was taken care of, but she hadn't been the kind of mother she'd wanted to be. It had only been when Scott had come home and helped her get her act together that she'd seen just what a lousy job she was doing.

She couldn't put herself and Alston through that again. She'd been through hell when she'd lost Ben and she couldn't do it again.

She felt panic rise up inside her as her heart sped up. She turned and gripped the side of the counter and forced herself to take the deep, calming breaths she needed to fight it down.

"I know I don't have the right to ask this of you, but I can't just walk away from you. I love you, Lacey. I want us to be together forever. I want to make a real family with you and Alston. I just need you to believe in us. Give us a chance."

She felt the tears as they rolled down her cheeks and then suddenly she was sobbing. It was as if she had lost Ben all over again, but instead of Ben it was now Scott she was losing. She wanted to believe that Scott would come home, but she couldn't. There was no guarantee that he would come back to her and she could not live with the fear of losing him.

"I can't do it, Scott. I'm sorry."

She turned around and threw herself in his arms and held him tight. If only she could hold on to him forever. If only she never had to let him go.

She pushed herself away from him, then ran from the room. Closing the bedroom door behind her, she curled up on the bed. She buried her head in the covers and breathed in the scent of Scott and cried.

CHAPTER TEN

"WHERE'S THAT TRAUMA BLOOD?" Scott asked as he quickly examined the gunshot victim lying on the trauma table.

The kid couldn't be over nineteen. He was just a boy. What could he have done to get himself shot?

They'd stripped him down at the scene and he could see two entrance wounds in the chest.

"We need to turn him over," he shouted to the nurse beside him.

Where was Lacey? There were too many inexperienced nurses in the room. She was in charge. She should be there to help.

He examined the kid's back and saw that there was only one exit wound. He would need to go to surgery. His job until the surgeon arrived was to stabilize the patient, and with the amount of blood this kid had lost it was going to take this whole team to do it.

"I've got the blood," one of the younger nurses called as she walked into the room carrying a red cooler.

"It should have been here five minutes ago. Let's get it going," he said as he looked up at the monitor.

He was tachycardic, and his blood pressure was low,

but it was holding. If they could get some blood into him he might make it.

"Where's X-ray?" he shouted across the room.

He watched as a young man pushed the machine into the room. Could he move any slower? Didn't he understand that this kid was going to die if they didn't get him stabilized soon?

He backed out of the room with the rest of the staff while the X-ray was taken, then quickly returned to the patient's side and checked out the screen on the X-ray machine.

"It looks like one of the bullets hit his left lung. He's going to need a chest tube."

"His oxygen saturation is dropping," the respiratory technician said.

"So is his pressure," said one of the nurses.

Scott looked up to see the pressure had dropped down to eighty over forty-four.

"Is the blood going? Where's Lacey?" he asked. "We need that blood going or we're going to lose him."

"I'm over here," he heard Lacey say.

He looked over to where she and another one of the nurses were setting up the blood to rapidly infuse.

"The blood is starting now," Lacey said.

"His oxygen stats are still dropping," the respiratory tech told him.

"Where's that chest tube tray?" he said.

"It's right here, Doctor," Lacey said beside him.

There was no missing the censure in her voice. Yeah, he knew he was being a jerk, but right now all that mattered was saving this kid.

He gowned, and then prepped the incision site. After

making the incision he inserted the chest tube, then began to stitch it in place.

He couldn't help but remember that night when he'd stood in a room just down the hall, when that drunk had grabbed the scalpel and held Lacey hostage. Just thinking about that night made him angry. Not just at the drunk, but at himself too.

He should never have kissed Lacey that night. No, that was the anger and pain in him talking. If he had it all to do over he knew he'd kiss her again.

The young kid's vital signs began to stabilize as they continued to transfuse him with multiple units of blood. As soon as the trauma surgeon arrived to take him to Theater, Scott left the room. In a few days he'd be back in Afghanistan, taking care of patients just like that kid, and some of them wouldn't be much older.

Lacey tried to ignore the rest of the staff as they gathered at the unit coordinator's desk and gossiped. She'd seen the looks some of the staff were giving her. Everyone was wondering what was wrong with Scott and they all assumed that she knew.

Of course she knew. The man was about to leave the States and return to the place where he'd lost his best friend. It wouldn't be easy for him to do that. And then there was the issue of the two of them—though if anyone understood why she couldn't deal with the danger he was going to be in, it was him. He'd seen her at her lowest, with an empty bottle of alcohol at her side. And he'd stayed by her as she'd crawled her way back up, she reminded herself.

"I just talked to Dr. MacDonald. He says that Scott is being redeployed to Afghanistan. He turned in his notice today," one of the respiratory techs was telling the group.

"Well, that sucks," one of the new nurses said. "Don't they have to hold your job open for you if you're deployed?"

"Dr. MacDonald said Scott told him he wasn't sure what he wanted to do when he returned, so he decided to turn his resignation in."

Lacey couldn't help but look over at the group. Why would Scott turn in his resignation? He loved his job working in the ER at the hospital. Was it because of her? They'd worked together before they'd ever become romantically involved, so that didn't make any sense.

"Don't you have something to do? You know…something like taking care of your patients?" the unit coordinator said.

"Thanks, Gloria," said Lacey, when the crowd broke up.

"No problem," the older woman said, then returned to her computer. "Maybe you could go talk to him? He's been impossible to work with for the last two days. I'm thinking there might be a mutiny if he doesn't stop biting everyone's head off."

"Where is he?" Lacey asked.

She'd take this one for the team. It was her responsibility as charge nurse to make sure everything ran smoothly in the department.

And this has nothing to do with the fact that I'm worried about him.

"He went into the doctors' lounge," Gloria said.

Knowing that she was the last person he'd want to see, she prepared herself. This was the problem with dating someone that you worked with. Things had a tendency to cross over between your personal and your private life if you weren't careful. They'd crossed that line the first time Scott had kissed her, and now they were paying the price.

Scott sat at the table, holding a soft drink in one hand while the other one tapped a beat on the table. He looked up and scowled as she walked into the room.

"You don't have to tell me. I was being a jerk in the trauma room and I owe everyone an apology," he said. "I've got it. You can go now."

"You were, and you do, but that isn't the only reason I need to talk to you," she said.

She saw the glint of hope in his eyes when he looked at her, and then it was gone. She was relieved that he had accepted her decision to end their romantic relationship. She'd explained her reasons for not continuing and she was glad he wasn't pushing back at her.

If only it didn't hurt so much to see him like this.

"What happened out there, Scott? That wasn't you," she said.

"I don't know. It was just that kid. He's so young— too young. He reminded me of all the kids I treated in Afghanistan. There were some like him—the lucky ones, who managed to survive—but there were just as many who didn't," he said. He ran his hands through his hair, then looked up at her. "And next week I'll be right back in the middle of things, trying to save the ones I can and having to deal with the reality of those I can't."

"I'm sorry," she said. "I don't want you to go. I wish—"

"What do you wish?" Scott said as he stood and moved toward her.

He ran a hand down the side of her face, and she wanted to turn to him but knew she couldn't.

"I wish I was different," she said as she stepped away from him.

Just two steps, but it felt as if she had run a marathon. It was so hard to walk away from Scott. If only she wasn't such a coward.

"The rumor is that you're not coming back here after you return from deployment. Is it true?" she asked as she took another step away from him.

If she was the reason he was leaving she had to stop him. She couldn't let that happen. She could easily get a job at another hospital. Besides, it had been Scott who got her the job working here, after she'd finally gotten her act together after Ben's death. If one of them left it should be her.

"I'm leaving all my options open right now," he said as he walked over to the recycling bin and threw away his empty drink can.

"If it's because of me, I can leave. It's not right that you have to give up your job," she said.

Why did this have to hurt so badly? But how much more would it hurt if she waited for Scott to return while all the time knowing that he might never make it home alive?

"There's no reason for you to do that. I've been thinking about making a change for a while now. This deployment has just changed the timing of things," he said as he opened the door and they both stepped out into the emergency room.

As they went their separate ways she felt the pain of knowing that Scott was already moving on and making plans for a future without her.

But that was what she wanted.

No, it wasn't what she wanted.

She wanted things to go back to the way they used to be. The way things had been before that one kiss changed everything.

Lacey opened her eyes to find her son making a goofy face, crossing his eyes and twisting his mouth into a crazy rendition of a smile. Laughing, she pulled him into the bed beside her and tickled him.

As his laughter filled the room she remembered a time when she would have rolled away from him in the bed, too tired and too depressed to play with her little boy. This kid and his crazy antics meant everything to her. That was why she knew she could never take the chance of being pulled back into that deep hole she'd fallen into after losing Ben. She needed the security of knowing that she and Alston wouldn't have to go through that torment again.

"Did you get your paper done?" she asked as she got out of bed and yawned, then headed to get dressed. Working the night shift was hard on the body but it worked well with Alston's school schedule.

"I need some help with my science," he said as she came out of the bathroom, where she had changed clothes.

"Okay, let's look at it," she said as they walked toward the kitchen. "What's it about?"

"We're working on our science projects. I'm doing parachutes, so I've got to write a paper on gravity." Alston said as he pulled a notebook from his backpack.

"Well, that sounds really interesting, but I don't know much about parachutes. Are you sure you want to do this for your project? We could find you one that I could help you with. What about something with seeds?"

"I only need some help with this first part," Alston said. "Scott's going to help me with the rest of it. Did you know he jumped out of a plane once? He knows all about parachutes."

Lacey felt her heart drop into her stomach. She'd forgotten that Alston didn't know about Scott's deployment. She'd have to tell him today. Or should she call Scott and let *him* tell her son? No, she was being a coward again. She would have to do it.

"How about we walk down to the library and see what books we can find on gravity?" she said.

The walk would be good for both of them. And it would give her a chance to tell her son that Scott was leaving. Maybe they would find another subject for his science project while they were at the library…

"That would be awesome. Can we get some ice cream too?" he asked.

"Sure. We'll have to stop for ice cream on the way back, though. I don't think the librarians would want us touching their books with sticky hands."

As Alston ran off to get his shoes she tried to think of the best way to tell her son that Scott would be leaving in a couple days. The two of them had a special relationship that shouldn't end over her and Scott's split. She knew Scott would never let that happen, though she would need to explain to Alston the change in her and Scott's relationship.

She'd spent so much time worrying about moving on and leaving Ben behind. But then she'd taken her first step toward a future with Scott and realized she wasn't moving on without Ben—she was just moving forward and taking his memory with her.

Scott had been the one to show her that she could do that. It had been when he had explained to the crowd at the awards banquet how Ben was still a part of the veteran program that it had hit her that moving on didn't mean leaving Ben behind.

And now that she was finally ready to see where the future could take them he was leaving—and she was too much of a coward to wait for him.

As they walked the ten blocks to the local library the constant jabber of her son lightened her heart—until she remembered that she would soon have to tell him about Scott's deployment.

Alston had been only five when his father had been killed, and with the resiliency of a child he had accepted the change in his life more easily than she had expected. There had been nights, though, right after Ben had first been killed, when she'd found him crying in his bed when he should have been asleep, but she blamed that on the fact that she had been too caught up in her own grieving to see the pain her son had been hiding from her.

Alston quickly found some books on gravity, and they spent the next hour putting together a paper.

She told herself that it was the cool temperature of the library and being surrounded by books that made her drag out the time as they went through the shelves of books, looking for something to read after they'd finished the paper, but she knew she was just postponing the inevitable.

Not for the first time she considered backing out and

having Scott tell her son that he was leaving, but she couldn't do it. Alston was her son, and she needed to be the one to break the news to him.

As they crossed the street from the ice cream store she took Alston's hand in hers while they both licked their melting cones.

"Mom, I can walk by myself," Alston whined. "You treat me like a baby."

"You *are* a baby. You're *my* baby," she said as she licked at a drip of ice cream running down her cone.

She might be a little more protective than some of Alston's friends' parents, but with all the things she saw in the ER, and after losing Ben, she felt she had the right to be a little paranoid.

"I'm almost nine. That is not a baby," Alston said as he tried to pull away from her.

They'd almost made it onto the sidewalk when she heard the loud racing of an engine. She looked up and saw a car speed through the red light and head straight for them.

Letting go of Alston, she pushed him toward the sidewalk.

The last thing she saw was her son hitting the concrete—and then there was just pain.

Scott rushed into the emergency room. He'd been in the process of going through his pantry, to dispose of everything that wouldn't be edible when he returned from deployment, when his phone had suddenly been flooded with text messages.

Assuming all the messages coming in were good wishes from people who had heard about his departure, he'd finished disposing of the food items into the trash before he'd picked up his phone.

He'd read the first text message, from one of the nurses in the emergency room at the hospital, and then gone on to the next message. None of it had made any sense. There had to be some type of mistake.

But when his phone had begun to ring and the caller ID had identified the hospital he'd grabbed his keys.

A hospital social worker had explained that there had been an accident and that as he was listed as Alston's next of kin they needed him to come.

"But what about his mother? Where is she?" he'd asked, even as he'd started his car and headed to the hospital.

After being told several times that she wasn't able to give any information concerning a patient's condition over the phone, he'd hung up and called the ER directly. When Gloria had answered she'd put him through to the ER doctor taking care of Alston.

He had listened carefully as the doctor had explained that Alston had fallen and had a radius fracture that would require a cast. He'd been pulling into the parking lot when the doctor had gone on to tell him that while the kid was going to be fine, Lacey had been brought in as a trauma and was being cared for by one of the other doctors.

None of it had made sense to his muddled mind. Alston had fallen, but Lacey had been brought into the hospital too.

By the time he made it to the trauma room it was empty. Empty packages littered the floor, along with blood-stained clothes. Recognizing the bloody shirt that declared the wearer a unicorn nurse, he headed to the doctors' station.

Someone was going to explain to him what was happening.

"Dr. Boudreaux," Gloria said, "thank goodness you're here. This is just awful. Alston is worried to death about his mother and we didn't know what you would want us to tell him."

"Gloria, I need you to tell me what happened." Scott made himself stop and take a breath. "Where exactly is Lacey?"

He listened to the unit coordinator as she told him everything she knew. There'd been an accident—pedestrian versus motor vehicle. They'd brought both Lacey and Alston in by ambulance, but Lacey was the one who had been struck by the car and her injuries were more serious.

He tracked down the nurse taking care of Lacey, only to learn that she had been rushed off to surgery due to internal bleeding.

He wanted to bust into the operating room and take over the case. It was at times like this when he wished he'd remained in surgery. But after Afghanistan he'd thought that working in an ER would give him a break. Now he was thinking of making more changes in his life—but none of it would matter if he lost Lacey.

Returning to the ER, he hunted down Alston's room. The boy rushed at Scott when he saw him and then he began to cry.

"Whoa, now," Scott said as he carefully supported the boy's arm, which was sporting a new blue cast.

"Have you seen her?" Alston asked when Scott had picked him up and put him up on the examining table.

A bright red scratch cut down across one side of the kid's face, but it wasn't deep and wouldn't scar.

"Not yet. She's in the operating room. But I made someone call inside the room and the doctor said she was doing better," Scott said as he examined the boy for any other injuries, even though he knew a thorough examination would have been done when Alston had first arrived.

"Hey, Scott," said a nurse dressed in a pair of bright pink scrubs, who was sitting in the corner. "Alston has been cleared by the doctor to be discharged. We were just waiting for you to arrive."

"Thank you, Amanda," Scott told the woman.

"I'll have them bring in the paperwork," she said as she left the room.

"Do you remember what happened?" Scott asked Alston.

"We went to the library to get some information for my science project. You know—the one on parachutes that you're going to help me do," Alston said.

The boy flinched as he moved his arm as if to make the shape of a parachute. Scott would have to see if they could get some pain medication for him before he was discharged. And the science project... Scott had forgotten all about his promise to help Alston with the parachute assignment. Had Lacey explained to the boy that he was leaving?

"What happened when you left the library?" Scott asked.

"Well," Alston said, "we went to get ice cream after we left the hospital, but we didn't stay at the store to eat it. Momma said that she had to talk to me about something on the way home and we could eat it while we walked. And then, just while we were crossing the road—and we crossed with the light, like Momma says you have to—this car came *speeding* up."

Scott backed away as Alston swung the arm with the cast around, indicating a car speeding past.

"And then Momma pushed me and I landed on the sidewalk."

As the boy took a breath after telling his story, Scott tried to piece together all the information.

"Then some people came up to me and they wouldn't let me see my mom."

Alston began to cry and Scott picked him up and hugged him. The kid had been through a lot already today, falling and breaking his arm, and now he was separated from his mother.

"As soon as your mom gets out of surgery the two of us will go see her—okay?" Scott promised him.

"She's really going to be okay?" Alston asked as he wiped his eyes and nose against Scott's shirt.

"I know the doctor doing the surgery and he said your mom is doing well. Now, I'm going to make some phone calls and see if you can go stay with Jason tonight. Is that okay with you?" Scott said.

"That's okay—but not until after I see my mom," Alston said.

After Scott had made some calls to his family, then to Lacey's mother in Florida, he found the nurse and asked for some medication for Alston's pain, then signed the discharge paperwork.

The two of them were quickly joined in the waiting room by Scott's mother and father, who had offered to take Alston to Jason's house after they'd made sure Lacey was going to be okay.

By the time Lacey's surgeon came out of the operating room Alston had fallen asleep. Picking up the boy, Scott carried him down the hall to the recovery room, where Scott had been given special permission to see Lacey.

"Alston, wake up," Scott said as he shook the boy awake. "Here's your mom. She's sleepy like you are… see?"

The boy opened his eyes and looked over at his mother. "She's really going to be okay?" Alston asked.

"She's really going to be okay. She just needs a nap right now," Scott told him. "I'm going to stay with her for the night, and if anything changes I'll call you. Okay?"

"Okay. Can I go to Jason's now?" Alston asked.

"Sure," Scott said, and he carried him back out to the waiting room.

CHAPTER ELEVEN

LACEY AWOKE TO the chattering of her son—something that didn't surprise her. She stretched, and it did surprise her to find an intravenous line in her arm.

Turning toward her son, she saw the bright blue cast on his arm and slowly the memory of the car speeding toward them returned—and with it fear for her son.

"Alston…" she said, her voice coming out in a croak as she tried to sit up and go to her son.

"He's okay," Scott said from the side of the bed.

Alston bounced over to her.

"Remember I told you she'd be sore after the surgery? We have to be careful not to touch her where she has that dressing on her stomach. We have to be very careful where she has that line in her arm too," Scott reminded her son.

"Sorry," Alston said, and he moved closer to her, then patted her hand gently.

"He's really okay?" she asked Scott as she ran her free hand over the large scrape on his face.

"I talked to one of the cops who worked the scene. The car was being driven by a high school kid who was paying more attention to his radio than to his driving.

If you hadn't pushed Alston out of the way... Let's just say it would have ended differently," Scott said.

"The cop said you saved my life, Momma. You're a hero, just like Scott—only you haven't gotten an award," Alston said, then turned to Scott. "I think we should go buy my mom a trophy. One of those big ones, like we won when we beat that soccer team last year—you know the guys with those ugly green uniforms."

"We'll have to see what they have in the gift shop. Why don't I take you down?"

When the nurse came in to give Lacey her pain medication, Scott took Alston downstairs to wait for Rayanne.

Scott had explained the circumstances of the accident as had been told to him by the police officer he had spoken to, but Lacey still couldn't understand what had happened. She'd just taken her son out for a trip to the library and an ice cream cone. It had been a spontaneous trip, a few blocks down the street from their house. Alston had said that they'd waited for the light, checked for cars, and stayed on the walkway that crossed the street.

She'd almost been killed doing something as innocent and safe as going to the library.

Scott had been right. You could get killed just as easily crossing the street as you could climbing a mountain.

Or working at a hospital in Afghanistan?

No, that was different. Scott would be in a lot more danger than she would ever be crossing a street. But did that mean she couldn't accept that risk?

She had to make a decision. She'd survived being hit by a speeding car. She'd been given a second chance. But was she brave enough to face a future with Scott in Afghanistan?

Alston had called her a hero. If he only knew what a coward his mother really was. It was as if she could see happiness just beyond her reach, but was too scared to grab it.

If Ben could have picked a man out for her and Alston she knew it would have been Scott. The man who had been there for her when she hadn't thought she could go on. But she was afraid to be there for him while he used his medical knowledge to take care of others. What kind of friend did that make her?

Scott stopped outside Lacey's hospital room and prepared himself. He was set to leave the next day, and this would be the last chance he'd have to see her before he left.

He heard a sound through the door that sounded like someone was crying, and pushed open the door. Lacey was sitting up in the bed while she cried into the covers.

Moving to the bed, he eased her into his arms. "It's okay," he said. "Is it the pain? I'll call the doctor and get your medicine increased if you're still hurting."

"It's not the pain," Lacey said. "It's me. I've been such a coward."

"You're not a coward. You're one of the bravest people I know," Scott said.

He rested his chin on her head and breathed in the sweet scent of her. He'd miss that scent while he was gone.

"No, I'm not. And I've been an awful friend, too," she said. "I've been totally irrational concerning everything. And I could have been killed just walking to the library."

He tried to understand what it was that she was saying, but she was beginning to ramble like her eight-year-old son.

"It's just the pain medication," he told her. "As soon as you get some rest you'll feel better."

"No, I won't," she said. "I've messed things up, and now you're leaving, and I didn't even get a chance to tell you that I love you."

"I love you too," Scott said, knowing that she wouldn't understand that he meant it in a purely *un*-platonic way.

"No," Lacey said as she drew away from him. "I *love* you, Scott. As in I'm *in love* with you."

Scott stepped away from the bed. With all the pain medication she had been given, did she even know what she was saying?

"You've had a hard day, Lacey. They've given you a lot of medication to help with the pain. We can talk about this after you take a nap," Scott said.

"It's not the medication. I know how I feel," Lacey said, then yawned.

Scott watched as Lacey's eyes closed and her respirations became even. Did she really know how she felt? Did she truly know how *he* felt?

He'd asked her to wait for him but he'd never come out and asked her if she would *marry* him. He'd been afraid that he'd scare her off if he asked too much of her, too fast, but he'd assumed that she must know where he was hoping the relationship would eventually go.

Lacey opened her eyes and looked across the room to where Scott sat in a chair, asleep. Had she really told him that she loved him or had it all been a drug-induced dream?

She lay in the bed and watched him. Drugs or no drugs, she knew what she wanted now. There'd be no more wasting her life. She'd spent too much time letting her fear of the unknown keep her from admitting her feelings for Scott. She wouldn't let him leave without telling him how she really felt.

He stirred in the chair, then looked over at her. "Do you feel better?" he asked.

"Yes. Can you come over here?" she asked as she moved over on the bed. "We need to talk."

"Sure," he said, and he stood and moved closer to the bed. "Look, I want you to know that I understand that you might not have meant everything you said earlier. I don't want you to think that I'm holding you to it. Pain medication can do funny things to people."

"Which things are you talking about?" she asked.

"Well, you said that you love me," Scott said.

"Yes, I did," she said.

"You said that you were *in* love with me," Scott said.

"Yes, I did," she said.

"And you said that you would marry me when I came back to the States," he said, his lips turned up into a mischievous smile.

"Scott Boudreaux—I never said any such thing. Besides, you didn't ask me to marry you," Lacey said as she pushed herself up in the bed.

"Lacey, will you marry me when I get back?" Scott asked.

He looked so hopeful, and she knew inside her heart that she was making the right decision for both of them.

"No, I won't marry you when you come back. But I will marry you before you leave."

She laughed as Scott collapsed back into the chair beside the bed.

"Are you okay?" she asked.

"Are you sure? I don't even have a ring for you," Scott said as he took her hand in his.

"I'm sure. That is if it's what you want?" she said.

She hadn't considered that he might want a big wedding.

"It's what I want. But how are we going to make it work? I leave tomorrow night!" Scott said.

"Well, the first thing we need to do is call your mother and your sisters," Lacey told him. "If anyone can get a wedding together by then it would be your family."

It took them more than a day, but with a change in flight and some phone calls Scott managed to get an extra day—which also allowed Lacey a little more time to recover in the hospital before she was whisked off to his parents' house by his sisters.

Instead of the usual bachelor party, Scott and Alston spent the night playing video games and eating pizza. According to Alston it was the best bachelor party ever.

Scott had felt it was important for him to get Alston's approval, but he hadn't been prepared for Alston's simple answer when he had asked the boy if he could marry his mother.

"I think my daddy would want you to marry my mom," Alston said.

"You do? Why is that?" Scott had asked.

"Well, my daddy loved you. And my daddy loved my mother. Doesn't that mean that he'd want you two to love each other?"

And that was that, as far as the eight-year-old boy was concerned. And Scott couldn't help but feel that Alston was right. That somehow Ben had had a part in him and Lacey falling in love.

As a surprise, Scott had managed to get the management of Baby Blues to open early, and his sisters had set up the courtyard there for the ceremony. He remembered how Lacey had loved the magical feel of the place. They might not have had a lot of time to plan the wedding, but they were only going to do this once and he wanted to make sure they did it right.

Now, pacing back and forth, Scott waited at the entrance, watching for the car he'd rented to arrive. As it turned in he stepped back and waited. When the car came to a stop, Scott opened the door before the driver could come around.

Lacey stepped out and the courtyard went silent. She wore a simple white dress that left her shoulders bare.

Louis Armstrong sang "A Kiss to Build a Dream On" over the speakers—the song he had requested. It would be their song from now on, and he could imagine it playing forty years from now, as they danced together with their arthritic joints and graying hair.

"It's all so beautiful," she said as she looked around the courtyard.

"Are you ready to get married?" Scott asked her.

"I'm ready," she answered as she slipped her hand into his. "I'm finally ready."

EPILOGUE

SCOTT STARED STRAIGHT ahead and reminded himself that he couldn't embarrass his wife. He'd spent his life taking on some of the most dangerous challenges around the world. He'd hiked the Alaskan mountains and dived in shark cages. He'd parachuted out of planes and been white water rafting on some of the fastest rivers in the world. But nothing had ever scared him like what he saw on the ultrasound machine.

"There are two of them?" he said for the third time.

"Yes," said the ultrasound technician. "There are two."

"And they're both girls?" he said, again for the third time.

"Yes," his wife and the ultrasound technician said both together. "They're both girls."

"But there are two?" he said as he turned to his wife. "We're going to have two girls? At the same time?"

"That's usually how it works with twins," his wife told him as the technician wiped the gel from her stomach.

How could she be so calm about this? Of course, in his defense, she had known about this for longer than he had. He'd been overseas when Lacey had learned they were having twins, and she had sneakily kept that information to herself.

He watched as the technician printed out a picture, then handed it to his wife.

"Here—hold this," Lacey said, and she pushed him down to sit on the table and handed him the picture. Then she pulled out her phone and snapped a photo of him.

"What was that for?" he asked as he looked down at the picture in his hand.

"I just wanted to make sure I got a photo of something I never thought I'd see," Lacey said.

"What?" he asked as he stood to follow her out of the room.

"I think, Dr. Scott Boudreaux, you have finally found your most extreme challenge," his wife said, then strolled out of the room, following the technician.

And, looking down at the picture in his hand, of the two little girls who would soon join his family, he had to admit that she was right.

* * * * *

THE NURSE'S ONE NIGHT TO FOREVER

JANICE LYNN

MILLS & BOON

To Macy

CHAPTER ONE

FOR THE HUNDREDTH time since Riley had arrived at the engagement party Dr. Justin Brothers found himself watching her pretend she was having a good time. She wasn't.

Which didn't make sense as he knew she and Cheyenne were close friends. And Paul was a great guy. Surely Riley was happy at their engagement?

Still, if ever a woman was faking it, Riley was now. Her eyes begged to be rescued, even though she was laughing at something someone had said.

Justin wanted to don some armor and do just that.

He knew better.

Riley King fought her own battles and would cut down any man who got in her way. Or maybe it was just him she cut down.

The only place she was relaxed around Justin was in the surgery suite. There, she'd give tit for tat. He loved working with her, watching her take charge and make sure everything went smoothly. It always did with Riley at the helm.

"Go talk to her."

Justin cut his gaze to his friend Paul. "You worry about taking care of your own love-life."

Faux-punching Justin's shoulder, Paul grinned. "This whole shindig is about my love life and how awesome it is."

A pang of envy hit. Was it only last summer that Justin had almost walked down the aisle himself? That he'd thought he'd found "the one?"

How quickly things changed.

Although Justin wasn't lonely, he wasn't opposed to meeting someone special and being in Paul's shoes.

His gaze went back to Riley. The curvy nurse who was so quick to put him in his place, had captivated him from the moment he'd met her.

"You like her."

"Never said I didn't," he reminded his friend, dragging his gaze from Riley yet again. "It's more that she doesn't like *me*."

Paul gave a look of disbelief. "Never known you to strike out."

"It happens." *Unfortunately.* He couldn't recall the last time prior to Riley, but she was a biggie.

Too bad she'd laughed when he'd asked her out. Laughed and told him no in no uncertain terms.

His gaze drifted back to her, taking in the body-hugging green dress that flounced at the hem and made his eyes pop. She had her dark hair pulled up, but several tendrils had worked loose and framed her pretty heart-shaped face. At work she wore scrubs and no-nonsense shoes. Tonight she had stilettos on that made her legs look a million miles long and gave a gentle sway to her hips when she walked.

Just looking at her had Justin struggling not to reach for his collar to loosen a few buttons. Riley made him hot.

Because she was hot.

And smart, and funny, and—not interested.

Only he'd swear she was…

From across the terrace her big green eyes collided with his gaze and she failed to hide the initial flicker of awareness. The same awareness *he* felt every time they were together but that she seemed to find easy to push aside and deny.

She'd had a bad break-up a year or two ago. He didn't know the specifics, but you couldn't work in the same hospital unit and not pick up on gossip. She didn't date. Perhaps she was still hung up on her ex. That theory made the most sense but, right or wrong, the thought of her wanting another man irked him.

Cheeks blushing a rosy pink, she averted her eyes, took a drink from her champagne glass, then pretended to listen to whatever her friend was saying.

The same way Justin was pretending to listen to what Paul was saying.

Justin grimaced and told himself to stop with the Riley fascination and acknowledge the woman Paul was now introducing to him.

The single woman who'd just joined them had a hopeful look in her eyes. If she triggered half the sparks Riley did, he'd consider himself a lucky man.

Too bad he felt nothing when he looked at the tall blonde and everything when his gaze wandered back to the brunette whose gaze was on him again…

For so many reasons surgical nurse Riley King hadn't wanted to attend her coworker's engagement party. But she adored Cheyenne, and hadn't been able to think of a single excuse that wouldn't have their close-knit work-group rallying to make sure Riley was okay.

This party was about Cheyenne—not a wake for expressing grief over Riley's jilting at the altar. She had to at least make a quick appearance, even if she knew she'd be one of the few solo attendees and would get looks of pity and offers of blind date set-ups.

No, thank you.

She didn't want pity, blind dates, real dates, or to be anywhere that had anything to do with the opposite sex and especially not with weddings.

Like this engagement party.

Still, she had to go on smiling and pretending she was having the time of her life, and that she wasn't hungry when she was actually longing to give in to the temptation of the yummy-looking calorie-laden appetizers at various locales on the beautifully decorated patio.

Even worse, she had to pretend that the engagement and wedding excitement didn't trigger flashbacks to sitting in her fancy white dress, alone on her wedding night.

Johnny's exit had just been more dramatic, but every man Riley had ever cared for had left, leaving her done with romantic involvements.

So why was her gaze constantly on the man on the opposite side of the party venue? The very gorgeous man she couldn't keep her eyes from straying to no matter how many times she dragged them away?

Hot, steamy Dr. Justin Brothers—the heartthrob orthopedic surgeon all the females at the hospital oohed and ahhed over twenty-four-seven.

Riley didn't *ooh* or *ah* over Justin. Much. Sure, he was tall, muscular in a non-gym-rat kind of way, and had the most amazing blue eyes and smile. But she knew his type. Male—which equated to love 'em and leave 'em.

Justin was one of those fast guys who didn't waste time before declaring, "Next!" From the moment he'd arrived on the Columbia Hospital scene, he had never been with the same woman twice. He wasn't interested in pretending he'd stick around.

Wasn't that what Karen, one of his more recent exes, had told Riley when they'd bumped into each other at the grocer's? Justin was fun while it lasted, but knowing that hadn't prevented the woman from being heartbroken when he'd moved on.

Riley did not want to be the next Karen. Or Nancy. Or Stephanie.

So what if she enjoyed their hospital banter? The way he made her fight laughter more often than not? Made her fight the awareness that, although she'd sworn off romance, her body was still young and hormonal?

Regardless, she wouldn't risk a repeat of what had happened with Johnny. Not ever, ever, *ever*.

That was why she'd told Justin no when he'd asked her to dinner.

Twice.

She hadn't been sure he was serious the first time, and had figured the second time had been about wounded pride.

But if ever she was tempted to date again, Justin would be the one to make her do it.

When Justin had come to work at the hospital six months ago she had felt good old-fashioned lust surge to life. Something she'd thought impossible to feel again. Something she hadn't wanted to feel again.

Which was why she avoided him when she was outside the safety of the hospital.

The less she knew about Justin, the better.

The more she thought of him as a player—no better than any other man who'd ever walked the earth, looking for a female's heart to crush—the better.

The sooner she snuck away from this party, the better.

Why had she thought she could attend an engagement party? Wasn't that like having all her shattered dreams tossed right into her face? A vivid reminder of her own engagement party?

Romantic happiness was like a vapor. Here one moment, gone the next. Riley had sworn off pursuing that elusive mirage. Life was so much better since she had.

She gripped her glass tighter. She should have known Johnny would invade her thoughts tonight. She *had* known.

Laughing a bit too loudly at a comment someone made, Riley wanted to fall through the floor. Surely enough time had passed that she could leave without being noticed?

She glanced at her fitness watch. Her heart sank. Had she really only been there just over thirty minutes? How was that possible when it seemed hours had gone by since she'd arrived a little late, with her roommate Cassie and her on-again, off-again boyfriend Sam?

An hour. She had to stay at least an hour.

Then she could go home, change into something comfortable, eat celery while telling herself it tasted way better than chocolate, grab her six-pound Maltese terrier, and lie on the hammock in her backyard to let the night sky and her loving dog soothe away her raw nerves.

Across the room, Justin Brothers clanged his glass, causing the crowd to hush."Can I have your attention, please?"

Oh, he had Riley's attention, all right. Way too often and almost non-stop since she'd arrived and seen him putting shame to every other man present in his tailored black pants and perfect-fitting light blue button-down shirt. He'd undone a couple of buttons at his throat and rolled up his sleeves to reveal tanned mid-forearms. He looked phenomenal. Someone should put him on a billboard.

Yep, her attention was had. Which was unfortunate. You'd think an engagement party that had caused an outbreak of botched wedding memories would douse her reaction to Justin, but he still left her feeling unsettled.

"We're here tonight to celebrate Paul and Cheyenne's engagement," he continued, glancing to where the happy couple stood next to one another.

Riley's gaze followed, taking note of Paul's arm around Cheyenne's waist, his hand resting at his fiancée's lower back as she smiled up at him with her heart and a lifetime of dreams shining in her eyes.

Once upon a time Johnny had held her and she'd smiled adoringly at him, oblivious to his cheating ways.

Ugh. Riley fought a wave of nausea and finished off the champagne she wasn't supposed to drink until after the toast.

Staring into her empty glass, she grimaced. *Oops.*

Moving away from the friends she'd been talking to,

she grabbed another glass from a nearby tray to participate in the toast to the happy couple.

Relationships always started with smiles and happiness. It was what came later that brought tears and heartache. Grief. Humiliation. Pity.

Drinking champagne inappropriately.

Poor Cheyenne.

Cheyenne wouldn't listen, though. Hadn't Riley already tried to warn her friend to no avail that she was making a mistake? Cheyenne had hugged her and told her that someday someone was going to come along to heal all the wounds Johnny had inflicted.

Which was naïve and completely ridiculous.

Riley did not need or want someone to come along and "heal" her. She *was* healed—and she had learned valuable life lessons her friend had yet to experience.

Riley prayed she never would.

Tightening her hold on her new glass, she focused on where Justin was still talking, giving his toast to the couple. He was Paul's best man and he was taking his duties seriously, delivering one heck of a spiel about love and commitment.

As if he knew *anything* about those things.

"So, let's raise our glasses to Paul and Cheyenne, celebrate their love, and wish them a long, happy life together."

Riley did wish that for her friend. She just didn't believe it was possible. Still, she raised her glass, faked a smile as she clinked her glass against the nearby guests' glasses, then took a sip. A long sip that almost emptied her glass.

When she looked back toward Justin her eyes collided with his blue ones, as they often did. Probably

because he was wondering why she couldn't stop looking at him.

Heaven help her, but it would be easy to fall into that
man's eyes and drown in their mesmerizing depths.

She ordered her own eyes to move, to look at the
pretty landscape surrounding the porch, the ornate
bushes, the small trees and colorful plants—anything
other than Justin.

Her eyes refused to budge, preferring to submerge
themselves in vivid blue.

Maybe he'd put a spell over her. Because not only
would her eyes not avert, but her ability to fake anything vanished.

She knew it because she saw concern flicker on his
face.

She didn't want his concern.

She was fine.

Better than fine.

Only…

Only nothing.

Shunning the emotions rocking her, she clamped her
armor and her fake smile back into place and raised her
glass to him in acknowledgement of his toast.

His gaze searching hers, he raised his glass back.

In unison, eyes locked, they took a drink.

Riley swallowed, wondering if she'd had too much
as her head felt dizzy. This glass was her third and
would be her last.

She rarely drank, so three glasses of champagne
had to be why her insides felt so topsy-turvy. If she
wasn't careful she would soon be quite tipsy. She'd
only ever been drunk once—and, really, did that night
even count?

Ha. That night counts for everything, the nagging voice that reared its ugly head from time to time reminded her.

That night had been the end of what she'd thought the rest of her life would be and the beginning of a very different reality.

A better reality, she reminded herself. She was strong and independent, with a job she loved, a home and dog she loved, and a good life. It was no big deal that she was faking smiles and just about everything else.

Sighing, then realizing she'd done so for real rather than just in her head, Riley jerked her gaze away from Justin, emptied her glass, and took in the partygoers around her.

Most everyone was paired up. Anywhere she went, she was one of the few singles. She'd known the engagement party wouldn't be any different. What she hadn't known was that Justin would attend alone.

On the few times she'd seen him outside the hospital he'd always had a beautiful woman on his arm.

Ugh. What good was it to not be looking at him if she was just going to keep thinking about him? She needed to stop.

She didn't know which was worse: the flashbacks to her almost-wedding or making googly eyes at Justin. One had left her battle-scarred. The other was like stepping into the line of fire, begging to reopen wounds better left alone.

"You okay?"

Riley choked on the champagne that hadn't gone down yet. She tried to look as if the liquid wasn't clogging her airway, but quickly gave up when doing so meant not breathing. She coughed repeatedly, attempting to clear the gurgling from her throat.

"I was before you came over here and startled me," she accused, once she could form a sentence, hoping her watering eyes wouldn't ruin her mascara. "Why did you sneak up on me that way?"

Watching her closely, no doubt wondering if he needed to do some kind of medical maneuver to clear her throat, he quipped, "You mean in that walking across the terrace in plain sight way?"

She coughed one last time, took a deep breath, and appreciated it when it didn't trigger further hacking. "Yeah, that would be the way."

"For the record, my question referred to before your excellent dying from pneumonia impersonation." His lips twitched. "Glad to see you made a quick recovery."

Riley rolled her eyes. She might enjoy their banter at the hospital, but at an engagement party, with three glasses of champagne flowing through her, thinning her protective armor, not so much.

"No thanks to you," she complained, reminding herself to keep her eyes focused on his face and not let them drop to that sexy V revealed by those loosened buttons. "You could have at least slapped my back a few times."

"And have you accused me of drumming up business by cracking a few ribs?" His grin was infectious, making his eyes twinkle. "I don't think so."

Why did the man have to be so good-looking? So—so *everything*?

"I said slapping my back, not breaking bones." Although she was fighting against smiling, she gave him a stern look. "Jeez, men and their having to flex muscles every chance they get…"

He was unfazed, and his eyes danced. "You don't want to see me flex my muscles, Riley?"

Um, yeah, she'd like to see him do that…

"Not that way," she denied, gulping at her big fat lie and wondering at what she even meant. This party, maybe him, too, had her so flustered she was making no sense.

"Is there some *other* way you'd like to see my muscles flex?" He pounced on her goof. "I'd be happy to oblige."

"I'll pass, since I see all the muscle-flexing from you that I want to see in the operating room, when you're pulling and tugging on patients."

"My talents extend beyond surgery."

Heaven help her, she was about to go into a coughing fit again.

"I'm sure they do," she managed to say, knowing he was waiting.

"You should let me show you sometime."

Riley refused to take him seriously. "Ah, poor Justin. Are you upset you don't have a date tonight?"

Eyes locked with hers, he shook his head. "Quite the opposite. I purposely came alone."

Surprised, and further flustered by his answer and his look, Riley stared at him. "Why would a muscle-flexing guy like you do something like that?"

"I was hoping you'd be here without a date."

The South Carolina humidity had just gone into overdrive and was drenching her skin.

Resisting the urge to fan herself, she tilted her chin upward. "What good would that do you?"

"Based on past experience? Not one bit." Looking way too charming, he gave a self-deprecating laugh.

"But a guy can hope you'll take pity and at least say yes to one dance."

Dance with Justin?

Riley gulped at the thought of wrapping her arms around his neck, of his arms around her waist. She'd need more than her hands to fan her if she agreed to that. Something along the lines of the jet blast from a Boeing 747.

"Maybe later," she answered, thinking that if she said no he'd persist, and that if she said yes he'd pull her onto the dance floor with the other couples now.

"I'm going to hold you to that."

Most likely he'd move on to one of the few other dateless women there, all of whom she'd seen talking to him at different points since arriving.

"Maybe you'd like to see the gardens? There's a small lake with a fountain just over that rise. I'm told it's worth the short walk." He gestured beyond the porch to a lighted walkway.

Getting away from the party appealed more than getting away from Justin.

She set her glass down on a table, then nodded. "Please."

Seeming surprised she'd agreed, he smiled. "You just made my night."

His smile was so genuine, so endearing, her breath caught. She fought against saying she'd changed her mind and was leaving the party she hadn't wanted to attend to begin with. Even though that was what a smart girl would do.

Her IQ was dropping by the second.

"You wish," she quipped, not waiting for him as she headed toward the path he'd pointed out.

He quickly fell into step beside her as they made their way along the cobblestoned walkway. Trimmed bushes, flowers, and solar-powered lights bordered either side, giving a sense of privacy and filling the air with the scent of sweet gardenia.

"I do, you know."

"Do what?" She didn't look at him, just carefully made her way along the path, thinking she should have gone for different shoes as four-inch heels weren't ideal for garden walkways.

When she'd chosen them she'd been thinking of how the extra height would make her look taller, feel thinner, more in control during what she'd known would be a rough experience.

"Wish you had just made my night," he clarified.

At his response, Riley stumbled, reaching out to keep herself from falling at the same time as he moved to catch her.

She fell into his arms. Literally.

Embarrassed, she glanced up, both cursing and blessing her heels. They'd caused her to stumble, but they also gave her the vantage point to more easily look into his eyes.

Blessing? She wasn't supposed to be looking into Justin's eyes—much less easily. Nor was she supposed to be pressed against his hard body.

Oh, my!

"Well, hello, there," he teased, not stepping back from where he held her.

Neither did she. Which was a problem. Why was she not removing her body from where it was plastered to his? And why, oh, why did he feel so wonderful? So solid and chiseled to perfection?

Not to mention that his spicy clean scent was pulling a wicked number... She'd gotten whiffs of that clean, all-man smell in the OR, but had never allowed herself to really take it in. Where was an alcohol pad when she needed one to block it out?

Unable to stop herself, Riley breathed in through her nose, filling her nostrils, her lungs, her being, with Justin.

Goodness, the man was intoxicating. His body, his smell. The way he was looking down at her.

His heart pounded hard against her chest as his gaze dropped to her mouth. She parted her lips, planning to apologize for falling, but nothing came out.

His hands trembled slightly where they pressed against her back. His throat worked as he swallowed, and then, surprising her, he closed his eyes.

The walkway lights flickered over his face, allowing Riley to see how the skin was pulled tightly across his cheeks, how he was struggling with something. Not something... With *her* and how their bodies were responding to one another.

"Justin?"

He opened his eyes.

"I feel as if I should be asking you if you're okay," she mused, still not moving out of his arms.

She'd thought it was his heart pounding against her chest. It wasn't. It was her own, banging so violently against her rib cage that he might be black and blue if he didn't step away.

He didn't. Instead, his hands moved from her lower back to caress her face.

"I'm good," he assured her.

She'd bet he was, and she wanted to know more.

Which scared her.

Terrified her.

Just as she'd worked up the strength to pry her body from his, he bent to touch his lips to hers. A soft brushing of his mouth, slow, gentle, in a show of great restraint because she felt the way his body tensed.

Lord help her for what she felt as his mouth coaxed hers to open, to allow him to explore to his heart's content.

Riley's head spun. That was how Justin made her feel. Spinning out of control.

A single moment or an eternity might have passed during their embrace. Riley couldn't have sworn one way or the other. Just knew that Justin's kiss took her beyond the realm of time, place, anything…

All that mattered was his kiss, how when she opened her eyes and looked into his what she saw weakened her knees. Mostly because what she saw there was reflected in her own for him to see.

But she didn't want him seeing behind her carefully guarded walls—didn't want anyone glimpsing behind her armor, least of all Justin.

What had she done?

She needed to run, to put as much distance between them as her high heels would let her.

But other than to tremble at the gravity of what was happening, her body didn't move.

Holding her close, he smiled. "That was worth waiting for."

Stunned at his admission, she blinked. "You were waiting to kiss me?"

Brushing a few loose hairs away from her face, he nodded. "You know I was."

No, she didn't know that.

Wrong. She *did* know.

She knew. And there was no more denying what she'd been denying for months.

What she'd been wanting for months.

Justin.

CHAPTER TWO

RILEY HADN'T INTENDED to go home with Justin.

Ha—even a few hours ago, when they'd been swirling and laughing on the dance floor, she'd still been telling herself their kiss had been a one-off.

So much for good intentions and all that jazz.

Here she was, in his bedroom, in the midst of something straight out of someone else's life, practically ripping Justin's shirt off his muscled chest.

He trailed hungry kisses over her throat, slid her spaghetti straps down her shoulders while her every nerve cell strained to be nearer to his talented lips.

She'd lost her purse somewhere. Possibly it was in the Jeep he'd driven them in to his apartment. Or maybe she'd tossed it somewhere between his front door and where they were now wrapped around each other next to his bed.

His big bed.

A big bed he'd probably brought countless women to.

Hesitation hit. Did she really want to be another notch on Justin's belt?

Abandoning their fumbling at his shirt buttons, her fingers lowered, tracing over the rich, smooth leather encircling his waist. Seriously, what was she doing? Feeling for literal notches on his belt?

She pressed her forehead to his chest, resting against the soft cotton material. Closing her eyes, she breathed in his amazing scent, full of spice and temptation.

It made women crave more.

It made *her* crave more.

Don't inhale, Riley. Do not inhale.

Wasn't that when she'd first lost her mind in the garden? When she'd allowed his scent to intoxicate her? Weaken her to his powerful sensory onslaught?

Swallowing, she clenched his belt and ordered her brain to use logic, not hormones, to calculate how she wanted to proceed.

Or not to proceed.

Unaware of her inner turmoil, he dipped his tongue into the indentation at the base of her throat as his fingers connected with her dress's zipper.

A moan rose from deep inside her chest.

She was here, in Justin's bedroom, the sole recipient of his many talents. Was she really going to tell him to stop?

He would. As wrapped up as he was in what was happening, she didn't question the fact that if she told him she'd changed her mind he'd stop.

Letting go of his belt, her hands went back to working those last few shirt buttons free. The time for stopping had gone. Just like her inhibitions, apparently.

Possibly this was happening because she'd been so emotionally raw at Cheyenne and Paul's party. And she'd drunk champagne while eating very little, because she was on yet another diet in the hopes of getting rid of the extra fifteen pounds she perpetually carried.

Or maybe she was here because what she'd seen in Justin's eyes when he'd kissed her, what she'd felt at his touch, had soothed the ever-present rawness Johnny's cruelty had dealt her.

"You taste good."

Was that why he was nibbling at her neck that way? As if her skin was nectar and he was starved?

"Sweet as honey," he continued, his lips miracle-workers at her throat.

"Too sticky," she murmured, finally freeing him of his shirt.

Wanting to look at what she'd uncovered, she attempted to take a step back. But she was too close to the bed to manage more than bumping against the king-sized monstrosity.

"Sticky sweet," he practically growled, prickling her more and more sensitized flesh with goosebumps.

His hands made their way beneath her dress, cupped her bottom, and pulled her against him.

Her entire body *tingled*. As if someone had hooked up a TENS unit and cranked the power full-blast.

Oh, wow.

He pressed against her belly, hard, tempting, promising great pleasure.

Riley wanted great pleasure.

She had heard about it, had dreamed of it a long, long time ago, but experience it? *Nada.*

Her ex sure hadn't delivered great pleasure.

Johnny had been okay in bed. Probably as good as Riley. Which should have her reconsidering what was happening now, because the last thing she wanted was Justin thinking her a dud between the sheets. She must be. Johnny wouldn't have strayed before they'd even made it down the aisle if she was any good, right?

But Justin wasn't acting as if he thought her a dud. He couldn't get enough, seemed to want to kiss her all over, touch her all over, as if he found her curves sexy rather than too fleshy. As if he found her irresistible.

Justin was *with* her, kissing her, grinding his body against hers. He was focused on her and making her feel good. He *wanted* her.

She'd regret it tomorrow. She knew she would. She knew herself too well to believe otherwise. She had to work with him, for goodness' sake.

But when his fingers hooked her panties and slid them down she couldn't lift her feet fast enough to shake free of the skimpy satin and lace material.

Not only was she doing this, but she was going to demand Justin make it worth every single recrimination she'd feel later.

With that thought, she pulled his belt free from his jeans, tossed it to the floor, then twined her fingers through the loops of his jeans and tugged him to her.

Eyes locked with his, she lifted her chin. "You only get one shot," she warned, with the bravado of a seasoned siren rather than a woman whose groom had been a no-show at their wedding. "Make it good."

Not looking the slightest bit worried about his making-it-good abilities, Justin grinned.

"I can do that," he promised, and then he did.

Slowly waking, Justin felt his lips curve when he recalled how he'd spent the night.

With Riley. Sexy, curvy Riley. With her long brown hair and big green eyes. Sweet and sassy Riley, who was all business at work, tough and forceful with her patients when they needed to be pushed, kind and gentle when they needed a soft touch, and always professional.

It was her smile that had first hooked him. When she smiled her eyes lit, dimples dug into her cheeks, and a genuine warmth exuded from her that soothed something deep inside him and yet left a raw achiness.

Last night, when he'd gone to her, he'd been thinking along the lines of chatting, going for a walk, strolling near the lake to admire the fountain, then heading back to the party to dance.

Never in his wildest dreams had Justin envisioned them heading to his apartment. To his bed.

Well, maybe in his wildest dreams. He just hadn't expected it to *happen*.

He wasn't complaining. He'd wanted her for months.

She'd been a firecracker and she had put on an impressive show. She'd met him touch for touch, kiss for kiss, demanding more until he'd given all he had to give, and then had still found the strength to give more.

He stretched his arms over his head, surprised his muscles weren't protesting his vigorous nocturnal activities. Instead he felt glorious—it was like the best runner's high.

Amazing what a night of phenomenal sex with the right woman did for a man.

And Riley was the right woman.

He'd suspected that from the moment they'd met, and finally she seemed to have quit denying there was something between them.

She hadn't said no, nor had she rolled her eyes and laughed. What she'd said had turned him inside out and shattered all doubts that they were meant to be a couple.

Anticipating the vision of Riley sleeping in his bed, her beautiful hair sprawled out on his pillow, he rolled onto his side and opened his eyes.

What?

The space where Riley should be lying was empty.

Was she already awake and hadn't awakened him?

Listening for sounds in the bathroom, or coming from the kitchen, he didn't hear the slightest creak.

With a rising sense of unease, he sat up and glanced to the bedroom floor where they'd stripped each other.

Riley's clothes were missing.

Empty bed, quiet apartment, missing clothes.

Reality gut-punched him, wreaking havoc with his earlier post-phenomenal-sex euphoria.

Riley was gone.

Why hadn't she woken him?

Getting out of bed, he grabbed a pair of shorts from a drawer, then made his way through the apartment, looking for some sign that she'd really been there and that he hadn't dreamed the entire night.

Surely she'd left a note?

A glass slipper?

Something?

Nothing.

She'd awakened, dressed, and left.

Raking his fingers through his hair, he considered his options.

He didn't have her phone number. Why hadn't he gotten it last night when he'd had the chance?

Because he hadn't expected to wake up alone. Not after the hot kisses they'd shared. The hot *everything* they'd shared.

Taking a pre-made bag of vegetables and fruit from

his freezer, he dropped them into his blender, along with a scoop of protein powder, poured in some almond milk, put on the lid, then pressed the button.

Why had Riley left?

She'd enjoyed their lovemaking. She hadn't faked her responses. Not the first time or the second. She'd have told him if he wasn't pleasing her. She'd not been shy in saying what she wanted, and he hadn't hesitated in giving her that and more.

No matter. He'd thought she was through denying the sparks between them, but now she'd made how she felt clear enough. He didn't need a flashing neon sign that her being gone this morning wasn't the making of a promising relationship.

He couldn't make someone want him when they didn't. He'd learned that almost before he'd learned to walk.

Feeling a fool, he raked his fingers through his hair, stopped the blender, then poured his smoothie into a plastic cup.

Rather than head downstairs to the condo complex's gym, he pulled out a chair at his kitchen bar and contemplated his relationship with Riley—starting from the moment they'd met. Even before then...

From the outside looking in, he and Ashley should have had it all had they married.

Only their idea of "family" had varied.

Justin had always wanted kids of his own, but planned to adopt as well. Ashley had known about the foster boys Justin was involved with, but the week before their wedding she'd told him she wouldn't be raising someone else's kids—not even his "little charity cases" whom she barely tolerated.

Justin had called off the wedding and several months later had relocated his job. He'd thought he'd focus on the boys until he met someone who wanted the same things he did—to have a big family, which included adopted and—Lord willing—birth children, and maybe a few foster kids along the way.

Then he'd met Riley.

An orthopedic nurse full of curves and sass who refused to date him but ruined his interest in every other woman.

They'd seen each other out socially a few times. But, determined not to let her get to him, as he had no desire to chase someone who claimed she wasn't interested, he'd done his best to stay away and had brought a date to each group event.

For the past few weeks he'd not even bothered dating because he hadn't been interested. And he'd known the reason.

Riley.

He'd enjoyed talking with her last night—enjoyed how, while the conversation had flowed vocally, their eyes and body had been communicating in a whole other language.

When he'd asked if she was ready to leave the party she'd not hesitated, immediately taking him up on his offer to drive her home.

Only the moment they were in his car he'd half-jokingly invited her to his place for drinks, to sit on his balcony and enjoy his view of the river.

He'd expected a flat-out no.

Instead, she'd agreed.

He should have known better. Maybe he had. But he'd been caught up in the way she'd been looking at him. And he'd barely gotten the engine turned off in the parking garage before they'd been all over each other, taking their garden kiss to another level of intensity.

Thinking back, he was surprised they'd made it to his bedroom. Had the elevator ride to his floor taken much longer they wouldn't have. The chemistry had been that powerful.

Probably because of how long he'd wanted her. How *much* he'd wanted her.

Frustrated, Justin downed the rest of his breakfast, then walked back into his bedroom so he could jump in the shower.

He'd really thought they had something special.

Too bad Riley had left.

"I wasn't expecting you to stay at Cheyenne's party after Sam and I left. How late did you stay?"

"Not too late."

Riley eyed Cassie from across the table and took a sip of her coffee. The hot liquid scalded her tongue, but she gulped the drink down rather than give any sign of unease.

"Daisy slept in my room most of the night."

"Did she?" Riley tried to make it sound as if it wasn't a big deal that her dog had stayed in Cassie's room. If Riley had been at home the dog would've been wherever *she* was. They both knew it.

"I'm not sure at what point she abandoned me," Cassie mused. "I'm guessing whatever time you came home."

Glancing down at the fluffy white dog, eyeing them in the hope they'd share some of their breakfast, Riley shrugged. "She met me at the door when I came in—"

at the crack of dawn "—and she wanted to go outside. She crawled into bed with me after that."

"Had Sam not had to be up early for work we'd have stuck around at the party, just so I could keep an eye on you and Dr. Brothers."

Her friend waggled her brows suggestively.

"I was enjoying the fireworks exploding between the two of you."

Ugh. Could they not just go back to talking about Daisy?

Reality had hit. Although Riley had been oblivious to everyone except Justin when they'd been talking, laughing, dancing, no doubt their friends and coworkers had seen them…had taken note of the fact they'd left together.

Double *ugh*.

"Was it him who gave you a lift home?"

"No." A creepy *I-know-what-you've-been-doing* taxi driver had brought her home.

"Too bad," Cassie mused. "You seemed lost in conversation with him when you waved me off and said you'd find your own ride."

Staring into her coffee mug, Riley shrugged. "He's easy to talk to."

Easy to do a lot of things with. Things she regretted, yet wasn't sure she'd have passed up, given the choice of a redo.

"Mmm-hmm?" Cassie teased. *"Talk to."*

Knowing they were destined to have this conversation at some point, Cassie scooped Daisy into her lap, threaded her fingers into the dog's soft white fur to rub her neck, then met her friend's curious gaze.

"You two could have started an inferno with those sparks flying."

An inferno was a pretty apt description of what they *had* started. Images of the night were definitely burned into her mind.

"I drank a little more than I should have," Riley admitted, searching for the words to appease her friend.

Sitting her coffee mug on the table, Cassie leaned forward. "You left with him, didn't you?"

Riley grimaced. "Do we have to have this conversation before I've finished my first cup of coffee?"

Cassie clasped her hands together and made a gleeful noise. "Which means you did!"

Riley's face instantly heated. Cassie was her best friend, knew all the details of her wedding gone awry. She understood when Riley said she wasn't interested in going back down that road.

"We all make mistakes," she admitted, thinking hers were typically super-sized.

"No!" Cassie gasped, her bottom lip going into a disappointed pout. "Dr. Brothers wasn't any good?"

"He was—*phenomenal*—good." She couldn't bring herself to say otherwise. "Just..." she stroked Daisy's fur "...I shouldn't have had sex with a coworker."

"There's no hospital rule about dating coworkers." Cassie dismissed her comment with a wave of her hand. "I'd know, since I'm dating a really hot emergency room nurse."

There *was* that.

"Justin and I aren't dating," Riley pointed out, staring at Daisy as if she was trying to convince the dog. "Last night was a one-off fluke. Nice, but no big deal."

"*Nice?* The man is gorgeous enough to make even

me look twice, and I'm gaga over Sam." Cassie shook her head. "I can't believe you're describing sex with Dr. Brothers as 'nice!' Guess he'd be too good to be true if he was the total package."

Justin *was* the total package. Witty, kind, attentive, gorgeous…*hot in bed.*

Stop thinking of him that way, she scolded herself, her temples pounding.

Still, letting Cassie think poorly of Justin didn't sit well.

"Last night was better than nice—way better. But it doesn't matter. What happened was one night. Nothing more."

Her friend sipped her coffee, obviously processing what Riley had said.

"I can't say this doesn't surprise me, because it does," Cassie began. "I thought— Oh, never mind what I thought. If that's all he wants it's his loss. You're a great catch."

Even her best friend assumed it must be Justin who didn't want to continue their relationship. Because no one in their right mind would assume a slightly chubby plain Jane wouldn't jump at the chance to be with him anytime he crooked his talented finger.

They were probably right. But she wasn't giving Justin the opportunity to be the one to say, *Thanks, but no thanks.*

She liked her life just as it was. She'd worked hard to get Johnny's voice out of her head, and on most things had succeeded.

She liked not having to worry about making anyone happy but herself. Not having to walk on eggshells because of her many flaws, or worry about starting over if the person she'd built her world around found some-one new and left her.

Riley reached for the small golden cross she wore at her neck and toyed with when she was nervous or agitated.

It wasn't there.

Her stomach knotted.

It had to be.

She touched her neck again, feeling around on her throat. Panic gurgled from her belly upward. No! She hadn't lost—

Riley's airway tightened.

Her necklace was gone.

Sitting Daisy down, she stood, patted her neck, shook out her clothes, looked around on the floor.

Nothing.

Panic rose, clogging her throat.

"What's wrong?" Cassie asked.

"My necklace." Riley fought back tears, tracing back in her mind when she last recalled having it.

"The one your mother gave you?"

Riley nodded, feeling bereft, as if she'd lost a part of her mother. Had she had it on the night before at the party? She couldn't remember—couldn't recall if she'd put it on after changing out of her scrubs at the hospital. Was it possible she'd lost it there?

She'd check at the hospital, call Cheyenne, see if any-one had found the necklace at either place. She hoped so. She'd hate never to wear the precious gift again. It had been the last thing her mother had given to her.

Or she might have lost it was while she was with Justin. Had she still had it on in his Jeep? At his condo? *In his bed?*

* * *

Justin scrubbed for surgery. He had two hip replacements on his schedule today. One on a fifty-two-year-old male with severe arthritic changes, and another on a thirty-year-old who'd had high-dose steroids administered repetitively in primary care that had resulted in necrosis of the hip joint. Both were total replacements, and would be mentally and physically demanding.

And emotionally. Because both meant being in the operating room with the woman he'd thought about almost non-stop since she'd left him.

Riley frustrated him. He kept telling himself to forget her. Then he'd remind himself that he'd been telling himself that for months and it hadn't worked. Had he really thought it would after Saturday night? After their sweet garden kiss and how much fun they'd had at the party? How much fun they'd had *after* the party?

Even the boys had commented that he wasn't his usual upbeat self during their fishing trip yesterday afternoon.

It hadn't been a fish he'd wanted to catch, but a woman he'd thought he'd hooked, but who'd gotten away.

He'd already gotten involved with one woman who hadn't wanted the same things as he did. Obviously Riley didn't either or she wouldn't have left.

He seriously needed to move on.

Maybe telling himself that would work this time.

Knowing he'd way over-scrubbed, Justin made his way into the operating room where he'd spend the next few hours.

Good thing Bernie Jones' hip would require all his attention.

* * *

Riley had been dreading this moment since she'd left Justin's. The moment they came face-to-face.

Well, not face-to-face, since they both wore surgical masks and were covered from head-to-toe.

Still, their eyes were visible beneath their protective shields.

Justin's eyes were expressive.

Usually.

Exactly as it should be—even if it did sting a little—he'd not bothered to look her way yet. He'd just entered the operating room and asked to start the check-in procedure.

What had she expected? For him to say something directly to her?

Hello, Riley, so how about Saturday night?

She didn't want him to do that—would have been mortified if he had. So why the disappointment that he was ignoring her?

Maybe it was lack of sleep making her crazy. Certainly, despite knowing she'd made the right decision, she'd struggled to keep her mind off Justin.

And off her missing necklace.

Yeah, that was why, when she finally had slept, it had been after tears shed over her lost treasure and nothing to do with Justin.

She needed to ask him if he'd found her necklace. No one had found it at Cheyenne's party or anywhere else. When she could get him alone, she'd ask.

Not that she wanted to be alone with him, but she couldn't very well ask if he'd found her necklace at his condo without raising a few eyebrows. They'd already caused enough eyebrow-raising on Saturday night.

She was working as the nurse overseer that day. Her job was to make sure everyone had what they needed, that a sterile field was maintained, and that everything went the way it should and was recorded accurately.

An anesthesiologist, his assistant, a scrub tech, a circulator, and a scrub nurse were also in the room, along with their patient.

"Bernie Jones, age fifty-two. Controlled hypertension and no other known health conditions," Riley informed the, starting the check-in while double-checking the patient's ID bracelet. "No known drug allergies."

"I will be performing a minimally invasive left hip arthroplasty," Justin began, and then proceeded to give a one-minute synopsis of what the planned surgery entailed. Sometimes that changed, as unexpected issues arose, but for the most part the hip replacements performed at this hospital were uneventful.

The man was an excellent surgeon. The best she'd ever worked with. Many of the other orthopedic surgeons, although talented, were moody, sometimes socially awkward. Not Justin. Everyone on the unit loved working with him.

Always upbeat, he usually chatted while performing whatever procedure they had going. Thus far today, however, he'd been all business.

Which was fine. Only…

Oh, no—no onlys.

Justin needed his full focus on his job and so did she.

The scrub nurse had the patient properly positioned. The anesthesiologist had the patient completely unaware of what was happening to and around him. And, with the patient lying flat on his back, Justin made an eight-centimeter incision. Once he had the incision made, he placed soft tissue retractors in front of and behind the femoral neck, exposing the hip joint.

"Scalpel."

The surgical tech handed Justin the cutting tool, which he took and released the capsule to expose the femoral head and the acetabulum. He studied the area a moment, made another tiny cut. When he was happy with what he'd done he used a protractor to work on the unhealthy acetabulum, removing bone spurs and diseased tissue.

Reminding herself that she was responsible for what every person in the room was doing, not just Justin, Riley pried her gaze away from his skilled hands and took in each member of the OR team. Anesthesia was closely monitoring vitals, and everyone else was attentively doing what they should be.

Her gaze went back to where Justin worked. He'd dislocated the hip and was inserting a large screw into the acetabulum. Once the screw was securely embedded in the bone he exposed the femoral head more fully and finished removing the capsule.

While the anesthesiologist chatted with his assistant about a recent sailing trip he had made, Justin painstakingly removed the femoral head with an oscillating saw, cleaned the acetabulum, then went about rebuilding the joint with prosthetics.

All in all, the surgery took just over two hours to complete.

When he was finished, Justin's gaze lifted and sought Riley's.

What she saw there had her stomach churning more than any bone-cutting surgical procedure she'd ever witnessed.

His eyes glittered with what she could only label as

hurt because she'd pushed him away—although more likely that was just his wounded pride she was seeing. But there was also curiosity as to why she'd done so. And something more that she could only think of as warmth—not that that made any sense.

None of what she saw made sense except the curiosity. He probably wasn't used to women walking away from him, so no doubt that did have him puzzled.

Leaving him had been her being proactive on preventing heartbreak. A pre-emptive strike. She'd left before he had.

Maybe if Justin hadn't been quite so handsome, had been something more ordinary than an orthopedic surgeon, not quite so fabulous, she might have risked a relationship. Doubtful after what Johnny had done, but maybe.

Someone so good-looking, so successful, was destined to break her heart if she gave him the chance.

"Good job," he praised the team, still holding her gaze.

Something flashed in the blue depths that suggested he saw more than she wanted him to see, that he knew she warred within. She wanted to look away, to mask her eyes from his. With each passing second her heart pounded harder.

Just as it reached the point of thundering in her ears, he broke contact and headed out of the operating suite.

"Wonder what was up with Dr. Brothers. He was quieter than usual," the recorder said as soon as Justin was out of the room.

Riley stared down at the surgical tray.

"But he's still a pleasure to work with. If only all

orthopedic surgeons were as easy to be with in surgery as that man," the assistant observed.

"If only all orthopedic surgeons were as easy on the eye as that man," the surgical tech teased with a waggle of her brows.

Riley said nothing and prayed that Sheila, the scrub nurse, wouldn't say anything either. Sheila and her husband had been at Cheyenne's party.

"Looked like you were all cozy with him on Friday night, Riley," said, Sheila giving her a knowing look. "I saw you leave together."

Ugh. Of course Sheila had seen. And now she'd mentioned that. In front of the whole team.

"Really? Lucky you..." The surgical tech sighed.

Rather than answer Sheila, or acknowledge the surgical tech, who looked amazed that Justin had been with her, Riley shrugged and went about preparing the patient to be rolled to the recovery room.

What could she say?

Why, yes, that was me, all cozied up with Justin. And guess what? The man is pure genius between the sheets!

Yeah, that wasn't happening.

Nor would she tell them that she'd left before he'd awakened and had the opportunity to tell her to leave.

Sheila was right, though. Justin had been particularly subdued. Normally he would have made chitchat, and most definitely would have said something directly to her. He'd have made small talk, teased her about Daisy and how she needed to get a real dog, or he would have lingered after surgery to chat for a few minutes.

He'd done none of those things.

As much as she hated to admit it, the fact that their

Saturday night escapade had created this rift in their work relationship, leaving things awkward, stung.

Justin was used to one-night stands, so what had happened shouldn't be a big deal. But the others were right. He hadn't behaved normally. He'd been as tense as she had.

Was it because she'd been the one to leave? Or could she have misjudged how casually he saw sex and Saturday night hadn't been quite as run-of-the mill for him as she'd thought?

CHAPTER THREE

IT HAD BEEN a long day, but Riley had made it through her first day at work after "that night," as she'd dubbed Saturday.

She wasn't sure what she'd expected, but she shouldn't have worried. Except for that lingering look after he'd finished the surgery Justin had ignored her. That would hopefully put to rest the rumors flying around that they were an item after being seen together at Cheyenne's party.

More than one person had questioned her about her relationship with Justin. The fact that people actually believed they might be an item floored Riley. Couldn't they see she was nothing like the women he dated? She wasn't tall, thin, bordering on perfect.

She'd be a sitting duck, just asking to be dumped again, if she got involved with Justin.

Grabbing her bag from the locker, she headed out of the nurses' changing area and down the long hallway toward the elevator bank.

Just as she got into an open car Justin stepped inside—then realized who she was, and paused midway to pressing his floor number. His jaw tightened, and for a moment she thought he was going to either wait for the next elevator or take the stairs.

Riley bit into her lower lip, telling herself to let him leave, but then heard herself saying, "It would be silly for you to get out."

He faced her. "You're sure?"

She nodded.

The elevator was empty other than the two of them, and it was with reluctance that Riley watched the door close behind Justin.

"You did a great job on the hip replacements today," she rushed out, feeling the need to fill the silence.

"Seriously? One minute you're sneaking out of my condo and the next you want to make small talk?"

"Fine…" she breathed, knowing she deserved his question. But how could she explain that she'd missed their usual camaraderie when she'd been the one to leave? "I won't say another word and we'll ride the elevator in complete awkward silence."

Her insides trembled. So did her lower lip. She felt Justin's shoulders sag more than saw them as she refused to look up.

"I'm sorry."

She didn't respond, just willed herself to be strong. But how could she hold tough when just being near him was setting her nerve-endings on edge? Setting her memories ablaze? When the taste of him lingered on her lips and in her mind? When she craved his mouth against hers?

Ugh.

She would not put herself through this. She just wouldn't.

"Hell, Riley…" He sounded as upset as she felt. "This isn't easy for me, you know."

That had her gaze lifting. "You think it's easy for *me*?"

His eyes searched hers. "Isn't it?"

Was that what he thought? She must be a better actress than she'd given herself credit for.

"People were talking about us today. I didn't like it." She hesitated, and then, glancing away, admitted, "More than that, I didn't like it that you didn't talk to me."

"I didn't know what to say."

"You normally have no trouble talking to me," she reminded him.

"I normally haven't had sex with you, then woken up in bed alone."

"There is that." Riley leaned back against the elevator wall, looked up—and lost her breath as her gaze locked with his emotion-filled one.

He really did seem to be struggling with this as much as she was. He looked as torn and confused about what had happened as she was, and wondering where they went from here.

She sank her teeth into her lower lip as she considered him—as she considered her own conflicted thoughts and emotions.

She'd looked into those eyes when they were filled with passion, had laughed with him, smiled at him, felt so at ease with him Saturday night.

His seeing her naked could have been so awkward—could have triggered so many negative memories of Johnny's harsh comments about her size and many other failings. Instead Justin had made her feel beautiful, sexy, confident. Not once had he looked at her or responded to her with anything other than complete and utter fascination.

And Justin being fascinated with her—her body, her

words, her desires—had been heady. Addictive. Making her want more. Lots more.

She still wanted more. As evidenced by the heat building inside her at being near him, alone, in an elevator, and knowing what he was capable of.

She gulped.

As if he had read where her mind had gone his gaze dropped to her lips and his eyes darkened. "Riley, I really am sorry. I—"

The elevator came to a stop and the door slid open. Two suited men boarded, nodded toward them, then went back to their conversation.

Justin didn't resume speaking—for which Riley was grateful. She didn't want the suits privy to their conversation. But she wanted to know what he'd been about to say.

When they got off the elevator they headed in silence toward the employee parking area. She bit her already sore lower lip as they walked near to one another and yet so far away.

She should have known this would happen. This horrible awkwardness.

She *had* known.

Justin had never been one for dancing around an issue, and he truly didn't understand why Riley hadn't woken him.

He'd had to bite his tongue in the elevator. He wanted to talk to her—needed to talk to her to understand what had happened between them. But he knew Riley wouldn't appreciate their having a serious conversation in front of others.

Once they got outside the building they'd headed

for the employee parking lot. Although only a few feet apart physically as they walked together toward their cars, miles separated them in every other way.

He couldn't hold back any longer. "Why did you leave?"

"There was no reason to stay."

Ouch. Did she truly believe that? "I can think of a few."

She sighed. "Don't look a gift horse in the mouth, Justin."

Confused, he stopped walking. "Not sure I follow."

"My leaving made things simpler for both of us."

"By…"

"By letting us not have to pretend what happened meant anything."

Having to remind himself that they were in the hospital's parking lot, Justin contemplated what Riley said. "Who says it didn't mean anything?" he asked.

Her gaze cut to his. She looked stunned for such a brief moment that he thought he might have imagined the flash of vulnerability.

"Good sex counts for something, eh?" she said.

His faltering ego surged a little. "You admit the sex was good?"

Her cheeks went bright pink. "Would you believe me if I denied it?"

"No." He knew better. "Which is why I was shocked to find you'd left. We could have spent the day together."

She shifted her weight, looking more and more uncomfortable with their conversation. No wonder. They were still standing in the employee parking lot.

"This isn't the best place to have this conversation," he admitted. "Maybe we could grab a bite to eat?"

Obviously shocked at his suggestion, she met his gaze and appeared ready to tell him no. It wouldn't be the first time.

"No strings attached," he added. "Come and talk with me so we can get past this weirdness between us. It seems neither of us likes it."

"I—I have to let Daisy out. Sorry."

He started to point out that they could meet up afterward, but she'd already taken off toward her car.

Well, that hadn't gone the way he'd hoped.

Then again, what had he expected? She'd left his bed without waking him.

Riley tapped her fingers against the steering wheel as she drove toward the park. She'd have plenty of time to hit the trail before sunset. She had to get out of the house and burn some of her nervous energy. And she needed to run as she hadn't exercised over the weekend.

Sex with Justin had burned more than few calories, though.

Ugh.

"I have to stop thinking about him," she said out loud, hoping that would make it happen.

Not true. She *needed* to think about him and figure out what his odd behavior in the OR meant. What his asking her to dinner meant. Even more, she needed to figure out why it mattered so much.

Shouldn't she just let it go? Not worry that their working relationship felt changed forever and just be grateful she'd escaped unscathed otherwise?

Only she didn't feel grateful. She felt bereft of his friendship.

So why had she refused dinner?

She gripped the steering wheel tighter. He'd said no strings attached when she'd hesitated. Why hadn't she gone?

For the same reason that for so long she'd only interacted with him at the hospital.

Justin was dangerous to her peace of mind.

To her peace of heart.

Seeing him in the elevator had flustered her, so that she hadn't even thought to ask about her necklace. She'd ugly-cried at the loss, so how could she have not remembered to ask? Then again, if he'd found it, he'd have told her, surely?

She pulled into an empty parking space, happy to have found one so quickly as the lot was almost full.

Daisy whimpered from the back seat, where she was inside her carrier.

"I know, girl. Give me a minute and I'll have you out of there," she promised, opening the door, then Daisy's crate. She snapped a leash to Daisy's collar. "We're going to work off some steam, aren't we?" she cooed as she put the car key fob inside the zipped pouch at her waist.

Car locked. Dog on leash. She ticked the items off in her head before turning toward the trail.

Were her eyes playing tricks on her?

Not twenty feet away Justin was stretching.

She'd not told him where she was headed. Had she subconsciously chosen this park because she'd gotten glimpses of him running there in the past? If so, was she crazy? Why would she *do* that?

He hadn't seen her yet. She could leave without him knowing she'd been there.

Instead, she took a deep breath and went to face what seemed inevitable.

Because she needed to ask him about her necklace—not because she'd latch onto any excuse to talk to him.

Justin stretched his hamstrings, then straightened, planning to take off down the trail.

Instead, he almost fell over.

"Riley!" he exclaimed when she jogged over to him. She must have parked on the far side of the lot. Then his gaze dropped. "Who do you have here?"

At his question, the living white mop that was wearing pink bows just above its ears barked.

Looking uncomfortable, Riley squatted down to pet the Maltese terrier with its big dark eyes. "Meet the infamous Daisy. She's here to protect me."

Wishing he knew how to make the awkwardness between them go away, he decided to keep it light, so he arched a brow at the dog that couldn't weigh more than six or seven pounds. "What's she going to do? Yap someone into submission?"

Still rubbing the dog's neck, with a slight smile Riley warned him, "Don't underestimate the annoyance factor of a small dog's bark. From experience, I assure you there are times you'll do most anything to quieten it."

"You run with her?"

"She's home alone all day while I'm at work. I'm not leaving her there again while I run."

Justin was impressed by her thoughtfulness. Was even more impressed that she'd come over to him and was carrying on a semi-normal conversation.

He eyed the dog, who had stopped barking and was now sniffing his running shoes. "She runs?"

"Sometimes." Riley laughed. "She's quite the princess, but I adore her."

Her confession eased the tension that he'd been carrying from the moment he'd realized she'd bailed on him and that had multiplied ten-fold after their conversation at the hospital. He still needed to unwind, though. And nothing did that the way running did.

"But no worries," she assured him, her pretty green eyes sparkling. "If we can't keep up with those long legs of yours we'll just lag behind."

She planned to run with him?

Earlier she'd told him not to look a gift horse in the mouth. At that time he hadn't agreed. Currently he was going to take her advice and go with it.

"For that matter," she continued, "Daisy gives me the perfect excuse if I fall behind."

He'd walk if that was what it took to spend time with her. They needed this. At least he did. From the moment he'd awakened to find her gone he'd been trying to figure out where he'd gone wrong.

"How many days a week do you run?" she asked as they fell into step beside each other, Daisy trotting along beside them.

Moving more slowly than he normally would, he shrugged. "Depends on my surgery schedule. Every day, if I can. I enjoy running. It keeps me sane. How about you?"

"I don't run because I *enjoy* it."

He glanced toward her. "Then why?"

"It's part of my weight-loss plan."

Her weight-loss plan? "I've seen you naked. You don't need to lose weight." Realizing what he'd said, worrying she would shut him out, he grimaced. "Sorry."

Jogging, Riley remained silent.

Wanting to move past what he'd said, he asked, "What kind of weight-loss plan are you on, Riley?"

"Low-calorie, low-fat, low-carb, regular exercise, water only—and weekly séances and exorcisms to rid me of the starving little demons inside me who love to eat. You name it, I'm trying it."

Thankful that she'd not clammed up, Justin felt his lips twitch at her reply. "How's that working out?"

"Not as well as I'd like—obviously. And I find no humor in it. Not everyone can look as good as you, Mr. Washboard Abs. Some of us have to torture ourselves just to maintain a semi-healthy weight."

"Thanks." Trying not to puff out his chest at her compliment, he grinned. "For the record, I think you look amazing."

She rolled her eyes. "Flattery will get you nowhere. I have eyes, a mirror, and thighs that are more flab than fab. But I'm working on that." She let out a sigh. "Thus the torture."

He gave her a skeptical look. "What exactly is it you're hoping to accomplish with all this torture?"

"To drop fifteen pounds."

From his vantage point beside her he let his gaze travel down her body, then shook his head. "You don't need to do that. You look great just as you are."

"Yeah, if you like chunky."

Did she really believe that? Despite her light tone, he realized that she did. She was always so confident at the hospital, and had seemed so in charge on Saturday night, that to hear the very real vulnerability shocked him.

"I don't know why you're under the impression

you're chunky. Take it from me—your curves are sexy as hell."

"I...um...thank you."

She didn't say any more, just ran in silence, but he could tell his compliment had both pleased and disconcerted her. Was it her ex who'd put the crazy notion that she was overweight in her head?

Justin wished she could see herself through his eyes—then she'd know how beautiful she was.

"Daisy does like jogging, doesn't she?"

Having teased her about the dog for months, he deemed that the safest topic. Not that he necessarily wanted safe conversation, but he'd tried being direct earlier and that had gotten him nowhere.

"I told you," she reminded him, smiling as her gaze dropped to where the dog was happily keeping up. "She's a good girl—aren't you?" She baby talked to the dog. "Of course she prefers riding to exercising, and I'll be having to carry her before we're done. Takes after her mama, don't you?"

Justin laughed. Riley obviously loved her dog. She talked about her at work often enough. He'd teased her into telling him about Daisy's adventures numerous times since learning of her pet. Seeing her with the dog now, introduced another side of Riley.

"How long have you had Daisy?"

"I adopted her from a local shelter after...last year. I went to the shelter planning to get a guard dog." She gave a self-derisive laugh. "I left with this sweetheart instead."

"So when I tease you and say that you should have gotten a bigger dog I'm not far off the mark?"

"I've no regrets over my choice."

Too bad she couldn't, or wouldn't, say the same about Saturday night.

"What about you?" she asked. "Do you have a dog? Or are you more a cat kind of guy?"

He shook his head. "No pets—which you know. You've been to my place."

There he went, reminding her of Saturday night again. If he really wanted to keep the tension down he was going to have to do better.

"True. I…" She winced. "Sorry. I wasn't thinking."

"No problem. Maybe I should get one, though—so I can train it to wake me up when beautiful women sneak out of my bed."

What was *wrong* with him? He wasn't supposed to be poking the subject with a stick.

"You foresee women sneaking out of your bed as a recurring event?"

"I didn't foresee it being an event *ever*," he admitted, hoping she wouldn't freeze. "I'd like to think any woman I'd invited into my bed wouldn't want to sneak out."

She gave a little shrug. "I woke up and thought leaving was the best thing for both of us."

"You were wrong. At least from my perspective."

She jogged beside him in silence for a few minutes. Then, "What would be different had I stayed there?"

Her question caught him off-guard. More the fact that she'd asked than the fact that he hadn't considered it. He had.

"I'd like to think you'd have given our coworkers a different response to their asking about us today."

She kept her gaze focused on the path ahead of them. "What kind of different response?"

Did she really not know? Or did she just want to hear him say the words out loud?

"I've not kept it a secret that I want to date you, Riley."

She turned toward him, stumbled a bit, causing him to reach out to steady her. She shook his hand away, then resumed her previous slow but steady pace.

"I didn't take you seriously."

"Way to deflate a guy's ego…" he half-teased.

"That's not what I meant. I—I meant the opposite, really. I'm surprised you want to date me."

Once again the vulnerability in her voice surprised him. It was what he'd seen glimmering in the depths of her eyes so brightly at Cheyenne and Paul's party— what had lured him to her despite his determination to stay away since she'd shot down his dinner offers.

"Why would that surprise you? You're smart, funny, beautiful…we enjoy talking with one another." *Enjoy so much more with one another.* "We have great chemistry. Why wouldn't I want to date you?"

She hesitated long enough to reinforce the fact that his response truly had caught her off-guard.

"I'm not like the women you usually date," she said finally.

He didn't see the connection between that and her saying no. That she wasn't like other women he'd dated was a huge plus in his eyes.

"I haven't dated anyone in a couple of months," he pointed out, "and the reason I want to date you is that you're different."

Her intake of breath was her answer. She hadn't considered that her being different was a *good* thing. How could she not see how crazy he was about her?

"You are different, Riley," he assured her. "In a great way. That's why I want to spend time with you."

Giving a warning to Daisy, she came to a halt, put her hands on her hips and regarded him. "Let's be real," she said a bit breathily. "Most women are different from the real-life Barbie dolls you date."

Jogging in place, he looked back at her. "I haven't dated a woman solely based upon her looks since I was a teenager." Had he even then? "Any woman I've dated has had more going for her than just looks."

But even if looks were a qualifier Riley had nothing to worry about. Everything about her appearance appealed to him. Her eyes sparked with a green fire that would dull any gem. A soft sheen of sweat glistened over her skin, giving it a healthy glow. And her body... Well, he knew how her curves fit perfectly against him.

Still, he wanted her to understand about Saturday night—that he hadn't meant things to proceed as fast as they had, that she was more to him than a one-night stand. How did a man go about saying that to a woman who seemed not to want any more than that without coming across all wrong?

"Such as?" she asked, and then, having obviously caught her breath, took off down the trail again, Daisy quickly taking a slight lead.

"The last woman I dated was a veterinarian who volunteers with a local Spay Your Pet program," he pointed out as he fell into step beside her, not wanting her to think he was a total loser.

But he didn't really want to discuss his exes. At some point he'd explain about Ashley, but he got the impression Riley would add his failed relationship with her to what she perceived as his revolving dating door.

"If I'd had a dog," he continued, "she'd have been handy to have around."

"You *don't* have a dog, though, so that couldn't have been your reasoning."

He might almost believe that was jealousy tingeing Riley's reply.

"Stacey was a nice woman," he defended. She had been. She'd also been in love with someone else. "My mother still volunteers at her Spay Your Pet program a couple of times a month."

"Does your family live close, then?"

"My parents live just south of Columbia. The rest of our wild bunch are scattered within a thirty-mile radius. We get together every week or two for dinner."

"You've always lived here, then?"

He nodded. He'd been lucky when he'd been placed with the Brothers family at such a young age and they'd adopted him. So many kids never got any family—much less one like he'd had.

"My family is close." In more ways than one. "I've no desire to move away. What about you?"

She hesitated a few seconds before answering. "I moved to Columbia for university, but I grew up in a small town close to the Florida state line."

"You never thought of going back after graduation?"

She shook her head.

"I'm glad you stayed. Otherwise we wouldn't have met."

She rolled her eyes. "You *sure* you're used to running? You may be suffering from lack of oxygen."

"Because I'm glad we met?"

She stared straight ahead, but rather than answer came to another stop.

"Need a break?"

She shook her head. "Nope. Going to give Daisy a drink. I should have when we stopped a few minutes ago. You go ahead—don't let us hold you up."

"I'm in no rush."

He knew better. If he took off he wouldn't see her again until they were back at their vehicles. If then. He wouldn't put it past her to find a way to leave without his knowing again…

CHAPTER FOUR

DAISY HAD BEEN as good an excuse as any to put a halt to their conversation. Riley recognized her action for what it was.

She couldn't figure Justin out. If she took him at face value he seemed too good to be true. And things that were too good to be true were exactly that. Not true.

Unzipping her pouch, Riley took out a small container of water and let Daisy lap from the lid. When she was done drinking the dog sat down and stared up at Riley with big eyes.

"Had enough, girl? I don't blame you. If I looked as good as you I'd demand to be carried too," she cooed, earning a few hand-licks as she picked her up and cuddled her in her arms.

"All you have to do is say the word?"

Riley blinked at Justin. "Pardon?"

"I'll carry you anywhere you want to go," he offered, his eyes full of challenge.

"You'll *carry* me?"

Grin on his face, he nodded.

"That would be humorous. Not that I'd do it to you," she added quickly, patting her thighs. "Wouldn't want to hurt the hospital's best orthopedic surgeon's back."

His smile fading a little, he met her gaze. "Don't do that."

"What?" she asked, not following what he meant.

"Insult yourself or imply that you aren't perfect."

Heat flooded her face, but she stood her ground as she stroked Daisy's fur. "Stating facts isn't insulting oneself and no one is perfect—least of all me."

"Then you were insulting *me* when you implied I'd hurt my back if I carried you?"

"I— Can we just get back to jogging?"

He studied her a moment, then challenged, "Hop on, Riley."

"What?"

"You heard me. I need to prove that carrying you is no big deal. My man card demands it."

She looked toward the evening sky and shook her head. "You're crazy."

"Think of it as part of my workout," he teased, leaning forward a little and lowering himself for her to hop on.

She rolled her eyes. "I should—just to teach you a lesson."

His eyes sparkled. "I'm always up for learning a new trick."

Something in the way his eyes glittered, as if he didn't think she'd do it, had her contemplating taking his challenge. Made her want to. How rebelliously teenagerish of her.

"Scared I'll drop you?" he pushed.

"No, that didn't cross my mind." It hadn't. "I just don't think Daisy would like me riding on your back."

"Think she'd be jealous? You could hold her."

His grin was full of mischief—as if he could read

her thoughts and knew she was tempted, as if he wanted to tempt her further.

"I'm all sweaty," she warned him, not believing she was even considering taking up his offer.

"It's summertime in South Carolina. Everyone is sweaty. Come on, Riley. Have some fun."

A vision of Johnny telling her to do the same, to "have some fun," echoed through her head. What was it he'd said? That she lacked spontaneity and he was glad he'd realized before it was too late?

She'd been grieving her mother's death. Of *course* she'd been "uptight" and "dull."

That didn't mean she was now.

She narrowed her gaze at this grinning hunk, pushing her outside her comfort zone.

"If you drop me," she warned, "'fun' isn't the word I'm going to use."

His eyes glittered. "If I drop you, you can use any word you like. Ready?"

It was probably because of Johnny's taunts that the silliness of riding piggyback with Justin through the park, even if only for a few yards, tempted her so much. Maybe Johnny had been right. How long had it been since she'd done something carefree and out-of-character?

When had she become boring?

She was content with her life, or maybe she'd just been treading water. But something about Justin made her entertain things she wouldn't otherwise consider.

That's not necessarily a bad thing, that nagging inner voice assured her.

Justin bent lower, so she could grab hold of him around his neck. "Your chariot awaits, ma'am."

She shoved aside the last bit of doubt and instantly felt lighter.

"Hang on," she told him, putting Daisy back on the ground. "I have to make sure we don't tangle up her leash."

"Can't have that."

"Now we're ready." She wrapped her arms around Justin's neck and hopped a little, to make it easier for him to scoop her legs around his waist. Once he had her up Daisy gave a yap, clearly not liking that Riley was on his back.

"Shh, Daisy—stop that."

But Daisy kept barking and Riley kept shushing.

"This may not work," Riley warned Justin when the dog didn't calm. "She's small, but she can make a person wish he was deaf."

"She won't bite?"

"She never has before."

"Then hang on."

With Daisy still yapping at his feet, Justin took off in a playful trot.

They wouldn't win any speed contests, but they weren't trying to go full force—more just having fun. Being with Justin *was* fun. It was also a bit nerve-racking to have her legs wrapped around his waist, her arms wrapped around his neck, for his skin to be against hers, to feel his body heat, his strength against her...

She *so* shouldn't be thinking the things she was thinking.

Daisy gave a few more yaps, but then settled, just looking up at them as she kept pace.

Justin made carrying her seem like nothing. But having her body wrapped around his, even in this innocent way, wasn't nothing—not when he made her feel *everything*. When their skin-to-skin contact, even though innocent, felt nothing of the sort.

Her thighs tightened reflexively.

"Put me down," she ordered after he'd gone a couple dozen yards. How could she be battling the urge to lean in and kiss his neck at the same time as feeling so childlike in their antics? "You've proved your point."

She might have worried that she was too heavy for him to carry, but he wasn't huffing or puffing or straining in the slightest. Which added *dainty* to the list of things he was making her feel. Had she ever felt dainty?

Laughing, Justin kept on jogging, his hands securely holding her legs at his waist. "Hang on and let me make it to the bridge. Man card on the line, remember?"

His man card had never been on the line. She knew exactly how manly he was—was haunted by memories of his manliness. And he sure wasn't laboring to carry her, which was a testament to how in shape he was.

Looking ahead, Riley eyed the bridge. It wasn't that far away, and he was making good headway in its direction.

"Okay. Since Daisy has hushed, and you seem determined to do this, to the bridge it is. Can't have your man card being revoked on my account."

"Phew, thank goodness for that."

"No one would believe this," she mused.

She didn't believe it. Who'd have thought earlier today that she'd be riding on Justin's back?

"Take a picture for proof?" he suggested, giving her leg a squeeze.

"Yeah, right. A picture of this—that's what I want. *Not*."

"*I* want one," he surprised her by saying. "Take one for me. I bet we look cute."

"'Cute' is not the word I'm thinking."

Being careful to hold on with one arm around his

neck, she dug into the pocket at her waist to pull out her phone. She didn't want a photo of them, but… But he said he did, so it would be rude not to take one, right?

He slowed to a stop as she held the phone up high, trying to get them at a decent angle.

"Here, let me."

Riley tightened her legs at his waist as he took her phone, held it farther out in front of them.

"Say cheese."

"Cheese!" she said, keeping her smile in place.

"Hmm, I couldn't get Daisy in," he said, holding the camera up again. "Let me try from a side angle." He snapped a couple more shots, then surprised her further by saying, "Now a silly one."

Even though she knew he couldn't see her face, she arched a brow. "As opposed to our non-silly ones?"

"Humor me?"

"I'm on your back, aren't I?"

He laughed. "That you are. Now, make a funny face."

She let go of his neck, held her arms out wide to her sides, kept her legs tight at his waist, and stuck her tongue out at her phone.

He clicked the screen a few times, then, laughing, pulled the photo up on her phone. "Hey, that's great," he said.

He held it up to where she could see.

"I hope the others are better, because there's nothing 'great' about that one." Although she had to admit seeing Justin's face contorted into his "silly" pose did warm something inside her.

Or maybe that was just the trapped heat accumulating between their sweaty bodies.

He swiped his finger across the phone screen and showed her the next picture.

"This one is good."

He was right. The photo on the screen was perfect. Justin's face was full of good humor as he smiled at the camera, his eyes twinkled, and the sheen of sweat outlined his muscular arms perfectly. Her own smile looked real, relaxed, and her eyes sparkled. Even her skin glowed.

Must be the South Carolina humidity he'd mentioned, she thought. Because if she admitted it was the man she'd have a lot of soul-searching to do.

He handed the phone to her. "You'll have to send me these."

She slid it back into her pocket without taking another look, although she knew she'd painstakingly go through all the photos later. She wouldn't be able to resist. Just as she seemed unable to resist anything Justin dangled her way.

"Just so long as you don't show anyone," she said.

Why she'd added the caveat she wasn't sure. It had just come out. Maybe as a protest against how he pulled her out of her comfort zone. Maybe because her heart was still pounding like crazy at seeing the photos, at how they looked like a "real" couple, at how happy she looked.

In both photos her face glowed with something that had been missing for a long time. Happiness. But her smiles in the pictures shouldn't impress her. They were just reflections of who she was: a woman content with her life—right?

Justin tightened his hold on her legs, then resumed his progress toward the bridge, almost as if he thought she was going to tell him to put her down again. She should. His carrying her was just childishness.

"Why don't you want me to show the pictures to anyone?" he asked. "Are you ashamed for people to know you were with me?"

Her stomach twisted. "It's not that." She scrambled for a reason. "It would just give the wrong impression."

"What wrong impression would that be?"

"That we're involved."

Another hesitation, then, "Aren't we?"

Riley closed her eyes. She was surrounded by Justin. He was filling all her senses. His smell, his strength, the sound of his breathing as he carried her the short distance to the bridge, the feel of his muscles working against her body...

"Life will be simpler if we aren't." The exposed honesty of her admission shocked her.

The fact that he didn't push her to elaborate shocked her even more.

Reaching the bridge, he relaxed his hold on her legs and Riley slid off his back.

When she was on her feet, Justin turned. "Anytime you want to be carried rather than going it alone, just let me know."

Rather than answer him, or any of the questions swirling through her mind, Riley scooped Daisy up into her arms and took off, tossing over her shoulders, "Race you to the end."

Justin was smart enough to know that Riley had hoped he'd take off and leave her when she'd issued her challenge. She'd certainly picked up her pace from their earlier jogging. But he knew she wasn't trying to win a race. She just wanted to make conversation difficult.

He was okay with that. Maybe he even needed a moment to gather his wits after holding her. He wasn't sure he'd ever be able to touch Riley without feeling his blood heat. Holding her, even on their juvenile piggy-back ride, had sent his insides into an adrenaline rush.

Her legs around his waist had given him instant flashbacks of a far more erotic wrapping of those long legs around him. Had sent him into an instant long-ing to take her back to his place and explore those legs at his leisure. To explore all of her. Her body and her mind, too.

He wanted to know what made her tick...what made her who she was. He'd learned a lot today. But he wanted to know more. Lots more. *Everything*, he admitted. He wanted to know everything there was to know about Riley.

And with time, he would.

Because, whether she wanted to or not, Riley liked him. She had admitted she didn't want to, which was maybe progress in getting her past whatever made her think she shouldn't. Surely, with patience, she'd real-ize liking him wasn't a problem? But her thinking she *shouldn't* like him, *shouldn't* want him, was a huge problem...

"By the way," she said now. "You didn't happen to find a gold cross on a chain?"

He glanced toward her. "No. Did you lose one?"

She nodded. "At some point over the past few days. I'd thought it might be in your Jeep or—well, you know..."

"I haven't seen one, but I haven't looked. It has sen-timental value?"

"It was a gift."

"From a man?"

"From my mother," she corrected. "She gave it to me for my graduation. That I've lost it breaks my heart." Her voice broke as she made the admission.

"We'll check the Jeep when we get back to the parking area. Maybe we'll find it."

Please let it be here. Please let it be here.

Riley ran her hands around the edge of the passenger seat, checking beneath it. Nothing.

"It's not here."

"I'm sorry, Riley. I'd hoped it would be so I could play hero and give it back."

"If you found my necklace I'd definitely think you were a hero."

He turned back to the Jeep. "Let's look some more."

She shook her head. "Wishing isn't going to make it suddenly appear."

Still, he checked over everything on the passenger side one more time.

"Thanks for checking, though."

"You're welcome. I'll look when I get home and give you a call if I find it."

"I— Okay, that would be great."

"I'll need your number." He studied her. "Is that okay?"

"I— Sure. I guess so."

"If you hand me your phone, I'll dial mine. That way you can send me those pictures."

"That's fine."

She took her phone from around her waist, but didn't hand it over. Couldn't hand it over.

"Riley…?"

Taking a deep breath, she thrust the phone his way. "Here. Just take it and get it done."

Staring at her a bit oddly, he punched in his number and hit "dial." His phone began ringing. He pressed the stop button, then handed her phone back.

"Now, no excuses. Call me anytime."

Riley slid her phone back into the pouch. She wouldn't be calling Justin. He was much too dangerous to her sanity and well-being for her to have anything more to do with him.

"Come on, Daisy," she said to the dog. "Let's go home."

Justin sought Riley the moment he entered the operating room. Funny how, when everyone was dressed in the same surgical scrubs and protective wear, his gaze still went to her in instant recognition, as if he felt her presence as much as saw it.

The surgical crew today was identical to the previous day's. That didn't always happen, but Justin liked this group. They worked well together.

"Good morning, Dr. Brothers," Sheila greeted him.

"It *is* a good morning," he echoed.

"Somebody is in a lot better mood than he was yesterday," the anesthesiologist teased. "Feeling lucky?"

Justin forced his gaze not to go toward Riley, to see how she'd taken the doctor's comment.

"I'm lucky every day," he countered as he allowed a nurse to assist him in putting on his personal protection equipment.

"Hear, hear!" the anesthesiologist cheered.

"Lucky in cards. Lucky in lottery tickets. Lucky in

races." With the last, Justin gave in and glanced toward Riley to see if his words had got a reaction.

"Remind me to have you to scratch off my next lottery ticket," she piped up, without looking up from the surgical tray she was inventorying.

Relieved that she'd joined in the conversation, he nodded. "Sure thing. I'll even let you borrow my lucky rabbit's foot if you want."

"Ew!" She glanced up, her eyes twinkling. "Please tell me you don't really have a rabbit's foot."

"Yeah, that would be gross, Dr. Brothers," Sheila added.

"Agreed—and I was speaking metaphorically. The only lucky foot I have is attached to the rest of me, and I've got two of them." He winked at Riley. "You're welcome to borrow one or both, though."

"I'm good," she countered. "Thanks, anyway."

"Better luck next time," the anesthesiologist put in.

Justin felt he'd been lucky *this* time. Riley's eyes had been expressive, had connected with his, and some warmth had passed between them. She hadn't completely shut him out after the day before. He'd wondered if she would when her only response after he'd texted her that he hadn't found her necklace had been: Thanks for looking.

Lord, how he wished he'd been able to find it and give it back to her, and erase the sadness he'd seen when she'd told him about losing it.

Surgical cap, lighted visor with face shield, mask, gloves, shoe covers, protective apron over the operating room scrubs he'd donned just prior to coming into the surgical suite—all in place.

Justin stepped over to his anesthetized patient and gave

his complete attention to the sleeping woman. "Cynthia Gibbons, sixty years old, left hip replacement," he began, and each member of the crew kicked into their professional role to make sure every aspect of Mrs. Gibbons's surgery went smoothly.

During the next two hours Justin worked, often chatting with the crew about whatever topic they happened to be on. Riley joined in. It almost felt like old times. Almost, but in some ways better.

Physically, she wound his insides tight…made him want what they'd had the night of Paul and Cheyenne's party. Not just the sex, but the easy flow between them.

Although he wanted the sex, too.

Desperately.

Giving himself a little shake, he pushed Riley from his mind and focused on the joint he was repairing. When he'd finished he straightened, and stretched out his spine and shoulders.

"Great job," he praised his team.

His gaze once again went to Riley and their eyes met. She'd been looking at him.

He was surprised when she didn't immediately look away. Instead her eyes sparkled with tiny green flames that burned holes right through him.

Plus—although it might just be the bright lights shining above the operating table—he'd swear that beneath her scrub mask she was smiling.

At him.

He caught himself whistling twice that afternoon, getting more than a few eyebrow-raises from his co-workers.

But later, when he went back to the recovery area,

planning to find Riley, he was disappointed to find she'd already gone.

So much for his belief that she was coming around to his way of thinking…

Riley didn't see Justin for the next couple of days as he wasn't on the OR schedule but working in clinic.

That didn't keep her from thinking about him. Nor did it keep her from looking at the photos he'd taken of them when she'd been riding piggyback.

Even though he'd asked her to, she'd not sent them to him. Something about sharing the pictures made her feel vulnerable—as if she would be giving him a part of herself, a part she needed to protect.

Stretched out on a hammock beneath two palm trees, she fiddled with her phone, flipping through the shots he'd taken, unable to keep herself from smiling. When she came to the one of their "silly" faces, she even snickered.

"What's so funny?" Cassie asked, plopping down on the hammock next to Riley and almost flipping them out as she sat on the edge, her feet barely touching the ground.

"Nothing." Face heating, Riley clicked her phone off as if she'd been caught looking at something naughty.

"Nothing?" Cassie asked, then shook her head. "You're not fooling me, you know."

Holding her phone close to her chest, Riley asked, "About what?"

Cassie rolled her eyes. "Why don't you just admit that you like him?"

"Who?"

From where she perched on the hammock, Cassie gave her the evil eye.

Riley sighed. "So I like him."

"What are you going to do about it?"

Good question.

"I'm not planning to do anything," she admitted, toying with her phone.

"Well, that's a crying out loud shame—because he likes you, too."

"How do you know?" *Eek.* That had been a lot of interest in her voice. Too much.

"You mean other than I saw how you two were eyeballing each other at Cheyenne and Paul's party?"

Riley sucked in a deep breath. "He's easy to look at. I'm not blind."

"If you don't see how he looks at you then you must be."

"How does he look at me?" She cringed because she'd asked, but she hadn't been able to stop the immediate question. Nor could she stop the way she waited with bated breath for her friend's answer.

"As if he wants to eat you up."

"That was just at Cheyenne and Paul's party…because we'd drunk a little too much."

"It's every time he's in the same room with you. It's been that way from the beginning."

Riley clicked her phone back on, pulled up the photos and handed the phone to Cassie.

Her friend's dark eyes widened. "When were these taken?"

"The other night when I took Daisy for a run. I bumped into him."

Cassie flipped through the photos. "You were having fun?"

Staring at the phone in her friend's hand, Riley shrugged. "I was."

"Justin looks like he was, too."

"He was." And if she hadn't already known, looking at the photos would have assured her that he had been.

"So what does this mean? And don't lie to me the way you keep lying to yourself."

Riley rubbed at her temples, started to say it meant nothing, but wasn't sure that was the truth. She *was* lying to herself, wasn't she?

"I wish I knew."

Cassie's expression softened. "Let me ask a different way. What do you *want* it to mean?"

"Justin says he wants to date me."

Still holding the phone, Cassie gave an excited squeal. "Then date the man! It's not as if he isn't a handsome, successful orthopedic surgeon who's a great guy and just happens to turn you on."

"There is that," Riley agreed, taking her phone back.

After watching her in silence for a few moments, Cassie asked, "Does this have to do with Johnny?"

"Ugh…" Now her temples really hurt. "Do we have to say his name out loud?"

"We don't have to. But since he's what's holding you back, we need to."

"He quit holding me back the moment he didn't show up for our wedding."

"Best thing that man ever did for you."

"True." She shuddered at the thought that had he shown up she would have tied herself to him for life. "I don't want to go through that again."

Cassie reached out and hugged Riley. "Johnny didn't deserve you. He never did. What he did to you on what was supposed to be the happiest day of your life was unforgivable. But it wouldn't happen again."

Trying not to cry, Riley inhaled and then blew out slowly. "You're right—because I won't let it."

She was content with her life, didn't need a man to be happy. But Justin...

Cassie gave her another squeeze. "It's been over a year, Riley."

"Not nearly long enough to forget what happened," she admitted, hugging her friend back, then pulling away.

"Don't forget it, but don't let it dictate your future," Cassie advised. "You deserve to be happy. And Justin makes you happy. If you don't believe me look at those pictures."

Cassie had left with Sam, but Riley stayed outside, lying in the hammock, enjoying the cool breeze. Daisy was curled in her lap and hadn't budged since a few minutes after Cassie had left. For that matter Riley barely had.

Reaching for her necklace to toy with the cross, she recalled too late that it wasn't there. Tears prickled her eyes. How *could* she have lost her necklace? She'd searched everywhere she could think of, had called around, and no one had found it—including Justin.

Justin. He was never far from her mind.

She picked up her phone and yet again looked at the photos that filled her with an equal mixture of confusion and joy. She should send them to him. He'd given her his number and she'd told him she would.

She glanced at the time. She'd been out longer than

she'd thought. He'd been in surgery early that morning. He was probably asleep.

She'd been in surgery just as early and *she* wasn't sleeping, her nagging voice pointed out.

Pulling up his phone number, she attached the pictures and typed a message.

Here these are. Sorry it took me so long.

Before she could change her mind she hit Send, then closed her phone and stared up at the stars dotting the night sky and peeking through the trees.

Almost immediately her phone dinged, indicating a new message.

Thanks.

Her pulse went crazy, obviously thinking it was going for some world record. Hands a little shaky, she typed...

You're welcome.

You in bed?

She should be in bed. *With him*, that nagging voice added. Riley grimaced and answered him.

No. Outside stargazing. You?

Same.

His answer surprised her. She typed again.

What?

I'm on my balcony, looking at the stars and letting go of the day's stress.

Bad day?

Not really. Just missed seeing you.

She closed her eyes. She'd missed seeing him, too.

Part of me wants to say that the day isn't over.

Even as she admitted it she surprised herself—and no doubt him. She was playing with fire and was going to get burned.

He messaged back.

I like that part of you. You should listen to it more often.

Despite her misgivings, Riley smiled.

You think?

I'd be there faster than you'd believe if you invited me.

I want to…but I won't.

I was afraid of that.

Don't be mad.

I'm not. I don't understand your reasons, but I do get that this isn't easy on you.

But it should be, shouldn't it? She bit into her lower lip. Should she try to explain her reasons to Justin? Really, it wasn't any of his business. Despite what had happened, they weren't dating.

He was texting again:

Giving in to one's desires? Easy as pie.

Are we talking dessert or the numerical pie? For the record, I never was good at math, so if you want to impress me, better make it dessert.

Why was she being flippant? Because she didn't want to discuss her reasons for being so afraid to give in to all the things she wanted to do with Justin? Because she was afraid? Or because she'd learned better than to take that risk when Johnny stood her up?

Any flavor you want. Just name it.

Sighing with a mixture of wistfulness and resignation at how Justin tempted her, Riley typed back.

I'll have to think on that one. Night, Justin.

Night, Riley. Text me if you change your mind. We could stargaze together.

Struggling with a mixture of giddy anticipation and leeriness, Riley reread her messages, typed some words…

Bring Key Lime!

Doing so made her smile even when she knew she'd never send them.

That was when it hit her. Prior to last Saturday she'd have thought Justin would have been out on a date. Never would she have assumed he'd be at home stargazing when he was off work the next morning.

She'd seen him with several different women over the months she'd known him. Why was he alone now? Had she misjudged him? Would a player really be alone on a Thursday night? Why was she so glad he was alone?

CHAPTER FIVE

"PLANS TODAY?"

Tell Justin yes, Riley ordered herself, even as she heard herself say rather sleepily into the phone that had just awakened her, "Nothing specific. Why?"

"I'm taking my Wilderness Group out on a kayaking trip in the Congaree National Park. One of the other adults canceled and I need a certain adult-to-child ratio."

Riley yawned and then, making sure not to disturb Daisy, who was curled next to her, rolled over in bed to look at her clock.

"I thought you might want to go," Justin continued.

"On a kayaking trip with your Wilderness Group?" She didn't even know what a Wilderness Group was.

"Nothing like a bunch of seven- and eight-year-olds floating down a river, right?"

"You've lost your mind."

He laughed at her comeback. "That means you want to go with me! I'd hate to disappoint the kids…"

Ugh. Justin was emotionally blackmailing her with the thought of seven- and eight-year-olds.

"How many kids are we talking about?"

"Nine signed up for the trip. I'm hoping they'll all show."

"You're taking *nine* kids out on the river?"

"They're great kids," he assured her. "Plus there'll be another adult there, and a guide."

Still, nine kids on a river… Sounded rather sketchy.

"You're sure it's safe?" Because she wasn't sure. They seemed too young.

"We'll have life jackets on the entire trip," he assured. "Besides, it's a slow float—not a white-water rafting trip. And the water isn't up as we've not had a lot of rain. We just need one more adult. Say you'll go."

"I'd be more a hindrance than help. Your seven- and eight-year-olds probably have more experience on a river than I do," she admitted. "I've never even been in a kayak."

"All the more reason for you to say yes. Experience something new. You'll have fun."

Maybe… Living in Columbia, she couldn't drive around the city without passing over a bridge with a view of people enjoying the waterways in various ways. They always caught her eye with their colorful floats and kayaks.

"You don't even know if I can swim," she pointed out.

Her mother hadn't been able to swim, but Riley had learned during the hours she'd spent playing at the community center, after her mother had dropped her off for the day while she worked.

"Guess if you can't you'd better not fall out of your kayak…"

"Justin!"

He laughed. "I'm teasing. Do you think I'd risk you or my Wilderness Group getting hurt? It's a fun outing—a trip to get the kids outdoors, get some sunshine and see nature—not some kind of survival of the fittest training. I've taken them out before. Several times, actually. They're experienced on the water, they respect it, and like I said they'll be wearing life jackets at all times. I just need another adult present to keep my ratio of adult to kids correct."

She couldn't disappoint nine kids. Plus, being outdoors, getting some sunshine and seeing nature sounded heavenly. Still, she was only a mediocre swimmer, and she really had never been in a kayak or a canoe. She wouldn't be much help, surely?

"You're sure I wouldn't be in the way?"

"If you say no I may have to cancel. You won't be in the way. You'd be doing us a huge favor."

Indecision tugged at her. A day on the river with nine kids. A day on the river with Justin.

"There's no one else you can call?"

"At this last minute? You're my last hope."

Justin's last hope or ruin nine kids' day? When she didn't have anything better planned than catching up on her laundry and doing some yard work.

"Fine," she agreed, feeling a weight lift from her when she did so. Because of the kids. Not because she'd agreed to go out with Justin. At least that's what she assured herself. "I can't have a bunch of kids disappointed because I was too chicken to float down a river."

"That's the spirit," he encouraged, merriment evident in his voice. "And that's the way to keep from disappointing a grown man who wants to float down a river with you today, too."

"You say that *now*..." Climbing out of bed, she looked at the lazily stretching dog. "A couple of quick questions: what do I wear and what do I need to bring with me?"

"Wear clothes you don't mind getting wet. A bathing suit with T-shirt and shorts over it is ideal. Swimmer's shoes. Bring a water bottle. Bring dry clothes to change into afterward. I'll take care of everything else."

"Can I bring Daisy?"

"The boys would like that. Let me see if I can rustle up a life jacket for her."

"Seriously?"

She'd been mostly kidding when she'd asked, so his offer surprised her. Who knew they made life jackets for dogs? Or that Justin would not only humor her but be concerned for Daisy's safety?

"Would it make you happy to bring her?"

Riley glanced down at the dog, looking up at her with her big dark eyes set in her cute, fuzzy white face. "Yes, as long as it's safe for her, it would."

"Then, yes, I'm serious. I want you happy, Riley."

It was a fitting statement for him to make, given her and Cassie's conversation on Thursday. Justin wanted her happy.

And if the smile on her face now was anything to go by, she'd say he'd got his wish. Which seemed to answer a lot of the other questions she'd been struggling with since waking up in his bed. Before that, even.

She'd been stressing over what to do about Justin from the moment her gaze had connected with his and he'd smiled, stealing her breath, making her hormones surge and upsetting the balance of her well-orchestrated life.

* * *

Riley met up with Justin and the others at Three Rivers Park, where a rental company had their kayaks ready and waiting. Justin had his own kayak, with a small cooler strapped to the back and a smaller waterproof supplies box strapped to the front.

Once in the river, the kids began having a blast, pretending they were pirates and that Justin was their Captain.

"Is Daisy okay, Miss Riley?" asked Kyle, the youngest of the boys, from his kayak.

The sandy-haired child had an impish smile and dark brown eyes, and he seemed to have made it his mission to keep a check on Daisy, never rowing too far away from Riley's kayak.

Supposedly she was keeping an eye on Kyle and one other boy, Jevon, who also stayed close to her kayak without her saying a word. Perhaps Justin had asked them to keep tabs on her? She wouldn't put it past him.

She glanced at her dog, wearing the life jacket Justin truly had come up with and looking absolutely adorable. Daisy was perched in the kayak, surveying the water with great interest, but not enough to be tempted to dive in at any point. She seemed content with taking in the scenery. Fortunately Riley had kept her kayak afloat thus far, with no tip-overs, and she and Daisy hadn't taken any spills into the river.

All the same, Justin had hooked her to Riley, so that the dog couldn't get more than a few feet away even if she wanted to. Riley liked it that he'd thought of all these extra touches to keep Daisy safe, and knew he'd done the same, likely much more, for the boys.

"Yeah, I think Daisy is feeling on top of the world," she told Kyle. "This life being captured by pirates doesn't seem to bother her."

Daisy was probably getting a big head with all the attention she was receiving from the kids—Kyle especially. The boys had been so excited to meet her, even if Daisy only looked at them as if they were crazy when they tried to get her to do tricks. Daisy's one and only trick was to sit, and she only did that when she wanted—which wasn't often.

The boy paddled his kayak closer and held on to the side of Riley's, keeping their crafts side-by-side as they floated along the gently moving river. Although there had been a few sections of water that her required paddling, they could have floated most of the trip like this, without any work other than making sure they didn't run ashore or run into the rare downed tree.

"Could have" being the key phrase. Because the boys weren't content with a leisurely float and were only happy if they were paddling. If not for the guide slowing them down to point out various turtles, birds, and other wildlife, they'd probably have already finished their trek.

"Captain Brothers didn't really kidnap you, did he?" Kyle asked, his expression telling her that he hero-worshipped Justin more than a little and wouldn't believe anything negative she said.

Smiling, Riley shook her head. "Shh, don't let the others know, but Daisy is the only real princess you guys are holding captive."

Kyle grinned. "I didn't think so. Captain Brothers is too nice."

"Pirate captains aren't usually nice, are they?" Riley couldn't resist teasing the boy.

"Captain Brothers is," Kyle assured her. "He's a *nice* pirate."

"That he is," Riley agreed—although she wasn't too sure about the pirate part. The more she learned about Justin, the more she admired him, and questioned her initial impression of him as a playboy.

Which didn't mean anything except that he was a good guy. Good guys existed. Who knew?

"Are you Captain Brothers's girlfriend?"

At Kyle's question Riley's face heated—and not because of the hot South Carolina sunshine. "No." *Not even close.* "We work together at the hospital."

In the way that impish little boys did, Kyle grinned. "Maybe you can be *my* girlfriend."

Not sure what to say, and certainly not wanting to encourage him, but knowing he'd meant the comment as a compliment, Riley smiled, part of her flattered that he'd do so. "Maybe… But I'm betting that when you grow up you'll have lots of much younger girlfriends."

With a cheeky grin, Kyle waggled his brows. "I have lots of girlfriends now."

"You rascal," she teased, wondering at what age boys even started having girlfriends, much less lots of them. Seven seemed young. Still, what did she know about kids? And Kyle was adorable and seemed so proud of his claim. "A girlfriend in each port, eh? You really are a pirate."

He beamed. "Captain Brothers says I'm his first mate."

There went another big dose of that hero-worship.

"That must mean you're special. Daisy sure thinks so."

The boy's grin widened.

"Kyle? Are you making sure Miss Riley isn't planning an escape?" Justin called from where he floated behind the group.

Both Riley and Kyle twisted to look behind them at the man they'd been discussing. Riley couldn't see Justin's eyes behind his dark sunglasses, but his smile was wide. She imagined his eyes were twinkling with mirth.

He'd stayed at the back the entire trip so far, saying he preferred to be where he could see all the kids and make sure no one got left behind or had any issues. The guide stayed in the front, leading their way down this somewhat shallow section of the Congaree River. Riley stayed near the back too, and Stan, the dad of a boy named Stephen, paddled in the middle of their small group.

Although Justin had said he needed her there, Riley wasn't so sure. One adult per three kids seemed a good enough ratio, although admittedly one adult to just over two kids was better. Not that she'd done anything other than help apply sunscreen to little faces and ears, and supervised as they'd applied it to other exposed body parts.

Honestly, after the length of time Justin had had to spend getting her and Daisy settled securely into their kayak, she was probably more of a hindrance than a help.

"Aye-aye, Captain!" Kyle called. "I'm questioning her."

"That he is!" Riley tried to hold in her laughter at Kyle's salute to Justin.

Kyle let go of her kayak and their boats separated.

She expected him to row ahead. Instead he stuck close, pointing out a turtle sunning itself on the bank and talking to her about everything from baseball to his favorite video game.

When they reached the place where the guide had stopped, ready for their lunch break, Riley stayed back until Justin had gotten out of his kayak, then watched him help a few of the boys pull their kayaks up on the bank so they wouldn't go floating away. She wasn't exactly sure how to get out of hers without tipping the kayak over—which she'd rather not do.

"I'll take Daisy," Kyle offered, wading out in the water to where Riley was trying to watch how the others were getting out of their kayaks. "That way she won't be scared of falling in when you get out."

"Good idea," Riley agreed, and unhooked Daisy's lifejacket from hers, and handed the dog to Kyle. At least if she tipped the kayak Daisy wouldn't get dumped into the water.

Once Kyle had Daisy, Riley contemplated again how to get out of the kayak. The kids had made it look easy enough, but every time she shifted her weight the boat tilted.

"Need a hand?" Justin offered, smiling down at her.

"Or two or three hands," she admitted, taking his outstretched one to balance herself as she attempted to get out of the kayak.

With him steadying her, she managed to land with her feet in the water rather than her rear-end.

"Oh, that's cold!" she exclaimed as the calf-deep water soaked her tennis shoes. Justin had told her to wear swimming shoes, but she didn't own a pair. These old tennis shoes had had to suffice.

"Feels good," Justin claimed, holding her hand and keeping the other on the rope attached to her kayak to keep it from floating away.

The sun was shining down hot on them, but goose-bumps prickled Riley's skin as she climbed ashore to join the others. From the cold water or from where Justin held her hand?

"Feels good if you're a polar bear," she mumbled as she carefully made her way through the river to the bank. "Thank you," she added, once they were on dry land.

Letting go of her hand to pull her kayak up on the shoreline, next to the others, he grinned. "You're welcome. Can't have my favorite girl taking a swim before the designated time. I'd have a revolt, with lots of boys diving in under the pretext of rescuing you."

Rather than answer she just smiled, and made her way over to where Kyle was cuddling Daisy. Once there, she glanced back toward where Stan and the guide had begun unloading the things bungee-strapped to their kayaks.

Justin's arms and face glistened in the sunlight with a deepening tan, and memories of his bare chest flashed through her mind. She didn't recall any tan lines on his arms, but there must have been. Next time she'd look closer…

Next time?

There would be no next time.

Justin laughed at something the guide had said and Riley's heart missed a beat. Face on fire, she dragged her gaze away from Justin's muscular arms and ordered her brain to never, *ever* go again where it had just been.

Fortunately Kyle, still holding a wiggling Daisy, wanted her attention.

"She wants to get down, Miss Riley, but I wasn't sure if I should let her," he told her, keeping a tight grip on the dog, who was doing her best to wrangle her way free.

Poor Kyle. Riley was impressed that he continued to hold on to Daisy, despite her escape attempts. Although only six pounds, Daisy could be a handful.

"It's probably best if we put on her leash since we're in a place that's strange for her," Riley told him.

She'd left the short cord that had attached their life-jackets to each other back in the kayak, but she had brought Daisy's leash with her in the fanny pack she'd filled with treats, her phone inside a sealed plastic bag, a small bottle of sunscreen, and a protective lip balm. Being careful not to dislodge any of the other items, she pulled out Daisy's leash.

"Does she need to leave her lifejacket on?" asked Kyle.

Riley nodded. "I don't think she'll go in the water, but let's leave it on just in case. I'll hook this to her collar and then you can let her down."

She attached the leash and Kyle set Daisy down— although it was more a case of Daisy leaping from his arms the moment he relaxed his hold.

Daisy sniffed the ground for a few seconds, but then, rather than run off, she got on her hind legs and danced around at Kyle's feet, making him laugh.

"She likes me," he said, bending to pet her and baby-talk to her before taking off toward the other boys when Justin called him.

"That she does," Riley agreed, walking behind Daisy

as she sniffed rocks, grass, a few stray bushes, then pulled against her leash with a backward glance that said *Come on*. Riley let the leash out, and wasn't surprised when Daisy went to the outskirts of the group where they were resting."Funny girl," Riley teased the dog.

When Daisy had finished her business she went back to the group and once again wanted to be the center of the boys' attention—which they eagerly supplied even though they were supposed to be listening to the guide talking about the Congaree National Park.

Not wanting to get the boys in trouble, Riley scooped up Daisy and stood beside Justin, listening to the brief talk about how the forest around them boasted the tallest specimens in the United States of at least fifteen different varieties of tree.

"Anything I can do to help?" she whispered to Justin when he moved away to start unpacking a cooler.

She wanted to be useful. Or maybe she just wanted an excuse to be near him, to watch him with the boys and marvel at this unexpected side to him.

Someday Justin was going to be a great dad.

The thought was like a punch to the uterus. Justin would be a great dad, but that was nothing to do with her. She didn't want it to be anything to do with her. She'd never be a mom—wouldn't risk failing a child the way her father had failed her. And after Johnny's betrayal she'd given up all thoughts of being a mother.

But she couldn't quite shake the image of a little boy with sparkly blue eyes, a quick grin, and his dad's dark sun-streaked hair...

"You being here is enough."

Justin was answering her question, unaware that her mind was casting him in a paternal role. Thank goodness!

"Just relax and enjoy the scenery," he said.

Not wanting to be in the way, and needing a moment to shake the image, Riley led Daisy to the water's edge to let her get a drink, then followed her as she explored their immediate vicinity.

Keeping a hold on Daisy's leash as the dog sniffed the ground near a wild rhododendron, Riley let her gaze go again to Justin. He was busy with the kids, leaving her free to watch from behind her sunglasses without worrying that he'd catch her.

The kids adored him. That much was easy to see. And no wonder. He knew each kid well, called them by their names, and obviously spent time with them on a regular basis.

Seeing him with them had brought to light the fact that there were a lot of things she didn't know about Justin. Other than that he was a great coworker, a fantastic orthopedic surgeon, a phenomenal lover, and that she enjoyed being around him.

Justin had motioned to the guide that he was ready, and the young man lined up the boys. Justin squirted sanitizer into their hands, then inspected them prior to letting the boys move along in their makeshift lunch line. Stan handed each kid a bagged-up sandwich, while the guide joined them and let each one pick a piece of fruit and a bag of chips. Each boy had their own water bottle with their name printed on it, which they'd had tied to their kayaks during their float and had removed at some point.

"All right, mateys—what do we do with our trash?" Justin gave the kids an expectant look that said they'd reviewed this often in the past.

"Bring it all with us," one said.

"Not leave any trace of it," another said.

"Eat it!" Stephen said, giggling, causing all the boys to burst into laughter and his dad to frown at him.

"Good answers," Justin praised, then eyed the giggling boy. "Except Stephen, who has to eat his trash or walk the plank." He winked at the kids. "The rest of you bag it up for us to take back with us."

"Yes, Captain Brothers!" they said in almost perfect unison, giggling as they said it.

Kyle tugged on Justin's sleeveless shirt, where it was poking out from beneath his lifejacket. "Stephen doesn't have to really eat his trash or walk the plank, does he?"

Justin laughed and rubbed the boy's head. "You think I should let him off the hook?"

Kyle nodded. "This one time, Captain."

Justin winked at the boy. "Guess we'll let him bag up his trash, too, then."

Kyle grinned. "Thanks, Captain."

"You're welcome." Justin returned his attention to the rest of the crew. "Now, you pirates—eat, cleanup after yourselves, stay where I can see you, and we'll be back on the river in thirty minutes, to plunder the rest of these waters for treasure."

When Daisy had thoroughly checked out her immediate surroundings, she eyed the boys who were gathering their food with longing, like the little scavenger she was.

"You can't have the boys' lunch," she warned the dog, but Daisy's expression said, *Yeah, right*.

Riley spotted an old log about twenty meters back from where the group was gathering for their lunch. Leading Daisy, she walked over to it, sat down on the log, and watched as Justin and the other two adults got the boys settled.

Even in this environment, where Justin was doing anything but trying to look sexy, Riley found him so. How could she not with the sunlight glinting off his hair, highlighting every natural hue? With his arm muscles perfectly displayed in his sleeveless T-shirt and life-jacket? With his easygoing rapport with the boys and how their eyes filled with adoration when they looked at him?

Ugh. She should not be finding his parenting skills sexy. His parenting skills were none of her business.

As if he sensed her thoughts were on him, he looked her way, grinned, then came over to her, held out the hand disinfectant.

"Can't have you picking up any germs on our trip," he teased, squirting a generous dollop into her palm. "I'd miss you if you had to call out of work."

She rubbed her hands together and held them out for his inspection, as the boys had.

He made a show of checking them. "Guess that'll do."

"Thanks, Captain," she replied, unable to resist the tease. "Good to know I pass muster."

His gaze met hers from behind his mirrored sunglasses and heat filled her at what shone in his face.

Lust and so much more.

Her insides trembled with the recall of what it had felt like to be the sole recipient of his attention.

She didn't need to hear his, "Oh, you pass muster, all right…" to know she wasn't the only one battling physical attraction.

CHAPTER SIX

RILEY DRAGGED HER gaze from Justin's face to what he held.

"Sandwiches are all the same, so I hope you like peanut butter and jelly."

"No problem. I know we captives can't be choosy. But are you sure you have enough for me to have one? I don't want to take anything away from the kids."

"I brought plenty for the kids—besides, even pirates' captives have to keep up their strength when they're expected to man their own ship."

"There is that." Her gaze dropped to the sandwich and her stomach growled. "I *am* hungry."

"Floating down the river works up an appetite."

Were they talking food or a different type of appetite? If so, the river had nothing to do with how starved she felt. Justin alone was responsible for the cravings rocking her.

Taking the sandwich and removing it from the bag, she eyed him before taking a bite. "You know, when you said 'floating,' I pictured a relaxing trip, enjoying the scenery—not all this paddling to keep pace with the kids. They seem to think we're in a race to get to the end."

"They always do." He walked over to the makeshift

lunch line and grabbed a sandwich of his own, some fruit, and a couple of individual-sized bags of chips.

Once back to where she sat, he joined her on the log. "Banana or apple?"

She took the apple and the bag of chips he held out. "Best sandwich ever. Thank you."

"Admit it," he said.

Taking another bite of her sandwich, she glanced toward him in question and purposely avoided looking at Daisy, who was expectantly waiting for a bite.

"You're glad you came," he clarified.

Chewing the bite she'd taken, she nodded. "Beats working in my yard any day of the week."

Even if her yard work wouldn't have left her wanting to wrap her arms around Justin's neck, to run her fingers through the damp hair at his nape and feel his lips against hers.

"What kind of yard work? I could help you," he offered.

Face warm, Riley avoided looking toward him. "Just cleaning up my landscaping, putting down some fresh mulch…that kind of thing. Why would you want to help with that?"

"You've helped me today," he reminded.

"This…" she waved her hand toward where the kids were sitting near the river, eating their lunches, with the two other adults sitting close, chatting about how great the weather was "…doesn't fall into the same category as yard work."

"Agreed, this is awesome, but I'd be glad to help you—especially since I've kept you from getting it done today."

She shook her head. "There's no rush. I'm just sprucing things up and doing some weeding and trimming."

"I could come later—or even tomorrow. With both of us working you'd get finished a lot quicker."

She eyed him from behind her sunglasses. "Did you just invite yourself to my house?"

He grinned a bit sheepishly. "Consider it more an offer of free labor."

Justin at her house. Doing her yard work. How could she explain that she didn't want him there for fear that she'd invite him inside?

"I wouldn't feel right, having you over to work."

"What are friends for?"

What, indeed? And was that what they were? Friends? Riley didn't recall ever having any close male friends. Not even Johnny. She'd planned to marry him, so he should have been her friend, right? But she didn't recall ever thinking he was her friend.

Which probably should have clued her in that she shouldn't marry him.

Still, he'd been hardworking—or so she'd thought—handsome, and he had claimed to love her. She'd been reeling from her mother's death and had been easy pickings for the suave salesman.

What was her excuse with Justin?

Johnny wasn't fit to tie Justin's shoes.

"Riley?"

She blinked at Justin, knowing her last thought was true. "Hmm?"

"Just making sure you're okay. You got quiet."

"Enjoying my lunch."

Seeming to take her answer at face value, Justin

stretched his legs out in front of the log. "It is nice, isn't it?"

She nodded, took another bite, and refused to think of what the conclusions she was drawing about the man next to her meant.

Besides, lunch *was* nice—as were their beautiful surroundings. Off in the distance she could see Columbia's skyline, and in the other direction lay the Congaree National Park. Gorgeous trees lined the river banks. The sky was a beautiful blue with the occasional dotting of a white puffy cloud. The sun was hot, but there was just enough of a breeze to make the day feel perfect.

The day *was* perfect.

"Beautiful," she said, and meant it.

They finished eating. Stephen's dad and five of the boys had waded into the water and were attempting to catch minnows. The guide had gone beyond the kayaks and was animatedly talking to someone on his cellphone. The other four boys were digging through rocks, looking for the fossils that they deemed highly valuable.

Spotting Daisy, Kyle came running over. "Can Daisy help us look for treasure?"

"Sure." Riley handed the leash over and watched him run off toward the other boys, Daisy in tow. "He is a cute kid."

"He is—although a bit of a Casanova, it seems."

Riley glanced toward a grinning Justin.

"I heard him ask you to be his girlfriend."

Riley waved off his teasing. "Sounds like Kyle has more than enough girls keeping him occupied currently."

"I hope so."

Wrinkling her brows at how serious his voice had grown, Riley glanced at Justin.

"Sorry. It's just that I doubt he has much of a chance to keep any girlfriend for long."

Wondering what he meant, Riley waited for him to continue. When he didn't, she asked.

"Kyle lives in foster care—has done on and off since he was two."

Riley's heart squeezed.

"All these boys do except Stephen," Justin continued.

"I didn't realize…"

She glanced out at the kids, watching them laugh and play. They looked so happy and carefree.

With further respect for the man next to her, she asked, "How did you get involved in their lives?"

"Long story short, Stephen is a bit accident-prone. Over the years I've reset a few broken bones. His dad and I hit it off. Three years ago he told me about how he wanted to do more, to provide good role models for foster kids. Knowing I wouldn't say no, he asked if I'd help start this group."

"Wow," she said, truly impressed.

Justin would have still been in residency back then. For him to have volunteered with any group during that busy time spoke volumes about the man and what he'd done with what little spare time he would have had.

How had she ever labeled him as a player?

Okay, so he had gone out with several women since she'd met him, but maybe he just hadn't found someone he wanted a long-term relationship with, and that was why it seemed he was always with a different woman at the social events they both attended.

"At least twice a month we take the boys out on an

excursion of some kind," he continued. "We try to do outdoors adventures, as most won't have that opportunity otherwise. But sometimes we just go for pizza and to the movies or the arcade."

"How many kids are there in your group?"

"We have ten, but it's rare all ten make it to an outing. That we have nine today is good."

Guilt hit her that she didn't make better use with her time outside of work. "Is it still the same ten boys as in the beginning?"

He nodded. "Our goal is to try to make a difference in these boys' lives—to give them positive role models and to follow them through until they're adults."

"Great goals—and how lucky they are to have you in their lives."

Justin shrugged. "It's the other way around. I'm lucky to have *them* in my life."

He certainly seemed to enjoy being with the kids. Still, Riley knew it wasn't all fun and games to organize trips for ten kids. At least, she didn't imagine it was. Reality was she'd never organized a trip for *one* kid, much less ten.

"Why did you call it Wilderness Group?"

One side of Justin's mouth hiked up. "Would you believe it's because they're wild?"

She glanced at the playing boys, then gave Justin a skeptical look.

He laughed. "Stan came up with the name before we even officially formed the group. We needed to call it something, but we wanted a name the boys would like being a part of—something that was for them. Wilderness Group sounds good to ten boys who are in and out of foster homes because they have parents who can't or won't take care of them."

Realizing what poor home lives they had, Riley stared out at the kids as they balanced on an old log, walking from one end to the other with their arms held out to their sides.

"That breaks my heart for them."

Justin nodded. "Mine, too—which is another reason I love doing this. For at least a couple times a month they get to do fun, normal kid things. Don't get me wrong—some of these boys are in great foster homes—but they've all known heartache none of them should have experienced."

Riley stared at him, amazed by the empathy in his voice, the affection she could hear for the boys. He truly cared about them and he was willing to do something to make their lives better. She didn't know anything about Stan's finances, but she'd bet Justin funded the group's activities without even thinking twice.

Because he was a giver rather than a taker.

Because he was so much better a man than her own father had been.

Her father hadn't thought twice about abandoning Riley and her mother, much less tried to do anything to lessen their financial burden. Thank goodness Riley's mother had loved her so much and had been able to take on extra work to provide for them.

Reaching up to tug on her necklace, Riley let her hand fall away in disappointment as she recalled her missing necklace.

What would her mother think of Justin?

Now, where had *that* thought come from? What her mother would have thought of Justin didn't matter any more than it mattered that Riley's father had skipped out. He'd just been preparing her for life—for men like Johnny who'd come along and then leave her, too.

Was Justin even for real? And, if so, how was it that he wanted to date a slightly plump, jaded about love, nurse like her?

"Captain Brothers!" Kyle shrieked, just as a loud cry of pain filled the air.

Riley's throat tightened as she glanced toward the boys.

"Man down! Man down!" Kyle motioned for them to hurry.

Justin leapt from the log and took off toward where the boys were now huddled around Stephen, who was lying on the ground and holding his bent leg against his belly. Blood covered his hands.

Heart racing, Riley ran to where Stephen lay. Blood gushed down his leg from a jagged gash on his knee.

"Get the first aid kit out of my kayak," said Justin.

Riley rushed to the kayak and grabbed the first aid kit from inside the supplies box. When she got back to the boys, Justin had taken off his lifejacket and his shirt. He'd torn a strip from the bottom of his T-shirt, exposing a sliver of tanned belly, then made a makeshift tourniquet and was now tying it to Stephen's leg to slow the bleeding.

Riley opened the kit, grabbed some gloves for Justin, handed them to him.

Hoping to help, Riley gloved up, too, and opened a packet of gauze and disinfectant.

"Thanks," Justin told her as she bent down beside him and began applying pressure to the wound with the gauze.

"Stan, will you get the boys to pack everything back into the kayaks?"

With one last glance at his son, Stan nodded, knowing Justin was trying to occupy the other kids rather than have them surrounding Stephen. "Come on, guys, let's give the doc some room while we make sure we leave this place the way we found it."

The guide, realizing something had happened, had ended his phone call and come over to check on them. His face paled at the sight of the blood oozing down Stephen's leg. It had slowed significantly with the makeshift tourniquet but hadn't completely stopped.

Wondering if the guide was going to pass out, Riley looked at him and gestured to the boys. "Maybe you could help the others?"

With one last look at the bleeding leg, the young guide nodded, then went over to where Stan had the boys searching for stray bits of trash in a game of seeing who could find the most.

Justin and Riley worked to clean Stephen's gaping cut, rinsing it with saline to make sure there was no stray debris or germs.

"Needs sutures," Riley observed, hating the pain that showed on Stephen's contorted face. Still, the boy was being a trouper.

Justin nodded, called Stan over. "Looks like we're going to be upping the scar count."

"Does that mean you're sewing me?" Stephen asked, tears streaking his face.

Giving the boy an empathetic look, Justin nodded. "I think so, buddy."

"I figured you'd need to when I saw how much he was bleeding." Stan sighed, then bent next to his son to kiss the top of his head. "It'll be all right. The doc is going to take care of you."

Not looking thrilled at the prospect, Stephen nodded nonetheless, as if he had already had this done repeatedly and knew the drill.

"I appreciate it," Stan told Justin, shaking his head. "Saves us from another run to the emergency room." Turning to Riley, he added, "Dr. Brothers has sutured this kid on three different occasions. He thought I'd asked him to help with the group because I needed another adult, but really it was just to have an on-site physician for my kid."

Stan patted his son's shoulder. Stephen had stopped crying, but his poor face was tear-stained and dirt-streaked.

His eyes were puffy and red as he told Riley, "I'm accident-prone."

"Just a little," Justin teased. "You ready for this, big guy?"

Wincing, and appearing to brace himself for what was to come, Stephen took his dad's hand and then nodded.

Doing one last thorough wash and inspection of the gash, Justin turned to Riley. "There's a vial of anesthetic and a syringe in there. Will you draw me up three milliliters?"

Riley did so, then changed the needle over to a small gauge and handed it to Justin.

He squirted some of the numbing liquid into the open wound, waited a few seconds and then, moving through the wound, began anesthetizing the area.

Dabbing the gash every so often, Riley kept the blood from obscuring the wound so that Justin could see it.

"Grab that suture kit and open it for me, please."

Riley got the kit, opened it, and held out the small packet while trying to maintain a sterile field the best she could on a riverbank, while also dabbing the wound to clear away the blood.

When Justin had the needle held in the needle holder Riley patted the area. Then, balancing the kit on her thigh, she pushed the edges of the cut together as best as she possibly could to make Justin's work easier.

"Thanks," he said as he pushed the needle through one side of the cut and then curved it around to come out on the other. He pulled it through, then began tying knots, wrapping the Ethilon in opposite directions with each loop. When he'd made several ties, he snipped the thread, then put in the next suture.

The cut was jagged and ended up requiring seven sutures to close it. When he'd finished the last one, Riley wet a piece of clean gauze and began cleaning dried blood from around the laceration.

"Nice work, Dr. Brothers." Despite his crude work area the sutures were perfectly placed, and the wound should heal nicely.

"Thanks. Stephen keeps me in practice—don't you, bud?"

Not that he didn't get plenty of practice in surgery, Riley thought, but kept her mouth closed.

"He's a trouper, for sure," the boy's father praised.

"'Cause I know the drill," Stephen informed them, looking up at them. "Do pirates have lots of scars, Captain Brothers?"

"Usually three or four, so you're good," Justin assured him as he removed the T-shirt strip from the boy's leg, watching the closed wound to make sure the bleeding didn't restart.

When it didn't, he turned to Riley. "Thanks for the assistance, Nurse Riley. We're going to have to either set you free or officially have you join the crew as an honorary medic. Which is it going to be?"

"Hmm…" She pretended to be considering his offer. "I may have to think on this one. Captive or honorary medic… Decisions, decisions…"

Having finished gathering the trash and stored all their belongings properly in their kayaks, the boys had come over to make sure Stephen was okay.

Kyle patted Riley's leg. "Being a pirate is a lot of fun."

"Says the kid with no ulterior motive!" Justin teased.

"Kyle just likes Daisy, right?" She smiled at the boy as she picked up all the pieces of dirty gauze, then turned her gloves inside out as she took them off, capturing the gauze inside.

"Daisy is pretty cool. When I grow up I'm going to have a dog, too."

Not as a child, though—unless one of his foster families happened to have one, and then he'd have to say goodbye to it whenever his time was up with that particular family.

Riley's heart squeezed at that reality. How many homes had Kyle been in over the years?

She fought the desire to hug the boy to her. Although he seemed a bit smitten with her, she didn't think he'd appreciate any show of affection in front of his friends.

That she even wanted to hug him surprised her. She'd never been around kids much—mostly felt uncomfortable when she was. The fact that she'd come today, was enjoying being with the boys and felt a connection to them was shocking.

Perhaps it was because she felt a kind of affinity with them? Because she understood what it felt like to have a parent abandon you.

"Is Stephen going to be okay?" the guide asked.

"He'll be fine. He has a lot of accidents and Captain Brothers always fixes him," Kyle piped up, before any of the adults could answer. "When I grow up I'm going to be a pirate captain doctor who has a dog!" the boy announced, and then, carefully holding on to the dog's leash, told Daisy to come on.

Riley watched him skip off, happy as could be and unfazed by what had happened to Stephen. Unfazed by *anything* that had happened to him up to that point in his life, or giving a good impression of it.

In the meantime Stan had helped his son up off the ground and was holding his hand as Stephen tried walking. The boy limped a bit, with a few grimaces, but had no real difficulties. Father and son went off to get ice from the cooler to put on the area.

"What's his story?" Riley asked as they walked away.

"Kyle's or Stephen's?"

She'd meant Kyle, but realizing Stephen must have a story, too, she felt her heart quicken. "Both."

"Stan and his wife adopted Stephen when he was four. He'd been in a dozen or so foster homes, but no one wanted to keep him because of all his accidents."

"That sounds ominous. Just how many accidents has he had?"

"During his lifetime?" Justin shrugged. "Hundreds, I imagine, based on what I know from the past few years."

"Why?"

"He has poor balance and he trips easily. His pediatrician isn't sure if it's from the drugs his mother stayed on while she was pregnant with him or if he suffered shaken baby syndrome or some other ailment. They haven't been able to pinpoint any specific abnormality that's causing the issue—they just know that he has balance and coordination issues, which leads to a lot of accidents for an active kid."

Watching Stan check on Stephen's gashed knee, his eyes full of love and concern for the boy, Riley mused, "I didn't realize Stephen was adopted."

"Stan and his wife fell in love with him during his stay with them as a foster kid. Fortunately they have great medical insurance, and the courts agreed Stephen was better off with them than in state custody."

"Thank goodness."

Justin nodded. "Stephen got lucky. Most of these kids aren't ever released from their birth parents long enough to be available for adoption. The ones who *are* released are often too old to be wanted by the time their birth parents sign over their rights. Most end up going from one foster family to another, with occasional time spent with their birth mother or father in between until they lose custody again."

Riley grimaced. "That's terrible."

Justin nodded.

"I wish I could bring them all home with me," Riley mused, not sure what she'd do with a bunch of boys, but knowing she'd smother them with love.

The knowledge stunned her. Johnny hadn't wanted kids and she'd agreed. Having been a child put through the agony of losing a parent had left her thinking she'd rather not, so going along with him had been easy.

Maybe because she'd never trusted that Johnny wouldn't leave.

Justin's gaze cut to her and he grinned at what she'd said. "Better not let Kyle hear you say that. He might offer to grant your wish. Rumor has it that his birth mother plans to sign away her rights and he'll be available for adoption."

How could someone not want a kid as precious as Kyle? "She's giving him away?"

"Honestly, since she's unable to take care of him, it's the best thing she could do for him. I can't imagine it's an easy decision for her or any parent, though." Justin's face tightened a little. "Kyle's not been back with her for over a year and has only seen her once during that time."

Riley couldn't imagine that giving up parental rights would be an easy decision. Nor could she imagine not seeing her own child more than once during a year's time. But maybe it wasn't nearly as difficult as she thought, since her own father had had no issue with walking away andnever looking back.

Kyle had no stability and apparently he never had. And he had a mother who didn't want him or wanted him but couldn't provide care for him.

Riley preferred to think it was the latter. Maybe because it was what she'd always wanted to believe of her father. That he hadn't left because he hadn't wanted her, but that he hadn't been able to take care of her and her mother.

She'd never believed it. Maybe in Kyle's case it was true, though…

"Is his foster family planning to adopt him?" She

hoped that, like Stephen, Kyle would find a family to love him.

Justin's eyes darkened a little and he started to say something, then changed his mind. "Not that I'm aware of. They're nice people, with two grown kids of their own, and have been taking in foster children for about ten years now."

Riley had grown up without her father, but her mother had always been there, had always wanted and loved her. Not once had she ever felt alone or unloved as a child.

Just as an adult.

Now, where had *that* come from? She was not unloved as an adult. But the truth was since her mother's death she hadn't felt connected to any other person than her friend Cassie.

She'd wanted to be—acknowledged that her engagement to Johnny, and her unwillingness to see what had been so obvious, had mostly been about that desire to love and be loved. But she'd looked in all the wrong places.

Maybe, despite knowing how much her mother had loved her, the fact that her father hadn't stung more than she'd ever admitted.

Maybe she had more in common with the boys than she'd thought.

"I want to be a pirate."

At her blurted comment, Justin raised his brows. "Really?"

"Can I join your club?"

Because the more she thought about it, the more she knew she needed to be a part of these kids' lives. On the surface, it was for them, but the reality was she needed to be involved for *her*—to make a difference in their lives the way her mother had in hers.

"Are women allowed?"

"Allowed and welcomed," he assured her, looking pleased. "The more the merrier. And you wouldn't be the sole female. Stan's wife would have been here today except something came up last-minute with one of their other foster children. You took her place."

"They still foster children even after adopting Stephen?" She wasn't sure why that surprised her—maybe because of all his accidents—but the fact that they did made her happy. "How many do they have?"

"Currently they have one birth child and two foster children in addition to Stephen."

Looking around at the group, already seemingly completely recovered after Stephen's accident, probably because it was par for the course, Riley felt warmth fill her.

"Thank you for inviting me. Today has been a very good day."

"It has, hasn't it?" Justin grinned as he reached out and gave her hand a gentle squeeze. "And the best part is that it's not over."

CHAPTER SEVEN

JUSTIN WISHED RILEY had let him pick her up from her place that morning. That way he'd have had an excuse to spend more time with her. As it was, she'd driven herself, and he needed to wait at Three Rivers Park, where they'd turned in their kayaks, until all the boys had been picked up by their foster parents or birth parents, whatever the case might currently be.

Knowing he'd be there a while, he'd expected Riley to leave soon after they'd unloaded from the old bus that had driven them back to their drop-off spot. But rather than rush off, she'd stuck around, talking to the boys and their parents as Justin and the guide unloaded the bus.

Kyle still stuck close to her and Daisy, showing the dog to his foster family and telling them about how Daisy had loved sitting on the bow of the kayak and how she liked him so much.

Justin wasn't surprised when the boy threw his arms around Riley's waist and hugged her goodbye. Nor was he surprised when she hugged him right back in a hug full of emotion that was easy for anyone to see.

Easy for him to feel because it hit him right in the gut.

Riley might not have spent much time around kids, but she was good with them, full of compassion and patience.

He liked that about her.

He liked a lot of things about her.

But then, he already knew that.

She'd liked the boys, too.

Ashley had never connected with them, never bonded with them. No matter how much Justin had tried to involve Ashley in this special part of his life she'd resisted, claiming to be too busy with her residency, and then with work.

It hadn't been until the end that Justin had understood why.

His little charity, she'd called it.

Maybe because he'd been adopted, and viewed "family" as not just being bound by blood, he felt things she never had. Either way, the boys were so much more than his "little charity," and having them in his life had been a deal-breaker. He knew firsthand what a group like his could make in a foster child's life.

Ashley hadn't understood that.

Riley did. After just one day with the boys she got it.

Justin had wanted to wrap his arms around her and spin her around in glee when she'd said she wanted to bring them all home with her. That was exactly how he felt. What he'd do, given the chance.

Which might be happening soon with Kyle, depending on what his birth mother decided. *Would she let Kyle be adopted?*

After he'd been loaded into his foster family's vehicle, Riley came over to where Justin was strapping his kayak to the top of his Jeep. She'd changed out of her wet clothes into dry shorts and a T-shirt. They were a little tight, and accented her lush curves in ways that heated him more than the South Carolina sun.

She leaned against the side of the Jeep and smiled up at him. Good grief, she did a number on his insides. He'd kissed her, made love to her, and he wanted to do all that and more again. And she was smiling at him as if she was happy to be here with him.

Did he dare hope he'd finally gotten through to her that she was special?

"I think I'm in love."

As he battled suddenly weak knees, Justin's ears roared at her claim. Insides quaking, he grabbed hold of the Jeep to steady himself. Not that he thought she was talking about *him*. He knew she wasn't. But her words had twisted his insides around, playing havoc with logic.

"I can't imagine Kyle's foster family not wanting to keep him," she clarified. "I just met him and I adore him."

Kyle. Of course she meant Kyle.

"They've been taking kids in for years."

But he knew they had no plans to keep Kyle. He'd had multiple discussions with them when news of Kyle's mother's intentions had been made known.

"For some, that's what they want to do. Give kids a safe place to go for a few weeks or months." Thank God people like them existed, to give love and care so freely. "But many of the foster families don't feel equipped to take on one kid or more forever."

Thank God the Brothers family had. He and his siblings had gotten the cream of the crop when they'd been made official family members.

When he adopted—whether it was Kyle, one of the other Wilderness Group boys, or a child he'd yet to meet—Justin wanted to give that same cream-of-the-crop family experience.

Riley leaned against his Jeep and sighed. "I guess that makes sense…but I don't know how you could take a child in and then just let them go."

He understood. Because it was something he'd battled with since becoming involved with the boys. Having spent so much time with them, it was only logical that he'd want to adopt one of them, should that become a possibility.

"Don't think harshly of them. It's what they signed on to do. Foster parents do a great service, taking in kids who have nowhere else to go until the state figures out what's best for them."

"You're right. I know you're right. But still…" Her lower lip disappeared into her mouth.

He watched her closely. "You couldn't do it?"

"Be a foster parent?" She shook her head, looking down at Daisy in her arms and scratching the dog's neck. "I don't know… I'm not that great with kids but today, being with them—well, I can't imagine turning my back on them."

Justin's insides shook at her confession. Was that why he'd felt such urgency for her to come with them today? To see how she interacted with the boys? To see how they interacted with her? Stan's wife had canceled on them, but they'd have been fine even if Riley hadn't gone with them.

He hadn't consciously been doing so, but if he'd been testing Riley she'd just aced the test.

And if she hadn't—then what?

Then nothing.

He'd never meant to become involved with anyone who didn't want a houseful of kids. Whether or not Riley wanted kids hadn't mattered. He'd been drawn to her and any "rules" he'd given himself about future romantic interests had been irrelevant.

"They'd be lucky to have you," he said, and meant it.

Her cheeks flushed a bright pink. "Ha! I know nothing about kids."

She looked so flustered it piqued his curiosity. "No natural instincts?"

"None."

He didn't believe her—not after having seen her with the boys. She'd opened right up to Kyle, had shown patience and kindness to the boy.

"I was an only child of an only child, so no siblings or cousins. And none of my close friends have kids," she continued. "If I do have natural maternal instincts they've not had any reason to come out."

"Until today?"

Her gaze lifted, and even though he couldn't see behind her mirrored glasses he knew her eyes were filled with surprise.

"You think I was being maternal today?"

Her question was raw—as if his answer mattered way more than it should, as if her merit was somehow being weighed. As it had at the party, her vulnerability shocked him.

"I think the boys, and Kyle in particular, brought out your protective instincts."

Considering what he'd said, and seeming pleased with the conclusions she drew, she smiled. "Maybe you're right."

"Haven't you figured it out yet?"

"What's that?"

"I'm *always* right," he teased, thinking that when it came to Riley he really had been. Right to think there was something special between them.

He might not be able to see behind her glasses, but he knew she was rolling her eyes, which didn't bother him in the slightest. She was smiling and so was he.

He glanced around the parking area. All the kids except Stephen and Jevon were gone. The boys were sitting on the lowered tailgate of Stan's truck while Stan dug through a bag on the passenger floorboard.

Justin hesitated. As much as he wanted to suggest dinner, or whatever Riley would agree to, he couldn't just leave Stan with Jevon.

"I can stay with Jevon until he's picked up," he told Stan. Or until he drove him home, which was sometimes the case when the boy was at his birth mom's. She'd forgotten to come get him for one reason or another more than once. "If you need to get Stephen home?"

Stan shook his head. "I got this. You go ahead." He gestured toward Riley. "Nice to meet any friend of the doc's."

"Same," she agreed, holding Daisy close as she took one last look at Stephen's bandaged leg. "Take care of that knee so you're all well by our next adventure."

The boy nodded and Riley told him and Jevon goodbye. As she and Justin made their way to where she'd parked she was quiet.

"Thinking about all that yard work?" Justin teased.

"There's still a lot of daylight left. I could help you knock it out this evening."

Ignoring his offer, she let Daisy jump into the driver's seat, then turned back to him. "Thanks again for inviting me today. I wasn't sure about coming, but I'm glad I did for a lot of different reasons. Today's one of those days I'll think back on and always be grateful I experienced."

Despite the multiple layers of sunscreen applied at various points throughout the day her nose boasted a rosy pink color, as did her cheeks. He couldn't resist brushing his finger across her face.

"You're serious about coming with us again?"

She didn't pull away from his touch, or remind him he had no right to touch her. He supposed he didn't, but when she stared up at him, lips parted, looking hesitant, as if she wanted all the same things he wanted, he kept forgetting.

She nodded. "I'm looking forward to it."

"So am I."

He didn't want her to get into her car and drive away. He knew it was going to happen, and that the fact she'd spent the day with him at all was nothing short of a miracle. But he wasn't ready for it to end.

"Anything I can say that would convince you to spend the rest of the day with me?"

She inhaled deeply and he wished he could see what was in her eyes.

"I had a really great time…" she began.

"Does that mean you're considering having a really great rest of the day?" At her hesitation, he added, "As friends. Nothing more, if that's not what you want. You planned to do yard work. Let me help you."

"But…but that means inviting you to my house."

Hearing the possibility that she was going to say yes in her voice, he grinned. "I'd have trouble helping you with your yard work without being in your actual yard."

"Why would you want to do yard work with me?"

Unable to stand not being able to look into her eyes a moment longer, he lifted her sunglasses from her face, stared straight into her beautiful green eyes and told the truth.

"I'm not sure you get what I've been trying to convey to you for months."

Her eyes not leaving his, Riley swallowed.

"I like you," he admitted. "I want to date you. Not just take you to bed, like I think you assumed after Paul and Cheyenne's party, but to take you to dinner, help you with your yard work, spend time with you in ways that have nothing to do with sex."

Her eyes widened.

"I don't care who knows," he continued. "For that matter, I'd like there to be something for everyone to know."

Her lower lip disappeared into her mouth again as she stared up at him. "You're serious?"

He nodded. "Very."

Her long lashes swooped down over her cheeks and she kept her eyes closed for a few seconds, then lifted them and met his gaze. "I'm not sure this is smart, but would tomorrow be okay?"

Joy filled him. "Okay for you to be my girlfriend?"

Her eyes narrowed, but no walls went up. *Hallelujah*.

"Okay to help me with my yard work," she clarified, sounding very much like the in-charge nurse he was used to seeing. "Lucky you."

Although she was teasing, he *felt* lucky.

"The other thing is debatable," she said, her eyes darkening.

He felt her pulling away. He'd thought… No matter. She was letting him go over the following day. For now, that would have to be enough. No need to warn her that he'd been on his high school's debate team and they'd always won. She'd know soon enough that he wouldn't give up easily.

"I'll take what I can get if it means getting to spend time with you."

With that, he leaned down and kissed her forehead. Her skin was warm beneath his lips. The touch was brief, but it felt right.

Just as Riley felt right.

"Special delivery."

Riley frowned through the peephole of her front door.

What had she been thinking, inviting him over? All night she'd tossed and turned, knowing that she had opened Pandora's box, was risking letting him in, risking the pain he could dole out.

Although she'd not recognized it at the time, she now knew Johnny hadn't been nearly the man Justin was. If Johnny's betrayal had gutted her so, how much more so would Justin's?

She'd considered canceling all morning, picking up her phone, typing out a message, deleting it, only to do the same thing again fifteen minutes later.

She opened the door and gestured to what he held. "What's that?"

He glanced down at the pizza box as if it had morphed

into something unrecognizable. Arching his brow, he gave a sheepish grin. "Lunch?"

"I've already eaten."

Her cup of yogurt that morning had to count, because she didn't have the heart to tell him pizza was not on her diet. But the aromas were delicious and tempted her almost as much as he did.

"It's pizza. It'll keep until you work up an appetite." His gaze met hers as he added, "Doing yard work."

"Of course." She moved back for him to come inside, hoping she hadn't made a big mistake. Knowing she had.

"Not that I agree that you need to be dieting, but I did order cauliflower crust, in case you were still doing that low-carb thing."

Stunned, Riley stared at him. He'd ordered a low-carb pizza?

"Why?"

"Because I didn't want you to have a reason to say no."

To him or the pizza?

"You make it impossible to say no," she admitted, pointing toward her kitchen. "Just set the box on the counter." Because she sure couldn't take it from him. Not with the way her hands were shaking.

Although Johnny had constantly pointed out her jiggly thighs, he'd certainly never put any of her dietary needs before his. Quite the opposite. He'd order her favorites and then taunt her as he ate them.

Why, oh, why had she said yes to marrying him? Had she really been that desperate for love?

Justin set the pizza down, then turned to face her. "That's the idea, you know."

Trying to clear her head of the past, wondering if she should be desperately clinging to it instead, she blinked at the man now leaning against her countertop. He looked more scrumptious than anything she'd ever seen in her kitchen. Her mouth practically watered as she eyed him in his shorts, a T-shirt missing its sleeves, and tennis shoes.

"Making it impossible for me to say no?"

He nodded.

"I'm realizing that."

He grinned. "Maybe we could eat a slice or two before starting on the yard?"

She nodded. It wasn't as if she was going to tell him he had to work on an empty stomach, particularly as he'd brought food.

Riley pulled a couple of plates from the cabinet. "Can I pour you a glass of water?" she asked.

"That would be great. You mind putting it into something that would be okay to take outdoors?"

She filled two reusable plastic water bottles, then handed him one. He'd already opened the box of pizza and removed a slice. Heaven smacked her nostrils.

"That smells so good."

He took a bite. "Tastes that way, too."

She eyed the pizza. "It would be rude for me not to have a slice."

His eyes twinkled. "It would."

"But just one…"

Justin wiped the sweat from his brow to keep it from running into his eyes, glancing around at their progress thus far.

He liked Riley's house—and her yard. The blue

house had been built in the eighteen-hundreds and renovated several times over the decades since. The front yard boasted large rhododendrons, roses, azaleas and other flowering bushes Justin couldn't name but knew that his mother would have a fit over. And in the back Riley had a private oasis of sorts, with a large eucalyptus tree draped in tiny lights that he imagined must look magical at night.

That she had those whimsical lights said a lot about what she hid beneath her no-nonsense self-protective layers. There was a fire pit, a bench, several chairs, and off toward the back of the yard in a shady area was an over-sized hammock, hung between two large oaks.

Riley spent a lot of time in her yard and it showed.

The house itself was well taken care of, too, with high ceilings and glass vents above the doors giving testament to its age. Hardwood floors covered with the occasional colorful rug ran through the whole three-bedroom house. At some point someone had converted the back porch into a small washroom, and a new bathroom was now connected to Riley's bedroom.

Cassie rented the second bedroom, and the third seemed to be a catch-all with an exercise elliptical, a few ten-pound free weights, a shelf filled with books—mostly from nursing school—and a computer desk. The walls were decorated with colorful matching flower paintings signed by Riley and Cassie.

Yeah, he liked Riley's house, inside and out. Just as he liked *her*, inside and out.

"Cassie's with Sam," she'd told him earlier, while they'd been eating pizza.

She'd eaten two slices, all the while talking about how

good it was, making him glad he'd gone to the trouble to search out low-carb pizza options prior to ordering.

His gaze ran over where she knelt now, pulling weeds from a flowerbed. She didn't need to diet, but if she thought so he'd do his part not to sabotage her. But he'd also do his part to make sure she understood that he liked her curves just as they were.

Perhaps sensing that he was watching her, she turned, glanced up at him, and smiled. His muscles clenched with memories, with elaborate longings. Not that he could act on them, no matter how she looked at him or tempted him. He'd promised himself he'd keep his hands off.

For today, at any rate.

So far they'd worked in her front yard and were making good progress. She'd purchased some mulch that she'd had stacked up next to a screened-in side porch. After weeding her landscaping, they'd spread the mulch around the knock-out roses and bushes in the front of her house.

"You want something to drink?" she asked.

"If you want to fill my water bottle up, that would be great." He'd almost finished what she'd put in there earlier.

She picked up the bottle and carried it inside, coming back out moments later. She handed it to him and surveyed their work. "I like it," she admitted.

"Me?"

"My landscaping," she corrected, giving him a teasing look. "Thanks for helping. Your strong back has made mincemeat of getting this done."

"I'm glad you let me help."

"Me, too." Taking a drink from her water bottle, she

motioned to the remaining bag of mulch. "There's only the one left. I think we'll dump it in this side bed, and I'll mulch what's left of the back beds some other time."

"Just let me know when and I'll help."

Rather than agree, she looked away, and seemed unsettled by his offer.

Fighting a sigh, because for every two steps forward she felt it necessary to take one back, he picked up the bag of mulch, tore the plastic open, and began sprinkling the mixture over the flowerbed she'd indicated.

While he did so Riley trimmed a bush, dropping the cut pieces into a previously emptied mulch bag.

A few minutes later, live music filled the air. "Your neighbors are throwing a party?" he asked.

She shook her head. "There's a bandshell not far from here, in a small park. Local groups play there most weekends. Some are really good."

"So you lie in that hammock and listen to your own private concert?"

"Sometimes."

Her face said he'd hit on exactly what she often did. He'd thought as much. From the moment he'd stepped into her backyard he'd felt her presence, felt her connection to the retreat she'd created there.

"Is that where you were when we were texting the other night?"

She nodded. "I like being out there. Whether it's the eucalyptus or just being outdoors, my backyard soothes me."

"Now I understand why I couldn't tempt you to my place. Your backyard is amazing."

She beamed with pride. "It's not big or fancy, but it's home."

And it was an extension of her. Strong, beautiful, yet promising a fantasy escape from reality.

"How long have you lived here?"

"A coworker and her husband owned it. I'd visited a few times they had get-togethers and always felt a connection here. I'd just gotten engaged when it went up for sale. Thinking it would be our first home, I put a big chunk of my savings into a down payment. Obviously, as I'm not married, the engagement didn't work out…"

Had her voice broken a little just then?

"But I've no regrets on the house."

She'd been engaged.

Justin had known she'd had a bad break-up, but no one had mentioned that she'd actually been engaged.

"I didn't know you'd been engaged," he said.

"Failed relationships aren't exactly a priority conversation topic." She sighed. "My break-up was rather traumatic," she admitted.

Which made him wonder even more about the man she'd been engaged to but ultimately hadn't married.

"But that relationship did make clear several truths—one of which you should probably know, as it seems I'm having trouble staying away from you and you seem set on our dating."

She was considering dating him.

"I don't plan to marry."

Which sounded as if she'd been the one to call off her engagement. What had the guy done? Or had Riley just realized she was making a mistake? Just as he'd realized when he'd called off his own wedding?

"A couple doesn't have to marry to have a committed relationship."

"True." Her face pinkened. "And I don't mean to

imply that you're even thinking in those terms. But, since you say you want to date me, it's only right to tell you that we wouldn't be headed in that direction. I'm not a get-married-and-have-kids kind of girl."

Justin *did* want a committed relationship with Riley. Maybe he'd want marriage to her someday, too. But the fact that she didn't want marriage wasn't a game-changer at this point in their relationship.

"What do you mean about kids?"

"I don't plan to have children."

"That's a shame."

"Because?"

"Because you were wonderful with the boys."

"I… Thank you. But that doesn't mean I should procreate."

"Procreating can be fun." He waggled his brows, trying to lighten the conversation, trying not to let his mind fall into a dark place where Riley was saying she didn't want kids. "Besides, there are other ways to have kids besides procreation."

"Such as volunteering with your Wilderness Group," she agreed. "Bringing more children into the world doesn't make sense when there are so many who need love."

Which Justin sort of agreed with.

"It feels weird to even be saying these things to you, but I just thought you should know how I felt—that, regardless of what happens between us, either of us can walk away at any time."

Since she was adamant that she didn't want the same things he did, perhaps Justin should walk away now. Not that he believed he could.

"Okay," he said slowly, trying to process the full

implications of what she was saying. "I appreciate you telling me how you feel."

Too bad Ashley hadn't, or they'd never have gotten so close to walking down the aisle. At least with Riley he knew upfront that she could never be the one.

Unable to resist, Riley tore off the corner of a pizza slice from the box she'd stored in her fridge earlier.

Mmm. That was amazing, even cold.

Justin had made an effort to get her what he'd thought would make her happy. Because he wanted her happy. Which seemed unbelievable, really.

Just as the fact that he was in her shower right now was unbelievable.

Had someone tried to convince her earlier that week that he'd be in her bathroom, naked, with her water sluicing over his buff body, she'd have laughed.

Justin was in her bathroom naked!

Chewing her pizza, Riley leaned forward and pressed her head against the refrigerator. What was she doing?

You're having a great day, her inner voice reminded her. *A wonderful day with a wonderful man who brought you low-carb pizza.*

That alone should buy him major brownie points. That and all the other thoughtful things he did. For her and others.

But she shouldn't have him here—shouldn't be wondering what he'd say if she walked into her bedroom and got into the shower with him?

"What am I doing?" she asked out loud, causing Daisy to look up from where she waited in hopes that Riley would drop some pizza crumbs.

"You talking to Daisy?"

Popping the last bit of pizza into her mouth, Riley spun. "Cassie! You're home!"

Surprised at Riley's odd reaction, her roommate gave a knowing smile. "Any reason I shouldn't be?"

"What? No, of course you shouldn't be. I mean, yes, you should be." Goodness, she was flustered. "I'm just surprised Daisy didn't bark when you came in."

Reaching down to pet the dog, Cassie grinned. "You're looking a little rattled. That have anything to do with the Jeep out front?"

Riley's face heated. "Oh, that."

"Yep, that." Cassie looked around the kitchen, even though it was obvious they were the only two there. "Where is he?"

"Who?"

"You know who. The owner of the Jeep. It's not as if I don't know who drives it."

On cue, the shower cut off and Justin began singing from her bathroom.

Cassie's eyes widened. "Oh, my. He's in your *shower*?"

"It's no big deal," Riley assured her.

"Right. Dr. Brothers is singing in your bathroom. No big deal."

"Okay, so it is a big deal. Sort of. But really, he's just there because he helped me with the yard. Besides, who else would it have been?"

Cassie walked over to the fridge, eyed the pizza box, raised a brow in surprise, then pulled out a cheese stick and peeled away the plastic. "The yard looks great."

"Yes, he was a lot of help."

"I bet he was." She took a bite of cheese.

"Cassie!"

Her friend laughed. "Sorry. Should I make myself scarce? If so, I can hang at Sam's tonight."

Riley shook her head. "It's not like that."

"The man is singing in your bathroom and you're blushing." Her roommate pointed her cheese stick at Riley. "Don't tell me it's 'not like that.'"

"Okay," Riley admitted, to herself and to Cassie, "so maybe it *is* like that…"

CHAPTER EIGHT

COMING OUT OF the bathroom, Justin walked into Riley's kitchen. "Nothing like that fresh from the shower feel," he said.

"Oh!" She jumped as he spoke, then frowned down to where Daisy sat at her feet. "That's twice in less than an hour you didn't bark. You're fired."

"Someone came by while I was in the shower?" He raked his fingers through his still damp towel-dried hair.

"Cassie came to grab some things on her way to Sam's."

"They're pretty serious?"

Riley laughed. "Depends what day you ask."

"Like that, is it?"

"Oh, yeah." She started pulling things out to prepare a meal.

"What are you doing?" he asked.

"Making us something to eat…"

He eyed the lettuce, cucumber, celery, and tomato. He wasn't opposed to salad, but he didn't foresee it filling him up. "I'd rather you go and do whatever you need to do and then we grab something."

She eyed him, then glanced back at what was on her countertop. "Not a salad kind of guy?"

"It's a nice first course," he admitted, watching her closely for any sign that his comment bothered her. That wasn't his goal. After working in her yard he'd need more than what was on her menu, though.

"Sorry." She gave a small smile. "I wasn't planning on company when I did my grocery shopping."

"No worries. We'll go somewhere—anywhere you like—and the next time you go grocery shopping you can plan for frequent company."

Her cheeks pinkened. "I could do that…"

"And I could be that company."

She laughed. "You think?"

"I hope."

Hesitating only a moment, she nodded. "Let me put this away, then give me a few minutes to get ready to go out."

She looked amazing to him already, but he knew she'd only blow off any compliment. "Sure, but I'll put this stuff away."

Her gaze lowered to the items, then she nodded. "Sounds good. Thanks."

Placing the items back into the fridge had only taken Justin a minute, and while she showered he wandered around Riley's house, looking at the few knickknacks she had sitting around—a few photos of her and Cassie, and a picture of her and an older woman who must be her mother.

She'd truly created a warm, comfortable home and he was sitting in an overstuffed chair, Daisy in his lap, when Riley came into the living room.

"You're beautiful."

She rolled her eyes. "You obviously got too much sun today."

The fact that she refused to accept his compliments frustrated him. "If that were true it would only explain this moment. What about every other one since the moment we met?"

"Justin—"

"I'm serious, Riley. I find you beautiful. Don't make light of it when I tell you so."

"I… Okay."

"I like how your shirt matches your eyes."

"I… Thank you."

"Good girl," he praised.

"Don't treat me as if I'm Daisy."

"I'm not. Daisy *expects* to be doted on. You're the exact opposite."

"You have a point," she agreed.

"For the record, I enjoy doting on you, Riley."

She sat down on the edge of a chair and motioned for Daisy to come to her. Daisy lifted her head, gave a look that said *Whatever*, then rested back against Justin.

"For the record, you've established that I'm the opposite of my very spoiled dog."

He laughed. "Maybe with time you'll let me spoil you."

"Don't hold your breath," she warned him.

For dinner, they ended up at a Mexican place, and discovered they had similar tastes in food.

"I don't eat out a lot, but I do love this yummy cheese sauce," she admitted, dipping a chip into the creamy mixture.

He could tell. Her face showed pure pleasure with

every bite, and left him more interested in watching her than in eating. Not that that was anything new.

They talked about nursing school, med school, how they'd both arrived where they were in life now.

Justin couldn't recall a conversation he'd enjoyed more—not counting his talk with Riley at Paul and Cheyenne's party.

"I think they're going to throw us out of here if we don't leave soon," Riley mused.

Justin glanced around and realized they were the last customers in the restaurant, and that the staff were putting chairs up on empty tables.

"I guess more time has passed than I realized," he admitted, standing and dropping some money onto the table.

"Our waiter was giving us the evil eye the last time he asked if we wanted anything else," she teased. "There was still one other occupied table, so I didn't respond."

"I missed that." Because he had been too caught up in the woman sitting across the booth from him.

Between their kayak trip, the yard work, and their long dinner, he'd spent most of the weekend with her. An unexpected pleasure, for sure. But he still didn't want it to end.

When they pulled into Riley's driveway she didn't immediately get out of the Jeep, so neither did Justin.

Maybe she felt the same way he did.

"I—part of me wants to invite you in."

His heart pounded at her admission. He wanted her to invite him in, but he also wanted her one hundred percent on board when that happened.

"I've mentioned how much I like that part of you.

Still, I understand." He did. Mostly. "I'll walk you to the door, then leave."

She picked up her purse from the floorboard, as if she was going to get out, but still hesitated. "I…maybe we could sit in the backyard for a while?"

Pleased by her suggestion, Justin jumped on the offer. "I'd love to. If you're sure?"

"I'm sure." She got out of the car, headed to the back of the house, then paused. "I'll need to let Daisy out first, though."

"It's okay," he assured. "I promise I won't force my way into the house."

Her gaze cut to his. "That's not what I meant."

"I know. I'm teasing, Riley. I don't want you so nervous about my being here tonight. I was trying to lighten the mood."

"Sorry."

"I don't want you sorry, either."

Her gaze lowered, as if she carried a heavy emotional burden, but then she smiled—albeit an obviously forced one. "Today was wonderful, but it may take me a while to get used to the idea of you at my house."

Earlier, he'd wondered if she'd been the one to call off her engagement—now he asked himself what kind of a number her ex had done to her? He reached out to take her hand and gave it a gentle squeeze that he hoped conveyed she was safe with him. He'd never intentionally hurt her.

He hadn't intentionally hurt Ashley, either. But he *had* hurt her when he'd called off their wedding. She'd been floored that he'd chosen the boys over her.

He should have told Riley about his own past engagement earlier, when she'd mentioned hers. Something had held him back, though, telling him to wait until the time was right to mention that he'd come close to walking down the aisle, too, only to realize he was making a mistake.

He'd tell her about Ashley, but not now—not when Riley was just beginning to acknowledge what was happening between them.

Then again, she'd made it clear nothing long-term would be happening between them, so what did it matter if he told her about Ashley?

Riley admitted that Justin had been as good as his word. Not once had he made any attempt to go inside the house or tried to convince her to invite him in.

She'd let Daisy out into the backyard with them and the dog was now sleeping in her lap. She and Justin sat on the bench beneath the eucalyptus, talking, laughing, and she had to admit it was easy to forget to be nervous that they were alone when everything about the moment felt magical.

Or maybe that was just her fairy lights, casting a glowing spell.

She'd always found her backyard soothing. Tonight, next to Justin, with the night sky clear except for the dotting of twinkling stars, and the eucalyptus-laden breeze caressing her senses, she thought her backyard was the most romantic place on earth.

"Thank you for today, Justin."

He grinned. "Thank *you*."

"I'm serious. Today, and yesterday, too, were wonderful. It's been a really fantastic weekend. The best I can recall in a long time."

"And we still managed to get your yard work accomplished." He took her hand into his. "You should hang out with me more often."

In the glow of the fairy lights she stared at their entwined hands. How could something so simple cause millions of nerve cells to come to life? Cause her to want more of him touching her?

"Thanks for helping me with the yard."

Seeming oblivious to what his handholding was doing inside her, he said, "You have a great place."

"I think so."

Okay, this was crazy.

She gave a nervous laugh. "I'm making small talk."

"Why? We've been talking just fine."

Further torturing her, he lifted her hand to his lips and pressed a kiss there.

"I'm going to take this as my cue to leave and go," he said.

Her gaze hung on his.

Tell him to stay. Tell him not to go, to kiss you. All over.

She swallowed. "I think I'm ready for you to go home now."

He studied her a moment, then nodded. "Goodnight, Riley. I'll see you at the hospital tomorrow."

He gave her hand a gentle squeeze, then let himself out the back gate.

Riley sat outside on the bench for a long time after Justin left and wondered exactly why she'd let him leave when they'd both wanted him to stay.

Wherein lay her answer.

Wanting him to stay wasn't what she needed to feel.

Only she wasn't sure she could *not* feel that and so much more where Justin was involved.

She needed to be careful or she was going to end up hurt.

Riley wondered how Justin would be at the hospital the next time she saw him. Would he make a big deal over the fact they'd spent the weekend together or would he pretend it had never happened?

Good was her answer. He was good. Great, even.

Without saying anything untoward, he let her know with his smile, his wink, that he wanted to say more but would take his cue from her and wouldn't push it.

Even now, in the midst of repairing a torn medial meniscus, his gaze would connect with hers every so often, and in those brief moments she knew he was smiling beneath his surgical mask.

"Scalpel," he said, and the surgical assistant handed him the instrument.

The surgery went without any issues. And when they were finished Justin winked, then left the operating room.

The crew cleaned up the suite, then moved on to prepare for their next surgery—a knee being replaced by another orthopedic surgeon.

Two weeks passed, and with each day Riley found herself depending more and more upon the calls and texts she had from Justin.

And the time she spent with him.

Her brain kept screaming for her to put a halt to whatever was happening between them, but her lips could never sever their ties.

Tonight he'd invited her to the movies with the kids, showing up in a large SUV so they could go to pick up each boy.

Besides Stephen, six of the other boys planned to go. Four were currently with foster parents, including Kyle, and the two others were with their birth parents.

One birth mother seemed to have gotten her act together—was holding down a job and living with family members.

The other... Well, Riley knew she was going to struggle to drop Jevon back at the junked-up little house where several other people besides he and his birth mother were living. It wouldn't be so bad, but two of the men living there had given Riley the creeps, and she was pretty sure they'd been carrying out a drug deal when Justin had pulled the van into a driveway crowded with vehicles.

Stan and his wife met them at the movie theater. Riley found her to be every bit as nice as her husband and liked her at once.

Justin bought hot dogs, popcorn, and drinks for everyone, and when they were settled into a row he and Riley sat at one end and Stan and his wife at the other, with all seven boys in the middle.

Riley leaned over and whispered, "You're a really nice guy, Justin Brothers."

"You only just now figuring that out?" He grinned.

"I'm a slow learner."

"I don't buy that—which means I'm not nearly as nice as you think."

"Probably not, but what you're doing for these boys is wonderful." Riley glanced at Kyle, who'd insisted upon sitting next to her, then back at Justin. "I hate that he's upset I didn't bring Daisy," she whispered. "I had to remind him multiple times that pets aren't allowed in the movie theater complex."

Justin chuckled. "I'll plan something soon that Daisy can attend."

"Or maybe I can bring Daisy to visit him." She frowned. "Is that allowed? For me to visit the boys?"

"It shouldn't be a problem. I can talk with his foster parents and set up something."

"I'd like that," she said, and meant it.

"They'll likely want me there, too, until they get to know you."

"Shh!" someone hissed from behind them.

Riley's face heated.

Justin laughed and gave an *uh-oh* look.

She turned back to the movie, intent on watching the space story and not being one of "those" people who talked all through a movie.

When Kyle reached over and grabbed her hand, lacing his smaller fingers with hers, Riley wanted to hug him for the sweet gesture.

When Justin took her other hand she smiled, but wasn't sure if she wanted to hug him too or pull her hand away. Not because she didn't want to hold his hand, but because of the heat zapping from his body to hers at the skin-to-skin contact.

Justin holding her hand made her heart pound. Her stomach twist. Made her want to hug him with nothing between their bodies. Made her very aware of how very domestic they appeared, with her in between Justin and Kyle.

She shouldn't be doing this. So why was she?

Grimacing at her thoughts, she stared at the movie

screen but could no longer concentrate on the alien life forms trying to take over the earth.

An alien life form was trying to take *her* over.

Or it sure felt that way.

She cut her gaze to Justin.

Popping a piece of popcorn into his mouth with his free hand, he was watching the movie with great interest. As if his holding her hand was no big deal and was not affecting him in the slightest.

At least one of them was enjoying the film.

Then, without looking toward her, he squeezed her hand, letting her know he was aware of her watching him. Maybe he was even aware of what was happening inside her, because his hand held hers a little tighter.

After the movie, they dropped the kids off at their respective homes. Jevon was their last passenger, and Riley's stomach knotted more the closer they got to where they'd drop him off.

The boy had moved to the front row of seats in the SUV, preventing Riley from voicing her concerns about bringing him back home to Justin.

Fortunately, when they got to Jevon's, although there were still several cars in the driveway, there was no sight of the creepy men. Justin walked Jevon to the front door, keeping his hand on the boy's shoulder while he talked for a few minutes to a harried-looking pregnant woman, with a baby on her hip and another tugging at her shirt-hem.

Riley couldn't hear what was being said, but saw the woman nodding a lot, then hugging Justin after he handed her something. Money, most likely.

How could Riley not like a man who did such good?

Sure, he'd break her heart if she let him, but the man was one of the kindest people she'd ever met.

When he pulled the SUV into her driveway Riley didn't hesitate, and nor did she question whether Justin would follow suit.

No one was at the house, so they let Daisy out into the backyard. Following the dog, Justin headed toward the bench where they'd spent hours beneath the eucalyptus tree and the fairy lights.

Riley hesitated, and then, heart pounding, asked, "Want to lie on the hammock with me for a while?"

"Absolutely. I've been waiting for you to invite me."

They'd spent several evenings in her backyard, but for whatever reason she hadn't asked him onto the hammock. Tonight she didn't turn on the fairy lights, opting for the twinkling stars and lying in the hammock. With Justin. Large tree limbs would partially block their view, but there would be plenty of sky shining through to gaze upon.

"You first," she told him when they reached the hammock, thinking it would be easier for her to get in if he was already there.

Justin climbed into the hammock, took Daisy from her, then patted the space beside him. "Your turn."

Being careful not to flip him out, Riley got into the hammock and snuggled next to him. She became instantly alert at the feeling of her body against his. Over the past couple of weeks he'd held her hand, kissed her hand, even her forehead, but he'd never kissed her lips or pressed his body to hers.

She wasn't sure why. Part of her appreciated it that he hadn't pushed. Another part—well, that other part was sorely disappointed and tonight seemed to be taking charge.

Although usually the eucalyptus filled her senses, Justin overpowered everything, with his long lean body, his spicy scent, his warmth…

"This is nice." He laced his hand with hers.

"It's one of my favorite places to be," she admitted, wondering if she meant in the hammock or his arms.

"In my arms?"

Had he read her mind? "In the hammock," she assured him, but wasn't positive she'd told the complete truth.

Which was a little scary.

A lot scary.

There was a light breeze that put the slightest chill in the air, making the warmth of his body next to hers more appealing, and she wrapped her arm around his waist, holding him tight, pretending she didn't notice the way his abs contracted beneath her fingers.

"Cold?"

Not really, but after moving nearer what could she say? That she was trying to get closer even though their bodies were already pressed side by side?

"I can go inside and get that quilt you keep on the back of the sofa if you want me to," he offered.

"I'm fine," she assured him, her fingers tracing a pattern over his stomach.

"Tell me about that quilt. It looks old."

Did he really want to talk? Because *she* didn't.

"It is old. It was my mother's. Her grandmother made it for her."

"You've mentioned your mother before—that she gave you the necklace you lost. I've noticed the photo you have of the two of you in your living area. What about your dad?"

Now she *really* didn't want to talk.

"What about him?"

"What does he do? Where does he live? Why are there no photos of him?"

Riley fought the stiffening of her muscles and the urge to tell Justin to mind his own business. "I don't know, I don't know, and he left when I was four. Any photos that existed of him were gone long before I was old enough to know what they were."

"Sorry."

"Don't be. I had a great mother and a great childhood. She worked hard. We were poor. But we never went hungry or without love. I feel blessed. It could have been so much worse—like with the boys in your Wilderness Club."

"I'm glad your mom was able to take good care of you." He paused. "What happened to her?"

Riley didn't feel like talking about her mother or the past, but she answered him. "She passed in an automobile accident, not long after I graduated from university."

"I'm sorry, Riley. She sounds like she was a great lady."

"She was. She'd have liked you."

She'd have adored him. Kindhearted, smart, handsome—what more could a mother hope for, for her daughter?

"Oh? Tell me more."

"She liked handsome men who talked a good game."

He strained his neck the better to look at her. "You think I'm handsome?"

She rolled her eyes. "You know you are, Justin."

"How would I know that?"

"A mirror?"

He laughed. "I don't think much about the way I look."

"Beautiful people usually don't."

"I'd argue with that. Some of the most beautiful women I know obsess about how they look. They pick themselves apart, seeing flaws where none exist."

"A lot of not so beautiful people do that as well."

"We do tend to be our own worst critics. Usually because someone has torn down our belief in ourselves."

She considered his comment and couldn't argue. Hadn't she been a wreck after the end of her involvement with Johnny?

"For the record, you have no need to pick anything. You're perfect as you are," he said.

"You're saying that because you want to date me?" she ventured.

He shook his head. "Because I *am* dating you."

Justin felt Riley stiffen in his arms and wondered if he should have kept his thoughts to himself. They'd had such a great time, the last thing he wanted was to put her on guard.

"*Are* we dating?" Riley asked.

Choosing his words carefully, he took her hand into his. "Yes, Riley, we are dating."

She lay in his arms for a long time, not saying anything, just holding his hand and breathing softly as they swung in the hammock.

"I never meant for that to happen."

"I did."

She didn't look at him, just stared upward at the sky peeking through the tree limbs. "But you've barely touched me the past few weeks and you sure haven't tried to have sex with me."

Her words were a mix of breathiness and accusation. He hugged her closer to him, wanting to calm the demons that made her doubt herself. "Not because I haven't *wanted* to touch you or have sex with you. Believe me, I have."

"Do you think you'll still want to date me after we have sex again?"

The uncertainty in her voice had him turning onto his side to face her. "Do you think I won't? Because that's a pretty easy theory to disprove."

"By our having sex?"

"Obviously."

"Is that a proposition?"

"Is it working?"

"No."

"Then I need to try harder."

With that, Justin rolled so that his body covered hers. He supported his weight on his elbows and stared down at her, giving her a minute to tell him to get off her if that was what she wanted.

Instead, eyes wide, she smiled up at him. "I don't know how you did that without toppling us out of the hammock, but I'm impressed."

"You only just now figuring out I have skills?" he teased, waggling his brows and trying to remind himself to take things slow. Easier thought than done, with his body stretched out over Riley's.

Daisy jumped down from the hammock.

"Hmm…" Her gaze lowered to his mouth. "I don't think Daisy was nearly so impressed."

Fighting the urge to flex his hips more fully against her, Justin replied, "Daisy needs to learn who's boss."

Riley's gaze lingered on his mouth. She *had* to feel his reaction, *had* to know how she was affecting him.

"I suppose you think you're an expert at teaching females you're the boss?"

What he thought was that Riley was an expert at shooting his temperature through the roof.

"She's a good dog…just needs the right encouragement."

"What did you give my dog?"

He grinned down at her. "The right encouragement."

"You're good at that, aren't you?"

"Giving the right encouragement?" he asked, knowing they were no longer discussing her dog.

"Getting females to do what you want them to do."

Riley lay still beneath him on the hammock. Their bodies were pressed together and he was propped up on his elbows so he could see her face. Good thing, otherwise he'd have missed the swirling emotions in her eyes. Emotions that conveyed the way he affected her, making her want to draw nearer and back away at the same time. He'd been patient, given her space, but maybe she needed the right encouragement too.

"Maybe. Let's see," he told her, his voice low, husky.

His gaze went to her lips, then back to her beautiful eyes. He wanted her to kiss him. He waited, wondering if she'd hold out for him to make the first move, or perhaps push him away. She stared at him, clearly warring with the voices in her head, then seemed to come to a conclusion—a good conclusion.

She wrapped her arms around his neck to cradle his head and she arched up from the hammock to kiss him.

Her mouth was warm against his…soft. Sweet. Promising so much more than a quick peck. Making him want to forget patience and take control.

But he wouldn't.

Riley needed to do this—to be the one in control as her mouth explored his.

Her fingers curled into his hair, cradling him, holding him close as their kiss deepened.

When she lay back she stared up at him, with wide eyes and plump lips. He'd never seen anything more beautiful than the sight of her beneath him, staring up at him in awe.

"Thank you," he whispered, bending to kiss the tip of her nose. He let out a breath he hadn't realized he'd been holding, in the fear that she'd tell him to leave. "Thank you for kissing me, Riley."

"You're welcome."

Her gaze met his, darkened with what he could only describe as passion.

"Do you want me to kiss you again?" she asked.

Was that a trick question?

"More than anything," he said.

Riley kissed him again and again.

Justin was the best man Riley had ever known. In so many ways. Kind, patient, tender… Even now, when she could feel how tense his body was, how every sinew was strained tight, his lips were gentle against hers, as if she was fragile and must be handled with care.

Perhaps she was.

Not physically, but emotionally.

"What I'm about to do may not work, and you may not forgive me," he warned.

Before she could do much more than register what he'd said, much less wonder what he planned, Riley gasped as Justin rolled them so he was on the bottom and she lay across him.

"I've no idea how you did that without us falling out," she admitted, holding on to his shoulders as if she thought they might still topple.

"That was the part you might not have forgiven. If we'd ended up on the ground because of my miscalculation."

"You calculated well."

"Apparently," he agreed. "As I have you against me."

"It's where I want to be," she admitted, wrapping her arms around his neck.

"Riley…" he groaned, his body contracting beneath hers, his hips arching upward.

Pulling him so his lips hovered just above hers, she smiled. "You know those skills you mentioned earlier…?"

He nodded.

"You're going to need them."

His eyes widened. "You're sure?"

"Positive. I want you."

"No regrets?"

Regret was inevitable. Surely he knew that? She wanted peace and contentment in her life. Being with him was utter chaos. At least it felt that way to her nerves. Yet she couldn't stay away—much as a moth was drawn to a flame, knowing it was flying to its demise, but flapping its wings with all its might to go down in a blaze of glory.

"I want you," she repeated. "Now."

"Here?" he clarified, still seeming afraid to believe her and giving her plenty of time to change her mind if that was what she wanted.

It wasn't.

Going in for another kiss, then another, she whispered against his lips, "You have those skills, right? Show me…"

CHAPTER NINE

"I'M NOT SURE what I did to my knee," Cassie mused, carefully climbing onto Justin's examination table. "Sam and I were at a restaurant that had steps and my knee started to hurt. I didn't feel or hear any pop prior to the pain hitting."

Justin dried his just washed hands and turned to his patient, doing his best to focus on her and not on the woman who'd brought her to this appointment. The woman he was absolutely crazy about and had spent every spare moment with over the past few months.

There were times when he still felt those walls she refused to let go of, that he longed to knock down completely, and felt her clinging to them as a protective shield, but they'd come a long way from her sneaking out of his condo.

"How long ago was it that you first noticed a problem?" he asked, sitting down on his stool and rolling toward Cassie, where she was sitting on the examination table.

"A week ago."

A week ago he and Riley had sat on a blanket, watching a band make use of the bandshell at the park near her house.

Unable to avoid doing so a moment longer, he glanced toward where she sat. Their gazes collided and she smiled. His heart quivered like a fish out of water. Because that was what it did when Riley smiled at him a certain way.

The way that said she knew what he liked and she liked it, too.

The way that said she wanted him.

She *did* want him. For the past couple of months she'd not pretended otherwise. Most of the time. Although she kept herself emotionally guarded, physically she held little back.

Flashing her a quick smile, he dragged his gaze from hers and forced himself to focus on her roommate. "Any improvement since you felt the initial pain?" he asked.

Cassie shook her head. "The pain keeps getting worse. It's not too bad when I first get up in the morning. But the more I do, the worse it feels." She frowned. "It's interfering with my work, my everything. And I don't feel safe driving—which is why I had Riley bring me today."

At the mention of her name, his gaze went back to the pretty woman sitting on the opposite side of the examination room. Sure, he knew she'd never let her guard down completely, but he was hopeful he would eventually earn her trust.

Which was an issue.

He'd still not told her about Ashley, and nor had she opened up about the details of her broken engagement. Talking about Ashley never felt appropriate while he was with Riley. Did she feel the same about her ex with him? Maybe they needed to forget their pasts, not worry about mistakes made before they'd even met.

Not that he bought that.

Nor could he shake the feeling that he was constantly trying to earn Riley's acceptance. Hadn't he learned as a child that you couldn't earn love? If so, his birth mother would have adored him.

"I've tried all the things we tell our patients to do, but not noticed much of a change," Cassie continued, oblivious to the fact that his attention had strayed.

Chiding himself, he forced his attention back on Cassie. Getting her to sit on the exam table with her legs hanging over the edge, he visually inspected both her knees, then grasped her right knee, placed his palm over her patella and, holding on to her ankle, put her leg through a passive range of motion. She had smooth movement, with no noises or reported pain, and he easily achieved greater than one-hundred-and-thirty-degree flexion.

He started to do the same to her left, but Cassie grimaced as he attempted to move her leg so he stopped. He'd only achieved about ninety degrees.

He quickly did varus and valgus tests, noting the difference in results, then palpated the patella, feeling along the tibial plateau for abnormalities. He checked for a fluid shift, noting she was positive for effusion on the left knee. He ran through anterior and posterior drawer tests, then an Apley test, checking the collateral ligaments and for meniscus tears.

Having her position herself so her legs swung freely off the table, he took a reflex hammer out of his scrub pocket and struck just below and slightly lateral to her patella. He didn't think she had any spinal issues, but wanted to make sure the deep tendon reflex was normal. They were symmetric, and within normal ranges bilaterally.

"Stand and walk across the room," he told her.

Grimacing, Cassie got off the table and hobbled toward the exam room door and back. Justin studied her gait, making note of how she distributed her weight.

"All your tests for tissue tears are negative, so it's likely just inflammation. I'd recommend pulling the fluid off, an injection, compression, ice and rest, followed by some physical therapy you can do at home or at a center—whichever you prefer."

Cassie nodded. "I'm willing to try anything."

Justin drew up the injection, pulled out a drape, antibacterial skin prep pads, gloves, and some anesthetic spray. He turned to Riley. "You okay with helping?"

Riley stood to wash her hands and put on a pair of gloves. She hadn't expected to participate in Cassie's treatment. But, since she'd asked Justin to see her today, she wasn't going to refuse.

"If you'll tell me what to do," she said.

With Cassie on the table, her leg slightly flexed, Justin pressed along the lateral condyle, looking for a good entry point. He marked his spot with the top of the needle cap, pressing just hard enough to indent the skin. Donning gloves, he cleaned the area with antiseptic preparation, then picked up the syringe.

"If you'll spray the anesthetic at the marked area, please?"

Riley aimed the anesthetic, spraying until the skin blanched, and Justin pushed the needle into the desensitized area.

Watching Justin in an office setting was a new experience. At the hospital they were usually in surgery together, with his patient asleep. His movements were just as efficient today as at any other time she'd seen him work. Something she'd had the opportunity to do in and out of the hospital almost daily these past few months.

Because she couldn't seem to stay away—had quit trying, for the most part. Every so often fear would remind her that she was playing with fire, that she was going to hurt both herself and Justin. Still, she couldn't stay away.

He injected a small amount of anesthetic, then switched the syringe over to an empty one. Rechecking the position, he pulled back on the plunger. The syringe filled with straw-colored fluid.

When he was ready, Riley handed the medication-filled syringe. Needle still in place inside the numbed area on Cassie's knee, he carefully exchanged the aspirated syringe with the medication one, handing the other to Riley. When he felt a pop, indicating the needle was where it should be, he injected the medication into the joint space.

"You okay?"

"Never better," Cassie said through gritted teeth.

"You're doing great," Riley praised her as Justin withdrew the needle.

Riley immediately covered the area with sterile gauze and applied pressure.

"Remember—compression, ice, and rest, then knee-strengthening exercises." He printed a home exercise sheet, and an order for formal physical therapy, and handed them to her. "I'm writing you a note. I don't want you on your feet much for the next couple of days. And you—" he turned to Riley "—I'll see tonight, when I bring dinner for all three of us."

"I *knew* I liked him," Cassie said.

"That makes two of us," Riley agreed, applying a bandage over her friend's knee.

Only eventually he'd tire of her and leave. Then what?

"Me, me! Please. I want to go next," Kyle called, bouncing and waving his hand as he waited his turn to have his photo taken in the oversized chair in front of the forty-foot-tall boy at the children's museum.

Riley smiled down at the excited boy who'd stuck so close to her most of the day. She loved these outings she took with the Wilderness Group, and had even taken Daisy to visit with Kyle a few times. His foster family was wonderful. She hoped they'd adopt Kyle if that ever became a possibility.

The Wilderness Group had done a big photo earlier, everyone included, and were now doing individual pictures. There were only two boys who hadn't been in front of the exhibit yet. And Stephen looked as if he couldn't care less as he and another boy discussed something they'd seen earlier in the day.

"Okay!" Justin laughed at the boy's exuberant request. "You're next. Need a hand climbing up?"

Kyle's forehead puckered. "I got this, Captain Brothers." Only rather than attempting to get in the chair, he turned to Riley. "Will you be in a picture with me?"

As in just the two of them? She looked to Justin for guidance and he shrugged, leaving it up to her.

"I think you're supposed to have an individual picture right now, but I'll be in a photo with you later, if you want."

Kyle nodded, as if he understood, but disappointment shone on his face.

Riley looked to Justin. As always, her heart sputtered—probably in disbelief that they were a couple and had been for several months. She barely believed it and yet she was living it.

She'd never thought she'd be in a relationship again. Had never thought she'd risk doing so. Was it possible she'd been wrong? That Justin was worth taking a chance on and wouldn't break her heart?

Part of her wanted to believe it was true. Another part warned her that she was being foolish and would deserve the heartache that would head her way if she fell for such nonsense.

"Smile," Justin told the little boy, who seemed to have gone from a bundle of energy to a flat tire.

Did having a photo taken with her mean that much to him? Goodness, but he was getting attached. She probably shouldn't encourage him, but she couldn't stand to see his disappointment.

Rather than try to get Justin's attention, Riley darted into the picture, spread her arms wide in a total photo-bombing pose near to where Kyle sat, and cried, "Cheeseburgers!"

Surprised, Kyle laughed, wrapped his arms around her neck from behind in a hug, and repeated, "Cheeseburgers!"

When she was sure Justin had gotten the shot, she turned and hugged Kyle. "Now, we better let him get a picture of just you, too, since he was nice enough to bring us here today."

Kyle nodded and gave a toothy grin.

Shaking his head, Justin chuckled, snapped the shot, then helped Kyle down. He took Stephen's photo next, then one of Stephen with Stan.

When he was done, he joined Riley where she waited and pulled up the photo-bomb picture. "Do you see his face? You made his day."

Kyle did look ecstatic at her silliness. For that matter, so did Justin.

"Good. He deserves lots of smiles."

"As do you."

Justin leaned in and planted a quick kiss on her mouth. Something he'd done a lot of the past couple of months. Lot of kisses. Lots of more than kisses.

"Not here in front of the kids," she scolded, but they both knew she didn't mind a light PDA.

Justin chuckled. "Afraid you won't be able to resist pulling me off to some private corner and having your way with me?"

"Have you looked around this place? It's crawling with kids—literally. There are no private corners. Now, are we going to see if this tall boy exhibit teaches us anything about human anatomy?"

"I'd rather hold out for a private lesson later."

Riley clicked her tongue. "Now, now, Dr. Brothers. What will the boys think if their leader doesn't forge their path?"

"That's he's lucky to be with you?"

She laughed. "Good answer—but let's go check out the exhibit with the kids."

"Wait, look at this first."

Riley glanced at his camera screen. After her photobombing he'd continued to snap photos, and had gotten one of Kyle hugging her. Gravity tugged at her insides at the sight of the emotion on his face, the freely given love.

"You know, for someone who once claimed not to

know anything about kids, you sure have let the boys grow on you."

She enjoyed the Wilderness Group, and was grateful to be a part of the boys' lives. They'd enriched her life—especially Kyle, who always sought her out and made her feel special.

"They're awesome kids," she said.

But perhaps she needed to pull back, not encourage Kyle so much. She didn't want him to get too attached to her. The last thing she'd ever want would be to hurt him.

"Agreed—and you're awesome with them."

Justin's compliment made her insides gooey. She did enjoy the boys, but it wasn't as if she was doing anything more than spending a few hours here and there with them.

They headed around to the entrance to the tall boy exhibit, where the kids could explore the human body structure inside of it.

"You'd make a great mother, Riley."

Justin's words struck deep, bringing old insecurities to the surface, and the words Johnny had tossed at her in the aftermath of their failed wedding.

Why would he marry an overweight woman like her? He wouldn't want to risk his kids taking after her. He wouldn't—

Riley stopped her thoughts, knowing her insecurities would choke her out if she let them. She wouldn't let them.

And, although his sentiments were so different from Johnny's, Justin's words cut into her, making her feel the need to set the story straight.

She stopped walking, turned to Justin, and shook her head. "No, I wouldn't."

He stared at her as if he didn't know what to say. He probably didn't.

"I won't have children," she reiterated, wanting to make sure he understood.

It was something she'd decided after Johnny had left her at the altar. She'd go through this life alone, because it was easier with no one to leave her again.

Only she was so involved with Justin, she wasn't really going it alone, was she?

Panic gurgled up her throat.

Justin's forehead scrunched, then his expression softened with compassion. "Sorry, I know you said— I just thought—"

He thought she'd changed her mind because she'd been hanging out with him and the boys. Did he not realize how she felt? How having a child would only set her up for pain? Why would she want children when everyone she loved left?

She'd been foolish to let Justin get so close, because sooner or later he'd do the same.

Justin's blood cooled. He shouldn't have pushed with that comment about Riley making a good mother. He'd known better. So, why had he?

She didn't want children.

Listening to her make her claim had brought back memories of Ashley. Which wasn't completely fair. Ashley hadn't been opposed to children of her own, just not fostered or adopted.

Riley didn't want either.

Even after spending the past few months with him and the boys her feelings hadn't changed. Would they ever?

He'd been so into Riley that he'd continued to pursue

their relationship even after she'd told him she didn't want children. He had no right to be upset now, at hearing her repeat what she'd said all along.

Only he was.

How could she spend time with him and Kyle and not want more? Not want to be a part of their forever?

"I'm sorry," he backtracked, knowing his comment had triggered what he usually did his best to avoid: Riley's walls. "I didn't mean to upset you. It's just that you're wonderful with the boys...with Kyle."

"I adore them, but that doesn't mean I want children of my own," she clarified, not meeting his eyes. "I told you from the beginning that I didn't."

"I know you did, but—"

She took a step back, causing him to realize that he'd sharpened his tone. Something he rarely did with anyone, and that he sure didn't want to do with her or the boys. He took a deep breath, then raked his fingers through his hair.

"But you thought I'd change my mind?" she asked.

"I've heard you say more than once that you want to take the boys home and keep them," he reminded her, fighting to keep the accusation out of his voice.

Riley didn't respond, just stared at him, shock and uncertainty shining in the green depths of her eyes.

What was wrong with him? he asked himself. He knew better than to push. He never pushed. Because so long as he didn't she wouldn't build new walls between them.

Right now, new walls were going up.

"I... Maybe we should talk about this later?" she suggested, not quite meeting his eyes.

She was right. They were at the children's museum

with the Wilderness Group, and they had been having a good time. A great time. Now wasn't the place to have this conversation.

His phone buzzed in his pocket and, grateful for the reprieve, he glanced at his smart watch to see who the message was from.

His lawyer.

It was a Saturday. If Mary was texting there must be news on Kyle's mother.

Heart thundering, Justin swallowed the lump that had formed in his throat. Would today be the day his life changed forever? If it did, what was Riley going to think about that change?

She knew how he felt about the boys, but he'd never told her he planned to adopt Kyle. She'd already said she didn't want marriage and children. He could live without marriage so long as they were committed to each other. But no children…

His heart ached at the thought.

No children wasn't a possibility for him. His whole life he'd planned to have kids—to adopt, to foster. Soon, hopefully, he'd be a father.

It was something that scared him, but it was a challenge he'd gladly face. He had a lot to learn, but if Kyle's mother signed the papers and the courts granted him custody Justin would do right by the kid. He'd love him and raise him to the best of his abilities. Just as his parents had adopted, loved, and raised him.

Which meant putting Kyle first—above his own needs.

But where did that leave his relationship with Riley? She didn't want children, but did that mean she wouldn't want *him* to have them either?

If not, did that mean it was time to let go?

If so, how exactly did he do that, when letting go was the last thing he wanted?

CHAPTER TEN

"WHAT ARE MY odds of success?"

Justin clenched his cellphone in his sweaty hand, waiting anxiously for his lawyer's response. He'd snuck away from the group as soon as he could to call Mary back.

On her way to prison, Kyle's mother had signed away her rights rather than leave the boy dangling in court custody indefinitely. Kyle was adoptable. Mary had already drawn up the papers and had them ready to go, so they could move quickly to make Kyle his.

Justin had always planned to adopt one of the Wilderness Group, to make one of the boys his permanently. Kyle had always reached out to him more than the others, had always seemed a bit different. That he would be Justin's seemed like fate.

"You have a great shot. Not as good as if you were married and bringing a two-parent household to the table," his lawyer warned him. "But as you've been involved in Kyle's life for several years and are financially solvent, and you have letters of recommendation from Kyle's current foster parents, and you're an upstanding member of society, the judge should grant your petition."

"When will we know something for sure?"

"Kyle's mother just signed the papers yesterday. These things don't always move quickly."

After as long as he'd been involved with the boys, Justin knew she was right—but he wanted answers. Wanted to know whether or not to tell Riley that Kyle's mother had signed her rights away and he planned to adopt him.

She'd told him she didn't want kids. If he adopted Kyle did that mean she'd not want to continue their relationship?

But she adored Kyle. He couldn't imagine her walking away. He didn't want to imagine her doing so.

"I'll call when I know more, but I thought you'd want to know she signed the papers and I filed your petition late yesterday afternoon. I didn't have a chance to update you then. We'll have more answers soon."

"Thanks."

"Good luck, Justin. I know how much this means to you."

Yeah, adopting had been his goal even before becoming an orthopedic surgeon had.

Justin hung up the phone, thought about pulling Riley aside now, because he'd really like to tell her everything, to share all the things he was feeling, all the *what ifs*, but thought better of it.

Maybe he would have, had they not just had the discussion they'd had, but not now. He was going to have a difficult enough time pretending that everything was fine for the rest of the afternoon without Riley also pretending. Not that he didn't want to shout to the world that Kyle might be his soon, but he didn't want to get Kyle's hopes up in case the judge decided against him.

If the adoption went through, his life would undergo major changes. Changes such as him needing to find a house with a yard for Kyle to play in, needing to make sure that wherever he moved was zoned for a good school system, making sure that when he signed on to be the boy's father he took that commitment seriously and put Kyle first.

Yeah, between Riley's declaration and his lawyer's call, Justin's focus would be shot for the rest of the afternoon. Good thing all they had left to do was the Flight Adventure and simulator. After that, the boys should all have rides home and he'd go and run to clear his head—because everything was a jumbled-up mess.

Or maybe it was just where Riley was concerned that he'd made a mess of things…by wanting what she'd said from the beginning that she didn't.

Riley pasted on a smile when Justin rejoined their group. They'd been having such a lovely time that she hated how things had gone downhill—hated even more how nervous she felt when she glanced toward him now.

"Sorry," he murmured, getting in line beside her as a museum worker talked to the group about aviation, then let each boy take a turn pretending to fly a plane in the cockpit that had been built into the side of the building, to give the kids a lookout over Columbia during their "flight."

Riley had never been in a plane. She'd never had reason to, so she was as fascinated as the boys. Or would have been had she been able to keep her eyes off Justin.

He'd pulled his phone out again, checking to see if he had any new messages.

"Everything okay?" she asked.

He turned toward her but didn't meet her eyes. "Fine."

"Was that the hospital earlier?"

"The hospital?"

Whoever it had been, the call had had his eyes darkening.

"No. Why?"

"You seem distracted. I wondered if something was up with a patient."

"No. Everything's fine as far as I know."

"Good."

Only, everything was not fine, because he'd gone from lots of PDA to barely acknowledging that she existed.

Then again, it might not have anything to do with the text and everything to do with the conversation they'd been having.

Justin was great with kids—obviously he wanted children. At some point he'd have to move on in order to have those things. Maybe it wasn't fair of her to hang onto their relationship knowing she didn't want them.

Why had she given in to her desire to spend time with him? Let him become a part of her daily life to the point where she couldn't imagine a single day without him in it?

Her heart hurt at the thought that soon she wouldn't need to imagine it. Because Justin was going to leave. And soon.

She felt it with every bit of her being.

Felt it and needed to brace herself for it.

He was tense the rest of the afternoon. He had been since his off-the-wall comment, but whoever had texted him had totally pulled him out of the game. And not just with her, but the boys, too.

He said all the right things, smiled at all the right times, but his eyes were far away, as was his mind.

At last, Riley hugged the boys goodbye, got into Justin's Jeep, and was grateful the wind made it difficult to talk, because that at least gave them a reason for silence.

When he pulled into her driveway she turned to him, searching for something to say that would erase whatever had changed between them.

"Thanks for going with us today," he said.

At least he was talking to her. "You're welcome. Thanks for inviting me."

Ugh. They sounded awkward—like two strangers forced into each other's proximity.

"Did you bring clothes to change into for our run?" she asked.

They'd planned to go to the park and get in a few miles, then head back to her place to clean up and go to dinner.

Justin grimaced, then shook his head. "Something's come up. I'm going to take a rain check on our run and our dinner plans."

He was canceling their plans.

Justin was canceling their plans.

And just like that she knew the end had started.

She nodded as if she understood, and reached for the door handle. She did understand.

She didn't lean over to kiss him goodbye and he didn't seem to notice—or didn't care if he did.

Her feet felt like lead as she trudged toward her house from the driveway. As if with each step she was giving into gravity more and more, becoming heavier and heavier.

Why couldn't she get the sick feeling of impending

doom out of her stomach? It was one she recognized, having felt it before and ignored it then. Could she afford to do so now?

But that night, as she lay in her hammock, breathing the eucalyptus-laden air deep into her lungs, wishing she had her necklace to draw strength from, every instinct told her she should worry. The same instinct that she'd ignored prior to her wedding day. Look where that had gotten her... Jilted at the altar.

Why wasn't she picking up her phone and calling Justin? Demanding he tell her what was going on? Better yet, why were tears rolling down her cheeks?

Because she was a fool and she had let him get too close.

She needed to rectify that immediately.

Riley had tossed and turned most of the night, struggled with dragging her butt out of bed that morning to head to work, and then been disappointed that Justin hadn't been on the schedule in the OR.

Disappointed or relieved? Because as long as she didn't see him she didn't have to deal with their changed relationship status.

Why hadn't he called or texted?

Then again, she'd not called or texted him, either.

She could have reached out to him but had instead waited to see what he'd do.

Why?

Because she didn't want to seem desperate to have his attention.

Because he'd made her uncomfortable with his questions about kids.

Because he'd been so distracted by whoever had texted him.

Because she knew he was leaving, and the sooner she accepted it, the sooner she quit wondering, the sooner she could start getting past the heartbreak that was about to rain down on her.

The day crept slowly by, but she made it—never feeling so happy to clock out, go home, shower, and take Daisy for a run.

She ran further than her usual distance, needing to push her body in hopes of clearing her mind. It didn't work, so after returning home she went to her other active therapy—yard work.

She was in the backyard, pulling weeds while Daisy inspected the fence line, when Justin arrived at her house.

"I missed you," he said.

He was there. She was glad he was there. But he shouldn't be. She needed to *not* get sucked back into those baby blues.

"Daisy, shush," she told the dog, who was yapping at Justin.

Daisy ignored her and kept on barking—wanting Justin to say something to her or to pet her, most likely.

She turned toward this man she was glad to see, but who looking at hurt. Hurt because she felt the tides pulling them apart. And as much as she needed to let go, she desperately wanted to cling.

When Justin stooped to pet Daisy she realized his eyes appeared tired, his face strained—and, despite his words that he'd missed her, he'd stopped just inside the gate rather than come over to her for a welcome kiss.

Did he think she was going to tackle him and lick him crazily, as Daisy was now doing?

"I missed you, too," she admitted, wiping her hands over her shorts and immediately regretting it.

He was clean and crisp in his light blue shirt and khakis, but she was a far cry from it. Other than grabbing a drink, she'd gone straight out to start gardening. She rarely wore gloves while digging around in her flowerbeds, as she preferred the feel of earth against her skin. No doubt dirt streaked her clothes.

"Where were you?" As the question slipped from her mouth she regretted the accusatory tone she heard.

Yes, she'd spent the past twenty-four hours tormenting herself with doubts, but taking that out on him wasn't fair and nor was it what she wanted to do.

"I left the office early and had dinner with my family."

Justin went to his parents every week or so for a meal, usually on the alternate weekend from when he did something with the Wilderness Group. He'd asked her to go several times in the past, but she never had. She usually spent the time catching up on her laundry and housework.

Why had he taken off work early to go today? Had it been a special occasion?

"That's nice. You had a good visit?" She purposely made her tone as pleasant as she could, when her nerveendings felt as if they'd been scraped with sandpaper.

Justin bent to pet Daisy at last, calming the dog's yapping and eliciting a happy panting. "It was a nice visit."

Ugh. Was she jealous of her dog? It wasn't like

she wanted to roll on her back and have him scratch her belly.

Well, no, but…

"My parents are doing well. My sister stopped by with her kids."

He did some more of his looking at Daisy rather than her. Made more small talk.

Looking down at her dirty fingernails, she kept up the awkward trend with a pleasant, "That's good."

"Spending time with family is good." Now his voice was coated with accusation.

She ignored his jab and went on the offensive. "Why didn't you call me?"

"I didn't think you'd want to come," he parried, looking up from where he knelt with Daisy. "You never have in the past."

Riley frowned at his comment, but also at the distance between them. Why was he so far away? Why had he stopped at the gate? Usually he couldn't wait to take her into his arms for a hello kiss when he arrived.

But usually they hadn't disagreed over kids and he hadn't gotten a text message, then shut her out.

"A guy gets tired of hearing no after a while," he added.

Riley flinched. She didn't tell him no often—and never with sex. Just with his attempts to put them into a more traditional relationship box.

Picking up Daisy, he straightened, stroking the dog's fluffy white fur as he said, "Dinner with family usually means a relationship is moving toward certain things. Things that you claim not to want. You've made it clear you don't want them."

Oh, yeah, there was accusation in his tone. Loads of

it. And despite his calm petting of Daisy, tension emanated from him.

Riley's knees liquefied, and all she could manage was a muffled, "Oh…"

Moving closer to her, his expression somber, he asked, "That *is* still what you want, Riley?" His narrowed gaze pinned her. "Or, more aptly, *don't* want?"

Feeling a bit woozy, she said, "I— You mean, marriage?"

His eyes not wavering away from hers, he nodded.

What *was* this? Riley wondered. Was Justin telling her he wanted marriage with *her*? Or was this his way of pushing her away?

Which didn't make sense.

He'd come to her house, not the other way around.

But there was something antagonistic about him that she'd never seen before—something dark and stormy, brewing just beneath the surface.

"I… I enjoy our relationship," she admitted. "But I've not changed my mind about marriage."

Just the thought of saying she'd even consider marriage had her stomach twisting. No way did she want to risk feeling again that horrible feeling she'd had when she'd been at her wedding venue alone, when she'd had to tell her guests that Johnny hadn't shown, when she'd had to pretend everything was okay when it hadn't been okay, when *she* hadn't been okay, and then walk away with her head held high even though she'd felt lower than low.

No, she wouldn't be risking that kind of rejection and heartache again.

Taking a step back, Riley inhaled deeply and ordered

herself not to let thoughts of Johnny invade a moment when she already felt defensive.

"Where is this coming from?" she asked. "What happened at the museum yesterday? Did your family say something? I feel as if you're wanting to fight with me."

"I don't want to fight—not with you or anyone—and of course my family didn't say anything. They've never met you. Why would they say something?"

His tone said that it was a problem they hadn't met her. Had he wanted her to meet them? He had asked her multiple times in the past, but he'd never acted as if it were a big deal when she said no. The thought of going had practically had her breaking out into hives.

"Why are you so against having children?" he asked.

Eyeing the way he held her dog, stroking Daisy's fur almost methodically, Riley winced. "What relevance does that have to anything? You've known from the beginning how I feel. Why are you making it a big deal now? If you want to break things off, then just do it."

Oh, heavens. Had she really just told Justin to break things off with her? Her heart slapped her for saying such a stupid thing. Logic told her to brace herself for his answer.

Because he'd not come to her house to make things right. He'd come to fight.

But Riley didn't want to fight. She wanted—Justin.

"I'm going to be a dad."

The earth stopped spinning and Riley's body jerked from the force of it.

"What?"

Putting Daisy on the ground, he walked over to the eucalyptus tree and placed his palm against the bark, as if to gain some magical power to continue their conversation.

"I should have said I *hope* to be a dad. If the judge approves my request, I'm adopting Kyle."

"That's wonderful!" she said, and she meant it, joy replacing her anxiety.

Momentarily forgetting their tension, she moved toward him, planning to throw her arms around him, but stopped as she recalled that they were at odds and reality hit.

Justin was adopting Kyle. He'd be a father.

Breathing became difficult… Air was not able to find its way into her contracted lungs. Her knees threatened to wobble, possibly to give out completely and let her drop to the earth, and her mind echoed with one thought.

Justin was going to be a father.

"Not everything is finalized," he continued, his words somehow making their way beyond the noise of her mind, "but after she met with the judge today my lawyer thinks it's going to be. The judge wants proof that I can provide Kyle with a stable life. I spent this afternoon at my parents' putting together an action plan for doing just that."

Justin was adopting Kyle. He was going to be a father. The thoughts continued to race through her mind.

"I want to do what's right for Kyle."

He *would* do what was right for Kyle—would be an excellent father.

"Which is why he's so lucky to have you," she managed to say.

He'd mentioned that Kyle might be up for adoption someday. She'd never considered Justin adopting him—

but perhaps she should have, knowing how involved Justin was with him.

She had no doubt Justin would take his position in Kyle's life seriously. The boy was blessed to have Justin wanting to be his father. She didn't find it hard to imagine him being a dad. Justin was wonderful with the boys and would be a wonderful father to Kyle and to any other children he might someday have.

Her uterus spasmed deep within her at the thought of Justin having more children, of another woman's belly ripe with his baby.

She never should have gotten involved with him. Look at her now, feeling possessive of what wasn't hers, longing for something that hadn't existed for more than a few fleeting moments.

"Riley?"

He interrupted her thoughts and she glanced up, thinking he looked way more perfect than any person had a right to. Definitely he was the closest she'd ever come to perfection—likely ever would come. Not that she was looking for perfection, or anything else. She'd been just fine before he came along. She'd be just fine when he moved on.

Only the thought of not having him in her life gutted her. Not being able to kiss him or touch him.

How was she supposed to forget how it felt to be as one with this man and just move on as if she'd never known that high?

Anger at herself for becoming so vulnerable to him hit her. Anger at herself, and at him too, for making her want things she was better off not wanting.

"Riley?" he repeated.

"Justin?" she countered, lifting her chin and focusing on her anger. It was easier to grasp hold of than the intense sadness of the fact that they were ebbing away.

Looking frustrated, he raked his fingers though his hair. "I'm trying to figure out where everything in my life stands at this point."

"Mainly meaning me and where I fit in?"

"Kyle adores you."

"I adore him too—but that has nothing to do with where you and I stand."

His gaze bored into her. "Doesn't it?"

A heaviness fell over her chest, her shoulders, weighing her down. Averting her gaze, she stared at her dirty fingernails, wondering why she found feeling the cold earth between her fingers so satisfying, wondering if there was enough dirt on the planet to get her through the heartache headed her way.

"I think we need to talk about Johnny."

Riley's jaw dropped. Um…*no*, they didn't need to do that.

Her fingers curled into her palms. "Why would we talk about my ex?"

"It's time you told me about what happened between the two of you."

It was probably past time. But things had been going along so easily and wonderfully she hadn't wanted to think about Johnny, much less talk about him. Who wanted to tell her lover that the last guy in her bed—the *only* other guy in her bed—had stood her up on what should have been the happiest day of her life?

Telling him now, when they were on the cusp of the end… Did it even matter at this point?

Riley took a deep breath. She didn't want to relive that horrible moment. But Justin wasn't going to let this drop. He thought he needed to know. And maybe telling him would amp up her defenses, because currently she felt so exposed.

"Johnny swooped onto the scene not long after my mother died." She'd felt so alone in the world, so lost... "After she was killed in that car wreck I was devastated." She'd never known a person could cry that many tears and live. "She was my best friend and I'd never felt so alone," she admitted.

She had been alone.

"Johnny was handsome, and charming, and in my grief I latched on to him for all I was worth. Because focusing on him made the pain of losing Mom seem less. I ignored all the things I should have seen—like the fact that he went through half a dozen jobs during the time I knew him—and I dove in heart-first. Because when I was with him I wasn't alone."

"He asked you to marry him."

"Yes, he asked me."

Needing to move, she walked over to the eucalyptus tree, broke off a tiny segment, and inhaled the scent that usually comforted her. Nothing could soothe her inner shaking, though.

"I said yes, and I thought I was the luckiest girl alive when he slipped that engagement ring on my finger."

It hadn't been much of a ring, but she hadn't cared. She'd cherished that thin gold band with a stone that had been a cheap imitation—much as Johnny himself had turned out to be.

"What happened?"

How did she even answer that? Reveal her most humiliating moment? Admit that she hadn't been good enough for Johnny to stay with her so she knew no one ever would. She sure didn't expect someone like Justin to.

"He failed to show up for our wedding."

How could she have been so blind to his true nature? So suckered in by the false compliments that only ever followed his tearing her down first? To his constantly borrowing money? Having her pay for things? She knew the answer, though. Grief had veiled all logic.

She looked at Justin to see how he'd taken her confession.

With a grimace, he narrowed his eyes, and his jaw worked back and forth as he processed what she'd said.

"He was in an accident?"

"That would have been easier in some ways," she admitted. "The truth is more sordid."

She gave a humorless laugh, recalling her utter humiliation when she'd discovered the truth.

"He didn't show up for our wedding because after our rehearsal dinner the night before he'd cashed in our honeymoon airline tickets—" that she had also paid for "—and run off with someone he'd been having an affair with for months."

Wincing, Justin stared at Riley in disbelief that any man could be so stupid. So callous. How did a man just not show up for his own wedding?

"I'm sorry."

Her distaste for marriage was beginning to make sense, as was the determined expression on her face as she stared up at him.

A smudge of dirt across her cheek told the story that she'd brushed her hair back at some point during the past few seconds, prior to putting her hands back on her hips and lifting her chin in defiance at what life had thrown at her.

Her ex really was stupid to have chosen another woman. That the man had hurt her, humiliated her, made her self-conscious about her weight and destroyed her confidence in herself, made Justin want to track him down and beat some sense into him.

Another part wanted to thank him—because had the man been smarter Riley wouldn't be single. And, as frustrated as he was, Justin wouldn't have wanted to have missed out on the past few months.

"Don't be sorry," she advised. "The woman he ran off with did me a favor. Apparently she wasn't the first person he'd cheated on me with, nor would she have been the last."

Her words were said with such fervor that he knew she believed what she said. Good—she *should* believe it. No doubt Johnny hadn't been faithful to the other woman either.

"Once the humiliation and hurt wore off," Riley continued, her chin still tipped upward, "I became grateful he didn't go through with our wedding."

Was that how Ashley had felt? *Grateful* that he'd called off their wedding because he wouldn't give up his involvement with the boys? At least he'd realized the week before that what they wanted from life didn't mesh, and hadn't left her standing at the altar alone.

But she had felt betrayed, because she hadn't understood how he could put the boys before her. He hadn't been able to explain that he loved them more than he did her, and that giving back to the foster program was something ingrained within him.

"There's something else I need to tell you," he began,

wondering how Riley was going to take his next revelation. He didn't want to tell her—knew doing so was going to make her even more prickly—but not to tell her would be wrong.

Not that he was sure it even mattered at this point. Everything in Riley's demeanor said she was already done with him and their relationship. What he was about to tell her would likely destroy any hope that remained.

Not telling her wasn't an option.

"Prior to relocating to Columbia, I was engaged."

If he'd had any doubt as to whether or not she already knew, he no longer did. Her eyes widened, shining with pure shock, and she took a step back, bumping against a tree branch.

"I was nearing the end of my residency, dating a beautiful fellow resident, and knew I wanted a wife and family," he rushed out, knowing he needed to explain. "That's not a good reason for getting engaged, but when she started hinting for a ring I gave her one."

He'd loved kids, wanted a houseful. He'd liked Ashley. They'd gotten along well during their residencies, and he'd believed they could have a good life together. Right up until the moment she'd made that comment about the Wilderness Group and opened his eyes.

"Ashley was a brilliant surgeon...fun. My friends liked her." The more he said, the more Riley's face paled, but he needed to get this out. "We got engaged. Our families were thrilled, as were our friends."

"Please tell me you didn't stand her up."

Riley's voice broke and he'd swear her lower lip trembled.

"No, not exactly. I called off the wedding after I realized I couldn't marry her."

Like Riley, he felt lucky that he'd had a narrow escape from what would have been a miserable marriage for both him and Ashley.

"It sounds as if she was perfect."

Riley's throat worked, and then she surprised him by walking back over to the garden bed where she'd been weeding when he'd arrived and staring down at the plants.

"Why couldn't you marry her?"

"Our definition of 'family' wasn't the same. She wanted me to give up the group...the boys. But they were my family, much more so than she was. I couldn't marry her."

Surely after having spent time with the boys Riley would understand? Despite everything she said she had connected with them, and had formed a special bond with Kyle.

"Honestly, from the moment she called them my 'little charity cases,' anything I felt for her vanished," he admitted, shoving his hands into his pants pockets.

After a few moments Riley dropped to her knees and went back to pulling weeds, as if she hadn't heard him.

Justin stared at her, thinking her reaction odd, waiting for her to say something, to do something other than just pull weeds. He wasn't sure what he'd expected, but not silence, and her going back to what she was doing as if they'd not just had a major heart-to-heart.

"How long before your wedding day did you call things off?"

"The week before we were to be married."

Her hands stilled. "At least you didn't leave her at the venue, waiting for you to arrive."

The extent to which Johnny had betrayed her hit

home. The man truly had let her go to the last minute before letting her realize what a loser he was.

Had he not realized until right before the wedding that Ashley only tolerated the Wilderness Group, and planned for him to give it up after they married, would he have gone through with *his* wedding?

"I wouldn't do that," he assured her, even as he simultaneously acknowledged to himself that he couldn't say the same about Ashley.

Her hands squeezed the dirt. "Of that I have no doubt."

There was an ominous overtone to her words.

"Meaning?"

Letting go of the dirt, she let it sift out through her fingers. "I'd never give you the opportunity to dump me at the altar."

"I *didn't* dump Ashley at the altar." Maybe he almost had, but he'd had a good reason. "She was fine." Not at first, but she had moved on. "She's planning a big wedding with her new fiancé."

Ashley had moved on, and from the outside looking in she seemed no worse for wear. But was that what Johnny thought about Riley?

Riley grabbed hold of a weed and yanked hard. "You keep tabs on her?"

"No, but we dated for a long time."

They'd been so busy with med school, then residency, that neither had realized they wanted different things. If only they'd spent more time talking they'd have saved a lot of heartache.

"She and my mother have stayed in touch."

That sounded chummier than it was. The reality was that they ran into each other at various events and chatted. Other than a rare phone conversation or birthday card, neither sought out the other as far as he knew.

"Your mother told you about your ex's wedding plans at your visit today?"

Riley yanked at the stubborn weed again, almost falling back when she lost her grip. Had he been closer, he'd have tried to steady her, but he was too far away so he just nodded. He realized Riley wasn't looking his way, and said, "Yes."

After he'd told his mother about his plans to adopt Kyle, she'd launched into tales of Ashley.

"You didn't find that odd? Does she want you to intervene and win her back?"

"No."

At least, he hadn't gotten the impression that had been his mother's goal. Nor had he found her comment odd—more reflective on how life changed.

"She was just musing about how Ashley was planning another wedding and I was planning to adopt, how we were both happy, and how things changed with time. She wasn't hinting that we should get back together."

"It's good to have someone to support you unconditionally."

Yes, it was. It was what he'd hoped to find someday—what he'd hoped to have with Riley.

"I'm blessed with a great family." Which was probably why it was so important to him to have a big family of his own. "Just as Stephen has been."

Riley's hands stilled.

"Things could have been so different," he continued, thinking back over what he could recall of his early childhood. "When I was placed with Mom and Dad they adopted me. I hope to do the same for Kyle—to give him what I've had."

And he wanted Riley to be a part of that. Even with the turmoil of emotions whipping through him, that remained clear. He wanted Riley in his life.

Moving to stand near her, he held out his hand to help her back to her feet. "I'd like you to be a part of my life—a part of Kyle's life."

She didn't look up from where she still tugged on the persistent weed, and nor did she take his outstretched hand. Her shoulders drooped a little.

Letting go of the weed, she held up her hand—not to take his, but to make a "stop" motion. "Don't say anything more. I let myself get caught up in a relationship with you when I knew better. That was a mistake. A big one. But that doesn't mean I have to keep making it."

Heart racing, Justin stared down at where she knelt on the ground. He was opening himself up to her, laying everything on the line and telling her he wanted her in his life.

She was calling them a mistake.

It wouldn't surprise him if she buried herself in the ground in an effort to block him out.

"Riley, I don't think you understand what I'm trying to say," he began, thinking if he could only make her understand she'd quit shutting him out.

"You're the one who doesn't understand. How could you? You've never felt the things I've felt…never been humiliated by the person you trusted most." She took a deep breath. "I'd like you to leave."

"Riley…" he began, knowing that leaving would be an even bigger mistake than either of them had made already. "Stand up and look at me. We need to talk this through. My leaving won't solve anything."

Surely she had to see that? Had to see that he wanted her in his life. In Kyle's life.

"Your leaving will solve *everything*."

Because she wanted to shield herself rather than face what was happening between them, rather than let him in.

"I want you to go," she continued.

He reached out to touch her, but she jerked away.

"Don't touch me."

Justin's hand fell. Riley was so far gone emotionally he'd never get through to her until she'd had time to think, to realize they were worth taking a chance on.

"I'll call later—once you've had time to calm down."

"I won't change my mind."

"About?"

"Us."

That was when it fully sank in. Riley was done. This wasn't just a disagreement. To Riley, this was the end. She'd just thrown away their relationship.

How could she do that? Be willing to do that? As if they didn't have something special? As if he didn't matter?

Perhaps for the first time he understood how Ashley had felt when she'd asked him those same questions. His answer had been easy at the time. He hadn't loved her.

Just as Riley didn't love him.

Although she'd yet to get that persistent deeply rooted weed, she began pulling stray bits of grass from the garden bed—as if nothing significant was happening, as if she'd grown bored with the conversation.

As if she wasn't tearing them apart.

Justin stared down at her, gutted, letting a myriad of emotions filter through him and settling on a mix of resignation and anger.

Why was he doing this? She didn't want what he wanted, didn't have the same feelings he did. He just needed to accept it.

"Fine—there is no us." Each word felt like a razor, scraping his insides before it left his mouth. "I guess there never really was. You have your life and I have mine."

He turned, quietly let himself out through her gate, making sure Daisy was safely on the other side, and walked away.

Like she'd said—problem solved.

CHAPTER ELEVEN

"Where are Riley and Daisy?" Kyle asked, as the boy realized Riley and the dog weren't waiting for them in the Jeep.

Justin had been dreading Kyle's question, but had known the boy would ask. Of course the kid would.

Riley hadn't missed a single excursion for the past three months, and if it was something the dog could go to neither had Daisy.

Kyle and Daisy had formed a special bond.

As had he and Riley.

The fact that she wasn't in the front passenger seat said everything, driving home what had been Justin's reality this past week and a half.

It's what she wants, he reminded himself.

What he wanted, too—because he was tired of chasing a woman who didn't want to be chased.

Justin checked Kyle's seatbelt, making sure the boy had gotten it secured properly. "Riley won't be here today."

Kyle's sandy brows rose and he stared at Justin from where he sat in the passenger side back seat. "Why not?"

Good question, and one Justin struggled with answering. Because he didn't understand exactly how they'd gone from talking to her telling him to leave. How had their conversation ended with them ending? He'd come to bare his soul to her and instead he'd walked away.

Maybe he shouldn't have left.

But he hadn't been able to stay when she was telling him to leave. Telling him not to touch her.

Oh, how that had hurt. That she hadn't been able to bear his touch. That she'd rather be alone than with him.

His muscles seized his ribcage, crushing inward. He put his hand on the roll bar, leaned in a little. "Riley's busy."

Probably working in her yard, running, or out doing something with Cassie. She and Sam were off again, so the two women had lots of time to console each other.

"Too busy for us?" Kyle didn't look as if he believed Justin.

"She has things to do, bud, besides just hang out with a bunch of guys."

The boy's forehead scrunched deeper. "Doesn't she like us anymore? I can tell her sorry if I did something wrong."

That the boy immediately thought it was something *he'd* done wrong broke Justin's heart. Especially since it wasn't Kyle who had messed up. Justin hadn't messed up either. Other than to want more than Riley did.

"You didn't do anything wrong," he assured him.

Getting Kyle beyond that, to where he didn't immediately question himself, and giving the boy the confidence to know he was worthy and wanted was something Justin would spend the rest of his life making sure happened.

Kyle considered him a moment. "Did *you* do something wrong?"

Justin laughed at the boy's perceptiveness. "Probably," he admitted.

After all, hadn't Riley accused him of wanting to fight moments after he'd arrived at her place? Had he gone there looking to fight with her? Knowing which buttons to push to get a rise out of her?

But why? Why would he do that? He hadn't wanted to fight with her. He'd had everything to lose and nothing to gain.

In some ways he *had* lost everything.

At the hospital, Riley had transferred out of the operating room to work on the orthopedic floor. With Cassie still out with her knee, she'd been able to easily make the transition, and thus far had managed to avoid providing care for any of his patients.

She'd probably asked not to have any of his patients.

She'd neatly shut him out of her life.

He'd been a fool to think something special was happening between them, that she was different…

Justin tapped the roll bar with the side of his fisted hand. He gave one last look at Kyle's safety belt, secured around his booster seat, then climbed into the driver's seat.

He'd not even gotten his seatbelt fastened when Kyle asked, "Did you tell her you were sorry?"

Sorry for what? Caring about her? Wanting her in his life?

Justin's gaze cut to Kyle's via the rearview mirror. "Unfortunately there's some things 'sorry' can't fix."

Kyle gave him an empathetic look. "My teacher at school says it's always a good place to start."

"Smart teacher." Justin started the Jeep and tuned the radio to a station he knew Kyle liked.

When they arrived at the bowling alley Stan was already there with the other kids. Including Kyle and Stephen, there were six boys. Maybe a few stragglers would still show.

Justin hoped so, as he always worried about the kids who didn't make it for their activities.

They'd reserved two lanes, so divided themselves into two groups to bowl. Stan took one team of three boys and Justin took the other.

The afternoon passed quickly enough, and soon they were eating pizza. The boys finished their meal, picked up their trash, then ran back to start another game while Justin and Stan divvied up what was left of the pizza to send home with the kids.

"You driving Kyle home?" Stan asked.

Stacking the boxes, Justin nodded. "I've made arrangements with his foster parents to spend some extra time with him. He seemed excited that I was picking him up."

"No wonder. He idolizes you." Stan grinned. "Have you told him yet?"

Justin shook his head. "I didn't think it would be fair to tell him before all the papers were signed, just in case something changes between now and then. If all goes well, he'll be mine next Monday."

Stan nodded as if he understood. And as the man had adopted Stephen, perhaps he did.

"I kept worrying that something would go wrong, that no one was just going to give me a kid as great as Stephen to love forever. I didn't even realize I was holding my breath until I could tuck him in that first night, knowing he was mine and we were his."

Yeah, that pretty much summed up how Justin felt. Like he was holding his breath.

He'd managed to turn his spare room into a decent boy's bedroom. Soon he and Kyle could go house-hunting and the kid could help him pick out their new home. Justin already had an agent looking, but so far nothing had appealed.

Because nothing had a magical back yard.

Ugh.

He had to get past everything to do with Riley.

"What's up with you and Riley?"

Turning toward his friend, Justin grimaced. "Not you, too?"

Stan laughed. "Kyle grilling you?"

Justin nodded and took a sip of his water.

"That kid is crazy about her and Daisy."

There was that…

Stan gave him a brotherly slap on the arm. "Maybe you should just marry her and keep her around permanently."

Justin choked on the drink he'd just taken and coughed to clear his throat. "That's *not* happening."

Stan looked disappointed. "Too bad. I thought you made a good couple. Is that why she's not here?"

"You have it wrong. She's the one who won't commit. Not me."

Not him. He wanted a committed relationship with Riley. *Had* wanted. Because he was past that now. Now he just wanted to give Kyle a wonderful life. Not to be with someone who shut him out with their first fight.

Wrong. She'd shut him out from the beginning. He'd just been too foolish to accept it.

Stan appeared shocked. "I've seen how she looks at you. She's in love with you. I'd bet money on it."

Justin's chest tightened at his friend's observation. "You've got that wrong, too, pal. That was lust in her eyes, not love."

"Maybe…but she sure fooled me." Stan looped his thumbs into his pockets. "I take it you're not together anymore?"

Justin shook his head.

"Sorry to hear that."

"It was inevitable." Riley had never wanted anything long-term.

"Again, I'm surprised. You two were much better suited than you and Ashley ever were. You never meshed."

Justin frowned at his friend. This was the first time Stan had ever commented on Ashley. "Seriously? Everyone always told me how shocked they were that we broke up."

Stan looked surprised. "I wasn't shocked you broke things off—just at how long you took to do so. On the few times she came to one of the Wilderness Group get-togethers you never looked at her the way you looked at Riley. Not once."

Probably not. Because he'd never felt about Ashley the way he felt about Riley. Which meant what?

Nothing. Because she'd never let her guard down long enough to risk love and he'd forever be walking on eggshells in case she shut him out.

She *had* shut him out.

"Call it lust or love or whatever, but you were

never heartbroken over your break-up with Ashley—unlike now."

Justin shook his head in denial. "You're just seeing nerves. Once everything is settled and Kyle is officially mine I'll be fine."

"If you say so." Stan's gaze went to where the kids were cheering as Jevon's ball knocked down half the pins. "Let's go see what the boys are up to."

Justin walked into the spare bedroom, his gaze going to the stuffed video character on the bed. Kyle's favorite. Justin had covered the bed with a matching comforter set, and hung a few posters on the wall, but the room was still bare basics because he wanted Kyle involved in the process of decorating. He'd just got a few items to make the kid feel welcome.

If he got to bring him home.

Maybe he just *thought* he was meant to have a houseful of kids.

Maybe his role was simply to run the Wilderness Group and he shouldn't try to take things further.

He'd always planned to adopt. But was it fair of him to project that onto the people in his life? To have projected it upon Ashley? Upon Riley?

Just the thought of her had his insides knotted.

He'd wanted forever. She'd wanted—not forever.

Not anything.

Raking his fingers through his hair, he went back to his own room and got ready for bed.

When he climbed between the sheets he was still restless. Because he couldn't get Riley off his mind. Knowing sleep wasn't going to happen, he grabbed his phone off the nightstand and opened his messages.

Nothing.

Not one word from her.

What was he thinking? She wasn't going to text him. If she'd wanted to talk to him she wouldn't have done everything she could to put space between them. So why couldn't he just forget her?

He tapped her number, pulling up her text messages and scrolling back to when she'd sent him the photos of them during that first run.

His jaw worked back and forth as memories assaulted him. Memories of how vulnerable she'd been—still was, he reminded himself. Memories of how kissing her that first time had felt, in the garden at Paul and Cheyenne's engagement party. Memories of their first night together in the very bed he now lay in.

No wonder his house felt empty.

No wonder every house the real estate agent had shown him had felt empty.

Because *he* was empty.

Empty without Riley.

He'd been a fool to hope he could change her mind. Change her heart.

Memories of the past flashed through him—memories of hoping he could change his birth mother's heart, could make her want him. He couldn't make Riley love him any more than he'd been able to make his birth mother love him.

He consoled himself that just as he'd made a new life with the Brothers family—a much better life than he'd had—he'd now do the same with Kyle.

Sighing, he went to put his phone on the nightstand and missed. His phone clanged down between the bed and the piece of furniture.

Sitting up in bed, he flipped on the lamp, and looked in the space between his bed and the nightstand, expecting to see his phone.

He didn't. It must have landed beneath the bed.

Getting up, he knelt on the floor and felt around for his phone, but still didn't see it in the shadows.

"Great," he muttered, opening the nightstand's top drawer and pulling out a flashlight.

Bending down, he shone the light into the shadows, spotting his phone where it had landed.

A golden glint reflected in the flashlight's beam was what he reached for, though. And his hand shook as he closed his fingers around the gold chain with its tiny cross.

He'd found Riley's necklace.

"Men are stupid," Cassie murmured, tossing a flower petal onto the ground.

As her friend stretched out on the bench Riley sat across from her in a chair, opposite the burned low fire in the pit. Daisy lazed in her lap, only opening her eyes long enough to look up and nudge Riley's hand when it stilled in stroking her back.

"Agreed."

"I mean, Sam should have called by now."

Which meant her friend was waiting for him to call. Riley fought against wincing. Would Cassie never learn? She and Sam had been doing this on-again, off-again for years.

"Don't you think it's time to call it quits for good with Sam?" she asked.

Cassie gave her an *Are you crazy?* look. "Why would I think that? I love him."

Riley frowned. "Then why aren't you with him?"

Cassie gave her a point-blank stare. "Why aren't you with Justin?"

Justin. She didn't want to talk about him. Or think about him. Doing either hurt too much.

"The two have nothing to do with each other," she assured.

Cassie had the audacity to snort. "Yeah, right. You've sniffed this eucalyptus one time too many."

"It's not the same," she defended, but even to her own ears her words sounded weak. Which didn't make sense. She didn't love Justin. "I do miss him," she admitted.

Of course she missed him. She'd had a great time with him.

And not just the sex. It was more the way he made her laugh, made her see the world in vivid colors, made her feel young and silly—beautiful, even. He'd made her step outside her comfort zone.

Ha. That wasn't what she missed. That was what had been their downfall. Him trying to push her beyond her comfort zone.

"Do you miss him with all your being? To the point that you'd do just about anything to hear him say your name? To see his smile? Hear his laughter? Feel his touch?" Cassie continued, her voice becoming more and more emotional as she did so. "'Cause that's the way I miss Sam."

Her roommate's words dinged at her like pointed darts, hitting their target. Riley did miss Justin in all those ways.

"If Sam hasn't called by tomorrow I'm calling him," Cassie announced.

Riley felt sorry for her friend. "Oh, Cassie, are you sure?"

"Absolutely. He's mine."

Cassie's certainty stunned Riley. "How do you know? I mean, you're not together…"

"We've had a fight." Cassie shrugged. "I don't like it, but it's what we do. Just like we make up. We do that really well, too."

Riley shook her head. "Aren't you afraid that someday you won't make up? That eventually he's going to walk away and not come back?"

Cassie gave her that look again. "Why would I be afraid of that?"

"Why *wouldn't* you?"

"Because he loves me," Cassie said, with so much confidence Riley couldn't question the sentiment. "Just as I love him. A disagreement—a thousand disagreements—won't ever change that. We'll always make up."

Riley stared. "I… I guess I understand that."

"If you feel about Justin the way I think you do, then you do understand. When you love someone you can't not make up because you can't imagine life without them."

Looking beyond her friend to her fairy tree, she saw the place where she'd rebuilt her life, established a home and found peace. Had she really made an oasis away from reality? Or a fort to hide within?

Nothing wrong with a home being an oasis or a place where one felt protected, she assured herself.

"You should call him," Cassie suggested. "As in right now—pick up your phone and call him."

Riley rolled her eyes. "What exactly is it you'd have me say if I did?"

"The truth. That you miss him and are sorry for whatever happened between the two of you."

"I didn't do anything wrong," she defended, although she wasn't sure she was telling the truth.

"You didn't do anything right or he'd still be here."

"Well, if that isn't the pot calling the kettle black!" she shot at her friend.

"You're right. I'm calling Sam." Cassie pulled her cell from her pocket and punched in Sam's number. Scooting into a sitting position, she got up, then hobbled toward the house. When she reached the back door, she gave Riley a pointed look, then said into the phone, "Hey, baby, I miss you…"

No doubt her friend would make up with Sam and they'd act as if nothing happened. Until the next time.

"That's not the life for me," she said aloud, causing Daisy to lift her head in question. "Who needs all that drama?"

Not that her relationship with Justin had been filled with drama. It hadn't.

She thought Cassie was crazy, but she envied her friend that faith in Sam. What would it feel like to be that loved?

Exactly the way Justin loved you before you pushed him away.

Oh, how Riley hated that nagging voice in her head.

Justin hadn't loved her. He'd—

Why had he even spent the last few months with her? There had to be easier relationships for him than one with a girl who was jaded about love and had been jilted at the altar, like her.

Yet he'd stuck by her, showered her with affection despite her struggling to give him any back outside of their physical relationship.

Why?

He could so easily have been done with her after she'd left that first night. Instead he'd reached out to her, nurtured their relationship, tried to make her feel safe.

But she'd been as prickly as a briar bush for fear of getting hurt. And ultimately she'd pushed him away. And hurt him. Hurt herself, too.

She closed her eyes. What had she done?

She needed to tell Justin that she missed him so much she felt as if she'd lost a part of herself. Not going out with him and the boys today had hurt so much.

Cassie's description ran through her mind. She did feel that way about Justin. All those ways. She couldn't imagine going through life without ever seeing him smile at her again, without hearing her name on his lips, without placing her hand over his heart and feeling the strong beat there. The beat that was for her.

Because Justin cared about her.

At least he *had*.

She had to go to him. She didn't know what would happen, but she'd tell him she missed him, that she was sorry she'd shut him out for fear of getting hurt. Tell him that being without him hurt. She didn't have a plan beyond that, but at least it was a start.

She'd only taken a few steps when she stopped.

Sitting in her driveway was Justin's Jeep.

CHAPTER TWELVE

FOR THE MILLIONTH time Justin asked himself what he was doing in Riley's driveway.

He hadn't had to bring the necklace to her tonight. He could have just given it to her at work the following day. So why had he gotten dressed and driven straight to her house? Better yet, why had he been sitting in her driveway for the past five minutes?

There was enough glow coming from behind the house that he knew he'd find Riley out back. Was she lying on the hammock where they'd made love? Or was she perched beneath the fairy tree she loved so much?

Bark. Bark. Bark.

Justin glanced through the windshield, made out Riley's outline in the dim light. Riley was there, holding Daisy, but bent to let the dog free. Daisy immediately took off toward him, yapping frantically and jumping up into the Jeep.

"Hey, girl," he greeted her when Daisy leapt up into his lap and began licking his face. Despite his tension, Justin laughed. "Yeah, I missed you, too."

He loved on the dog for a second, then took a deep breath as he glanced back toward where Riley had been standing.

She was gone.

Great. Had she gone into the house, or around back again? He'd wondered if she'd let him in, or if she'd take the necklace and then tell him to leave again. He had Daisy. She'd have to talk to him long enough to get her dog back, to hear him out as he told her what was in his heart.

"Okay, girl, let's go talk to your mom and hope she's as happy to see me as you are," he said, before moving her from his lap to the passenger seat. "What are the odds she'll greet me like you did? Jumping in my lap and licking my face would be one heck of an ice-breaker."

"Is that what you want?"

Shocked at the unexpected question, Justin glanced up. Riley stood near the driver's side.

"Me to jump in your lap and lick your face?"

Stunned that she'd heard his comment, that he'd not known she was there and had said something so stupid, he scowled at Daisy. "Don't you know you're supposed to give me notice when someone walks up to the car?"

"Apparently she was too busy licking you to notice."

"Apparently," he agreed, taking in everything about Riley.

She wore a loose T-shirt and yoga pants. Her hair was up in a ponytail and not a speck of makeup covered her face.

"You're beautiful," he said.

Not exactly what he'd meant to say, but true.

"Thanks, but I'm still not doing a Daisy impersonation by jumping in your lap and licking your face."

Justin stared at her, not quite able to believe that she

was teasing him. Or that she hadn't told him to leave. It was what he'd been expecting.

Maybe—just maybe—she'd listen to what he had to say. If he could find the right words, that was. He sure hadn't during the time he'd been sitting in her driveway, wondering what he was going to say now that he was here.

"But I will hop in for a ride, if you're okay with that?" She looked at him in question, waiting for his response.

Justin swallowed. Maybe he hadn't really gotten out of bed and found her necklace. Maybe instead he'd just drifted off to sleep and was dreaming.

"Hop in."

She started to climb in, then paused. "I'm going to put Daisy inside." She looked uncertain. "Will you wait for me?"

Forever.

Forever?

Grateful he hadn't said the word out loud, for fear she wouldn't come back outside, he nodded.

She scooped up the dog, talked to her the whole way to the house, then let her into the screened-in side porch, closing the door and making sure the latch caught.

What was she saying to the dog? Probably warning her to send out a search party if she hadn't returned within a reasonable amount of time.

He leaned back against the headrest, stared up at the sky, and tapped his fingers against the steering wheel.

Forever. That was what had echoed through him when she'd asked him if he'd wait. But she didn't want the same things he did. Not just that, but she specifically *didn't* want the things he dreamed of.

Would she ever?

If not, how far was he willing to go to keep her in his life?

How much was he willing to give up?

"You okay?" she asked, climbing in beside him and fastening her seatbelt.

"Not really," he admitted, knowing he hadn't been okay since their disagreement at the children's museum. "Where do you want to go?"

"Anywhere. Just drive."

Justin started the engine and took off down her street. The wind noise made talking impossible unless they wanted to yell at each other.

He drove them down toward the river, through several sections of town, and kept driving until he realized he'd circled back to near her house.

Rather than go into her driveway, he pulled into the neighborhood park and killed the engine near the bandshell.

They'd walked down here and sat in one of the carved-out seats in the natural amphitheater built into the hillside and listened to bands on more than one occasion. Tonight the only light shining was the moon, but it lit the path down the hill.

"Walk with me?" he asked.

She hesitated only a second, then nodded.

He met her on her side of the Jeep, and then, knowing he might be slapped down, took her hand into his.

She didn't pull away.

Her hand felt small in his—small, warm, soft, and yet capable.

She'd been hurt so badly. He couldn't imagine how she'd felt being stood up at her own wedding. No wonder she refused to give anyone the opportunity to hurt her again.

They walked down to the empty bandshell, and before he could suggest it Riley sat on the edge of the stage. Without letting go of his hand. Instead, she held on tight, as if she was afraid of letting go.

"I've missed you."

Her softly spoken words were the sweetest music that had ever played on that stage.

Humbled by her admission, he lifted her hand to his lips and pressed a kiss there. "Not nearly as much as I've missed you."

"I'm sorry."

Her words sliced into him, ripping his insides to shreds. He remembered how he'd balked at her self-preservation on the day Mary had texted him. Shame filled him.

"I'm the one who's sorry. You were right. I came looking to fight that night. I didn't realize—not even after you pointed it out."

Her hand shook in his. "It doesn't matter."

"It does," he corrected, knowing that he couldn't stop until he'd told her what was in his heart. "It mattered enough that it drove a wedge between us."

"Because I let it." She took a deep breath. "No, I did more than let it. I drove it as deep as I could."

"Because I scared you?"

Her lower lip trembled, as if corroborating her next statement. "I'm terrified of you."

"I don't want you to be scared, Riley. That's not how I want you to feel about me."

He stepped close, wrapped his arms around her. She didn't pull away. Instead she leaned into his arms, resting against him. *Forever*, he thought again. That was how long he'd wait for her. How long he'd fight for her. How long he'd be hers.

"I don't want to be afraid anymore."

His heart knotted at her sweet admission. "Tell me how I can help," he said. "What I can do to make things right. I'll do whatever it takes."

Looking down at her hand in his, she gave a little squeeze, and said, "Then love me."

Riley couldn't believe she'd made the plea. That she'd let Justin guess at how vulnerable she was.

Guess? *Ha*. She'd pretty much spelled it out for him.

"That's all?" He laced his fingers with hers. "I thought you were going to ask me to do something difficult, like slay dragons or thwart evil masterminds."

"No evil masterminds or dragons. It's just my own insecurities imprisoning me."

"Then let me free you." He squeezed her hand, looked into her eyes. "I love you, Riley."

Riley's heart leapt at his words. His very unexpected words. Johnny had tossed the phrase at her so freely, never meaning them. Justin had never spoken the words to her before. Not once. Until now.

Wanting to believe him, but unable to foil her fears, she pressed her forehead to his. "You're sure?"

"You doubt me?"

Her hands shook and she held on to his tighter. "No, Justin. I don't doubt you."

She'd doubted herself—doubted that she could handle losing someone so precious. She almost had.

"You have no reason to doubt me, Riley. I'm yours."

Hers? Was it even possible?

"For however long you'll have me." He swallowed. "Longer than that. Whether you'll risk loving me, risk letting me be a part of your life or not, you are a part of mine and always will be. Because my heart is yours."

Riley's eyes stung. Tears trickled down her face as she admitted, "I love you, Justin. Kyle, too. But I—what if I can't do this? What if I lock up every time we start getting closer and push you away?"

He kissed her hands, held them tightly within his. "Then I'll love you through it."

Was it even possible?

"I used to want children, a family, but then…"

"But then you got left at the altar and decided being alone was safer than risking that devastation again?"

Her insides quivered at what he was saying, at how exposed she was making her heart.

Then again, her heart was more than exposed. Her heart was Justin's.

"I can't believe I haven't told you why I was in your driveway," he said suddenly.

Confused, she watched him reach into his pocket and pull out a gold chain. Realizing what he held, disbelief hit her. Her breath caught all over again.

"My necklace!"

"I found it earlier tonight. It's been beneath my bed." He took her hand, pressed the necklace into her palm and closed her fingers around the chain. "The clasp is broken, but I'll have it repaired."

The chain had been in his pocket, and the metal was warm against her skin. Or maybe it was the warmth emanating from within her because he'd found her precious gift.

Oh, Mama, she thought, squeezing the chain. *How I wish that you were here...that you could know Justin.*

"I can't believe you found it after all this time. I thought I'd lost it forever." Her eyes watered as she looked up at him. "Even worse, I thought I'd lost *you* forever."

His eyes glittered with the reflection of the moon. "*You* are my forever, Riley."

Justin kissed her—a kiss not quite like any they'd shared. A kiss that was full of the ever-present heat, but also full of possessiveness and giving. *Love,* she thought. *That's what is there.* It had been there all along, but she'd been too defensive to accept it.

Never again. Come what may, she'd lay her heart at his feet, risking him trampling it or lifting it high. She'd take his precious heart and cherish the gift of his love.

EPILOGUE

"HE'LL BE HERE," Cassie assured Riley, rearranging her veil.

Understanding why her friend felt the need to re-assure her, yet again, Riley resisted being annoyed at her friend's repeated comment. Her friend's unneces-sary comment.

Justin *would* be here.

As long as there was breath in his body he'd be there for her and for Kyle and for any other children who came along.

Still, she did currently question her sanity at not in-sisting they just go to the county clerk's office and say their vows there.

"You ready?" asked Cassie.

"Ready for this to be over."

Riley looked in the mirror one last time. She'd not lost that fifteen pounds she'd meant to lose before today, but it didn't matter. What mattered was how Justin's eyes lit up when he looked at her…how when he looked at her what he saw was everything he wanted.

Cassie scowled at her answer. "This is the best day of your life. Enjoy it."

Riley laughed. "Which means tonight is going to be the best night of my life, right? That I *will* enjoy."

Catching on, Cassie widened her eyes, then giggled. "*Now* I understand your rush. Let's get this show on the road."

"Thank you," she told her friend. "For being here with me today, and the last time I planned to do this, too."

"I wouldn't be anywhere else." Cassie leaned in for a quick hug, taking care with Riley's dress and makeup. "Who would have thought you'd be married before me?"

"Just by a few weeks," Riley reminded her.

Cassie held up her left hand, flashing her diamond solitaire. "At which time you get to return the favor and walk down the aisle with me."

But Riley wasn't walking down an aisle, *per se*. Just taking a car down to the bandshell, where their friends, all the Wilderness Group, and Justin's family were waiting.

And Justin.

He'd be there.

Cassie helped Riley into her car. It wasn't a long walk, but far enough that she wasn't making the trek in a wedding gown.

A parking spot had been reserved for her near the top of the amphitheater, just out of view of the stage.

"About time you showed up," Sam said as he helped Riley out of the car. "Your groom is nervous you're not going to show."

Riley shook her head. "He knows better. The only place I'm going is wherever he is."

Simple traditional bridal music began playing. Sam

leaned over, kissed Cassie, then kissed Riley's cheek before going to take his seat.

Cassie hugged Riley one last time, then moved forward to where she would make her way to Justin. Riley couldn't see the stage, so she waited until the music changed before moving forward.

She moved to the top of the hillside, where she looked down at her guests, all of whom had stood at the change in music and turned to face her.

A flashback of stepping out at her previous wedding hit her—that moment when she'd appeared in order to tell everyone that the groom had bailed and there would be no wedding.

But the rising panic died as quickly as it had come to life as her gaze settled on the wonderful man standing on the stage waiting for her, with a sandy-haired imp standing next to him in a matching suit.

Mine, she thought as she made her way to her soon-to-be husband, who was smiling back at her with his heart in his eyes.

Her heart. Her family. Today and forever.

And it was.

* * * * *

COMING SOON!

We really hope you enjoyed reading this book. If you're looking for more romance, be sure to head to the shops when new books are available on

Thursday 20th March

To see which titles are coming soon, please visit

millsandboon.co.uk/nextmonth

MILLS & BOON

Coming next month

HEART SURGEON'S SECOND CHANCE
Allie Kincheloe

Dread pooled low in Rhiann's stomach as the door to the exam room opened with a slow and ominous creak. Broad shoulders in a white coat filled the space and her eyes roamed the doctor's familiar form, taking in the subtle changes time had wrought. Three years ago, he hadn't had those deep lines etched into his face. His dark hair had a little more silver at the temple than she remembered, but he was as lean and handsome as ever.

Dr. Patrick Scott stepped into the room, his eyes looking down at the screen of the silver laptop in his hand. His movements carried the spicy aroma of his cologne into the small room, those pleasing notes covering the harsh anti-septic and teasing a part of her that had gone dormant since her divorce. But on top of the overtly masculine scent, he brought with him a wave of sadness that hinted at tragedy.

"Hello, Mrs. ... Masters, um..."

His deep gravelly voice trailed off and his sky-blue eyes jerked up to meet hers when he recognized her name. The slight fake smile he'd had on his lips when he opened the door faded fast. From the ice that frosted over his gaze, the animosity he held for her hadn't eased since she'd last seen him.

The exam room door shut behind him with an audible click and the laptop clattered slightly as he set it roughly on the counter. "What are you doing here?" An uncharac-teristic coldness in his tone sent a shiver coursing down her spine. Patrick's voice had always held such emotion, the rich timbre broadcasting his feelings with the simplest words. In all the years she'd known him, Rhiann had never heard this distant tone.

Rhiann hugged the baby in her arms close to her chest, tears filling her eyes as she fought to keep her emotions from overwhelming her. She'd wished the time since they'd last seen each other might have given Patrick clarity and soothed the raw edges of his anger, but clearly not enough time had passed. Now she could only hope that he was professional enough to put their personal grievances aside and focus on her child's best interests, and she needed to keep a clear head today, so she stuffed her feelings away as best she could. She had known coming here was a risk, but there was no other way or she'd have explored it already.

"I need your help. Well, he needs your help. This is my son, Levi. He has a heart defect and the cardiologist at St. Thomas wants to do surgery to fix it. But if anyone is cutting my baby open, I want it to be the best surgeon I can find." She paused to swallow down an oversized lump, "And that's you."

"You expect me to save someone you love. How ironic." A single dark eyebrow raised as he stared down at her, his expression unreadable and as cold as marble. His eyes searched hers, for what she didn't know. Just as she was sure he was about to tell her to leave, to scream at her like he had the last time she saw him, his gaze flicked down to the baby in her arms, and the ice in his eyes melted the tiniest bit.

Continue reading
HEART SURGEON'S SECOND CHANCE
Allie Kincheloe

Available next month
www.millsandboon.co.uk

MILLS & BOON

THE HEART OF ROMANCE

A ROMANCE FOR EVERY KIND OF READER

MODERN

Prepare to be swept off your feet by sophisticated, sexy and seductive heroes, in some of the world's most glamourous and romantic locations, where power and passion collide.
8 stories per month.

HISTORICAL

Escape with historical heroes from time gone by. Whether your passion is for wicked Regency Rakes, muscled Vikings or rugged Highlanders, awaken the romance of the past.
6 stories per month.

MEDICAL

Set your pulse racing with dedicated, delectable doctors in the high-pressure world of medicine, where emotions run high and passion, comfort and love are the best medicine.
6 stories per month.

True Love

Celebrate true love with tender stories of heartfelt romance, from the rush of falling in love to the joy a new baby can bring, and a focus on the emotional heart of a relationship.
8 stories per month.

Desire

Indulge in secrets and scandal, intense drama and plenty of sizzling hot action with powerful and passionate heroes who have it all: wealth, status, good looks…everything but the right woman.
6 stories per month.

HEROES

Experience all the excitement of a gripping thriller, with an intense romance at its heart. Resourceful, true-to-life women and strong, fearless men face danger and desire - a killer combination!
8 stories per month.

DARE

Sensual love stories featuring smart, sassy heroines you'd want as a best friend, and compelling intense heroes who are worthy of them.
4 stories per month.

To see which titles are coming soon, please visit

millsandboon.co.uk/nextmonth